"Fascinating. . . . Marcinko . . . makes Arnold Schwarzenegger look like Little Lord Fauntleroy."

—*The New York Times Book Review*

"Blistering honesty. . . . Marcinko is one tough Navy commando."

—*San Francisco Chronicle*

"Marcinko was too loose a cannon for the U.S. Navy. . . . *Rogue Warrior* is not a book for the faint of heart."

—*People*

And by Richard Marcinko

LEADERSHIP SECRETS OF THE ROGUE WARRIOR

"Look out, Bill Gates. . . ."

—*USA Today*

"Bracing, gutsy, tough-talking, empowering. . . . Should be required reading for managers who want to weed out prima donnas, transform the lazy, and motivate the troops."

—*Publishers Weekly*

THE ROGUE WARRIOR'S STRATEGY FOR SUCCESS

"Picture Rambo in pinstripes. . . . Marcinko's style is inspirational; his (literal) war stories are entertaining; and sprinkled throughout are useful business insights."

—*Publishers Weekly*

Photo by Roger Foley

ROGUE WARRIOR®

SEAL FORCE ALPHA

RICHARD MARCINKO
and JOHN WEISMAN

POCKET **STAR** BOOKS
New York London Toronto Sydney Tokyo Singapore

This book is a work of fiction. Names, characters, places and incidents are products of the author's imagination or are used fictitiously. Operational details have been altered so as not to betray current SpecWar techniques.

Many of the Rogue Warrior's weapons courtesy of Heckler & Koch, Inc., International Training Division, Sterling, Virginia

A Pocket Star Book published by
POCKET BOOKS, a division of Simon & Schuster Inc.
1230 Avenue of the Americas, New York, NY 10020

Originally published in hardcover in 1998 by Pocket Books

ISBN: 0-671-00072-1

First Pocket Books paperback printing January 1999

10 9 8 7 6 5 4 3 2 1

Cover art by Franco Accornero

Printed in the U.S.A.

Once again, to the shooters . . .
and to
Gunnery Sergeant Carlos N. Hathcock II, USMC (Ret.)
A True Warrior
and
An American Hero

—Richard Marcinko
—John Weisman

The Rogue Warrior® Series by Richard Marcinko and John Weisman

Rogue Warrior
Rogue Warrior: Red Cell
Rogue Warrior: Green Team
Rogue Warrior: Task Force Blue
Rogue Warrior: Designation Gold
Rogue Warrior: SEAL Force Alpha

Also by Richard Marcinko

Leadership Secrets of the Rogue Warrior
The Rogue Warrior's Strategy for Success

Also by John Weisman

Fiction

Evidence
Watchdogs
Blood Cries

Nonfiction

Shadow Warrior (with Felix Rodriguez)

Anthologies

Unusual Suspects (edited by James Grady)
The Best American Mystery Stories, 1997 (edited by Robert B. Parker)

For orders other than by individual consumers, Pocket Books grants a discount on the purchase of **10 or more** copies of single titles for special markets or premium use. For further details, please write to the Vice-President of Special Markets, Pocket Books, 1633 Broadway, New York, NY 10019-6785, 8th Floor.

For information on how individual consumers can place orders, please write to Mail Order Department, Simon & Schuster Inc., 200 Old Tappan Road, Old Tappan, NJ 07675.

PRAISE FOR THE BEST-SELLING *ROGUE WARRIOR®* SERIES by Richard Marcinko and John Weisman

ROGUE WARRIOR: DESIGNATION GOLD

"The most colorful, hell-raising, bomb-throwing, ex-SEAL commander of them all is back in another fast-moving, fictional adventure. . . . Marcinko and Weisman add new plot ingredients and push them to the limits of military technology. . . . Half the fun is Marcinko's erudite commentary on the incompetence of U.S. military services, the complex and ultimately frustrating mechanics of international politics, and the manly art of protecting your ass."

—*Playboy*

"The salty soldier of fortune raises enough homicidal hell to get himself expelled from Russia. . . . hard-hitting."

—*Kirkus Reviews*

"Readers partial to Marcinko and Weisman's fierce brand of escapism will find this bottling to be vintage and undeniably potent."

—*Publishers Weekly*

ROGUE WARRIOR: TASK FORCE BLUE

"A lot of fun . . . shootings, double-crosses, and all manner of derring-do. . . ."

—*Houston Chronicle*

"Extremely lively. . . . Not for the squeamish, politically correct or saintly."

—*Lincoln Journal-Star* (NE)

ROGUE WARRIOR: GREEN TEAM

"So much action that the reader scarcely has time to breathe."

—Newgate Callendar, *The New York Times Book Review*

"Liberally sprinkled with raw language and graphic descriptions of mayhem, *Rogue Warrior: Green Team* is the literary equivalent of professional wrestling."

—*Detroit Free Press*

ROGUE WARRIOR: RED CELL

"In a field of wanna-bes, Marcinko is the real thing: combat veteran, killer SEAL, specialist in unconventional warfare."

—Sean Piccoli, *Washington Times*

"A chilling, blood-and-guts, no-nonsense look into clandestine military operations told like it should be told. It doesn't come more powerful than this."

—Clive Cussler

ROGUE WARRIOR

"For sheer readability, *Rogue Warrior* leaves Tom Clancy waxed and booby-trapped."

—Richard Lipsyte, *Los Angeles Times Book Review*

There are three strategies for victory, those being the Water Strategy, the Earth Strategy, and the Fire Strategy.

—General T'ai Li'ang, *The Li'ang Hsi-Huey* (374 B.C.)

THE *ROGUE WARRIOR®*'S TEN COMMANDMENTS OF SPECWAR

- I am the War Lord and the wrathful God of Combat and I will always lead you from the front, not the rear.

- I will treat you all alike—just like shit.

- Thou shalt do nothing I will not do first, and thus will you be created Warriors in My deadly image.

- I shall punish thy bodies because the more thou sweatest in training, the less thou bleedest in combat.

- Indeed, if thou hurteth in thy efforts and thou suffer painful dings, then thou art Doing It Right.

- Thou hast not to like it—thou hast just to do it.

- Thou shalt Keep It Simple, Stupid.

- Thou shalt never assume.

- Verily, thou art not paid for thy methods, but for thy results, by which meaneth thou shalt kill thine enemy by any means available before he killeth you.

- Thou shalt, in thy Warrior's Mind and Soul, always remember My ultimate and final Commandment. There Are No Rules—Thou Shalt Win at All Cost.

Contents

Part One: **The Water Strategy** *1*

Part Two: **The Earth Strategy** *127*

Part Three: **The Fire Strategy** *297*

Glossary *383*
Index *391*

Part One

THE WATER STRATEGY

Chapter

1

THE PILOT, WHOSE NAME WAS ARCH KIELLY, BLINKED THE cargo bay lights twice, then twice again, to signal he was descending to thirty thousand. Once there, he'd crack a hatch, depressurize, then lower the C-130's ramp. That was so we could jump at twenty-nine thousand five hundred—the minimum height we'd need to carry us to within striking distance of our target.

I was so preoccupied with checking the cargo straps on the assault craft (it was tied down astride the double-tracked rollers) that I got caught pants-down inattentive when Arch turned the interior lights off. He did that for a perfectly good tactical reason: so no one would be able to see anything untoward from the western shore of Borneo, five and a half miles below, just in case anybody happened to be looking in our direction, which was, of course, up.

So, I was blindsided (literally) by the sudden blackout. Then Arch the fucking pilot did something else I hadn't remembered he was going to do (although he'd told it to me in simple declarative sentences during the preflight briefing): he banked sharply to starboard as he brought the plane onto a due north heading. Surprise. Doom on Dickie. Which is a polite way of saying in Vietnamese that I was being fuckee-fuckeed. One second I was checking the quick release harness on the ICRRC, an acronym that stands for Improved Combat Rubber Raiding Craft for those of you who aren't familiar with SpecWarspeak. The next, I'd lost sight of everything and everybody else as the plane's interior went completely lightless. It was like, *WTF?*

Then he plunged the nose earthward, dropped the right wing about forty-five degrees, and knocked me completely off balance. I rolled around in the dark like a fucking pinball SEAL, caromed off a bulkhead, got turned around the wrong way (is there any right way in these situations?), tripped over the rollers, lost my balance, and went skidding face first into one of the hard-cast, H-shaped, reinforced aluminum mounting beams that support the plane's forward seating module. It was like, *slip, s-l-i-d-e, SMACK—whaap.*

Oh, that *smarted.* Belay that. It fucking *hurt.* Instant agony. My oxygen mask was knocked askew. My goggles were spun halfway round my head. My helmet strap cut off my air. Now, those of you who know me at all, know that I have a unique relationship with pain. In actual point of fact, I have an existential relationship with pain. By this, I mean that I see pain not as a vague, generalized physiological concept to be explored; not as a cryptic, enigmatic problem to be analyzed; but as a real-time, essential, individual challenge; a subjective, personal confrontational *experience.*

Pain is an ordeal; a physical encounter to be lived through, relished, and explored, *crack* by *smack* by *whaap.* My pain exists so I can demonstrate to you, my constant and gentle readers out there, that I am inexorably . . . alive.

Which is probably why that precise, painful, and even Heideggerian instant was exactly the second the C-130's crew chief—who was waiting for his cue—received said signal from the pilot and cracked open the port side hatch. I heard a Perot-size giant sucking sound, and felt the accompanying tremor as the Hercules lost pressure and its interior temperature dropped about 106 degrees in four and a half seconds. Oh, fuck me very much one more time! Was I ever inexorably, existentially, alive.

I struggled to readjust my helmet, mask, and goggles, but the environment wasn't making things easy for me. One problem: it was dark, remember? Another problem: I was wearing a shitload of equipment, and it was difficult to move quickly since I kept catching my straps, loops, lashes, or laces on one of the 130's numerous interior hooks, hangers, pylons, or braces every time I tried to shift my body position.

You do not, after all, jump out of an aircraft at twenty-nine point five thousand feet to go kill bad guys wearing nothing but skivvies, sneakers, and a K-Bar knife. Everything you plan to use, you must carry with you. And when your operational plan calls for a thirty-mile parachute ride followed by a ten-to-fifteen-mile boat ride, followed by who-the-hell-knows-what, you have to carry enough for contingencies. Contingencies, hell—there's the omnipresent Mr. Murphy to worry about, so you have to go out of the plane loaded down with more junk than you'll find in the Brigade fucking Quartermaster catalog. And things get even more knotty, intricate, complex, when you are operating, like I am, in the black. (No pun intended. What I'm talking about right now are black—as in untraceable—ops.)

Which is why I wore a wet suit (generic, French-made) covered by your basic black Nomex flight coveralls (German manufacture). Over those sat a UDT-style life vest (also in basic black), as well as a Brit Royal Marine CQC (that's Close Quarters Combat) vest equipped with class-III body armor and a flotation bladder, not to mention pockets that held twenty or so pounds of lethal goodies that ran the gamut from plastique (in this case an RDX-rich Czech Semtex) and Bulgarian pencil detonators to a point-and-shoot digital electronic camera (it produces bits-and-bytes computer images on a three-and-a-half-inch disk rather than using conventional film), and half a dozen extra magazines for my pistol, each of which contained vintage East German–manufactured frangible Plus-P load ammo.

From the starboard side of the padded pistol belt around my waist was suspended the ever-fashionable ballistic nylon tactical thigh holster containing a Portuguese knockoff of a Heckler & Koch USP 9mm semiauto pistol. The compartment usually reserved for a spare magazine held a suppressor for the pistol. Suspended from my waist's port side and cinched around my left thigh sat a ballistic nylon mag-holder for six thirty-round magazines (filled with the same Kraut ammo that was inside my pistol mags), so I could reload the suppressed HK MP5-PDW I would be carrying. My belt also held a canteen of water, a pouch holding a pair of small but powerful bolt cutters (British), my first-aid kit (also French), and a K-Bar assault knife in a Kydex sheath. I've already told you about the oxygen mask (Japanese) and helmet (Israeli). I don't think I mentioned the O_2 bottle, navigational chest-pack, and radio.

My normal weight is in the 220-pound area. If there'd been a scale on this flight, I'd have weighed somewhere in the 270 range. And I wasn't even three-quarters loaded up yet. The point of all this inventory description is to illustrate that there were a lot of possibilities when it came to the "materials that catch on protuberances" category.

I noticed that my fingers were going numb under the Nomex gloves. Now, I don't care whether you've jumped from thirty thousand feet once, or whether you've done it a couple of hundred times like I have: when they depressurize the fucking plane, it gets real goddamn cold, real goddamn fast. Even with the coveralls and the quarter-inch-thick neoprene foam wet suits below 'em, we were suddenly in a d-d-d-deep freeze.

I could sense my guaranteed fog-proof Bolle combat goggles frosting over on the outside, which would have made it hard to see the O_2 connector in front of my nose—if I could have seen anything in the blackness. I stumbled through the plane until I found an oxygen outlet. I identified it by Braille, fondled the nozzle, shoved it *sans* foreplay into the female connector, and (unlike the president) inhaled as deeply as I could.

Nothing happened. I sucked again. Nada. I tried a third time. *Bupkis.* This particular oxygen outlet wasn't working. But no O_2 at thirty thousand feet is a course of action frowned upon in every one of the military's field manuals and instructional course materials—not to mention the long list of personal do's and don'ts I carry in my Slovak brain.

So I fought my way aft in the darkness, found a second nozzle, and rapid-switched. Of course, *that* one was screwed up, too. It was right then I realized that my old and constantly consistent nemesis, Mr. Murphy of Murphy's Law fame, had stowed away for the ride.

I yanked the tube connector out of the plane's oxygen supply and shoved it into the O_2 bottle strapped to my chest along with the altimeter, compass, large digital readout watch, Magellan GPS module, and secure radio. I inhaled, and was rewarded with a lungful of oxygen. At least I'd be breathing when we went off the ramp. Of course, after that, things might get sticky. There were twenty minutes' worth of air in the bottle strapped to my chest. We were jumping at twenty-nine-thou five hundred. The estimated descent rate given the air temperature, crosswinds, humidity, and load, was eighteen feet per second. You need oxygen until you pass below ten thousand feet. Well—this was combat, and in combat we might get away with a twelve thou ceiling.

Okay, *you* do the math. Twenty-nine five thou minus twelve thou, divided by eighteen feet per second, gives us approx 972 seconds (I'm talking fast because I'm using up oxygen) which, divided by sixty, comes to just over sixteen minutes of air. So if we jumped in the next three minutes, I'd be hunky-dory. If not? Sayonara, Dickie—it would be hypoxia city.

You say you don't know about hypoxia? Well, lemme explain. The condition is a manifestation of pulmonary insufficiency. That's a twenty-dollar way of saying that your blood ain't gettin' enough oxygen. The manifestations include cerebral vasodilation, and changes in sensorum ranging from confusion to narcosis. In the kind of two-bit plain English I understand, this polysyllabic soufflé means that if I jump from too high an altitude I don't get enough oxygen in my brain (that's the cerebral vasodilation stuff), and I can also experience (here come the sensorum goodies): confusion, drowsiness, sluggish reaction time, loss of muscle control, blurred vision and a confused, almost drunken thought process. Bottom line: if something goes wrong, I can kill myself because my reaction time and sensory perception mechanisms will be off-kilter. Not a favorable condition for the old Rogue Warrior to be in.

Arch turned the emergency lights in the cargo bay on, and everything was all of a sudden bathed in dim red. Now I could see again. There were eight of us making the jump tonight, a HAHO—that's High Altitude, High Opening—insertion, which would take us on that aforementioned thirty-mile airborne parasail, followed by the ten-mile boat ride. And all that—*that* was going to be the easy part. Because after our half-the-fun-is-getting-there fun, we'd have the second part of the good time. To wit: assaulting a ship whose crew was augmented by *zhongdui*—Chinese naval commando reconnaissance units—who were, the intelligence reports surmised, probably almost as well trained as we were. *Zhongdui* notwithstanding, we'd take the ship down and send it to the bottom before they could get any message to the outside world that they'd been attacked.

Not that executing any of the above would be a problem. Not with the merry band of hop-and-pop shoot-and-looters I had with me tonight. Tonight, I was traveling with *Warriors*. Over there, Duck Foot Dewey ran a second swipe of Russian duct tape around his magazine pouch so it wouldn't come open midair and leave him *sans* ammo for the suppressed HK submachine gun secured to his chest. Just to his left, Gator Shepard checked the tape that wound around the tops of his Adidas GSG-9 tactical boots. The shock of jumping out of a plane can rip your boots right off. That's not a good idea when the outside temperature's about fifty below zero, Fahrenheit. Lose your bootie like that and you get to play "This Little Piggy Froze Solid."

Next to Gator, Half Pint Harris fondled his swim buddy Piccolo Mead's rucksack, pulling on it hard to make sure it wouldn't separate when the chute opened. Hunkered down just across the aisle from Half Pint was Chief Gunner's Mate Eddie DiCarlo—I call him Nod, as in Wynken and Blynken—taking a long and loving last look at his suppressed Heckler & Koch MP5-PDW before he stowed it in the padded scabbard that would ride on his right thigh. Leaning against the bulkhead just aft of Nod was Master Chief Nasty Nicky Grundle, whom I'd rescued not three weeks ago from a drab training assignment in Hawaii. Nasty's web gear was being checked over carefully by his new swim buddy, a former UCLA linebacker named Boomerang, the only West Coast surfer-puke in my current group of shooters.

Boomerang (he pronounces it "Boom-rang") had earned his nickname during BUD/S. Had he ever. The first time he went through training, he broke his ankle the fifth week. So they held him back until the next cycle. The second time around, he broke his collarbone at the end of the sixth week. This time they tried to wash him out. But the sonofabitch refused to go. He kept coming back for more. And the third time through, he graduated at the top of his BUD/S class—with two broken toes and a cracked rib.

I'd tell you more about Boomerang, but I see that Arch the pilot just blinked the red lights three times. And that whining noise you hear? That's the sound of hydraulics. The sonofabitch is lowering the ramp. And over there, the crewmen are unfolding the tracks so the ICRRC package—specifically the Kevlar-reinforced rubber assault craft, engine, fuel bladder, communications package, and assault gear, all lashed together in one ingenious, parachutable bundle—can roll right off the end of the ramp.

Arch blinked the lights thrice again. That was the get-ready sign. The next signal—the green jump indicator—would be roughly five minutes from now.

Shit—I wasn't ready to go-go-go yet. That was on the one hand. On the other hand, there was that old Rogue Commandment that had to be observed. You know the one. It goes, "Thou hast not to like it—thou hast just to do it."

And, there was much "it" to do. So, I scampered up to the cockpit, gave Arch a thump on the shoulder, a hearty "fuck you, cockbreath," and an upraised middle finger to show how much I cared.

Arch handed the controls to his copilot and swiveled in his chair. "Fuck you, too, asshole," he said through his mask. I could see the smile in his cobra's eyes. "Just stay in one piece, huh?"

I nodded. "I'll try."

He extended his big, gloved hand. "If there's ever anything else I can do—just call. I'm in the book at Kadena—there are lots of Kellys, but only one spelled my way, with an *ie.*"

"How come?"

"We come from the Cuban Kiellys. Grandpa was a Rough Rider who stayed behind. Over the years, the spelling got changed."

I grinned behind my mask, took his hand and clasped it. "Well, Kelly with an *i* and an *e,* don't make any fucking offers you don't mean."

His eyes grew serious. "I never do." Arch swiveled, settled back behind the wheel, made sure he had his feet firmly on the pedals, then nodded to his copilot that he was assuming control.

I plugged my Magellan into the navigator's satellite data display. His radar had our target ship on the screen. It was some 125-odd miles from our current position, traveling due north at a steady six knots an hour.

What was our current position? Well, we were over water now—the South China Sea to be precise—west-northwest of Belitung Island, about 200 miles south of the equator, and 110 degrees east longitude. FYI, we'd flown out of

Guam eleven-plus hours ago on this here MC-130E Combat Talon aircraft, which had been custom painted for us in a dull, black radar-defeating stealth paint. The craft itself bore no identifying markings whatsoever. Neither did anyone in crew. Even so, I can tell you (don't breathe a word of this, okay?) that the plane—as well as its crew—came from the Air Force Special Operations Command's 353rd Special Operations Group, First SpecOps Squadron, based at Kadena Air Base, on Okinawa.

I'm not usually a big fan of the Air Farce. But these guys knew what the fuck—they were pros. So far as I was concerned, Lieutenant Colonel Arch and his aircrew could fly me A^3, which stands for anyplace, anytime, anywhere. He was the type you wanted on a mission like this one. He'd get the job done, *sans* complaint, no matter what it took. I'd known that the moment we'd met: he had the look of a stone killer in his eyes, and he'd never said anything that wasn't in the affirmative.

Once we cleared Guam, we'd climbed quickly to our cruising altitude, the Combat Talon's operational ceiling of thirty-three thousand feet, and headed south by southeast on a route that would take us just under four thousand miles. We skirted Palau, cut a wide swath past Mindanao, refueled from an unmarked tanker over the Makassar Strait, then flew due west over the Borneo jungle before turning north for our final approach to the target. We'd stayed away from radar sites and flown (we hoped) between Russian, Chinese, French, and Israeli satellite passes. We'd maintained strict radio silence. This mission had to be fucking stealth all the way.

I stared through the pilot's windshield. It was the perfect operational milieu: there were no lights to be seen anywhere. I turned away, plugged my Magellan into the naviguesser's console and pulled the latest information from the navigator's forward-looking radar into my own. Then I plugged into the EWO—that's Electronic Warfare Officer—console, and dumped his target information into my own unit, too. That way, I could set a heading after we'd jumped—a course that would bring us down exactly where we had to be. The info loaded, I punched a series of commands into the unit and watched as it responded properly.

Then I turned the Magellan off, waited fifteen seconds, switched it on again, and repeated the cycle. I see you waving your hand out there. You say what? I'd just checked the GPS once, and I was wasting time? Hey, bub—remember the old Rogue's Eighth Commandment. Thou shalt never assume. So I didn't. I double-checked to make sure that the information I'd transferred was stored properly, and that it was displayed the way I was going to need it displayed. I peered down at the screen. Everything was copacetic. Now I knew there was at least one thing Mr. Murphy couldn't screw with tonight: my Magellan system.

The navigation and target info elements secure, I slid down the ladder rails, found the remainder of my own web gear, pulled it on, double-checked all the straps and Velcro closures, shrugged into my reserve chute, then attached my weapons scabbard, rucksack, and all the other miscellaneous goodies necessary for the night's activities. I punched the display screen of my Magellan and called out the coordinates of our target ship to my shooters so they could program their own GPS units. When I got "OK" signals (and a chorus of "Fuck you very much, Skipper") from everyone, I clambered astride the assault craft and clipped my harness straps to the big, black thirteen-cell Vector assault chute I'd ride tonight. I pressed my thighs up against the Kevlar-reinforced rubber.

"Hey—does that feel good, sir?" Nasty Nicky Grundle shouted. If his voice hadn't been muffled by the oxygen mask he wore I would have sworn that he'd spelled *sir* with a *c* and a *u*.

I nodded affirmatively, then did a pretty passable Rin Tin Tin humps Lassie against the gunwale. Ooh—it *did* feel good. Still laughing, Nasty and Boomerang released the tie-downs and began to slide the ICRRC package aft, holding it steady with a pair of safety straps secured to a pintle in the forward cargo area while I waddled behind, looking not so much like your generously endowed Richard as a fifteen-foot rubber-cocked Dick.

I hand-signaled the guys to circle wagons and watched as Gator, Nod, Half Pint, Duck Foot, and Pick flanked the ICRRC, then began to edge slowly aftward, their progress hampered by the hundred-plus pounds of equipment that each man carried.

I looked up to see the air crew chief's face, obscured by oxy mask and goggles, waving Boomerang and Grundle off. They gave the crew chief a thumbs-up, backed away from the ICRRC, and joined the other swim buddies. Seamlessly, they were replaced by two crewmen whose coveralls were crisscrossed by long yellow nylon safety harnesses secured to the aircraft's bulkheads.

We moved aft until we came to the ramp hinge. There, the crew chief signaled a halt. I looked down. There was nothing to see—only blackness and the void. I raised my eyes and looked out horizontally, and saw a constellation in the moonless night. The Southern Cross? Perhaps. Who knew. Certainly not I.

And then the two green lights came on and blinked twice. I drew my right hand across my throat. The crewmen nodded and unhitched the safety lines. I put my whole weight against the ICRRC, screamed a heigh-ho Silver and a hearty "Fuck-you" as I r-o-l-l-e-d it toward the void, tossed the crew chief the bird, and lumbered off the ramp, pulled by the weight of the assault craft.

Normally, I like to throw a hump and watch the plane disappear behind me. But tonight that was impossible—jumping attached to the ICRRC meant a static opening—that is, with the chute's line attached to the plane—and it came real fast. Some invisible giant hand grabbed me by the nuts and slammed me up against the gunwale of the ICRRC two or three times, then took me by the helmet, tried to twist my head in a complete three-sixty like something out of *The Exorcist,* gave up, and finally slapped me up against the boat face first half a dozen times so I'd feel VMA—very much alive. Then, as suddenly as it had started, it was over, and, the ICRRC hanging under me, the descent smoothed out.

I retrieved a red-lensed minilight from a pouch on my chest, tightened its lanyard loop around my wrist, then checked the steering lines and risers to make sure there were no tangles. I counted cells and saw thirteen. The chute appeared to be in textbook perfect condition. Compass heading was north-northeast. I put some of my weight on the steering line and swung the chute twelve degrees to the right, sending the ICRRC and me due north. Altitude was twenty-nine six and falling. I heard flutter around me and looked for the seven other canopies. Nada. Well—it wasn't cause for concern. After all, they were jumping with dark chutes and without lights.

Besides, every man with me tonight had made hundreds of HAHO jumps. They knew they had to key on the infrared strobe lights strapped to my ankles. And if they missed the IR lights, or the strobes died, each man had a Magellan GPS unit on his chest. And if their Magellans crapped out, and they missed my strobes, they'd have a very, very long swim.

But this was no occasion to dwell on failure. In fact, failure is a word I do not recognize. I have only one way to deal with my life, and with my missions: I attack, attack, attack.

And so, I rolled my head back and looked up at the stars. There are times when Warriordom is perfect—and this was one of them. Believe me, there are few experiences as exhilarating, energizing, or invigorating as jumping out of a perfectly good aircraft at an excessive altitude in order to initiate a mission that will stretch one's physical, mental, and operational capabilities way past the 100 percent mark.

And this Mission Impossible would certainly stretch our operational capabilities. We had been tasked by the powers that be (in this case the White House) with carrying out a stealth-quiet component of national policy. As long as I have a couple of minutes here, let me give you some of the background.

According to those solons in charge of things back in Washington, it is crucial to keep our relations with China on an even keel these days. First of all, China has the potential to become a superpower—and you play politics with superpowers differently from the way you do with other nations. Then there is the economic factor. China, you see, is one of our biggest overseas trading partners. From oil companies, whose investments in China total billions of dollars, to American telecom corporations, where tens of thousands of jobs depend on their selling equipment to the Chinese, to industrial machine toolmakers who hope to modernize Chinese plants, to toy manufacturers who buy cut-rate goods there and sell them at top-dollar prices here, China is important to the American economy. How important? Our trade deficit with China was more than fifty billion smackeroos last year. That gives the Chinese a lot of *crout.*

And, of course, there is also the Machiavellian ingredient. During the Cold War, China was our way of keeping the Soviets off guard. That was one of the major reasons Richard Nixon resumed relations with Peking back in 1972. If the Sovs had to keep a million Red Army soldiers on the Manchurian border, that was a million fewer potential adversaries for NATO to face in the West. Today, there may be no more Soviet Union. But the Russians still want to expand their sphere of influence—and one of the most pragmatic ways to keep them bottled up is to employ the Chinese trump. But these days, Peking—which is now spelled Beijing—is a much harder—and wilder—card to play.

So much for history. Now let's look at the current situation. One problem we are facing is a recent rapprochement between Moscow and Beijing—a potentially dangerous political situation because it means that they could coordinate policy to work against the United States. Another complication: the Chinese are finding new ways to flex their political and economic muscles. They've just taken control of Hong Kong, which adds billions of hard currency dollars to their economy. And they're looking for new ways to expand their influence in Asia and elsewhere, all across the Pacific Rim.

One way the Chinese have done so is through weapons. They are the number two weapons exporter in the world—second only to us. Moreover—and more dangerous—the panjandrums in Beijing haven't bothered to act within "conventional" borders. Over the last year, they have started shipping nuclear missile components (a clear violation of U.S. nonproliferation laws as well as the nuclear non-proliferation treaty they'd signed not two years ago) to Pakistan, Libya, and Iran.

Now, it has been obvious to me for some time that the Chinese have decided to use their new-found position and clout to squeeze the United States whenever possible. The problem is that we have not pushed back.

Let me pause here long enough to give you a theory about international relations. It is a concept propounded by Colonel Arthur "Bull" Simon, the Warrior who led the famous 1970 raid on the Son Tay prison in North Vietnam and who, in retirement, was hired by Ross Perot to rescue Perot's people in Iran, back in 1979.

"Bull" used to preach to us SpecWar youngsters. "If history is any teacher," he'd growl, "it teaches you that when you get indifferent and you lose the will to fight, some other sonofabitch who has the will to fight will take you over."

Those are words we should all take to heart. But "Bull" Simon's real-world experience wasn't held in very high esteem by most of those in the current administration. Our latest national security adviser, the newly installed Director of Central Intelligence, and the secretary of state are all practiced in the fine (and cowardly) art of appeasement. You—yes, you out there. You *what?* You want an example of appeasement?

Okay. At the most recent Sino/American ministerial (a ministerial is when our secretary of state and their foreign minister get together and palaver), SECSTATE hesitatingly—almost apologetically—brought up the matter of the slaughter of students at Tiananmen Square, the use of prisoners to make consumer goods, the torture of political dissidents, and the persecution of Christians.

The Chinese foreign minister slammed his palm on the table and said, quote, "The allegation that anyone died at Tiananmen is a lie. Your other assertions are also without basis in reality."

And what did SECSTATE do? SECSTATE did nothing. SECSTATE swallowed hard. And did nothing. The exchange made all the nightly news programs. I felt sickened when I saw it.

And that wasn't the worst. The worst was that the matter of nuclear smuggling was never even brought up. The fact that SECSTATE lacked the *cojones* to confront the Chinese upset me. I was even more upset when I learned from a very good source that our secretary of state had evidence to the contrary in her briefcase. But instead of using it, she sat there and said nothing.

Officially, therefore, the United States had no reaction to China's provocations. More to the point: our secretary of state has requested that the Chinese consider a schedule of summit meetings over the next three years, the first one to take place in six months. The Chinese have taken SECSTATE's request under advisement. Dammit, we didn't set the agenda—we simply made a request.

What did SECSTATE's disastrous performance tell the Chinese? It told 'em we weren't serious. It indicated we didn't have backbone, determination, or guts. It demonstrated weakness. And weakness is something that should never be revealed—not to other people, and certainly not to a nation like China, which is intent on creating a hegemony in its part of the world.

On a clandestine level, however, I am happy to report that not everyone in the administration assumes the same puppylike, belly-exposed, all-four-feet-in-the-air position that our secretary of state, the CIA director, and the national security adviser seem to adapt so regularly.

It had taken three weeks or so, but the president had

finally been convinced (browbeaten may be a more accurate word, but I wasn't in the room) by the Chairman of the Joint Chiefs and SECDEF—the secretary of defense—that Beijing couldn't be allowed to operate unchallenged, especially when it was selling weapons of mass destruction to states that sponsor terrorism directed at the United States.

Indeed, after carefully working his way around the State Department, the CIA, and the NSC chairman, SECDEF actually convinced the president to sign a national security directive that authorized covert military action if it could be proved without possibility of error that the Chinese were in substantial violation of the nonproliferation treaty. SECDEF argued that by acting covertly—by leaving State, CIA, and even the NSC out of the loop—diplomacy could proceed unabated. The president could still hold his regularly scheduled summit meetings with the Chinese—smiling warmly, acting nicey-nicey at the state dinners, but still let 'em understand that we weren't going to be pushed around.

That was where I came in. As you know, five months ago, the JCS Chairman, an Army four-star and lead-from-the-front warrior named Crocker, had me detailed to his office as his ASR—that's Attack SEAL-in-Residence. I'd gone after a bunch of no-goodniks in Moscow and the Middle East (you can read all about it in *Rogue Warrior: Designation Gold*).

Now, my cage had been unlocked once again. The deal was simple: roughly six weeks ago, FORTE satellite surveillance had detected what appeared to be a shipment of nuclear missile components. It tracked them on a long, meandering odyssey from a location deep within China to the Chinese coast. There, after a two-week period in which the missile components were moved from warehouse to warehouse on an irregular schedule—it appeared the Chinese were trying to confound surveillance, which they must have suspected, by trying to play a version of those street-corner shell games. Anyway, the components were finally loaded on what appeared to be a freighter named the *Nantong Princess,* which was moored in Shanghai harbor. The vessel sailed before any HUMINT—that's HUMan INTelligence—could verify the FORTE's assessment.

But the United States knew for certain the ship was not a commercial craft. That fact had been determined by National Security Agency SIGINT (SIGnals INTelligence) monitoring of its shortwave radio broadcasts, as well as its ELINT—ELectronic INTelligence—and TECHINT—TECHnical INTelligence—capabilities. And we knew that it was making a series of stops all around the Pacific Rim, starting in Pusan, South Korea, and ending at Karachi, Pakistan. Further investigations by No Such Agency, the Defense Intelligence Agency, and a couple of other alphabet soup groups that I'd go to jail for ten years for just mentioning, confirmed BRD—that's beyond a reasonable doubt—that the *Nantong Princess* was in fact a military vessel, manned by Chinese naval personnel augmented by *zhongdui* naval recon forces, and therefore a legitimate target for yours truly.

Since Chairman Crocker and I are not only on a first name basis (he calls me "Dick," and I call him "General") but also see the world eye-to-eye when it comes to taking action, he had asked me to come up with a tactical operation plan to make the freighter and its nuclear shipment disappear, but give the Chinese absolutely no opportunity to blame the United States.

Six hours after he'd made his request, I'd shown up at his office with precisely the kind of KISS (that's Keep It Simple, Stupid) operation I like the best. I'd take a small group of men, carry out a covert assault on the *Nantong Princess* in an isolated area during its leg from Jakarta to Singapore, and send it—and its cargo—to the bottom.

And the Chinese? Oh, they might have their suspicions. But I would leave not a trace of evidence to link the U.S. of A. with anything that might happen in the South China Sea. After all, the shipping lanes between Jakarta and Singapore are known to harbor pirates. The waters are filled with sharks. Ships have been known to disappear without so much as the well-known trace. *That* is known as deniability.

The plan I laid on the Chairman's antique desk wasn't a new one. In fact, it was one I'd taken off the shelf from my Cold War days and adapted to the current requirements. The Cold War plan called for a concentrated electronic bombardment of the target vessel to cut off all communications. I wouldn't have that luxury—I'd have to sever the comms myself. The Cold War plan called for a quick extraction by chopper. I'd modified that element, too: we'd extract by submarine. We'd have a beacon and would be able to summon it into the area once we'd completed the sensitive portion of our mission. And the old plan was paid for out of funds supplied by the Department of Defense's Special Operations budget. This one would have to be black funded. To do that, I suggested that the Chairman funnel some of the $50 million in Russkie money I'd sluiced off to him not three months ago, when my old friend Colonel Avi Ben Gal of Israeli Army Intelligence and I stumbled onto a couple of dozen of Moscow's secret bank accounts, during an operation we'd staged in Paris and the Middle East. The bucks (they were Swiss francs, but it would be simple to convert 'em) were easily accessible, no one would ever be the wiser—and best of all, we wouldn't cost the U.S. taxpayer even a single tax dollar. The man actually footing the bill would be Viktor Grinkov, a nasty, unscrupulous, greedy piece of work who currently ran the Russian interior ministry. It was his money—and he had made it clear through a series of backchannels he was upset at us for purloining it.

I laid the OPLAN on Chairman Crocker's desk. He indicated for me to Park It, then donned half-glasses and began to read. When he'd finished, he asked me half a dozen pointed and specific questions, listened as I expanded on the elements he'd queried, then asked me to wait outside while he made a call on the secure phone that sat at his left elbow.

Four minutes later he'd cracked the ornate wood door himself and beckoned me inside. "I like the funding part," he said, smiling. "SECDEF does, too." He paused. "There's only one element I'd like to change," he said.

I'm always open to suggestion if it makes the OPLAN better. "General?"

"I want you to exfil differently. The submarine commander should have no idea where you've been or what you've been doing. So change the pickup position by at least sixty or seventy miles—more if you can, even if it means taking on an additional fuel bladder. I don't want any submarine's log giving out the relative position where your goddam target went down."

I thought about it. Made a lot of sense. Gave us more deniability—and kept the sub's CO out of the loop. "Can do, sir."

"Good." He tossed my op-plan at me—I caught it one-handed—then pointed his thumb and index fingers in my direction in his trademark "Colt .45" fashion and said, "Then, go get 'em, Dick." Then he added the qualifier. Here is the Rogue Warrior's First Law of Covert Operations: There is always a qualifier.

Unlike most, this one was simple but direct. "Don't fail, don't leave any pecker tracks, and don't get caught," is what the Chairman told me, his face serious.

So, as is usual in my life, there was going to be no wriggle room for error. I had to stage my assault in a totally stealth fashion. I had to take over the ship before any message could be sent out. And I had to neutralize the whole fucking crew. That is a politically correct way of telling you I wasn't going to be taking any prisoners tonight.

Don't look so shocked. War is not nice. And this, no matter what you might think, was war.

Back to the business at hand. After all, there was work to be done—to wit, I had to guide us to the second phase of the mission and set us down ten nautical miles due south of our target. I pressed the switch on the Magellan GPS unit that sat next to the altimeter on my chest pack. The screen illuminated, but I saw no information. No distance to target. No heading. No latitude. No longitude. No nothing.

WTF. I pressed the on/off switch again. And again, the display came up blank.

Let me pause here for just a few seconds to explain the kind of unkosher pickle I was in.

Looking for a single ship in the South China Sea can be a problem *if*: *if* you are coming from the air; *if* it is night; *if* the ship does not want to be found; and *if* you do not know where the fuck you are relative to the target. Am I making things plain enough for you?

Yes, I had a compass. I could steer north, south, east, and west. I had an altimeter. I knew how high I was. But without the Magellan, which gets its signals from a GPS, or Global Positioning Satellite, I had no way of knowing where I was in relation to the target. I had no course to follow. No glide path to glide along.

My men had Magellans. But I couldn't use their units to help me because we had no way of making contact. Sure I was carrying a radio—but it and all its gear was stowed securely in my chest pack, and there was no way to use it. More to the point, even if I pulled it out and set it up, my guys' radios were in *their* chest packs.

Now, both you and I know that the Magellan was working just fine not ten minutes ago. But that was then and this was now and I was being screwed with by Mr. Murphy more than I wanted to be.

Okay. Let us be logical here. The batteries were working. That I knew because the screen lit up. But the antenna obviously wasn't working. *Why* wasn't it working? I stared at it and tried to be logical. And in staring, I had an epiphany. Y'know, as my old shipmate Doc Tremblay has told me more than once, sometimes I do have fartbeans for brains. The goddamn thing wasn't working because I'd forgotten to plug the antenna, which was located in my helmet, into the unit.

I reached inside my flight suit, brought the connector wire

out, plugged it securely into the Magellan's base, and turned the power on once again. Bingo. Full display. Now, perhaps, it *was* time to sit back and enjoy the ride.

Six thousand feet and descending through thickening clouds. My oxygen had barely lasted through fifteen five, and by the time I'd cleared ten five I was feeling the effects of hypoxia. That is to say, I felt sluggish and drowsy, my muscles wouldn't react very quickly, and my vision was blurred. What's the problem? The problem was that I wasn't making the turns I had to, when I had to—and I was therefore drawing all of us off course.

I fought my body with my body—tried to regain control over myself. But I wasn't having any luck.

Fuck it—I yanked on the right steering line and went into a tight, corkscrewing turn that dumped me fifteen hundred feet—from just above eleven thou to nine thou five—in just under a minute. It worked—the thick air was like a slap in the puss. I was back in control. I caught a thermal, gained a little altitude, and checked my instruments to see how much I'd screwed up.

It wasn't as bad as it could have been. Despite my problems, we'd made progress—some tailwind action had brought us farther along the track than I'd anticipated. That was good—the less distance we had to travel on the water, the better off we'd be. I looked down toward the choppy surface a mile below my boots. Like the Pacific, the South China Sea is an unpredictable, often nasty place. And that's when you've shipped out in something that's measured in the hundreds of tons. Our craft was less than twenty feet in length. It was powered by a single, although powerful, outboard motor.

There was a change in the sound of my parachute. Have I ever explained that you can tell from the way the air passes the foils what your chute is going to do? Well, you can. And from the way things currently sounded, I was about to pick up some crosswind.

I looked up—not much to see. Then, suddenly, the

ICRRC and I were yanked to port. Jerked hard. Crosswind, hell—that was a fucking wind shear. I pulled hard on the steerage lines and risers to bring us back around. No response. I hung on the lines with all my weight. Still nothing. Then I looked up and realized that one of the outer cells had buckled.

That was bad juju. Very bad juju. That is an understatement. You do not want your chute to buckle and collapse, because the chute is what keeps you from hitting the water at about 120 feet per second. And hitting water at 120 feet per second produces the same nasty result as hitting concrete at 120 feet per second. Am I making the point to you through ironic use of numerical repetition? Good. I think the Naval Special Warfare technical term for the condition I am describing is: "go splat."

I was not fucking about to go splat. Not tonight, anyway. I used the ICRRC as a platform, hoisted myself up, stood on the gunwales of the fucking boat, grabbed a handful of the starboard-side risers, and began to hoist myself up them, as if they were a climbing rope. That maneuver sent us into a spin—corkscrewing the ICRRC and me down at an accelerated speed.

But it also filled the leading edge of the canopy and the stabilizers with air. I could fucking feel the difference.

Now all I had to do was reverse the spin. How to do that? Let go the risers and drop—letting my harness absorb the shock—would probably work. I released my grip and dropped. As I hit—hard—I perceived that I'd made an ever-so-slight miscalculation about the weight factor and its consequences. You—the asshole laughing out there—you're ahead of me, aren't you? *You* realized I hadn't factored in the weight of the ICRRC, and so it wasn't my harness that bore the brunt of my six-foot drop, but my nuts—an eye-crossing, testicle-squeezing jolting kick that left me feeling like I'd be singing falsetto for the next couple of weeks.

I checked the compass and worked the steering handles to bring me back to a correct heading. That done, I began my final approach check, as I was under three thousand feet now and descending rapidly toward the water's surface. I heard the flutter of other chutes and looked around to see one, two, three, four shadows closing up behind me. I hoped the rest of my crew was there. But there'd be no way to tell until we all hit the water.

And then it was on us and things happened all at once. The water had what looked like a three-foot chop—more than I would have liked, but not as bad as it could have been. I cut the ICRRC package away at twenty-five feet. It dropped like a stone but landed right side up and ready to go. Then I released my combat rucksack so it wouldn't drag me down like a sea anchor when I hit the water.

Suddenly, instead of coasting the last four yards to the surface, I soared skyward. The big cargo chute caught a gust of air and, unfettered by the weight of the ICRRC package, began to lift me up and away. Shit. Fuck. I was at about ten yards—and sixteen, maybe even eighteen miles an hour—when I cut away. I dropped like the proverbial goddamn thrown stone. Which is to say, I slapped against the choppy surface face first and careened forward like one of those rolling bombs used by the World War II Dam Busters. My left foot caught in my rucksack line, which caused me to ball up and soar ass over teakettle, then flatten out and smack the surface in a painful belly-whopper. The momentum flipped me twice, then—somehow, I saw what was coming—I managed to grab half-a-lungful of air before my hundred-plus pounds of equipment sank and dragged me below the surface.

I struggled against the weight, my legs scissoring and my arms windmilling. Maybe it's the fact that I come from a down-and-out coal mining town in Pennsylvania, but I wasn't enjoying a lot of upward mobility right then.

Time to get serious: I grabbed the inflate tab of my CQC vest and yanked it. There was a satisfying *hiss,* the fucking thing filled with air, and I fought my way up, spitting seawater as I breached the surface like a goddamn killer whale.

I sputtered, and cursed at nothing in particular, then started to flail toward the ICRRC, which bobbed in the two-and-a-half-foot chop perhaps a 150 yards away. By the time I reached it, my lungs were heaving and I was sweating into my wet suit despite the fact that the water temperature was in the low seventies. Believe me, it is not easy to swim, even with a flotation device on, when you're lugging half your body weight in soggy equipment.

I lashed my rucksack to the gunwale hand-lines and cut the umbilical cord that secured it to my harness. Then I inflated my UDT vest to give me more buoyancy, then began the laborious process of removing the craft's drop package, so we could turn this useless lump of reinforced rubber and Kevlar into an assault craft.

The weighted pallet was first. I sliced the nylon netting with my K-Bar. The pallet sank away just as it had been designed to do. Next, I carefully sheathed my knife (I've seen people slice through rubber raiding craft during the boarding process before, and I wasn't about to do that and turn myself and my men into shark feed tonight), grabbed the closest hand-line, pulled myself up, muscled over the gunwale, heaved myself into the boat, and performed one of my more improbable rolls onto the floorboards, which is to say I managed to land face first and smack my nose—*thwap-slap*—against the forward thwart cleat.

WTF. Or, as the long-suffering, hard-working chain-smoking dweeb editor is so fond of misstating, "no pain . . . no pain."

I shrugged out of the CQC vest and secured that, too. I was about to begin my boat equipment check solo when Nasty Nicky Grundle's size twelve paw grabbed the hand-line, and he heaved himself over the gunwale with a grunt, and a friendly, "Fuck you very much, Skipper."

My extended middle finger told him that he was number one with me, too.

Nasty shrugged himself out of his equipment and secured it. Then he began to unbolt the 155-horsepower outboard motor that lay on its side, secured to the floorboard. He was about halfway done when I heard splashing and looked up to see Boomerang, Gator Shepard, Nod DiCarlo, and Half Pint Harris sidestroking toward the ICRRC. About twenty yards behind them, Duck Foot and the Pick played catch-up. That was eight out of eight. We'd be at full strength tonight.

I found the engine mounting brackets and motor bracket in their compartment and fitted them into place on the ICRRC's stern transom. Then I reached down and helped Nasty steady the outboard. He took the driveshaft, I held the cowling, and we lifted in unison—the goddamn thing was a heavy mother, too. Carefully we slid the motor over the engine mounting brackets, attached it to the outboard bracket just behind the transom, and tightened the clamp screws firmly.

Boomerang freed the thirteen-gallon fuel bladder from its stowage cradle in the bow, humped it aft over the two thwart tubes, and began to secure it in position adjacent to the engine. Thirteen gallons was one point nine times the amount of gas we needed to get to our target, and then to our final extraction point. Despite that huge safety margin, if there had been room on the ICRRC I would have brought a second fuel bladder with us. Things go wrong: bladders can leak; fuel gets used up faster than you foresee; or maybe Mr. Murphy decides to put in an unscheduled appearance. Bottom line: gasoline is something you don't want to run out of in the middle of a goddamn ocean.

My other merry marauders tied their rucksacks to the hand-lines, clambered aboard, then set about making our minicraft into a seaworthy man o' war. They didn't spend a lot of time talking to one another—they just Did the Job. That is common in units like mine. That is to say, units in which the men have worked together for so long that they don't need to speak, they simply converse in a kind of nonverbal, body-language shorthand.

Suddenly it began to rain. The sort of slow, steady,

drenching rain common to the tropics. The hair on the back of my neck stood up as I sensed a shift in the surface wind. Just another couple of Murphy elements to factor into the morning's events. I glanced at the luminous Timex on my wrist. It was just past 0100. I knew that sunrise was at 0650. By then, the *Nantong Princess* had to be in two pieces, sitting on the bottom in seventeen hundred feet of water.

Chapter

2

0127. Under most conditions, the ICRRC is ruled to be a tremendously seaworthy craft. The operative word in the previous sentence is *most.* I could tell that tonight was going to be an exception to the rule. We were overloaded by perhaps three hundred pounds—which meant we rode precariously low in the unruly, growing chop and huge arythmic swells. We were being buffeted by crosswinds, which were compounded by the rain squalls. The motion under way was not unlike the worst of the old-style roller coasters: long climbs as the waves swelled, followed by kidney-shattering drops into the troughs. You know those seventeenth-century Japanese woodcuts, with the stylized ocean waves that look like claws, waiting to rake a boat to shreds? Well, those artists knew WTF they were depicting. It is not a pleasant sensation to look up and see waves hovering ominously twenty-three feet above your head. I'm talking about waves that are about to crash over—and into—your tiny fucking craft. Oh, yeah, we were taking on enough water to make baling a mandatory and full-time operation.

The op-sked—which as you have probably already figured out stands for operational schedule but could tonight also stand for optimistic schedule—called for us to maintain the ICRRC's top speed of eighteen knots over the whole run to the *Nantong Princess.* Eighteen knots minus the *Nantong*'s six meant we'd be able to close on her within an hour and a half.

Of course, the ocean does not always cooperate. Right now, for example, despite the fact that I was running the outboard at full throttle we were barely making eight knots. According to my Magellan, the *Nantong Princess* was eighteen nautical miles due north of us, cruising at a steady six knots. Our net forward progress—by which I mean our closing distance—therefore, was a miserly two knots an hour.

Have I told you that fucking sunrise was at fucking 0650? Have I mentioned that by then I had to have fucking sunk the fucking Chinese ship? Have I explained that the *Nantong* fucking *Princess* was eighteen fucking miles ahead of us and that we didn't fucking have nine fucking hours of fucking sailing time? Am I making my emotional state clear to you? Good. I always like to be clear, unambiguous, explicit, precise, direct.

0214. The rain stopped as suddenly as it had begun, and we picked up seven knots of speed. I checked the Magellan. Now the Chinese ship was sixteen and a half miles ahead of us if its pace had remained steady. That gave us just over two hours to close the gap. Maybe the window of opportunity hadn't closed down on us—but the bottom rail was resting on our fingers, metaphorically speaking.

0249. The engine coughed, sputtered, and died. After I finished a pretty passable imitation of my old platoon boss, Chief Gunner's Mate/Guns Everett Emerson Barrett, whose ability to tweak the F-word into a string of compound, complex run-on sentences containing all its known mutations is legendary in Naval Special Warfare, I settled down and began to try to see what the problem might be.

We checked the fuel line from the bladder. It was unobstructed. There appeared to be no extraneous water in the engine or exhaust system. Then I opened the cowling. Mr.

Murphy had somehow loosened one of the spark plugs—it sat dangling at the end of its wire. Nod dried it off, sprayed it dry with compressed air, and pressed it home. Half Pint played the part of snipe—pumping fresh gas into the line, priming the engine, adjusting the choke, then finally yanking the starter cord. The engine coughed, sputtered, then erupted into a welcome, throaty growl, Nod shut down the choke, tweaked the throttle, and we Tally-Ho'd.

0317. We progressed through the swells at sixteen-and-a-half, seventeen, seventeen-and-a-half knots. The Chinese freighter was only six or so nautical miles ahead of us now. We couldn't see it, but it was almost as if I could sense the fucking thing out there—waiting.

0331. We pulled within two miles. As the ICRRC crested the swells, we began to see the *Nantong Princess*'s underway lights twinkling in the distance. Not every time we crested, but every fourth or fifth time. It was enough to prime our sense of anticipation.

0340. We started to feel the ship's wake under the ICRRC's floorboards. That really told us we were getting close. I could see a change come over my men. Before, they'd pretty much kept to themselves, staring out at the water, each man lost in his own thoughts. The wake, which meant that action was close at hand, brought them out of their individual reveries and made them come together as warriors.

Boomerang and Duck Foot, my lead climbers, checked out the rolled caving ladders and the collapsible painter's poles they would use to snag the ladders in the freighter's rail. The rest of the group ran weapons checks, locked and loaded, and secured their combat gear. Gator attached a hundred-foot nylon line to the boat's bow ring. We'd have to secure the ICRRC to the freighter so we'd have a way to extract once the scuttling charges had been placed and armed.

0355. The wake was much reduced now—it was as if we were dead-heading. And then, all of a sudden, we were on her. Somehow, it always happens like that. One instant you're out there—all alone. The next, you come on your target—wham.

The fantail loomed ghostlike in the darkness—a fucking modernistic skyscraper topped by a railing. We could feel the power of her screws now, and we got the blast of heat from the *Nantong Princess*'s discharges. Her name, in yellow Chinese and English letters a foot high, spread out above me like a gap-toothed smile.

I was wet. I was cold. I was tired. And I hurt like hell. But my whole body ignored the whole nasty package. Why? Because I'd just gone into automatic, preaction sensory overload.

No, I am not bullshitting you. I am not giving you some kind of Warrior pseudo-psychobabble. This stuff is real, folks.

Before you go into battle, several things happen to you. Your breathing gets shallow. Your legs may feel a little shaky. Sometimes there's a slight feeling of nausea. And you always experience a huge adrenaline dump.

Those who haven't gone into battle before try to fight or even deny these signals. But those of us who've been there many times let our bodies take the lead. What we are experiencing is the same temporary queasiness every great actor or tenor feels before he goes onstage; the same knot-in-gut feelings pro football players get before the Super Bowl, or tennis pros undergo at Wimbledon. So I let my heart race. I allowed my breathing to go shallow. I felt the bile rise in my throat. And then, as quickly as it had come over me, the wave of sensation faded, subsided, evaporated. I knew my body and my soul were ready for any challenge—and I prepared to go to war.

0358. In the world of commercial shipping, the *Nantong Princess* could not be considered a big vessel. It looked like your everyday tramp steamer—perhaps 250, 260 feet in length, with a beam of 35 feet or so. We're talking about a displacement here of somewhere close to 2100 tons.

But from where we sat on the water, she looked like a fucking behemoth. We eased up close and pulled alongside. Nod was at the throttle, working hard to keep us even with the dark steel plates. That's a lot harder than it might seem. You're in a tiny craft that is fighting the ocean. The ship also creates its own currents—a contrapuntal situation in which the sea pulls you in one direction and the shock waves caused by the ship pull you in another. So your craft moves forward, sideways, and backward simultaneously.

You, there. Yes, you—the one with the thick glasses, the plastic pen protector in your pocket, and your hand flapping like a fuckin' pennant in the wind—you say what I've just described is impossible according to the laws of physics? Listen, bub—if you haven't been there, then S^2 (look it up in the Glossary) and keep reading.

The good news was that we had the power to move at eighteen knots so that keeping up with the ship, which was going at six or so, wasn't a problem. Keeping our ICRRC in an even course, however, was something else.

Now, you are probably wondering how we could make our approach so brazenly—we were perfectly visible in the open sea, after all, and our outboard was roaring at full throttle. The answer is that ships make a, well, shipload of noise. The turbines that drive the engines roar. The ship itself rolls and moans and groans. And there are large numbers of decibels of ambient noise: the screws churning, the bow cutting through the water, the sound of the waves and wind. All of these elements served to mask our approach.

Moreover, we were on a small, dark craft. And frankly it is hard to see anything at night, especially on the ocean, and especially if it is just before 0400, when most of the folks on board are asleep, and those who aren't, aren't at their top form. To see us you would have had to: 1. be in precisely the right place at the right time; 2. be looking for us; and, 3. be the winner of this week's fuckin' lucky club. Get the point? Good.

0401. I gave Nod a thumbs-up. He brought the ICRRC in close to the ship's low, port side amidships rail. Boomerang and Duck Foot extended their painter's poles with the caving ladders attached, reached up, and tried to hook the rail. This is more difficult to perform than describe, because the ship was moving in one rhythm, we were moving in another, and there is a current that flows alongside the ship that has its own syncopation. There is a Naval Special Warfare technical term for this continually mutating chain of events. It is called entering the FUBAR Zone. Entering the FUBAR Zone can be lethal.

See, when the rail was low enough to hook, we were too low by three feet to hook it. When we were in the right position, the rail was four feet above where we could reach because the ship was riding a different set of swells than we were.

Did you know that you cannot take over a ship if you can't get aboard? Well, I was learning this basic fact of warfare here and now. I waved Boomerang and Duck Foot off. I needed three more feet of height.

I hooked a thumb in Duck Foot Dewey's direction. "Get up on Boomerang's shoulders and try it from there—JUST GET UP THE FUCKING LADDER AND DO IT NOW!!"

"Roger, Skipper." Duck Foot clambered onto the forward thwart, then stuck his leg over Boomerang's shoulder.

"C'mon, dude." Boomerang helped Duck Foot straddle his neck. That was the easy part. Standing up was something else. Remember, we were bobbing up and down, and in and out, and side to side. There was pitch and there was yaw. There was roll and there was heave.

Swaying like a fucking drunk, Boomerang struggled to his feet just as the ICRRC hit a bad swell. "Fuuuck—" He went over sideways, launching Duck Foot ass-over-backward, toward the gunwale. Nasty and I made simultaneous diving tackles. I got hung up in the caving ladder—split my lip, smacked my nose, and missed Duck Foot completely. But Nasty grabbed him by the boot just as he was s-l-i-d-i-n-g overboard.

I spat blood and slammed Nasty on the shoulder. "Nice shoestring, asshole."

Nasty grinned and patted Duck Foot's balaclava'd forehead. "Aw, Skipper, I'm kinda used to having him around.

He's so cute and small—it's like having my own fuckin' hamster."

Duck Foot smacked the big SEAL hard enough to bring tears to his eyes. "And fuck you back very much, too," he said.

0402. No time for small talk—we were vulnerable down here, and if we didn't get up the goddam ladder soon, we were going to be visited by Mister Murphy. Duck Foot hoisted himself on Boomerang's shoulders. He snagged the rail on the second try, secured the hook, and started up the caving ladder. Gator and Pick covered him with MP5s.

One of the reasons my men and I pump a lot of iron is that climbing a caving ladder while boarding a ship under way calls for humongous upper body strength. The ladder itself is made of stainless steel cable, with titanium rungs. The fucking thing swings like a goddamn pendulum, and each increment is painful. Climbing a caving ladder is hard enough when you're doing it in training. But in combat, when you are carrying weapons and other equipment, it is a motherfucker.

I could see the strain on Duck Foot as he made his way inch by painful inch. But he never stopped. The sonofabitch just kept moving until he'd reached the top. Then he looked down, saw that he was covered, and he rolled over the rail.

This is the most vulnerable time. The man on top is unprotected, and if a crewman decides to come out on deck for a smoke, there can be trouble. But for once, Mr. Murphy decided to stay in his bunk. By the time Duck Foot unsheathed his MP5, Boomerang was already pulling his long frame up the caving ladder.

Two men on top—we weren't home free yet, but we were a lot better off than we had been ninety seconds ago. Duck Foot lowered a rope and I tied the second caving ladder to it. He pulled it up and snagged a scupper. Pick and Half Pint scampered up—one went fore, one moved aft. Now we had some fucking firepower up there. Gator and I went next. He had the coil of nylon line that was attached to the ICRRC's bow ring.

I grabbed the cable side rail, slid my boot onto the highest rung I could reach, and pulled myself upward. Fuck me—that *hurt.* By the fifth rung I knew I was in the midst of a very existential experience.

0409. Nod, wheezing and sweating, rolled over the rail and collapsed in a heap, hyperventilating. I gave the kid a few seconds to catch his breath. While he dry-heaved I stared down at the water. Two dozen feet below us, the ICRRC bobbed alongside in the current.

0410. We were forty-fucking-five minutes behind the op-sked I kept in my head, so it was fucking time to go to fucking work already.

I gave hand signals and we split into two prearranged groups. Yes, I know just like you do that we were all wearing radios, and we all had wire lip mikes and earpieces so we could communicate securely and quietly. But you don't want to use a radio unless you absolutely positively have to. Radios are particularly Murphy prone. They develop static and crackle at the most inconvenient times. They spontaneously spout loud feedback. And if you press the transmit button and you happen to be close to a TV set or another radio, you can often give your position—or at least your presence—away because your transmission will leak and "print" on that other set. That was why, according to my op-plan, we'd maintain radio silence until the last possible minute.

Okay—Nasty, Boomerang, Half Pint, and the Pick, my Red Squad, headed aft, toward the stern, where the interior ladderway to the engineering compartment was located. They knew their way because they'd studied detailed satellite photos and memorized their route. Simultaneously, Gator, Duck Foot, Nod and I—Blue Squad—would take down the bridge.

It's about to get busy, but let me explain a little bit here about boarding and neutralizing tactics. Your primary objective in any ship-boarding operation is to capture the bridge. If you are in control of the bridge, then you are in control of the entire ship. The EMERGENCY STOP control is always located on the bridge—which means you can bring the vessel to an absofucking complete stop. The captain's quarters are generally close by, too. So is the comm center, the radar room, and—often—the officers' quarters as well.

That is the up side. The down side is that there's likely to be more action—even at this hour—in the vicinity of the bridge than anywhere else aboard the ship. The current NAVSEA (NAVal SEA Systems Command) operational manual for what in SpecWar we call VBSS/H, which stands for Visit Board Search and Seizure operations against potentially Hostile shipping platforms, calls for a minimum of four shooters and two backup shooters when assaulting even the smallest ship's bridge. The assault force generally has an eight-shooter unit in play, plus at least one heliborne sniper uuit.

Cautiously, we moved forward along the weather deck, toward a ladder that I knew from the same series of satellite pictures led to a passageway just off the bridge where the *mo-sin-tin-shang* had his station. *Mo-sin-tin-shang* means radio operator in Chinese.[1]

---

[1]Yes, I know I'm not consistent about using the officially approved, Beijing standard, *Hanyu Pinyin* phonetic transcription spelling that the Chinese Communists foisted on the world some years ago. But you see, the Chinese Communists aren't very nice or moral or honorable people. And despite the fact that this administration has decided to pussyfoot around that fact and grant them most favored nation trading status, the Chinese government uses slave labor to produce goods it sells abroad; it condones torture; it is one of the most repressive governments on the face of this planet; and it clandestinely sells weapons of mass destruction to unstable regimes all over the goddam globe. That makes the Chinese more than a potential adversary in my book. They are a fucking threat to my country. So there's no way I'm going to play their game—not politically, or militarily. And there's no way I'm going to follow the spelling and pronunciation rules imposed by these totalitarian assholes. Besides, I'm the fucking Rogue Warrior, and I can fucking do what I fucking want.

Now, the SIGINT guys at No Such Agency had provided me with good, but not complete, intel. By that I mean, I knew which passageway I had to be in to neutralize the radio operator—but not which precise compartment the *mo-sin-tin-shang* worked in.

0412. Up the ladder. At the top were two companionway doors side by side. I picked the forward-most one—the one closest to the bridge—reached down, and tried the handle. It was unlatched. I lifted the lever slowly, released the catch without a sound, and moved inside.

The lights were dim, but I could make out six louvered wood compartment doors lining the narrow, puke yellow passageway. Unlike the clean sea breeze outside, the air in the passageway was stale. I wrinkled my nose and inhaled. The unpleasant mélange was a fetid mixture of cigarette smoke, sweat, garlic, BO, and Chinese grunge. Obviously, this crew didn't spend a lot of time policing their quarters—or themselves.

We moved slowly and deliberately. I had the point, my suppressed MP5 in low ready, my finger indexed alongside the trigger guard. Behind my right shoulder I could sense Nod's submachine gun. His field of fire complemented my own—and protected my left flank. Behind Nod came Duck Foot, his eyes scanning left-right, right-left as he moved cautiously, MP5 at the ready, breaching shotgun in a quiverlike sheath across his back. Gator Shepard brought up the rear, his back almost touching Duck Foot's.

My first concern was the radio room. We had to silence the ship—cut it off from the world. I checked the doors. None had any lettering. That told me these six compartments were probably officers' quarters.

Damn—this was going to knock us even further off schedule. I used hand signals to tell Gator and Duck Foot to deal with the six compartments while Nod and I continued onward. Gator's head went up-and-down once, Duck Foot gave me a single thumb-up and Nod and I moved off.

No, it wasn't a Good Idea to split my force in two. But

guess what—I had no choice right now. The satellite pictures I'd seen told me my gang of eight was up against three dozen or so Chinese. And experience has taught me that satellites don't always give you an accurate picture when it comes to personnel counts. After all, they can't gather the crew on deck for a yearbook photo. They shoot a series of images over a period of time, and then the intel weenies who insist they know how to make sense out of pigeon entrails tell me what they think they see.

So you tell me three dozen, mister intel-man, and I'll tell you I'm gonna add 20 percent—maybe even a few more points than that—to your guesstimate. So far as I was concerned, we were up against five-to-one odds, minimum. That meant each of my men and I were going to have to carry his own share of the operational weight—plus the extra heavy five-to-one ratio SOS—which as you can probably figure out, means sack o' shit.

Now, things weren't as bad as they might seem. The general rules of maritime room clearance—the ones I was talking about a few paragraphs ago—were written for two-man, not four- or six-man teams. Why? Because with the exception of such areas as the bridge, the crew lounge, the mess deck, and the engineering sections, most of the compartments aboard a ship are tiny. Try to put four or six men inside at one time and you'll probably end up shooting your swim buddy.

That was the up side. The down side was that we were going to have to deal with each compartment as we worked our way to the bridge because I didn't want anyone nipping at our heels. That's a general rule of all tactical teams: you never leave an unsecured area behind you. It may take more time—but your men stay alive.

0413. The end of the passageway was either a T or an L—it was impossible to tell from my present position. Didn't matter now, anyway—too much to do first.

I took the left side, so I could see forward, and cut the pie, moving so as to protect myself as I came around. Glanced back—it was a dead end. No doors. No hatches, no passageways.

Moved into the passageway to my right, now. Step by step—heel, toe. Heel, toe. My eyes scanning, MP5 in low ready. Trigger finger indexed. Breathing steadily so I wouldn't hyperventilate.

Three doorways on my port side—nothing to starboard.

Behind me—where Gator and Duck Foot were—I thought I heard the *crack-knuckle* sound of their MP5 hammers falling in three shot groups.

First door. Nothing. Second door—Chinese characters on it. I looked down at my left hand where I'd inked my clib sheet. The characters didn't match. Third door. Three characters in bold strokes. I checked. Double-checked. They matched. I searched for hinges and saw none—which meant the door opened inward.

My eyes told Nod which way I was going, and what he had to do.

Nod gave me a single affirmative nod of his head and backed away, toward the first of the three doors. He'd take down each room, one by one, while I dealt with the communications shack.

I dropped, peered under the door, and checked for illumination. There was weak, blue-green light coming from the room.

I rose. Held the MP5 in place against my shoulder with my right hand. Left hand on doorknob. S-l-o-w turn.

It was unlatched. I nudged it inward, slow but deliberate, until I got it a third of the way open.

From the doorway I could see three targets inside—three *mo-sin-tin-shangs*.

Immediate threat—the *mo-sin-tin-shang* hunched in front of the old-fashioned green-on-black computer screen, behind a desk/console to my left. He was awake and alert. And he was in close proximity to a bank of buttons and switches that I didn't like the look of at all.

Secondary threats—the other two, who were sacked out

catching *z*'s on the lumpy lower racks of two small messy bunk bed units bolted to the bulkhead on the opposite side of the compartment. One was in skivvies and an aged yellow T-shirt. The other slept in a puke green uniform that looked like pictures I've seen of Korean war–era marine utilities.

I slid inside, my MP5 up, my sight picture forming nicely. This, my friends, is what it's all about—all the pain of getting here; all the wet, and the cold, and the unwelcome presence of Mr. Murphy—none of that fucking matters anymore. Why? Because it's *Show time,* ladies and germs.

Maybe it was the movement—maybe he sensed me the way people sixth-sense threats. Computer-man swiveled in his chair. Reached for something lying on the computer table.

Time freezes in situations like this one—to the participant everything takes place in slo-motion (or, in this case, slo-*mo-sin-tin-shang*-shun); almost like freeze-frame photography. And yet, things happen so fucking fast—no time even to think, just *react* and *do.*

Didn't waste a millisecond—I sight-acquire-fired. Caught him midreach with three of my frangible 147-grain noname hi-shock bullets right in the head. He went down as if he'd been mule kicked. Hit the desk face first—what was left of his face, that is—clattering the keyboard and knocking what he'd been reaching for—a small semiauto pistol—off the desk into a corner.

One down. I kept moving, closing space between me and Threats Two and Three. You never stop moving; never give up any space. Don't allow the opposition any edge at all. They were moving now—shifting from sleep to wake at the strange sounds.

You can sleep through almost anything if you're accustomed to it. Trains running next to your bedroom window, barking dogs, you name it—if it happens regularly, your brain programs itself. That's why folks who can sleep through a goddam hurricane hear people breaking into their houses—because the sounds of the break-in play differently on that piano they keep in their subconscious.

So what happened? Threats Two and Three came up from their bunks as if they'd been hit with a jolt of electric current. Talk about your dropped-jaw stare. Well, I must have been a fucking sight, too—blood from my split lip running down into my balaclava. All in basic black *sans* pearls, and MP5, up, aimed, and ready to go-go-go.

Left-side bunk rolled out onto the floor. I saw where he was going: the ladderback chair where a pistol belt hung. I stitched him with two three-round bursts and he stopped moving. Now the right-side bunk man—the puke green utilities—moved. He was reaching for something wedged above him.

Had to stop him quick. Fixed his chest dead center in the bright Trijicon night sight front blade and squeezed off a three-round burst.

Nothing. The hammer fell, but no shot. The sound of that hollow *click* rang in my ears louder than a fucking flash-bang explosion.

Fuck me. I racked and tapped and ratcheted the action just like I'd done more than a thousand times in CQC training sessions. An unfired shell ejected—another one went into the chamber and the bolt slammed closed. I squeezed the trigger. *Click.*

I saw the *mo-sin-tin-shang* in the bunk doin' the loco-*mo-sin.* He realized I was doomded—as in doom on me—and he obviously wanted to help the situation along. I dropped the MP5 and launched myself at him—a full-bore, horizontal lunge that took me across the seven feet of compartment—to strike him in the throat, keep the sonofabitch quiet, and keep him away from whatever it was he wanted so badly.

I managed to grab Mr. *Mo*—after all, in situations like this you should be on a first name basis—by the Adam's apple—his call for help was squelched into a silent gulp—

but he used my momentum to carry me—*slam, wham, damn*—Slovak noggin-first into the effing bulkhead.

Talk about seeing fucking stars—it was July Fourth, New Year's Eve, and fucking Coronation Day all at once. My head was dingdonging like the goddam bells of Saint Paul's. My eyes were crossed from the pain of sudden, traumatic neck compression—and that's *my* neck we're talking about, not his.

This guy must not only have studied the martial arts, but he'd also read Sun Tzu, because he sure followed the old bastard's advice for winning, which goes, "When your enemy is weak, become strong."

First he clawed at my eyes. Neck pain be damned—I pulled back and his fingers missed. But he still raked my face and scratched the hell out of it. Then he set about tearing the balaclava off my head—got it about halfway, wrapped his hands around the material, and tried to apply it as a tourniquet to my throat—no doubt to staunch the blood from my split lip and lacerated face.

When Mr. *Mo* realized that it wasn't working—that was after I managed to bring my knee up into his nuts hard enough to make him gag—he tried to remove my right ear with his teeth while he struggled to lay his wily (or wiry, take your choice) Oriental hands on—now I could see it—the nasty-looking stiletto that was wedged in the springs of the bunk above his own rack.

I'm not big on stilettos—unless I'm the one wielding 'em. So it was time to change the venue. Now, I am a big chap, and I outweighed Mr. *Mo* by at least sixty or seventy pounds. But since we were rolling around in a tightly restricted area—namely his bunk, which was maybe six feet by a foot and a half, and he was a persistent little rodent, he had the immediate advantage. Plus with every wriggle, writhe, and wrestle, he was moving closer and closer to the damn pig sticker.

Oh, there was also the noise factor. Frankly, I not only had to kill this sonofabitch—I had to do it quickly, and without letting him make any more fucking noise than he already had made.

Time to get serious. I wrapped him up with my arms and legs and rolled us both off the bunk, landing on top of him with all my weight. That did two things. First, it took him away from his weapon. Second, it knocked the wind out of him—at least long enough for me to work my left forearm under his neck and try to crush his windpipe.

He fought back, but he was losing strength and I was gaining it. Frankly, some of that is size, some of it is diet, and some of it is the fact that I wanted to kill him *mo* than he wanted to kill me—in other words, simple Froggish determination.

Reached with my right for the K-Bar. Wrestled it out of its sheath and brought it up. He tried to fight it away, but I was on top of him and his arms were pinioned. Slammed the blade into him just under the rib cage, and cut upward in a twisting motion, toward the lungs and heart, until he stopped struggling.

Rolled off him. Took his head in my hands and twisted sharply to break his neck—just to make sure he'd stay down.

Clambered onto hands and knees, sweating and out of breath. But no time to rest. Too much still left to do. This was the effing radio shack—there was still the whole goddam bridge to worry about.

First, I had to disable the commo gear. I lurched over to the console and gave it a quick once-over. There was the usual ship-to-shore shortwave shit. Oh, the writing was in Chinese, but the equipment is universal.

Then there was some other stuff that you usually don't find on commercial freighters—like the scrambler fax, the military model SATCOM receiver, and the ultra–high-frequency comms unit.

I disabled them all. Cut every goddam wire in the room, too. Then I edged back into the passageway. After the rest of my work was finished, I'd come back and collect all the papers, logbooks, files, and other sundry intelligence I'd observed.

0415. Nod was nowhere to be seen—and the passageway doors were all shut. I edged up to the nearest one, cracked it open, and peeked inside. One T-shirted, skivvy-clad body was sprawled facedown on the bed. The nicely placed group of bullet holes in his side told me he wasn't going to be waking up. A second corpse with an equally small three-bullet pattern in the dead center of its chest stared at me with uncomprehending eyes from the deck, and I slid the door closed, impressed with Nod's work. I was glad to see that he'd been spending time at the range.[2]

I got just about halfway down the short leg of the L, when Gator Shepard's face appeared peeking around the corner.

He hand-signaled, his left thumb and index finger making a circle. That meant everything was cool—unless he was Brazilian, in which case he was calling me an asshole.

I decided to accept the American interpretation. Nod silently materialized behind me. He is v-e-r-y spooky that way. "How many down?" I mouthed silently. Gator showed me eight fingers. Nod displayed four. That meant we'd dealt with fifteen so far—that left another thirty or so.

I wiped the blood from my face, rearranged my balaclava, stuck a fresh magazine into my MP5, and quietly racked a round I hoped hadn't been fondled, groped, or otherwise disturbed by any of the Murphy clan into the chamber.

---

[2]Now, that may sound cold. But different people see things in a different light. I remember running into my old friend Bert Hickman, a marine sniper, small weapons expert, and internationally ranked skeet shooter, on the day Egyptian President Anwar el-Sadat was killed by a group of fundamentalist assassins. It happened, you'll remember, as Sadat reviewed the October War memorial day parade in Cairo. I was heading for the gym to blow off some steam; Bert was coming from his daily workout. We passed one another at a trot. "Whaddya think about Sadat?" I called to him, shaking my head in disbelief.

"Great hit, great hit," said Bert, never stopping.

0416. Gunfire erupted from somewhere in the stern as we cleared the last of the passageways prior to entering the bridge area itself. *Okay, ladies and germs, that will end the stealth portion of our show this evening.* It was time to go to full-auto, kick-ass rock-and-fuckin'-roll.

No need for radio silence anymore. I pressed the transmit button on my radio. "Sit-rep?"

Boomerang's voice came right back at me. "Got us a lively little firefight here, Boss Dude—"

"Where's here?"

"Forwardmost section of the engine room."

Fuck. "Bad? Anybody down?"

There was a pause. "Nah—we're all okay—brought down six of them, too, before they started shootin' back. But it's gonna slow us down some."

That was bad news. After the engineering space, Nasty, Boomerang, Half Pint, and Pick had to deal with the security contingent, the crew's quarters, and the mess deck. Yes, I know that they had a demanding assignment. Yes, I know that under normal circumstances a full sixteen-man platoon would be employed. But y'know, there are times when you have to operate full-tilt boogie with what ya got on hand. That's how it was right now—and besides, I'd put those four shooters up against any full goddam SEAL platoon anywhere, anytime, anyplace. I winced involuntarily as a burst of gunfire ricocheted in my radio earpiece. "WTF, Boom'rang?"

The motherfucker actually laughed into his mike. "Hey, Boss Dude, I'd love to talk some more but it's gettin' busy here—we gotta go and play some games with these assholes."

Yeah, well I was about to have my own mitts full. I waved at Nod, Duck Foot, and Gator—"Let's *move* it."

No time for subtlety now. Three doors between us and the bridge hatch. They were metal, not wood; they were solid, not louvered—and each of them had one line of Chinese characters stenciled on a rectangular plate above the transom. These obviously weren't everyday living quarters but VIP accommodations or something like that.

I kicked the first door in. Dark compartment, two tables and maybe eight, nine, chairs—blackboard with Chinese writing on it up against the wall. I licked the MP5's 110-lumen bright white Sure Fire combat light around, sweeping the bulkheads, corners, floor. All clear.

As I searched behind DNO—that's Door Number One, but all you *Let's Make a Deal* fans out there probably knew that already—Nod and Duck Foot hit the second door, and Gator went for the third. As I came out of mine, a burst of automatic weapons fire knocked Gator from his doorway. He kind of exploded out and away as rounds cut holes through the metal. He landed with an ominous thud on his back in the passageway.

I moved to where he lay on the deck, grabbed him by the collar of his CQC vest, and dragged him out of the direct line of fire. A second volley of shots came through the compartment door, and I threw myself on top of Gator as the rounds ricocheted up and down the hallway—didn't want him getting any more hurt than he already was.

"I'm okay, Skipper." Gator rolled onto his side to dislodge me.

"Hold it, will you?" I held him down and ran my hands over him until I was satisfied that there were no holes, and no signs of blood. I rolled off him and pulled him to his feet. A third volley came through the door, sending Gator flat on his belly.

"Shit, the cocksucker surprised the hell outta me again." He hunkered down and picked up his weapon. "I can take care of this, Skipper. You keep going."

No way. There was more than one man in there, I could tell from the volume of fire. Besides, I wanted all my men in one piece and didn't need any goddam bad guys nipping at my heels. More—these assholes really wanted to keep us out of their compartment. Even in the height of battle, that made me inquisitive about what might be inside. I motioned toward the door. "Duck Foot—"

"Yo."

I pointed at the shotgun scabbard on his back. "Kill that fucking door!"

Duck Foot pulled his breaching gun—a cut-down Remington 870P Magnum, with thirteen-inch barrel and built-in standoff device—out of the scabbard strapped to his back. The weapon was loaded with five Def-Tec TKO frangible slugs. The TKO is made of powdered zinc—it disperses on contact. But before it disperses, the fucking stuff will disintegrate the hardest lock cylinders, hinges, or reinforced dead bolts.

Duck Foot scurried to the right side of the door, careful to crawl under the bullet holes so his movement would be masked. I stood well to the left side of the door frame, protected by the heavy bulkhead. I pulled a frag grenade from my vest, yanked the pin, and held the spoon down firmly, then gave Duck Foot a single nod of my head.

Duck Foot put the tip of the standoff device between the door handle and bolt assembly, then pulled the trigger. *Whaaaam*—the metal buckled—but the door stayed where the fuck it was.

The explosion was answered by gunfire. Fuck—a long burst of automatic fire came through the door and bounced around the metal passageway bulkhead like goddam pachinko balls, sending all four of us to the deck yet another time. I brushed a sharp sliver of copper-coated lead from my CQC vest. I saw that something had cut through the ballistic nylon of my tactical holster. Bummer. But on the bright side, I'd managed to screw with Mr. Murphy by not losing physical control of the grenade.

My delight was interrupted by Duck Foot's scream. "Oh, goddam—" he shouted.

I looked over. He'd caught a couple of ricochets. One sliced him across the lower arm. The other caught his left cheek like a scalpel pass. The fucking thing about bullets is that when they hit metal, they flatten out and they get real sharp—especially if they're copper-jacketed in the first place. They can do some nasty damage.

Obviously, he wasn't too bad off. Because bleeding or not, Duck Foot thrust the shotgun around and blasted the lock again. This time I sensed motion—so I kicked the door, and as it opened five, six, seven inches, I softball-pitched the frag grenade inside—hard enough, I hoped, to bank it off an interior wall or two and take it back into the center of the room.

Despite the insulation provided by the door and bulkhead, the fucking concussion blast was potent enough to shake us up and send pieces of shrapnel into the door. I hoped it had done more damage to the assholes inside.

It was time to see for ourselves. Gator kicked the door in. It opened wide. Firing from a kneeling position, he hosed a long burst from right to left through the thick smoke, washing the compartment down with his MP5.

No response.

He flicked his Sure Fire on. The bright white light reflected off gray/mustard/black opaque smoke. As it dispersed, I could make out a body. It was wearing the Chinese version of BDUs—in other words combat clothes—and a bulletproof vest. Vests, however, are little protection against frag grenades in small, metal-walled compartments. Next to the corpse was a mangled AK—the weapon had taken a heavy hit from the grenade blast, too. Another body, also in combat gear, with a machine pistol in its motionless hand, lay sprawled near the first.

There was no movement. But I had to make sure no one was playacting. Cautiously, I made entry, approaching with MP5 at the ready position. I kicked the weapons away from the corpses. Then I swept the corners of the room with the light and MP5's muzzle. The beam picked up something and my finger tightened on the trigger. It relaxed when I saw two more bodies. They lay partially concealed by a small wood desk. I approached, kicked the pistols away from their motionless hands, then made damn sure they were dead.

Now I focused on what the hell all these stiffs had been so desperate to keep us away from. There was a humongous fireproof, six-foot-tall, three-foot-wide, three-foot-deep combination-lock document safe strap-welded to the far bulkhead, right next to one of the compartment's two well-used, metal-frame single beds.

This was probably the intel compartment—or maybe it was where the political cadre lived. Either way, there was no time to waste on it now. Our cover was completely blown, as they keep saying on *NYPD Blue,* which meant we'd lost tactical surprise, and we were gonna have to grind out the rest of the mission against full opposition. I punched the transmit button on my radio: "Let's move-move-move—we gotta get to the bridge."

Oh, Dickie could see that this was going to be a long fucking morning.

Chapter 3

WE SECURED THE SHIP AT 0453, ENGAGED THE AUTOPILOT, AND dropped the *Nantong Princess*'s speed to a leisurely five knots. The crew had totaled thirty-eight, including a security force of six *zhongdui,* who had actually turned out to be *zhong*dweebs. Despite the fact that they carried the very best equipment the Chinese manufactured—everything from their bulletproof vests, to their small arms, to the flame retardant uniforms they wore were domestically produced—they'd lacked the will to fight. That, plus the fact that we'd taken them completely by surprise, and they hadn't been very well trained in emergency battle reaction procedures. The ship's company had suffered the predicted 100 percent mortality rate. My own injuries were much lighter. Duck Foot was going to need eight or nine stitches on his cheek and an equal number on the fleshy part of his left forearm. Half Pint lost the tip of a finger—he had no idea how he'd done it, but his fucking TAC glove was soggy with blood—and he was never again going to tell me I was Number One by tossing me the bird. From now on, all he'd be able to muster was that I was Number Two-thirds.

We wrapped the wound as best we could, and I told him that his new assignment during the extraction was to play the role of chum. That's not as in *buddy,* but as in *shark bait.*

Me? I had my usual complement of postcombat dings and dents, but there was nothing a couple of generic aspirin, a healthy dollop of Bombay Sapphire, and a soak between a pair of warm thighs couldn't cure in a jiffy. And oh, yeah—Nasty'd managed to turn his ankle as he dropped down a ladderway into the engine compartment. You ask what he turned it into? He turned it into instant pain. We splinted him with some metal shelf strap from the ship's machine shop, taped it securely, and gave him the radio handle "Hobble Grundle."

I sent Hobble, Gator, Duck Foot, Half Pint, Pick, and Boomerang down into the hold to check the cargo and start placing charges. Nod DiCarlo, whose background includes hefty doses of covert work and psy-ops in such picturesque locations as Panama, Iraq, Lebanon, and Bosnia, joined me for the intel sweep. I extracted one of the two watertight duffels stowed in my vest. Eddie plucked one from his.

In the way that you see things for the first time after looking at them forever, I saw as I smoothed out the creases that the duffels had been manufactured in China. Now, is that poetic justice, or ironic justice?

We began with the bridge: the *Nantong Princess*'s log, her radio frequency plot, master navigation chart, and complete file of maps—they all went into the bag. By the time we cleared the master's cabin, followed by the first mate's compartment, Nod was grumbling, "Yes, sir, no, sir, two bags full, sir." And he was spelling it—emphatically—with a *c* and a *u.*

Two bags full? Yeah—there were probably a hundred pounds or so of papers, books, and other miscellaneous items in the duffels. We probably took too much—I mean, I even stripped the dogtags off the *zhongdui* corpses. But it's hard when you don't speak the language—and where the *Nantong Princess* was going, we wouldn't have a second chance. Besides, I'd rather err on the side of complete than incomplete.

Proud as Blackbeard or Long John Silver with my booty haul, I left Nod to deal with the second mate's compartment, mess deck, and radio room, pulled the second duffel from my vest, and made my way back to the cabin where the big safe was located. The *zhongdui* corpses held nothing of interest for me except their ID cards and wallets. I noticed that each of the corpses bore a small, blue tattoo of a malevolent dragon entwined around an anchor. They'd had the work performed on the backs of their hands where thumb and forefinger came together. I took pictures of the tattoos to add to my intel files. The two Chinese officers—they be ossifers, har, har, har, because they be dressed like 'em, laddie—had no papers on them at all. Nothing in their wallets except Chinese, Korean, and Japanese currency, along with a bunch of Singapore fifty-dollar bills. Nothing in any of their pockets, either—other than:

1. one soggy (yecch!) handkerchief;
2. two ballpoint pens; and,
3. two packs of Marlboro cigarettes and a pair of cheap butane lighters.

But neither was holding any sort of ID card. Nor did either wallet contain a driver's license, or any of the other government-issue identification/credential/documentational detritus you normally find in military/official wallets. That made me suspicious. People who wear uniforms, especially officers, always carry some kind of official paperwork to show who they are, who has to salute 'em, and indicate where they can and can't go. The lack of IDs and other paperwork told me they were on a covert mission of some kind. I snapped their portraits with the digital point-and-shoot camera. We'd wash the images through a DIA computer and see if they'd piqued anyone else's interest.

I went through the cabin inch by inch. The closets held a

spare set of permanent-press uniforms, two sets of anonymous civilian trousers, cheap belts, and extra nylon shirts. Nothing inside the shoes. No hidden compartments in the closets—I ran my fingers carefully over all the walls and seams. There were two imitation leather briefcases. I turned 'em upside down. Out of one fell a crumpled sheet of notepaper with Chinese (Japanese? Korean?) writing. It went into the duffel. The other held detailed city maps of Pusan, Jakarta, and Singapore. I unfurled each one and looked to see if there were any marked locations thereon. It is a fact, folks, that even the most intelligent of intel officers will once in a while mark a map of an unfamiliar city with the location of an upcoming secret assignation, thus giving folks like me a big step up when it comes to setting up an ambush in order to hunt and kill way beyond my normal bag limit of bad guys. These maps may have been well used—the stress tears on the seams betrayed that little infobit—but there were no markings. They went into the duffel anyway.

I found nothing under the thin, lumpy mattresses (or inside 'em, either). The desk was bare. I checked under the faux-Naugahyde desk pad. Nada. Checked the single drawer and found half a dozen Korean girlie magazines, two well-used *Playboys,* and a couple of computer printouts written in Chinese characters. The printouts went into my duffel bag.

Obviously, the safe held everything of importance. Now, if Machinist's Mate First Class Stevie Wonder had been along on this mission he could have had fun cracking it. But the goofy-looking ex-marine wasn't around. He was back in Washington, taking the chief's exam. They only give it once a year these days of downsizing and limited promotion opportunities. And despite the fact that he hadn't studied for the test—he'd been too busy giving me a hand in the Middle East to do any serious book work—there'd been no way I was going to let him come play shoot-and-loot with me when he should be working a number two Dixon Ticonderoga down to a nub on multiple choice and essay questions so he could win a long overdue promotion to E-7.

Hey, whether the Navy knows it or not, the Navy needs chiefs like Boy Wonder—and I wanted to see him promoted. So he was there, and I was here, and there was this goddam gray steel security safe to be cracked and peeled like a *li'tzhou*—which is how they said chestnut on this vessel.

I used my Sure Fire to examine the safe carefully. You don't want to play with something that might be booby trapped, and if this had been my safe, it would have been booby-trapped.

But then, not everyone is me. And there was no sign of spooky-dirty-nasty-nasty in the vicinity.

So I began to do a methodical TTB—top to bottom—exam. The lock was your garden-variety, military/government issue combination lock—you know, the kind that go *"right four times past zero to thirty-two, then left three times to eighteen, then right twice to fifty-nine, then left to zero—and open, sesame."*

The CLIQ—combination lock in question—was mounted on an escutcheon plate that measured about ten inches square. To the left of the CLIQ, a single handle would work the door's locking bolts once the tumblers had been released. The door itself was recessed into the body of the safe. Looking into the recess, I could see the door assembly had been fitted with fireproof gaskets.

In the old days, you'd crack one of these babies by playing with the combination—listening through a stethoscope or electronic eavesdropping device as the tumblers fall into place uno by uno. But that takes time—and sensitivity. And time and sensitivity are two qualities I don't have a lot of. And so, eschewing foreplay, I extracted a can of explosive foam out of my CQC vest, screwed the plastic nozzle into place, and very carefully sprayed a thin stream of foam around the circumference of the combination lock so that the sticky foam seeped behind the face of the dial.

Then I stuck a Chicklet-size wad of Semtex explosive at the bottom of the dial, right at six o'clock. I inserted a fifteen-second nonelectric firing assembly device into the plastique, activated the damn thing, and got my Slovak ass out of Dodge, into the passageway.

When the smoke cleared, I went back inside. The CLIQ had been blown clear across the room. I ratcheted the handle left to right, the locking bolts released, and—open fucking sesame—the door swung wide.

I started at the top shelf. There was cash—thirty, maybe thirty-five, two-inch-thick bundles of Uncle Sam's well-used hundred-dollar bills. I stuffed the money into my duffel. It's nice when the Chinese decide to help us pay down the national debt, don't you think?

There were three thin ledger books. These went into the duffel, too, as did half a dozen thick file folders crammed with papers.

But it was what I found on the third shelf that made me gasp. There were two ring binders, each about an inch thick. The covers were white, with a one-inch-wide diagonal orange stripe running bottom left to top right. Each binder was emblazoned with the seal of the United States Department of Defense. One binder had the words NUMBER ONE, the other was labeled NUMBER TWO. Each bore the notation:

TOP SECRET
SKYHORSE
BIG BROTHER
TECHNICAL MANUAL

There is a common literary phrase for my reaction as I picked the fucking binders up as if they were red hot—which, in a sense, they were. It is: *holy shit.*

Let me digress here just long enough give you a short primer on classification. Despite what they do in Hollywood and on the TV, or regardless what mumbo jumbo nonsense some of the espionage/military/techno/spook novelists write in their books, there are three—and only three—security classifications for documents and projects.

- There is CONFIDENTIAL. ("Material which requires protection and the unauthorized disclosure of which could reasonably be expected to cause damage to the national security.") Confidential materials are flagged with a blue tab.
- There is SECRET. ("Material which requires a substantial degree of protection and the unauthorized disclosure of which could be reasonably expected to cause serious damage to the national security.") Secret materials are flagged with a red tab.
- And there is TOP SECRET. ("Material which requires the highest degree of protection and the unauthorized disclosure of which could reasonably be expected to cause exceptionally grave damage to the national security.") Top secret materials are flagged with an orange tab or a yellow tab, depending on which department or agency you work for.

That's it. Full stop. End of line.

Now, in order to further protect information from unauthorized disclosure, the top secret classification is often accompanied by either a code word designation, or by utilizing a systemic organizational approach known as compartmentation.

Let's define code word first. Simply put, code words are cryptonyms used to identify sensitive intelligence data, or programs. For example, in the 1960s, No Such Agency and the Navy ran a joint top secret program to eavesdrop on Soviet military communications by having SEALs plant listening devices on the telephone cables that ran across the bottom of the Gulf of Finland, just outside Leningrad harbor, from the Soviet naval base at Sosnovyy Bor, to the military regional headquarters at Zelenogorsk. That top secret program was referred to by the code words Ivy Bells. This one was obviously called Skyhorse.

Next comes compartmentation. In Navyspeak, compartmentation is (and I'm gonna quote directly here, but because of security considerations I can't tell you what I'm quoting from): "The establishment and management of an organization, network, system, or project so that information about the personnel, internal organization, or activities of one component is made available to any of the other components only to the extent required for the performance of assigned duties." So it is altogether possible to have code word clearance to one part of a compartmented project, but be segregated from the rest of it. In other words, you might be cleared to know about Skyhorse, but not another compartment of Skyhorse, which has an even more closely-held series of code words.

Got it? Good. Because you're going to have to know all this stuff cold in just a few pages.

Okay, now, here am I, standing aboard a Chinese freighter, in front of a Chinese document safe, and I am holding in my hands, three top secret, code word classified technical manuals for a project that is so sensitive that even I have been compartmented completely out of it. Talk about irony.

I grabbed the binders, laid them out on what was left of the desk, and scanned. Shit—it all looked real enough to make me very, very nervous. What made me even more nervous were the highlighted sections, most of which had notations, handwritten in Chinese characters, in the margins.

Now, I'm going to tell you a little bit about the Big Brother project. I can only tell you a little bit because that's all I know.

In the past, you may have heard me refer to the concept of C^2W.[3] Today, that C^2W system has been expanded and improved into something they're calling C^4IFTW, a mouth-filling acronym that stands for Command, Control, Communications, Computers, and Intelligence For The War-

---

[3]C^2W, pronounced sea-square-w, stands for Command and Control Warfare. It is when you combine operational security, deception, psychological warfare, and physical destruction in order to deny, influence, degrade, and destroy enemy command and control capabilities.

rior.[4] C^4IFTW is an integrated system that allows folks like me to enjoy real-time information on the battlefield without having to go through layer upon layer of intel weenies, staff pukes, recalcitrant middle-level managers, and other bureaucratic impediments to my mission.

With C^4IFTW I can plug in, download, and get the info I need—everything from real-time pictures, to target designation, to thermal imaging, to satellite-assisted maps—delivered when I need it. That technology is available to me, as a SEAL commander, right now.

But that's not the whole picture. C^4IFTW is a compartmented program. SEALs like me get to see the most basic form of the system. But way up the ladder is a highly developed version of C^4IFTW, which—because even the code word cryptonyms are classified—I've only heard about and couldn't until right now confirm is the Big Brother project, which as I have just learned was codenamed Skyhorse.

According to the current RUMINT,[5] Big Brother employs many elements of the old C^2W system. Which means, if I've been hearing the urinal gossip right, I can not only get tactical intelligence, but I can also screw with my enemy's phone and radio capabilities, fuck up his radar and other imagery, and destroy his own command-and-control capabilities. Best of all, this Big Brother C^4IFTW fits into suitcased-size packages (two of 'em, I gather from the manuals in front of me now), can be run by battery power if necessary, and totals no more than a hundred pounds in weight.

Or at least, that's what they're saying. Me, I have no idea, because as I told you I'm not fucking cleared to know about

---

[4]You guys think I'm making this up, don't you? Well, I'm not—you can find C^4IFTW in the United States Department of Defense's current *Dictionary of Military Terms,* a publication of the Joint Chiefs of Staff.

[5]RUMor INTelligence.

Big Brother, although it now appeared that the Chinese weren't under the same goddam restrictions as I was.

I began to skim the manuals. It didn't take me very long to realize that the fucking system was more powerful than rumor had it. You could, very easily, take over a goddam country—at least a small to middle-size one. Places like Saudi Arabia, or Kuwait, Guatemala, Honduras, Cuba, or Syria would be simple. Germany, France, or even Russia would be tough—but perhaps not completely out of the question.

Using Big Brother you could tap into everything from secure military communications to local air traffic control, to police band radios, cellular phones, and shortwave broadcasts. Monitor—hell, you could fucking broadcast over the air on radio and television if you wanted. You could monitor telephone networks—even calls on the new digital phones. You could program the fucking target and acquisition radar on ground-to-air and ground-to-ground missile systems. You could command and control military aircraft and do target assessments as well as any goddam AWACS aircraft. You could broadcast secure comms by covertly utilizing secure transponders on NSA satellites—or French, Brit, Israeli, Chinese, or Russian intelligence birds, for that matter. There is a SpecWar technical term for the capabilities of what I was looking at. It is: *Fuuuuck*in' incredible!

My reverie was rudely interrupted by Nasty's urgent growl in my earpiece. "Skipper, you better get down here fast—"

"Where are you?"

"Aft cargo area—the second athwartships compartment."

I climbed down one staircase and three ladders, and worked my way aft. I could see that the men had done a thorough job of searching the cargo. Every box, carton, crate, chest, and container had been opened and examined. I stepped over a pile of porcelain lamp bases. It occurred to me it was a good thing we'd hit the ship now—because it was more than three-quarters empty. It would have taken us a goddam week to sort through everything if we'd done the takedown just after it had left Shanghai. But secure in the knowledge that the missile components were still aboard from FORTE scans—not to mention solid intelligence that the Chinese had arranged to sell missiles to the Pakistanis—we'd let it cruise through the busier sea lanes, preferring to take the ship down during the most isolated portion of its voyage. So the *Nantong Princess* had unloaded cargo at Pusan, Korea, Yokohama, Japan, and several other ports.

They'd discovered the missiles quickly. There were six large missile containers; the selfsame housings our crateologists had said contained medium-range strategic missiles. The huge wooden containers were mislabeled, of course. But a box that holds a missile looks just like a box that's been built to, well, hold a missile. I saw that the nuclear warheads were packed separately, in precisely the same way we ship our own nuclear missile warheads.

Those were the missiles I had expected to find. What surprised me were the six French-manufactured GLCMs—Ground-Launched Cruise Missiles. The fucking Chinese hadn't even bothered to conceal 'em—they were packed in the same sort of tactical watertight containers that I use to transport my ordnance when I'm operating maritime. The containers were all marked with Chinese characters.

I scratched at my beard. I knew the Paks weren't interested in Cruise missiles; they already had hundreds of them, courtesy of the former Soviet Union, North Korea, and France. No, the Paks had bought medium-to-long-range strategic missiles from Beijing. But what we had here were half a dozen medium-range tacticals whose range was no more than 500, perhaps 525 miles. And they were French, not Chinese. Where the hell had they been going?

Well, there was no time to answer that question because it was only one of many I had to deal with. I was equally perplexed, for example, by the crates of Russian AK-47 assault rifles, concealed inside rough wood containers marked in English, EXPORT—Zelinograd Machine Tools/ MVD. The letters MVD were disturbing. MVD, friends, stands for *Ministerstvo vnutrennikh del,* which in English translates as Ministry of the Interior. From my recent experience in Moscow, I knew that MVD was the former Soviet Union's most corrupt government agency. It was involved in everything from the smuggling of nuclear technology to drug peddling.

But that's another story. Let's get back to my search. I opened more than a dozen boxes of Soviet Army surplus SKS semiauto rifles concealed in crates labeled as toys from the Moskva Toy Company. There were cartons of various caliber Tokorev and Makarov pistols whose cartons identified them as mushroom soy sauce. There were similarly camouflaged cases of twenty-year-old Soviet claymore mines and grenades, as well as roughly two and a half tons (!) of Semtex plastic explosive, packed in easy to handle and conceal ten-kilo (twenty-two-pound) blocks, and four to five tons of Bulgarian, Russian, Ukrainian, and Czech surplus ammunition, carefully wrapped in thick black plastic, packed on pallets, and labeled as pig iron.

Cruise missiles? Russian weapons? Eastern-bloc ordnance? This wasn't making much sense. The Chinese sell more than a billion dollars' worth of these very same goods every year—so why the hell would they be buying and/or shipping Russkie stuff when they have literally tons of the very same materials sitting in warehouses in Shanghai and Guangzhou? In point of fact, over the past decade China has been included pretty high up on the world's Top Ten Weapons Dealers list. Remember? Last year they were, as the old *Billboard* magazine might have put it, number two with a bullet.

The "toy" and "machine tool" crates were all stencilled in Cyrillic. I ran my hand over the rough wood of one of the crates we'd cracked open. I don't read Russian, but I understood enough to realize that the stencil read: "Crate Number 15 of 15." I peered at the weapons inside, then ran the numbers on my mental tote board. The crates of "machine tools" and "toys" contained enough small arms and munitions to supply a small army or a large guerrilla force for more than a year from the look of it. And I was examining only a small portion of the total shipment. Don't forget: we'd hit the *Nantong Princess* late in its cruise.

"Pull a bunch of serial numbers off these things," I told Gator. "Let's see if we can find out where they came from."

Y'see, even then, even that early in the story, the situation just didn't compute. There was something hinky about this deal. And the nettlesome truth was that I had no idea what said hinkdom might be. But I realized looking another four yards down the athwartships compartment there was no time to stop and smell the cordite right now.

Why was there no time? Because I saw it wasn't the nukes or the weapons Nasty had called about. It was the two Haliburton aluminum cases—each about the size of a big Pullman suitcase—equipped with integral casters and combination locks.

Nasty was hunkered near one of the cases. He'd picked the locks and opened them flat, like clamshells. The insides were made of thick black foam, hollowed out to hold the contents: a bunch of sophisticated, black-box electronic devices. Some had small screens. Others had dials and buttons. He'd pulled the contraptions out of their numbered foam repositories, spread them out in a semicircle around him, then laid the neat, bundled, color-coded wiring in a separate pile so he could take an informal inventory.

I bent down to take a closer look. There were nine component modules in one case, and twelve in the matching one. Each piece was marked PROPERTY OF THE UNITED STATES OF AMERICA in small letters. I saw two softcover black books the size of combat Bibles sitting in one of the suitcase's rigid foam cutout compartments. I plucked one of them from its nook and opened it. The title page carried a serial number. The frontispiece bore the globe, torch, and satellite-track logo of the Defense Intelligence Agency. Above the title was the word "SECRET." The text, printed in eight-point type, was a comprehensive listing of satellite frequencies and orbital data—ours, and everyone else's, too. I'd seen one of these before on the desk of my old friend Tony Mercaldi. Merc had referred to it as his satellite cheat sheet. I riffled through the book quickly, then started to examine everything else that was packed in the cases.

I looked over each piece of equipment, although there was really no need. I knew what we'd found—a Big Brother unit with all its technical manuals. It was an absofuckinglute intelligence disaster for the United States—and that is a goddam understatement.

Boomerang picked up a radar-defeating unit that could turn a plane, or a small boat, into a stealth craft at the flip of a switch. The box wasn't much bigger than your average Watchman. Boomerang examined the module very carefully. He looked up at me and inclined the rectangular box in my direction. "Hey, Boss Dude, seems to me we got ourselves some real evil fuckin' stuff here. Downright nefarious, in fact." He giggled in that perverse, son-of-a-beachy way only California surfers can. "I sure hope we get to play with it."

Chapter

4

0634. WHILE NOD TOOK DIGITAL PICTURES OF THE CARGO—more evidence for the Chairman and secretary of defense—I set up the Big Brother's secure piggyback SATCOM unit on the *Nantong Princess*'s flying bridge and broke radio silence. Yes, I knew I was dangerously behind schedule. And yes, I knew I was acting contrary to my mission directive. And yes, I knew that I'd probably piss some people off.

But that's part of what Rogue Warriordom is all about. When you suspect that your country is in jeopardy, you have to act. Decisively. Right now. And you have to be willing to suffer the consequences of your actions.

But as you know, there are very few consequences I haven't already suffered. Besides, I wanted to know WTF was going on—after all, it isn't every day that, whilst on board the ship of an adversary nation, you come across a piece of the most sophisticated equipment your country produces. So, before we extracted and I sent this ship and its cargo to the bottom, I wanted answers.

Now, at times like these, it might have been nice to have had one of the Chinese *ts'ing-po kwan-koon*—that's intelligence officers—on whom to perform a little *suen-man,* which is how they say interrogation in these waters. But as you already know, the *Nantong Princess*'s company took 100 percent casualties, and there was no one to *suen-man.*

So to get answers, I bounced a signal back to Washington. My first priority was calling Chairman Crocker—he had to be told what I'd discovered.

I dialed the secure line on his desk. The phone rang twice. Then a woman's voice answered. "Sixty-eight twenty-four."

The extension number was right. But the voice was unfamiliar. I waited. She repeated the number. I asked, "Who is this?"

"To whom am I speaking?"

There was no way I was going to tell her who I was. "I'm calling for Chairman Crocker."

"He's unavailable. May I take a message?"

"When will he be back?"

"Much later." I heard her hand cup over the receiver, and there was silence for a second or two. Then the voice came back at me. "Who *is* this?"

She was probably trying to run a trace. It was time to go. "I'll call back," I said, and hung up.

Now, you probably want to know how the Chairman could be out of touch when there was a critical mission in progress. The answer is twofold. First, my mission was covert, not clandestine. During *clandestine* missions—like the abortive Tehran rescue mission led by my old colleague and friend Charlie Beckwith—the entire Joint Chiefs sit in their situation room and bite their nails until they learn what had happened. But *covert* missions aren't supposed to be happening at all, and any undue attention might attract unwanted suspicion. And so, the Chairman was following his regular schedule—whatever it might have been—and certainly didn't bother to sit by the phone.

In fact, he was not expecting to hear from me until I was safely aboard the submarine that had been sent to pick up an anonymous SEAL unit engaged in a need-to-know training exercise.

But I still needed help—and advice. So I tried another secure telephone. To be precise, I dialed the secure phone that sat on the left-hand side of the desk that belonged to my old DIA compadre, Anthony Vincent Mercaldi. Merc and I have played games together since Christ was a mess cook and Saddam Hussein wasn't trying to build nukes. If there was anybody who'd know WTF, or not raise any waves asking around if he didn't, it would be the Merc. I made the call to Tony the same way I'd called the Chairman: by sneaking aboard the handiest No Such Agency SIGINT bird (the project designation for this one is code-worded Tracee Wink, and that's all I'm going to say unless you all have the same security clearances I do) and stealing a free ride.

How'd I do that, you ask?

Well, first I found the satellite's general location by checking the handily supplied DIA book of frequencies, trajectories, and orbit paths. Then I set the transponder frequency on which I wanted to broadcast into the six-pound Big Brother transmitter unit. While I did that, Duck Foot unfurled the unit's sixteen-inch metallic satellite dish, which looks like a tiny umbrella blown inside out by the wind.

We eyeballed the predawn sky and held the dish at a sixty-degree angle, pointing due north. Once Big Brother located the transponder, it automatically attached itself to the signal like a hooker sucking cock or a gigolo sucking clit (that's a little bit of EEO irony for any of you politically correct readers out there), caromed it nicely off the NSA/Australian station at Pine Gap,[6] and straight back

---

[6]Pine Gap is located approximately eleven and a half miles southwest of Alice Springs, in the remote, dry-as-a-bone geographical center of the Australian outback. It was first built in the late 1960s (more construction was added later) and resembles a lunar colony in a 1950s sci-fi movie. The buildings are all single-story preformed concrete units. Dozens of radomes hold dish antennas. Other receiving devices pluck SIGINT information from the skies and also capture Soviet (and now Russian) and Chinese telemetry information from missile tests, as well as monitor the French, whose nuclear test zone was north of Australia in Tahitian waters. Pine Gap is staffed by between four hundred and five hundred permanent personnel, as well as a few dozen specialists, who rotate in and out depending on changing mission requirements.

through the SIGINT designator at Vint Hill Station just north of Manassas, Virginia, and on to the Pentagon.

It was just before 1900, one day earlier, on the tenth floor of the DIA building above the Washington Metro stop at Clarendon, Virginia. The phone rang twice, the signal as clear as if I was calling from the next office.

Merc's voice answered. "Mercaldi."

"It's me. We gotta talk. I've come across a real big brother of a problem and I need information about that big brother real fast."

There was a stunned pause on the other end. Then he growled, "What the fuck, Dick, you're not cleared."

"I may not be fuckin' cleared, but I have the fuckin' thing here in fuckin' front of me." I even quoted to him from the effing technical effing manuals, and read him the effing print-order numbers on the effing DIA effing satellite guides.

"Whoa—I don't think you should say any more right now," Merc cautioned.

"Why not?" I told him on what equipment I was transmitting and heard him suck air in disbelief.

"You're shitting me."

"Now, would I do something like that, especially from where I am right now?"

"Where are you?"

"I am somewhere," I said. "And that's all I'm gonna say."

That shut him up. Then he asked for a description of the suitcases. I heard him making notes. Then I asked if he knew how all this here equipment came to be outside the control of the government of the United States.

Merc said simply, "I have no goddam idea at all, but you can believe that I am going to find out."

"Yeah, well if you do, try to do it without leaving any signs pointing in my direction."

Merc saw the logic in that. No sense letting anyone know any details. Especially when it was too early in the game for IFF, which is MILSPEAK for Identification, Friend or Foe. At which point, the pleasantries completed, he told me to finish my goddam work, get my goddam team together, and haul my goddam recalcitrant SEAL posterior to safer territory. "You *are* going to exfil from wherever the hell you are, aren't you?"

I told him that his irony wasn't appreciated, and that in a few hours we'd be in a better location from which to call him. In truth, my team and I were scheduled to have departed some half an hour ago. "Contact me as soon as you've secured after exfil," Merc said. "I'll have answers for you, Dick. I promise."

1012. I could fill you in on all the painful details of our extraction, but I can encapsulate the previous three and a half hours by saying simply that it was a very irksome experience for all of us. We sent the *Nantong Princess* and its cargo of missiles and weapons into fifteen hundred feet of water. We salvaged more than two hundred pounds of intel materials—more than we might have had to, but then since I don't speak or read Chinese, I couldn't tell what was valuable intel, and what was common trash. So I schlepped it all—at least as much as fit in our four watertight duffels—before our explosive charges broke the *Nantong Princess*'s spine in two, and we sent her to the bottom.

Anyway, the duffels, plus the Big Brother suitcases, filled the ICRRC to overflowing once again. Which, in turn, sat us dangerously low in the water. Which also meant that we had to proceed at a safer, slower, and hence less fuel-efficient rate than we'd planned to be doing.

Which meant—are you beginning to comprehend the situation here? Right: we blanking ran out of blanker-blanking gasoline two motherblanking miles from our blankety-blank-blanking rendezvous point, and sat bobbing like a blanker-bleeping cork for half an hour until the blanking submarine commander decided that since we weren't blankin' moving anymore (he could see us clearly on his bleeper-blanking state-of-the-art radar) and since we were signaling regularly—even, perhaps, somewhat frantically—on our Official United States Navy SEAL Mark 4 Mod-3 homing device, he might (yawn, stretch) just as well c-r-u-i-s-e over and pick us up.

Now you might want to know why he didn't move as soon as he sensed our predicament. The answer to that question has two parts. First, since he had no idea what our mission had been (remember—he had simply been assigned to pick a SEAL unit up at a predetermined spot in the middle of the ocean), he probably felt no urgency to come and scoop us out of the water because perhaps sitting and bobbing up and down like a fucking cork was part of our OPLAN (Operational PLAN). Second, and perhaps even more important: coming the extra two miles wasn't on his checklist. And as you all know, nuclear submariners don't do diddly-squat unless it is on their checklists. And so, after our kidney-perforating journey, we sat and heaved (and pitched, and moaned), and tossed, and rolled while he sat, and sat, and sat, watching us through his camo-spotted periscope.

1021. Aboard the USS *Scorpion.* Before we went below, we pulled ourselves out of our assault clothes and deep-sixed most of them over the side, too. We'd been zipped in those wet suits for almost a full day. There are, as you can imagine, no built-in toilet facilities in 'em. So we were pretty goddam ripe. (And that, as the famous old Sino-detective Charles Chan might say, is a velly *flagrant* understatement of the facts.)

In fact, I asked the chief of the boat—he is the sub's top enlisted man—for a hose to be brought topside so that we could clean ourselves up. At first, he'd balked; there was no hose denoted on his clipboard. But after one delicate whiff of *moi,* he was only too willing to comply, whether the fucking thing was down in black-and-white or not.

1030. I showered properly, changed into a set of borrowed blue coveralls emblazoned with the submarine's logo and a name tape that bore the word VISITOR, and made my way to the conn. The CO was there, hunched over a huge nautical chart. He was a compact, muscular guy, built like a punt returner or running back. He let me stand around as he finished drawing a line on the clear acetate atop the paper, then looked up and extended his hand in my direction.

"I'm Dave Brancato. Nice to see all youse guys safe 'n' soun', Captain," he said in an accent that took me back to the North Jersey days of my ute. Then he cut to the chase. "Sorry about not coming to get you sooner," he said matter-of-factly. "I guess I screwed up. So whadabout some hot cawffee?"

I thought about a wry, Roguish response. But to be honest I was beyond mix-ups right now. If I wanted to fret, there were things a lot more consequential to fret over. Besides, it wouldn't do me any good to complain. First of all, this was his boat, not mine. Second, like I just said, there was too much to do.

"Apology accepted," I said, shaking his hand. "And since you probably don't carry Bombay Sapphire, coffee'd be just fine." I paused. "Look, Dave, I'd like to get my guys fed, patched up, and bunked down—they've been on their tootsies for a couple of days. But I need your radio compartment all to myself because I have to get on a secure backchannel line to Washington ASAP."

His bull neck moved left-right and his expression turned to frown. "No can do, Captain."

Y'know, I do not like to hear the NCD words, which is exactly what I told Captain Dave.

"That's not what I meant," he said. "We're talkin' capabilities here, not will ya/won'tcha." He explained that *Scorpion* wasn't equipped for backchanneling. His particular sewer pipe was one of the older boats in service, and the comms package hadn't been upgraded yet. Probably never would be, he said bitterly, because *Scorpion* was scheduled for decommissioning in about eighteen months. You want to know why? Why don't you tell them, Captain Dave.

"Sure, Dick. It is because, thanks to this president, the Navy's environmental appropriation has tripled, while its war-making capabilities have been halved."

So, instead of the latest generation satellite burst transmitter and other high-tech goodies, the *Scorpion* had only the circa 1993, William Jefferson Clinton LFM (Let's Fuck the Military) budget cutback model, a *vox odious* radio/telecom system known as AUTODIN, for AUTOmatic DIgital Network. No bells. No whistles. No frigging backchanneling capabilities, either.

If I used AUTODIN, every one of my sensitive syllables would have to be caromed back to Washington through the cryptovault at the Navy's Pearl Harbor SUBOPS—SUBmarine OPerationS—message center. And any message that moves through a cryptovault can be steamed open, as they say in the "flaps and seals"[7] trade, and copied. Thereafter, it can be examined at leisure by the folks who run the message facility, or turned over to No Such Agency, or even, in some cases, to the local CIA or State Department gumshoes.

I told Captain Dave, *"non vorrei per tutto l'oro del mondo,"* a piquant, North Jersey Italian way of saying I wouldn't touch his AUTODIN with my ten-foot dick. No, I had to transmit to Washington without creating a ripple—or an echo.

That capability was nestled comfortably inside my Haliburton aluminum suitcase. All I needed was fifteen minutes of surface time, and the run of Captain Dave's bridge undisturbed by lookouts or any other sundry personnel save my own men. I wanted to run Big Brother's satellite uplink in private, although I obviously wasn't going to say anything to Captain Dave other than that I vanted to be alone.

---

[7]"Flaps and seals" is the intelligence term for the tradecraft of covertly opening, reading, copying, and then reclosing someone else's mail.

"Heey, I know that. I watch the classic movie·channel when we're in port. Greta Garbo, right?" Dave Brancato grinned. "Well, privacy ain't no prob if you don't mind a little cool salt spray frizzin' your French braid."

First priority: Chairman Crocker. I made the connection, but the same female voice answered, "Sixty-eight twenty-four."

I disconnected. Sorry, ma'am, but I like to do my explaining person to person, not through intermediaries.

I called the Merc. From whom I got very little satisfaction when I finally got hold of him—after three attempts and five hours. He'd swept DIA's computer network and come up dry. Then he'd gone into the Pentagon's net. Nothing there, either. So he called an old contact at Motorola, whose skunkworks (which is a kind of generic spook way of describing Motorola's clandestine operations division), held the contract for Big Brother.

Merc learned nothing until he gave up the numbers on the DIA satellite guides. Then he was told that the particular unit he was talking about had been part of a black project and Motorola couldn't say any more unless Merc could recite the proper code words—which, of course, Merc couldn't do. End of discussion.

Merc paused, and I heard him clap his hand over the receiver, as if someone had stuck his nose into the office. Then he picked up again: "So I figured maybe, it being technology, they'd know something about it at DITSA."

DITSA is how we in the defense establishment pronounce the acronym for DTSA—the Defense Technology Security Agency. They're the folks who make sure we don't send the wrong technogoodies overseas.

"So I called a guy we've known forever—you know the crazy Armenian."

Did I ever. His name is Ron Mardigian, and he's a stand-up guy. I'd done a lot of business with him over the years. "I know of whom you speak," I said.

"Well," Merc continued, "then you know how weird things must be, because he gives me this big song and dance about the fact that we're almost total strangers and why the heck am I calling him about this. And then he says, 'I really can't talk to you on the phone. Come on over for a face-to-face,' he says. And we're talking on our scrambler units, Dick—we're already on fuckin' secure phones! Then he says to call him from a pay phone but don't use the one in the lobby, and don't use any names."

That was strange. "And so?"

"So I jump the Metro to the Pentagon Annex. And I used a pay phone in the station, and I called, and told him, just like he axed me to, 'It's me—I'm here.'

"So Ron, he actually friggin' whispers, *'Go up the escalator and wait.'* And six minutes later the crazy motherfucker shows up wearing this Great White Hunter hat—you know—the ones with the big wide brims—and sunglasses, and he grabs me by the collar, and drags my butt down the street."

Mercaldi paused, as if he was checking the connection. Then he began again. "Now, first I figure he's just being your normal secretive paranoid Armenian, y'know. But then I realize he's really *spooked.* I mean he is *scared.* So I ask him what the fuck, y'know? And he says, 'Look, if we're gonna talk about this I want to do it far, far away from all prying eyes and microphones and all the other, more subtle observational devices we both know about.'

"Then he pats me down. For chrissakes, Dick, he fuckin' pats me down to see if I was carrying a goddamn wire. And then, when he's satisfied I'm clean, he grabs me by the lapels and says, 'Okay, who's this for?' "

I interrupted. "You didn't tell him anything—"

"I told him it was for a friend in the navy," Tony said.

" 'A friend.' That's all you said?"

There was a pause on the line. "Well, I said it was for a friend who was a SEAL," Merc admitted. "But, Dick, there are a lot of SEALs."

Right. But not very many of us would be asking about Big

Brother. And not many of us have known Mardigian the paranoid Armenian for fifteen years, either. "So what did he tell you when you said a SEAL?"

"He rolled his eyes and said there was no way he could help me, because if my friend was the same friend he was thinking of, he worked for the Chairman, and this wasn't a matter for the JCS. He takes me by the friggin lapels again, and whispers, 'From what I can see, the JCS was locked out of this one. Hundred percent.' "

Goddammit, Mardigian knew exactly who Merc had been talking about. My cover was blown. "Merc, *c'mon*—"

"Hey, Dick, what's done is done, okay. But I kept at him. I really leaned on the sumbitch. Played the old friendship angle for all it was worth."

"And?" I was getting inpatient.

"It took almost an hour, and we must have walked two miles, but DITSA-man finally gave me something. He admitted they had a file on the Big Brother deal."

Here is a fact of intelligence gathering. It is that once you get your foot in the door, or put your nose under the tent, or insert your dick in the—well, just fill in whatever portion of the anatomy makes you feel good—it's easier to get the rest of you inside. "So you pressed him some more, right?"

"Bet your ass. And a half mile later, you know what he says? He tells me—lemme give this to you just how he said it—'So,' he says, 'a special delivery orange-tab pizza comes over from the National Security Council. Extra-extra large, with all the toppings.'

"Okay, I can play along, so I ask precisely what toppings were on it. 'Oh,' he says, 'it had your National Security finding, it had your CIA spook-work, it had your No Such Agency tag, your presidential memo, yadda-yadda-yadda. All code word. All compartmented.' "

The Merc paused. "So I asked him to let me have a slice, y'know? And he says, 'Forget it, it's too hot to slice.' Then he tells me never ever to bring up the subject of this particular pizza, especially at my shop."

"You ask him why?"

"Bet your ass I did. He goes back into pizza code. Tells me it has something to do with a 'new recipe.' Something to do with China and the Russkies—and the dough's been reformulated without any DOD help at all. Then he says, 'Besides, it's already in the oven over at the White House. Been baking for some time from the look of the paperwork.' And that was it. He wouldn't go any further. Told me to keep my nose out of it, and don't bother to call him for any more information."

"Do you have any idea who's behind it?"

"No idea whatsoever," Merc said. "For all I know it's one of those hush-hush freelance things they're doin' so many of these days. From the way the Armenian was talkin' I know it's got a presidential priority, and that it's probably being handled out of the NSC adviser's shop."

"Can you poke a little further?"

"Fuck no." Merc's voice took on a suggestion of alarm. "I may have poked too far already. I think I'm hearing clicks on my phone I never heard before. And I'm starting to see the same people following me—and we're only talking about the last six, eight hours here, Dickie. I'm gettin' as paranoid as Mardigian, and paranoid like that ain't where I want to be. So I think this is one of those F-two[8] situations, y'know?"

I came away from my conversation with the Merc even more confused than I had been before. You see, my entire military career has been built on a foundation of what you might call core values (in the marines they probably call them Corps values). One of the most basic of these is that you do not give aid and comfort to your enemy.

Under that aid-and-comfort rubric, I for one would certainly put giving away one's most sophisticated technology. Now, if anyone would know WTF, it would be Chairman Crocker. But until he picked up his own fucking secure

[8]File and forget.

phone, I wasn't about to say a word. I'd grab a combat nap—then try him again.

In the meanwhile, I was just plain old-fashioned confused. Why, you ask? Because here I sat, with hundreds of pounds of documents I couldn't read, and two suitcases containing state-of-the-art techno-goodies, and I had no effing idea what was going on. You can therefore understand my befuddlement.

Now, the good news was that I had a three-and-a-half-day cruise (we were headed back to Guam, from where we'd fly home) during which I would have some uninterrupted time to probe, assess, and—hopefully—unravel these conundrums while I called Chairman Crocker's office in the hope that he would answer his own goddam phone. The bad news was that for the next few days I wouldn't be able to act, except by remote. That was troubling, because as you know, I tend to be a hands-on sort of person.

I dropped from the sail into the conn, manhandled the Big Brother suitcase along the narrow passageways to my quarters, stowed it with its mate, then climbed into the rack for a combat nap.

I don't think I'd managed to close my eyes all the way when a rude set of knuckles rapped a smart paradiddle on the bulkhead outside my compartment.

"Come—" I rolled over, sat up—and slammed my head against the ceiling as the sub surged forward in rapid acceleration. The blow brought tears to my eyes and a hiccough to my "Yo—"

A bespectacled first-class stuck his close-cropped head into the compartment and tried not to react to the look of anguish on my face. But he was stifling a huge smile when he said, "The CO requests your presence in the conn, Captain Marcinko."

Gingerly, I probed my now-tender forehead with callused fingertips. There was probably going to be a fucking lump the size of a chestnut.

I lay back on the tiny rectangular rubber foam widget that passes for a pillow on sewer pipes and listened to the insistent throb of tom-toms between my temples while I tried to focus my eyes on my watch dial. Holy shit, I'd been asleep for eight hours. Some fucking combat nap. I groaned and rolled out of the rack. "Tell him I'm on my way."

"We just received this—ooh, *that* looks real nasty." Dave Brancato stared at my forehead and shook his head sympathetically. He held the message out to me between two thick fingers. "I'm already doing a steady forty-two knots, so I guess we have about three and a half hours until the chopper comes from Singapore for you."

I looked. I read. I groaned. There are times when despite the best of intentions to continually be innovative, clichés say it all.

This was one of 'em. Because today there would be no rest for the weary. Now, I probably shouldn't tell you precisely what the message said because it was classified top secret. But I can give you all gist a hint.

My cruise to Guam was being interrupted, courtesy of CINCPACFLT—Commander-IN-Chief PACific FLeeT. He, in his four-starred wisdom, was TADing me (TAD, you'll remember, is a navyspeak acronym for Temporary Additional Duty, although SEALs refer to it as Traveling Around Drunk) to Yokosuka, the huge joint American-Japanese navy installation near Yokohama.

Once there, I would (I think I'm all right quoting directly here): "advise, counsel, and offer crisis management assistance at the specific and immediate request of Japanese National Police Inspector Toshiro Okinaga, to the HN (host nation) tactical response forces during the ongoing critical and time-sensitive crisis environment currently taking place at Yokosuka's sole fast-food franchise location."

Would you like me to translate that into English for you, folks? Okay. It means that CINCPACFLT wanted my butt in Japan so that I could help a Japanese National Police SWAT team take down a bunch of tangos who had taken a bunch of U.S. Navy personnel hostage at the Yokosuka Navy base McDonald's.

How had CINCPACFLT learned that I was aboard the *Scorpion?* The answer to that question lies far above my pay grade. But I would venture to guess it had something to do with the secure communications facility that is run out of the office of the Chairman of the Joint Chiefs of Staff; a comm unit that can instantaneously connect him with anyone, anywhere in the world.

That being the case, why had the Chairman and CINCPACFLT interrupted the last leg of a sensitive and critical mission to TAD me Japanward? Good question—and if we hadn't been under way at flank speed, I would have gone into the sub's sail with my handy secure transmitter and asked Chairman Crocker that precise question.

But that was impossible. Captain Dave had his orders on paper. And remember what I told you about submariners—they do not change things that have been written on paper.

Now, as to why I was being sent to Japan, the answer is kind of complicated, so bear with me for a few paragraphs of what the old editor calls literary explication, will you? And no, don't go skipping this stuff, because it may turn out to be significant a little further on.

First, the Navy's rapport with JMSDF (the Japanese Maritime Self-Defense Forces) has always been good. So, given the opportunity, CINCPACFLT will go out of his way to help his Japanese counterpart.

But that relationship alone would not have been enough to cause CINCPACFLT to send me humping and thumping to Yokosuka. He acted because of political considerations. You see, putting the Navy aside, our relations with the Japanese were for a while in what might be called a shambles. Moreover, that condition was caused mainly by the United States, not the Japanese.

You want specifics? Well, for one, the Japanese were outraged when it turned out that my colleagues over at

Christians In Action (you probably already know that's what we SEALs call the CIA) knew of, but didn't bother to warn the Japanese about, the Aum Shinrikyo cult.

You say you don't remember the Aum Shinrikyos? They were the no-goodniks who placed canisters of the nerve agent Sarin on five subway trains in Tokyo back in 1995, killing twelve and injuring another fifty-five hundred. Well, it turns out that the CIA knew that Aum Shinrikyo cultists had been testing Sarin as well as Tabun and other deadly chemical-biological agents at a ranch they owned in Australia. They even knew that the Aum Shinrikyos had been able to build an explosive delivery device for their Sarin gas, and that they'd managed to smuggle it from Australia to Japan.

But here's what: Langley never bothered to pass any of the above information to its Japanese counterpart, the intelligence agency called the Cabinet Research Office, better known as Naicho. Naicho was notcho happy.

Then there was the matter of our American military personnel raping that twelve-year-old schoolgirl on Okinawa. The Okinawans overreacted (not without provocation, I might add). They tried—unsuccessfully—to evict all Americans from their island. That is not the kind of relationship you want when it's strategically imperative to keep our air bases and other military installations on foreign soil.

And so, to help bolster the harmony between *Amerikajins* (that's us gringos) and *Nihonjins* (that's the Japanese), a memo went out twenty-two months ago over the signature of the previous White House national security adviser.

Let me show it to you in its entirety. And please remember that the acronym POTUS stands for President Of The United States.

MEMORANDUM

THE WHITE HOUSE

WASHINGTON

SECRET

UNCLASSIFIED WITH REMOVAL OF TAB A

To: Secretary of Defense

From: NSC Adviser

Subject: U.S.-Japanese military cooperation

1. POTUS directs immediate implementation of the American-Japanese Protocol formulated at December's Japanese-American Protocol RIG meeting.

2. All GOJ requests for assistance in the areas of crisis management, risk assessment, and counterterrorism are to receive a Priority One designation from the DOD and all of its related agencies.

3. SECDEF will devise, develop, create, define, and execute a Doctrine of Jointness that will allow the United States Government and the Government of Japan to bolster their mutual goals and objectives, as defined by the JAP RIG.

4. Refer to E.O. 1297/b-2 [TAB A], for specific guidance on implementing this policy directive, including key areas of bilateral cooperation, and unilateral initiatives.

SECRET

As I said, that memo was written twenty-two months ago. Today, there is a new national security adviser in residence in the West Wing of the White House. His name is Matt Thompson. After less than half a year on the job he considers himself the Metternich of the twenty-first century, and he is vehemently opposed to any strategic cooperation with the Japanese because it might interfere with the pro-China direction in which he has single-handedly moved our foreign policy.

Now, I am not one of your political creatures. I don't make foreign policy—I'm only the animal who carries it out. And so I'm not as current on these things as I might be (although I can guar-on-tee you that by the end of this book I'll be as up to speed as any NSC adviser, columnist pundit, or talking head on TV news). But I do know a few details. Like the fact that Matt Thompson is an old friend of the president's. By old friend, I mean they were college roommates. And so he, more than most in this administration, has the ear of the commander in chief.

From what I've read and seen, the NSC adviser has been pushing a policy that tilts the United States away from its traditional Pacific Rim allies—countries like Japan, Australia, Singapore, the Philippines, and South Korea—and inclines it firmly toward Beijing. His reasoning? Well, an op-ed in the *Asian Wall Street Journal* a few weeks ago opined that the administration was wisely and shrewdly acting the way it was in order to reverse China's current policy of rapprochement with the Russians, after an estrangement that has lasted more than a quarter of a century.

A Sino-Russo alliance, the article argued (it was written by some retired State Department suit turned consultant), would "disrupt the vital balance of power so fragile today on the Pacific Rim." And so, to neutralize this new Moscow-Beijing partnership and preserve harmony and tranquillity, the United States would have to shift itself out of its old, confrontational stance and develop a new and much more symbiotic relationship with China. It certainly looked to me as if our NSC adviser was receiving his operating instructions from the op-ed page of the fucking *Asian Wall Street Journal.*

And now, as Paul Harvey says, comes the other side of the story. You see, despite his close relationship with the president, Matt Thompson's wasn't the only opinion represented in the administration. The secretary of defense and the Chairman of the Joint Chiefs of Staff had their own points of view, which they argued both forcefully and publicly.

While it wasn't Chairman Crocker's style to write op-ed articles, he did do interviews from time to time. And whenever he was asked, he said he believed that our strategic relationship with Japan was just as vital—perhaps even more vital—to American interests as our economic relationship with China. He told anyone who would listen that he believed the United States could not afford to lose its bases there.

For his part, SECDEF loves giving interviews, and he's good at it. And during each one, he never lost the opportunity to make the point that with the Philippines gone, America has no ability to move quickly without our facilities on Japan and Okinawa. Whenever he testified before Congress, he invariably reminded the Armed Services Committee members that American weapons makers—whose workers vote—receive a goodly chunk of the $44 billion Japanese defense dollars spent annually.

SECDEF is also a veteran of the kind of war of attrition politics in which you chip away at your opponents. To explain that in real English, it means that an orchestrated series of leaks has been trickling out for the past couple of months, each one detailing an embarrassing tidbit relating to Matt Thompson's China policy and each one chipping away at the president's approval rating. And since we have a president who governs by poll, not conscience, I can report that SECDEF has been able to persuade the president not to act precipitously. Which means—for the present, at least—that DOD has managed to maintain its steady course with the Japanese, despite considerable public bitching, moaning, whining, and sniping from NSC Adviser Thompson's office.

That's the background. So, the political trenches being

dug the way they are these days, when CINCPACFLT gets a request from the Japanese, he probably calls the chief of naval operations, who calls Chairman Crocker, who says, "You bet—act on it pronto."

Why? Because CINCPACFLT knows that by doing so he will make his boss, the chief of naval operations, happy. For his part, CNO is ebullient because he knows that when he does anything that pisses off the NSC adviser, he is going to make the JCS Chairman and SECDEF euphoric.

Amazing how politics works, ain't it?

Anyhow, that's part one of the equation—the political factor. Part two—the personal element—is that I was summoned because it was my old friend Toshiro Okinaga who'd requested my assistance forthwith and chop-chop. Tosho was now, as you can see, an inspector, which is the equivalent of a one-star general, with the Kunika. Kunika is a special action unit of the Japanese National Police. It is in charge of all Japanese counterterrorism operations these days.

Some more background is probably in order here. Not so very long ago, I led the life of a peripatetic teacher, a *ronin,* wandering the globe inculcating students in the deadly arts of Warriordom—specifically proficiency in counterterrorism—to all who would listen (and who had the right security clearances).

Among those with whom I interacted was one Toshiro Okinaga. At that point of life he was a sergeant in Kunika, although he'd managed since then to just about take over the fucking organization. Tosh's English is frawless—the result of four years at Notre Dame (B.A. in political science), then another two for his M.A. in criminology, at the University of Indiana.

But I didn't like him because he spoke like me, chased pussy in his spare time like me, and could match the most energetic young SEAL pup Kirin Ichiban beer for Kirin Ichiban beer over a long night of pub crawling, like me. I wasn't fond of Tosho because he could use polysyllabic words to impress the bureaucrats and draw flowcharts diagramming risk assessment possibilities that influenced legislators. I admired Tosho—and liked working with him—because the man was a Warrior, a real samurai, whose dedication and commitment to improving himself and his men's abilities to make war never ever stopped. He also understood that you never ask your men to do anything that you won't do or can't do. And so, yes, Tosho was a superb pistol shot. And, yes, he was a seventh-degree black belt who knew the difference between dojo martial arts and down-and-dirty-on-the-street fighting. And although he hated heights, he'd learned to fast rope from choppers, rappel down the sides of skyscrapers—and even jump out of perfectly good aircraft. He trained with his men, always pushing them further than they thought they could go.

And when things got real, he was the first one through the door. He volunteered for the tough assignments and the high-risk operations, and because of his dedication to sweat-in-training, he'd seldom lost a man in battle. But perhaps most important is the fact that Tosho has never stopped thinking like a sergeant, even though he now wears the equivalent of a star on his collar. And so, thinking like the sergeant he once was, he'd put in a call for me, because just as I have a Safety Net of chiefs to help me through the rough spots, Tosho has a safety net of counterterrorism shooters to help him through major crises. Frankly, I'm honored to be at the top of his short rist.

Still, Tosho's crisis couldn't have come at a worse time. To be honest, the last thing I needed right now was any kind of diversion—moreover, one that could end up being time-consuming. No, what I wanted was a smooth cruise to Guam, a fast flight back to CONUS—the CONtinental US—and a long investigation to discover WTF was going on *in re* the matter of Big Brother technology, all those Russkie weapons, and the Chinese.

That was on the one hand. On the other hand, part of the responsibility of being a Warrior—an important part of the informal Code of the Warrior—is that you do not let down a fellow Warrior when he asks for your help. And so, I woke my men and gave them a sit-rep. Bottom line: I'd go to Japan. They'd go home.

Did I suffer abuse because they had not been invited to join in the festivities? Hey, is my dick big?

Oh, yes, they complained. Oh, yes, they protested. And when none of those techniques proved persuasive, they sulked, and glowered, and grimaced, and threatened. That's the way it is when hunter/killer shoot-and-looters are denied their fair share of hunting and killing and shooting and looting.

But to be honest, they had a two-part mission equally critical to my own. First, I tasked them with getting the Big Brother equipment back to Washington without attracting any notice. After all, no one, with the exception of Tony Mercaldi at DIA, knew I'd taken possession of the Halliburton suitcases and their contents. And I wanted to keep things that way.

Second, they'd have to start snooping and pooping, which is the SEAL way of saying they'd start making quiet inquiries about what we'd found—and who was responsible. In the same way SEALs recon hostile territory all over the world, my men would go to work as soon as they arrived back in CONUS. They'd check the lay of the land. They'd make studies and observations. They'd look for signs of hostiles—and identify 'em when they found 'em. And then, when I got back, they'd report what they'd discovered to me.

Chapter 5

I WAS SNATCHED OFF THE *SCORPION'S* DECK BY A PAVE LOW chopper's winch line just after 1500 and flown to Singapore. There, I caught a C-20A, which is the early 1980s, no-frills, military version of the Gulfstream III, for the hop to Yakota air base. We landed with nothing in the fuel tanks but fumes. But we landed. From Yakota I jumped a Navy Bell 212 and touched down a few minutes later on the VIP chopper pad at Yokosuka.

I didn't like what I saw as we came in. You could see swells of heavy, black smoke blowing across the expanse of stowage sheds, bunkers, and fuel tanks that ring the Yokosuka installation. Closer in, base traffic was Gordian-knotted—marines and SPs frantically waving at frustrated drivers. Things were worst as I flew over the wide road leading to the knot of "creature comfort" stores, which included Yokosuka's McDonald's—a hub of activity for sailors and visitors alike. We came in at about eight hundred feet, and from the numbers of police, medical, and fire equipment I saw on scene, I knew the news was not going to be good.

Tosho was waiting for me as I bounded through the hatch,

sitting on the fender of a navy gray HumVee, waving at me with the balaclava he'd pulled off his head. He hadn't changed since I'd last seen him—still the same compact little Japanese fireprug, although he'd gone a bit more gray up top. He was wearing black coveralls tucked into GSG-9 boots, a Point Blank bulletproof vest, and the kind of Velcro-rich close-quarters combat tactical rig that cops call SWAT-wear. On his thigh, I could see the butt of an old SAS-type Browning High Power pistol peeking through the ballistic nylon holster flap and thick nylon restraining strap. The narrow band of skin around his eyes—the only part of his face that would be unprotected by either Nomex balaclava or protective eyewear—was blackened from soot, giving him the bizarre appearance of a Japanese Panda in SWAT gear.

Whether the news was going to be good or bad it was still wonderful to see him again. I grabbed him around the shoulders and gave him an old-fashioned Slovak bear hug and a warm "Fuck you, asshole!"

He grappled like a sumo wrestler, slapped my arms away, wrapped me up, held his wide stance and—*"Roguee-sahhhnng!"*—lifted, taking me clear off the ground and spinning me around. He dropped me back onto what the Kennedys might call terra firmer, stepped back and squinted, jut-jawed at me. *"Kon-nichi-wa, Gaijin*—Welcome back, Dick—I just wish it was under better circumstances."

I didn't have to ask for a sit-rep because by the time the Navy Hummer had brought us the five hundred yards to the hostage site, I could see for myself what had happened. My old nemesis Mister Murphy had happened.

I jumped out of the Hummer, stepped back, and looked around to get my bearings. I knew this site—which is probably one of the reasons Tosho had called for me. I'd brought Red Cell here during its heyday, and Tosh and his guys and me and mine had played games at this very same Mickey D's. I'd been the baddie, and Tosho and his shooters had learned how to take down an American-style fast-food restaurant, with its huge reefers, walk-in freezers, open kitchen, and big storage areas.

They were just about to open a bunch of McDonald's in Tokyo and other Japanese cities back then, and Tosh had wanted to see the best way to deal with potential problems. It makes sense, doesn't it? The more you know about the sites you're going to have to deal with, the more effective your response can be.

Well, Tosh knew all about McDonald's—and exactly how to take 'em down with minimal collateral damage. This McDonald's was a charred shell. Shards of nominally shatterproof glass lay everywhere—they'd exploded out, so I knew the blast had been huge and had originated from inside the site. There was little that remained of the still-smoking interior. Forensics crews poked and probed through the debris, looking for body shards. The Kunika shooters in their black Ninja gear sat in tight knots, talking quietly among themselves. Across the way, a company of shell-shocked Marines in combat gear was being debriefed. A row of fire-blanket-covered bodies—some of them still smoldering—lay on the ground. I looked at Tosh and frowned. "What the hell happened, Tosh?"

"It was a *Jibaku*—they suicide-bombed the place." His expression showed the anguish he was feeling. "I tried to wait for you, Dick—told the navy not to push." He shrugged helplessly. "But Admiral Gray—he's the base commander. He overrode me."

That made no sense at all. "Why the hell did he do that?"

"You want the real reason? It's because CNN was broadcasting live, and he was afraid of appearing indecisive, so right on camera he ordered the marines to take it down. I thought his PAO[9] was going to shit."

"You mean MERF did *this?"* I knew the commander of the Marine Emergency Reaction Force based half an hour north of Tokyo—a hell of a Warrior named Shellhammer. He would never have screwed up so badly.

---

[9]Public Affairs Officer.

"No, the MERF wasn't getting here fast enough for the admiral, so he used what he had on hand—the base guards."

"What about you and your guys?"

"I told you, Dick. CNN was on scene. Broadcasting live, by satellite, back to the U.S. The tangos had sent out a list of demands—"

"About?"

"Islands, Dick."

"Islands?"

"The Senkaku islands. There are eight of them—uninhabited, rocky islands. They lie south of Okinawa, just to the northeast of Taiwan—and they're claimed by both China and Japan. The Chinese call them the Diaoyus."

"What the hell does this have to do with anything?"

"It has to do with oil, Dick. Huge fields of it, according to the American oil companies. Japan has to import all of its oil. If we developed the fields just off the Senkakus, we could expand them into something comparable to what the Brits did in the North Sea."

"And the Chinese want to do the same thing."

"Sure they do. Which is why ASDF[10] is always running surveillance flights. We've got E-2Cs overflying the islands on a daily basis."

"What's the American reaction to that?"

"Until recently, it was just fine. After all, if the Chinese took the Senkakus, they'd be within easy striking distance of Taiwan. We're talking two hundred, two hundred fifty miles maybe."

"So, what the hell precipitated this clusterfuck, anyway, Tosh? Seems as if the United States has no overt involvement here."

"It's a little complicated." Tosho shifted his weight before continuing. "See, America has always been neutral on the subject of the Senkakus," he said. "Your government has

[10]Air Self-Defense Force.

always referred to them simply as 'the eight disputed islands.' But last week, the White House spokesman began using both the Chinese and Japanese names, which made real headlines here and caused Beijing to go ballistic. The Chinese position has always been that no matter how the dispute went, the islands were always to be called by their Chinese name. The terrorists' first demand was for the United States to apologize, and either resume its policy of neutrality or refer to the islands by their Chinese name alone."

"So this wasn't a group of Japanese?"

"Oh, they were Japanese, all right. Maoists, no less—they call themselves the Red Seeds, and they support China." He paused. "Inscrutable, aren't we?"

He scratched under his CQC vest collar, found something that was bothering him, discarded it, then continued. "Besides, it didn't matter who the hell these tangos were. There was no way the admiral was going to let Kunika control the situation—not with the White House watching and some West Wing idiot on the cellular to him." Tosho wiped at the sooty ring around an eye with the back of a gloved hand. "That would have been . . . un-American," he said bitterly. "Not in the John Wayne tradition." Tosho was full of nasty surprises today.

"The White House?"

"Somebody from the national security adviser's office was watching the CNN broadcast. Whoever it was called Admiral Gray directly—actually got him on the cellular and demanded a sit-rep. The admiral started to explain that things were under control. Then he told whoever it was that you were on your way here to help us handle the situation—that you knew the base from your Red Cell experience." Tosho's face darkened. "From what I heard of Admiral Gray's side of the conversation, things got bad. The White House staffer obviously told him to move it—*right now.*"

"Didn't he object?"

"Not from what I heard. He just stood there, nodding

'yessir, yessir, yessir' into the cellular. And the point that was being made, Dick, was that the White House wanted this thing over and done with before you got here." Tosho wiped at the grime on his face. "Oh, man, talk about screwing with the chain of command. It was inconceivable—"

Actually, it wasn't inconceivable at all. During the Somalia crisis, one of the president's closest public relations advisers regularly called the SpecWar Ops Center in Mogadishu and countermanded the on-scene commander's orders. He got away with it for two reasons. First, most White House reporters didn't believe his actions were significant enough to report, even though said adviser's orders probably caused the deaths of several Rangers and Delta troopers. Second, the adviser was much too good a source—he was extremely close to the president and first lady—to be trashed in public. There is, you see, a journalistic technical term for White House reporters without sources close to the first family. That term is *unemployed.*

"Damn it." Tosho nodded in the direction of the charred shell that had once been the base McDonald's. His thumb hooked toward the medical technicians loading bodies. "Talk about your textbook clusterfucks."

I walked over and took a closer look at the corpses. Three were still covered by blankets. I lifted the edge of one, then another—and saw the charred remains of a child, her tiny form frozen in pain. Oh, Christ—there had been kids inside. And now they were dead. It angers me to see children murdered and fuels my rage against those who perpetrate such deeds. It hurt even more to know that these were Navy children—they were my family. They would be avenged. I would find out which schmuck at the White House caused this and I'd deal with it—on *my* terms.

I stepped back and examined the scene critically. I saw where it had gone wrong from evidence that I could read like a fucking primer. The Marines had staged over there—well within sight of the McDonald's back door, not to mention the security camera that was mounted above it.

Then they'd come around the corner and charged straight ahead, like the fucking Light Brigade, in a keep it stupid, simple, frontal assault. And while they'd been trying to toss flashbangs that couldn't penetrate the tango-resistant windows McDonald's installs overseas, and making a lot of ambient noise in the process, the terrorists calmly murdered the nine American and three Japanese hostages, then blew the McDonald's up—themselves included.

This is what happens when some equivalent form of Grade-A, Extra-Large, ruby red, government-inspected sphincter—e.g., the WHA, or White House Asshole—is allowed to commandeer a situation about which he has no knowledge, no background, and no ability. Then you have your C^2CO idiot[11]—COs like Admiral Gray, who don't have the balls to tell that WHA to get fucked unless he has a piece of paper in his hand signed by the commander in chief. So they kiss ass, say, "Yes, sir," and end up getting people killed.

And then you know what happens afterward? Said C^2CO spends considerable time and energy trying to lay the blame on the poor schmucks who got stuck holding the short end of the stick because of all those bad orders, flawed intelligence, and institutional stupidity. Please be so kind as to allow me to pause here just long enough for a brief Rogue Rant. Okay? Thanks.

Y'see, there is an unfortunate mode of thinking prevalent among so-called leaders these days. That trend can be summed up in three letters, CYA, which as you probably can guess, stands for Cover Your Ass. CYA means that officers care more about their careers than they do about their men. There is an old Marine Corps tradition that in the field, officers eat only after their men have eaten. There is an old Navy tradition that officers are responsible for the welfare of their men—totally responsible. Most of today's

[11]You will remember that C^2CO stands for Can't Cunt Commanding Officer.

officers don't give a damn about their men. They want to put in their eight hours a day, then retire to the golf course or the real estate office or the PC so they can check their stock portfolios.

Well, this is a situation I cannot abide, and lately, I have taken to acting, rather than bitching, when I come across it. And so, I looked around to see whether Admiral Gray was in attendance so that I could have five or six choice words about the sanctity of the goddamn chain of command with him before I pounded his pencil-dicked pus-nutted C^2 ass into the yellow Jell-O that he was. Yes, I knew that he wore a star and I didn't. But there are times when that Just Don't Matter—and this was one of 'em.

Tosho saw the Roguish, stop-me-before-I-kill-again look in my eyes, knew me well enough to realize what I was contemplating, and backed me up against the Hummer with his very solid forearm. "Bad idea, Dick—what's done is done."

Maybe yes, maybe no. Between Admiral Gray and whoever had called from the White House, a dozen people had been needlessly killed today. And believe me, I'd find some way to even the score. But in the meanwhile, I had to make tracks for Washington. There was a lot to be done, on a number of fronts, and this untimely diversion had postponed what I knew was a more critical, and long-term, issue.

"Okay, Tosh, you're right. Why not just take me to Narita, and I'll grab a plane for Washington."

Tosho dropped his arm. "Actually, I wish you'd stay a little while longer, Dick. There's still work to be done."

I wondered aloud what that was. Things at Yokosuka seemed pretty much over. "Fact is, Tosh, you didn't need me here at all."

"Not for this fiasco. But since I've discovered who's responsible, I thought you'd like a piece of the action when I go in to clean 'em out," Tosho said, guiding me toward a black Ford Bronco that had windows tinted as darkly as any Florida drug dealer's, and a roof that sprouted half a dozen kinds of antennas.

I looked back toward the charred corpses. I thought about the dead children. I thought about Admiral Gray. "You've got yourself a deal," I said. "I'll get a later flight."

Tosho cracked a grim smile. "Good." He opened the right-hand driver's door and stepped onto the running board. "Just before my shooters and I arrived here, my intel people intercepted a *saishotanchishingo*—that's what we call a whatchamacallit"—he fought for the English words and smiled when he came up with the right ones—"a minimized radio signal, between the hostage-takers at McDonald's and a control post. We were able to locate where the signal came from. It's a warehouse northwest of here."

"And?"

"And I had the place checked out—discreetly. By the time things went sour at Micky D's, I was pretty certain that what we'd come across was one of the Red Seed's headquarters."

"One?"

"They work in cells—just like the Japanese Red Army did. Compartmentation. It makes us have to work harder digging 'em out. Anyway, there were three *saishotanchishingo*s in all. It was enough to tell us this was the place where they staged for this nasty little exercise. It's—" He looked at my apprehensive expression and answered the question I'd been about to ask: "No—believe me, this was a piece of intel I had no intention of sharing with Admiral Gray."

He stuck his thumb toward the opposite side of the Bronco. "So come aboard, sailor. Given the way things were here, these assholes are probably gonna try to scamper soon, so we have to hit 'em, hit 'em before they do."

I clapped Tosho on the back with the flat of my hand. "So—'lay on, Macduff—' "

Tosho jumped right in. " 'And damn'd be him that first cries, 'Hold, enough.' Shakespeare, right? *Macbeth.* Fifth Act, final scene."

I hate the kind of people who can go on *Jeopardy* and win, don't you?

Tosho climbed behind the wheel and slammed his door shut. I opened the passenger door and started to get in when I realized there was someone in the rear seat.

I paused, but Tosh didn't give it a second thought. "Dick, this is Alixe Joseph. Alixe—Dick Marcinko."

I pulled myself up, swiveled my arm over the seat back, and offered my hand. "Hi."

I got a firm, dry handshake in return. "Hi yourself. I'm Alixe Joseph."

There was what might in pre–politically correct times be called a pregnant silence in the vehicle. I turned back and took a look. Alixe Joseph was an attractive woman in her midforties. She had an oblong, impish, yet cherubic face, set off by the kind of low-maintenance frizzed hair that isn't so much styled as it is shampooed, blown dry, and left alone. She was wearing a black, double-breasted, Italian hand-finished blazer and narrow-legged matching trousers, and a soft, ivory-colored silk blouse with a high cossack collar and pearl buttons.

The presentation in toto was a woman's version of those Princeton or Dartmouth bespoke-tailored alumni who do not pass GO, who do not collect $200, but proceed directly to the foreign service exam, or meander over to Langley to be fluttered,[12] then backgrounded, vetted, and cleared as TS/SCI[13] spooks. The only difference is that the male version is usually completed with fancy striped shirts from some stiff-upper-lip shirtmaker on Jermyn Street in London and the requisite loud, veddy English wide tie, instead of the hand-stitched, pearl-buttoned ivory silk tunic worn by Ms. A. Joseph.

But, she bore indeed all the other outward paraphernalia of senior spook or diplodom. She had a sensible, under-

[12]That's CIAspeak for polygraphed.

[13]Top Secret/Special Compartmental Intelligence clearance requires the Agency's most comprehensive background check.

stated steel-and-gold Rolex on her right wrist. The top of a vermeil Montblanc fountain pen for writing all those fifty-dollar words peeked discreetly behind the raw silk poof atop her blazer's narrow breast pocket. She was probably wearing old-fashioned shoes, too—the kind of $350 Ferragamo flats that woman diplomats, spooks, and Wall Street lawyers all favor.

I leaned over and snuck a glimpse. Yup.

"So, Alixe," I said, "do you work with the Christian brethren and sethren at Langley, or with all those foggy bottoms over at State?"

She laughed—and her blue eyes twinkled when she did. That was a good sign. "Neither," quoth she. When she saw the puzzled expression on my puss, she added obliquely, "But I quick-checked you out in my shop when Tosho requested your presence on-scene, and Tony Merc says to say, hi—and that he'll vouch for me."

For one of the few times in my life, I was struck dumb. I know hundreds of DIA gumshoes—and svelte, stylish Alixe Joseph was decidedly not type casting. I was impressed, and said so.

"I'm part of a new program," she said by way of explanation. "It's compartmented (isn't everything these days?). But we can talk about my component-specific element. I'm part of DHS—for Defense HUMINT Service."

I'd heard RUMINT about DHS. It had been created last year at the new SECDEF's direction. The nice thing about having an ex-senator running the Pentagon is that he has friends on Capitol Hill who actually believe that the armed services should be used for more than playing traffic cops in Bosnia, pretending to be social workers in Haiti, working like Boy Scouts during forest fires in Montana, or killing goatherds on the Mexican border. Activities such as preparing to make war, for example. Well, SECDEF believes in being prepared for war, and he used all his connections on the Hill to further that belief. And so, DHS got itself a three-year program, all quietly appropriated and advance funded.

The monies had been slipped into funding bills that the president didn't dare line-item veto, either.

I told her what I knew. She cracked a smile and made with the fifty-dollar words. "Oh, was *that* fortuitous—it means that our money is impregnable, locked in by Congress, and no matter how he tries, Matt Thompson and his White House mafia can't touch us."

And why would he try, I asked?

Because, Alixe explained, much of DHS's mission was to penetrate the huge Chinese intelligence apparatus that had been expanding all across the Pacific Rim ever since the death of Deng Xiaoping. She was based in Tokyo, worked out of the embassy. But her AO lay from Korea in the north to Indonesia in the south, and her job was to develop agent networks that would help us learn what Beijing was up to, as well as keep an eye on everything else that might affect America's defense stance on the Pacific Rim.

It was a formidable assignment. She must have had a hell of a background to get it, too—although she was spook-usual in her discreetness about what she'd done before.

What she did say was that her job was, these days, being made more difficult because of a political dispute between the Pentagon (read SECDEF) and the White House (read NSC adviser Matt Thompson). It was no secret that the NSC boss wanted the Pentagon, particularly DIA, to keep its nose out of anything having to do with his unique brand of China policy, a China policy that would be supported solely by the CIA's findings.

Of course, Alixe added, the new DCI just happened to be Matt Thompson's old buddy from Yale. They'd even worked together at the same left-of-center think tank in Washington, and they saw eye-to-eye when it came to dealing with our potential adversaries. Can you say "appeasement"? It appeared that they certainly could—and did, on a regular basis.

Now, let me step aside here for a minute and recap because Matt Thompson, whom I have never met, is becoming irksome. First, he advocates tilting our policy away from

Japan and toward China. Now, I believe we need to have an even-handed policy. Japan, after all, is a potential adversary in the economic sense, and we must maintain wariness. Though vigilance is one thing, jettisoning the Japanese, which is what he'd like to do, is something else altogether. And now I learn that he had been lobbying against DIA's HUMINT-gathering operations, one of the most important of which is focused on China. Not good. We've learned in the past that CIA estimates can be absolutely wrong. Like the ones Langley did just before the fall of the Soviet Union, which predicted that communism would be the dominant system in Russia right through the twenty-first century.

So—let me put this in Roguespeak—fuck Matt Thompson. What the hell does he know anyway? He's just another goddam academic who'd never bothered to hump his ass out into the field and lay it on the line. I told Alixe Joseph that any HUMINT capabilities at DIA were positive steps so far as I was concerned.

She nodded in agreement. "Especially because DIA's always been prohibited from recruiting agents and running nets—CIA would never let it happen." Alixe Joseph pointed her thumb and forefinger in my direction in a strangely familiar gesture. "That was true until Chairman Crocker and the new SECDEF came along. They did some heavy lobbying—convinced Congress to come up with the money and provide us some political juice. The problem is that CIA isn't doing the kind of job we need. You know the problems we faced during the Gulf War."

Did I ever. Here is some RUMINT for you. Hank Trott, the self-important CIA supergrade assigned to coordinate intelligence with Norm Schwarzkopf's staff, never even went to Riyadh. He stayed safe and sound back at CENTCOM headquarters in Tampa, Florida, playing tennis and swimming laps. When the commander of Schwarzkopf's J-2[14] complained, Langley grudgingly sent a working

[14]The intelligence directorate of Schwarzkopf's joint staff.

group overseas. But they sent it to London, not Saudi. Go figure.

Well, ever since, DOD has been trying to break into the HUMINT business so it can provide military field commanders and the Joint Chiefs with the kind of intelligence that warriors need. And I'm glad to see it has finally succeeded—even though I could have used folks like Alixe Joseph years and years ago.

"Anyway," Alixe Joseph continued, "I set up shop out here last year. They gave me embassy cover—POLAD[15] to the defense attaché to be precise." She pursed her lips. "Sometimes I think it would have been easier working NOC.[16] The way the embassy keeps trying to insert itself into my business is unbelievable. Anyway, things are complicated." She brightened. "But Tosho and I have managed to keep ourselves busy." She slapped him on the shoulder. "Haven't we, buddy?"

Blue dashboard light flashing, Tosho nosed the Bronco around the traffic, moving slowly toward Yokosuka's main gate. "Alixe got here just as the Chinese took over in Hong Kong," Tosh said. "Since they did, there's been a lot of new activity all over Japan—none of it good."

"Certainly, the Chinese have been expanding their intelligence activities here," said Alixe Joseph, continuing Tosh's thought in a way that told me they'd been spending a lot of time together. "That would be natural, given the power struggle after Deng died. Problem is, the hardliners in Beijing—and they're the ones who control the security and intel operations—are flexing muscle. They've been actively recruiting agents, and I think they've even been smuggling weapons—although we haven't found any concrete evidence of it yet, have we, Tosh?"

"Nope," he said. "But I pulled Alixe into the loop today because the group that blew up the McDonald's is Chinese

---

[15]POLitical ADviser.
[16]nonofficial cover.

sponsored. I'd hoped to have one or two for us to interview." His face grew grim. "No such luck."

Alixe's expression told me she was still optimistic. "Maybe we'll still get the opportunity," she said.

"How does Beijing insert its intel apparatus?" I asked. Frankly, I'm not a China expert, and I was glad to run into someone who could explain.

"They use students, journalists, businessmen—anyone who comes in contact with outsiders on a regular basis." She pursed her lips. "In Hong Kong, they used Xinhua—that's the New China News Agency—to infiltrate more than six hundred agents into the territories in the eight months before they took over. And remember what happened after the last Brits pulled out—it wasn't pleasant."

Tosho picked up: "For the six months before the Brits left, the Hong Kong bureau of Xinhua was run by a guy named Li Chimen. But if Li is a journalist, then I'm one, too."

"What he really is," said Alixe Joseph, "is a colonel in the People's Liberation Army." She flipped open the leather secretary that sat next to her on the Bronco's seat, retrieved a series of black and white three-by-five surveillance photos, and handed them to me.

I peered down. Li was a tall, lean man with a long, angular face, with prominent cheekbones and a cruel, thin-lipped, aristocratic mouth above which sat the sort of pencil-thin mustache common to villains in the sorts of World War II war movies currently in vogue on cable TV. I studied the photographs. Li was always dressed impeccably. His demeanor was properly military—he stood erect and straight. But I could make out something of the panther to his stance, too. I sorted through the photos until I found a close-up and I could get a close look at the dark, penetrating eyes below the visor of his PLA hat. The man was a shooter. I could see it in his eyes. I handed the pictures back to Alixe. "What's his story?"

"Li's background is special forces—a real operator from what we've been able to tell. My defectors tell me he ran infiltrations into Taiwan and the coastal islands—he's *zhongdui.*"

"A naval special commando—"

Alixe's head came up, her expression showed surprise. "You know the term?"

I wasn't about to explain. I shrugged her question off. "SEALs like to stay current on the opposition."

She accepted the justification. "Anyway, according to current RUMINT he's also worked covert programs in Libya, Sudan, and Tehran, too—probably helping them set up training camps for who-knows-what kind of organizations. These days he's got a new assignment: assistant to the director of *Er Bu*—"

"That's how the Chinese say 'Second Department'—of the PLA's Military Intelligence Department," Tosho interjected.

Alixe Joseph steadied herself as Tosho jumped the curb. "We call it the MID."

The big Ford threaded the needle between a pair of parked police cars, pulled back onto the roadway with a thwump, drove through the main gate, and accelerated toward Highway 16, which I knew led from Yokosuka northeast, skirted the harbor at Yokohama, then proceeded due north to central Tokyo. "Li does most of the dirty work for another real sonofabitch—a major general named Zhu Linfan." She retrieved the leather binder again, flipped it open, found the page she wanted, and tapped her well-manicured finger atop a newspaper photograph of a round-faced, cold-eyed Oriental in PLA uniform. "Zhu was the colonel who stopped things cold at Tiananmen Square back in 1989. He was the enforcer for Chi Haotian—the one-star at Tiananmen who went on to become defense minister. Zhu was Chi Haotian's top thug—Li is his."

Tosho turned his siren on to speed things up and had to shout to make himself heard. "Anyway, about a year ago, Li turned up as Xinhua's bureau chief in Singapore. After three months there, he was 'posted' to Seoul. Guess what: after two months in Seoul, he went to Jakarta to spell the bureau chief there for a month. Then it was back to Beijing for three or four weeks of 'editorial meetings'—and then, bingo—he turns up here in Tokyo as Xinhua's bureau chief."

Alixe Joseph interrupted. "Not just shows up, Tosh—remember?" She slapped the back of my seat. "It was like he had a goddam press agent. Three articles in the *Asian Wall Street Journal* trying to debunk the Xinhua-espionage angle. A series about Li on NHK—that's one of the local TV networks, Dick."

"Don't forget about the love tap in *Asahi Shimbun* business section," Tosho said. "It amazed me that nobody bothered to do any digging on the guy. Where are all those alleged investigative journalists?"

I grinned. "The operative word there, Tosh, is *alleged."* I dimly remembered reading the *Journal* articles at the time. But something else jogged my memory, too. "Weren't they written by the same piled-higher-and-deeper asshole who's been writing about China and Japan lately?"

"Asshole is right," Alixe Joseph said. "His name's Bentley Brendel. Retired out of the State Department about fifteen years ago. James Baker hired him back as a consultant on China policy during the Bush administration—right after Tiananmen. He lasted two months, then he jumped ship. Bush's policy was too hard-line, I guess."

"But he still flaunts his Republican creds," said Tosho. "The man has no shame."

Alixe Joseph continued. "Then Warren Christopher's people hired him during the first Clinton administration—gave him an office on the seventh floor at Main State, and a deputy assistant secretary's title. He stayed about a year."

So Bentley the DAS was a political chameleon. I mistrust animals who change color—or sides. "What's he do now?"

Tosho grunted. "From the look of it he mints his own money."

His comment brought a bitter smile to Alixe Joseph's face. "He's put together a consulting firm that handles Asian business deals," she said. "But all he really does is deal with Beijing. You want to build a cement factory in Guangzhou? For the right price Bentley will get it done. You want to open a soft drink factory in Shanghai? You go see Brendel Associates. But bring your checkbook." She shook her head in disgust. "What peeves me so much is that he's considered *the* expert on U.S.-China relations. I mean, he testifies up on Capitol Hill. There are rumors he even still consults at the White House—although when I checked through channels about it, I was told he may have come in once or twice to help the NSC adviser out, but he wasn't on the list of NSC consultants—and he hasn't been issued a White House pass."

"But he still has lots of friends in high places," said Tosho.

"He's certainly made my life more difficult," Alixe Joseph said. "I was sent here to work with the Japanese. Like I said, ever since Li Chimen arrived, there's been a lot to keep Tosho and me busy. Beijing is probing, Dick—they're testing our capabilities; hunting for our weaknesses."

"Any luck hitting back?"

"I'm running two networks here, and a couple of others elsewhere, that are producing some results," she said, animatedly.

"Enough to take a chunk out of Li Chimen?"

"Not yet," she said. "But I'm starting to nip at his heels. I know that because I lost one of my better doubles[17] just about two months ago—and I'm pretty sure Li was involved."

She went on, "But it's tough. Building networks takes time, and coddling, and money, and I'm not being given a lot of those things these days." Her expression grew dark. "And, y'know, it seems as if every time I try to take some countermeasures, or Tosho attempts to get proactive, some supergrade at State, or the Agency, or the White House, starts screaming and yelling about 'disrupting the vital

[17]double agents.

balance of power' in the region." She shook her head. "Well, that phrase is something that Bentley Brendel manages to work into almost every article he writes, too."

I knew that. I'd seen the phrase in the *Asian Wall Street Journal* article on Sino-Russkie-American relations. She looked at me intently. "Some coincidence, right? Hey, Dick, you and I both know that *that* sort of 'coincidence' seldom happens in our business."

I nodded. She was right.

"Well," Alixe continued, "I have another 'coincidence' for you. Seven weeks ago, right after my double was murdered, Li Chimen said, 'Sayonara, Tokyo.' He's moved on."

"And not back to Beijing, either, I'm willing to bet," I said.

Tosho grinned. "That's the kind of bet they taught us not to take at Notre Dame," he said. "No, Li was 'promoted' again. He's been appointed Xinhua's interim Washington bureau chief."

Tosho's assembly point was well away from the target—a warehouse in an industrial zone just north of Suginami-Ku. The warehouse was under discreet observation by a platoon of Kunika's best sneak-and-peekers. All the roads going in and coming out had been blocked. But Tosho's infiltration route began more than two miles away, in a quiet, uninhabited area. That showed sound planning.

There is one crucial element of a tactical-team mission that often escapes the planners: the approach. Whether you are staging a drug raid, executing a high-risk warrant, or rescuing a hostage from a bunch of tangos, if you fuck up the approach, the chances are that you will FUBAR the operation. Most often, the approach screwup occurs because the staging area for the raid is too close to the target, the bad guys hear you coming long before you hit the door, and they either destroy the evidence, kill the hostage, or blow themselves—and you—to the well-known smithereens.

SEALs regularly practice this SpecWar stratagem. Indeed, our staging often takes place hundreds of miles from our actual insertion point. But many cops do not. So I was glad to see that Tosh's shooters were far enough away so that their preparations weren't going to attract any unwanted attention.

On the drive over, Tosh had made a long phone call, rattling in machine gun Japanese to someone in his office. I saw the results when I showed up: a full set of combat gear, size Extra-Extra Rogue, was waiting for me. A tall, lanky kid in black BDUs, rappelling belt and harness, body armor, thick fast-roping gloves tied to his belt, and a balaclava bunched around his neck, held out a tactical holster in which sat a Glock 19 with night sights. "Hey, Captain Marcinko—remember me?"

I pulled the pistol out, opened the slide to make sure that it was unloaded, and locked the gun open as I looked carefully, examining the angular face, the Marine haircut, and the uneven smile. He was familiar—but he'd changed his appearance since I'd seen him last. "Yoshioka, right?"

He shook my hand. "You got it, man. It's been a while."

Indeed it had. Yoshi was one of the Kunika shooters who'd helped me secure a load of stolen Tomahawk nuclear missiles from a lunatic-fringe right-wing no-goodnik named Hideo Ikigami.[18] Back then he'd been a long-haired punk rocker who favored black leather and motorcycle boots. Now he was as close cropped and gung ho as a Recon Marine. And from the way he'd bulked up, I could see he'd been working out on the weight pile regularly, too.

I let the Glock's slide go forward and tried the trigger action. It was nice and smooth—staged well, and had about a five-pound pull. I sight-acquired-dry-fired a few times to get the front sight picture embedded in my brain and my subconscious. If you can visualize the correct sight picture

---

[18]If you want to read all about it, you can go out and buy *Rogue Warrior: Red Cell.*

in your head, then you'll always hit your target, because you won't have to waste time trying to remember the right sight picture when you're in combat and the bad guy is shooting back at you.

Yes, I know it sounds very Zen. Well, there's nothing wrong with that—we're in Japan, aren't we? And besides, the technique works, which is all that counts. Hey—don't skip this part because, as the old chiefs used to say, you will see this material again in a few pages.

Okay. You start with the pistol at your side. You bring it up as if to fire, and you align the sights. You memorize that front sight picture. Really *visualize* it. Burn it into your brain. After as many repeats as necessary, you try the same exercise with your eyes closed. When the gun comes up into the same position whether your eyes are open or closed, you are ready. I practiced the exercise a dozen times more with my eyes open. Then I closed my eyes and brought the pistol up to its combat position. I opened my eyes. The sights were perfectly aligned—fucking sight picture was *there*—embedded in my subconscious. I repeated half a dozen times with eyes closed—and came up with a perfect sight picture each time. Now I knew that whatever I pointed the pistol at, no matter what the conditions were, I'd hit.

Next, I fieldstripped the gun to check it over. It was in perfect shape, so clean you could eat off the fucking thing. I looked at Yoshi. "This yours?"

He smiled. "Right on. Sweet little puppy, ain't it?" He handed me five seventeen-round magazines and two fifty-round boxes of Hydra-Shok 147-grain ammo. "I brought an MP5 and four loaded mags for you, too, Captain. Just let me know when you want them, sir."

The "sir," just in case you were curious, was spelled with an *s* and an *i*. Polite kid, huh? I loaded all the magazines and gave Yoshi back the surplus bullets—except for one, which I saved for later use. Then I climbed out of my blue submarine coveralls and pulled on a black Nomex jumpsuit, then shrugged into the Class-III CQC modular bulletproof vest, and strapped on knee and elbow pads. (That was a real luxury. We Froggish types don't generally get to wear pads. We are, after all, maritime creatures—amphibians—and it is hard to swim in knee and elbow pads.) The Velcro belt came next. To that, I attached my tactical holster, knife sheath, bolt cutter case, and two double magazine holders, into which I stuffed the Glock mags (mag number five went into my pocket, along with the spare round). On the vest's Velcro strips I hung my radio case, grenade containers, and flashlight lanyard.

I stuffed the pair of extra-large, soft leather-palmed Nomex gloves into a thigh pocket and secured the flap. Losing your gloves before an assault is a no-no. I hung the helmet they'd given me off my tactical holster. It was a Japanese large, which was still slightly small for my Yankee-size head and I saw no need to put it on until absolutely necessary.

Finally, I retrieved the last of the Glock magazines and shoved it into the pistol, pointed the muzzle in a safe direction, cocked and locked the weapon, dropped the mag, topped the mag off with the round I'd saved, reinserted it into the butt, and slid the Glock into the tactical holster. I secured the flap, checked the strap, then ran a second Velcro strap over the top and secured it, too. Hey—I've been there, and it ain't a Good Thing when your Glock drops out of its holster after you've flipped upside down on a rappelling line because you wanted to be able to quick-draw and so you didn't secure the fucking gun tight enough, then Mister Murphy got hold of it, and yanked it out.

I tugged at my Velcro as I watched Tosho, who was lovingly double-checking the Browning before he restowed it. "Y'know, sometimes I think it would have been easier to be one of those Roman centurions. All they had to worry about was their chest plate, a helmet, a short sword and shield, and those stupid-looking leg protectors."

"Oh, you would have made one hell of a centurion," Tosh said. "No—better—you'd have made a world-class gladiator, real Coliseum material." He saluted me in the old, straight-armed Roman fashion. "Hail, Penis Erectus, omnipotent warrior."

I saluted him with my middle finger. "May the God of War be with you my old and trusted friend, all-powerful Flatulence." I stretched and yawned. "Speaking of which, when can we get this circus maximus under way, Flat, my man? I've gone almost twenty-four hours without killing anybody."

Tosho tapped the transmit button on his radio, muttered something into his wrist mike, listened for an answer, and checked the watch on his left wrist. His face turned serious. "Thirteen minutes, Dick," he said.

Chapter 6

SINCE WE'VE GOT A LITTLE TIME ON OUR HANDS, FOLKS, LET ME talk a bit about what's gonna happen here. You can label this particular kind of operation whatever the local nomenclature happens to be—because whether you call it a SWAT op, a Delta hit, or a SEAL Team Six shoot-and-loot, the dynamics are basically the same. We are talking here about a special operations unit action against a fortified position. To succeed, all the elements must be delivered in one swift punch. Only that way can relative superiority, or RS, be achieved.

What's RS? It's when a small but dynamic attacking force wins out over a larger but more conventional force. The most critical elements for gaining relative superiority are: one, time, and two, violence of action. In other words, the longer you take to hit your target without decisive, dynamic action, the more prolonged your area of vulnerability—or AV—becomes, and the more chance there is that Mr. Murphy is gonna take advantage of the situation. And if he does, he will move you and your men directly into the FUBAR Zone, which is a Bad Place for you all to be, because the FUBAR Zone is where you get dead. And listen up, out there: do not forget any of this RS and AV stuff because you're going to come across it again in a few hundred pages and there'll be a quiz.

I see you. Yeah, *you*—the one slouching in your chair with the Nike ball cap on backward and the hand lolling in the air. You *what?* You want me to stop speaking in generalities and give you some specifics? Hey—let's all say this together, shall we?—*"Fuuuck you,* asshole!"

Okay, okay—it was a good observation despite the fact that you look stupid with that hat on backward.

So, here is a specific. When we assaulted the *Nantong Princess,* our PV, or point of vulnerability, occurred at the precise instant of our insertion onto the ship. That is, at the point we transitioned from the ICRRC, clambered up the caving ladder, and rolled over the ship's rail. If we'd been observed right then, we might have been repulsed. Why? Because we were stretched thin. There was only one ladder. There were a limited number of angles from which to fire defensively. And most important, there was no way to achieve violence of action and overwhelm the crew.

So we acted dynamically; remember how insistent I was that we all GET UP THE FUCKING LADDER—NOW! Because once we'd gone over the rail and had enough men up there to achieve our critical mass on deck, there was no way the crew could stop us. We'd overcome our area of vulnerability quickly. Thereafter, *we* controlled the situation. Why? Because we enjoyed the element of surprise. Moreover, our speed, ingenuity, and violence of action gave us the advantage, even though the *Nantong Princess*'s sailors outnumbered us almost five to one. *We could not fail.*

Here, Tosho had tried to provide his force with as many tactical advantages as he could so that they could achieve relative superiority quickly.

- He had real-time photographic surveillance—television cameras with long lenses—that showed him any movement around the location's exterior.

- He'd obtained a set of plans for the warehouse's interior.
- He was using thermal imagers to try to pinpoint the locations of the tangos inside.
- He had obtained good intelligence on the size of the opposition—there were no more than a dozen of 'em in there right now.

But it wasn't going to be an easy op. After all, they had automatic weapons, and possibly they also had biological or chemical agents, which is an element that all tactical teams should factor into their assault equations these days.

CW/BW agents cause problems. The possibility means that the assault force should wear gas masks at the very least—and full protective gear at the most.

Now, it is hard to stage a tactical op when you are encased in CW/BW gear, which is some of the most cumbersome clothing ever invented. So, Tosho had made an executive decision today: we'd wear the masks, but not the coveralls. I saw no signs of grumbling from his troops. That told me they were M^3s, which as you can probably guess stands for massively motivated motherfuckers.

The assault force would strike in two waves. One wave would fast-rope from choppers and come down from the roof. Simultaneously, the other would go through the front door—preceded by a huge garbage truck equipped with a monster snowplow.

Operational security would be maintained by a secondary, larger force of Kunika shooters backed up by national police. They would seal off the warehouse and set up an unpenetrable cordon sanitaire. Tactical security would come from the five sniper teams Tosho had deployed. He had four static two-man teams, and one airborne unit.

I walked over to where Tosho was running the numbers one last time with his assault team leaders. Alixe Joseph stood out of the way, her arms crossed, playing FOW—which you can probably guess stands for Fly On the Wall. From the engrossed look on her face she obviously spoke fluent Japanese as well as Chinese because, ever the exemplary spook sponge, she was absorbing every nuance.

The shooters were working from a two-by-three-foot surveillance photograph over which a sheet of clear acetate had been laid. I couldn't understand the Japanese characters Tosho was writing with an erasable marker, but the numbers, arrows, lines, *X*s and *O*s that gave the acetate the look of a football coach's playbook made perfect sense to me.

Tosho finished palavering, then looked over at me. "See anything you'd change?"

I looked intently. The one weak spot was entry—it was a big fucking warehouse, there were lots of areas to clear, and the assault team was only forty-six men. "I'm worried that they could hole up inside—especially if they've built a safe room or some other fortified area."

Tosho nodded. "Concerns me, too. We have blueprints, but these guys have occupied this place for a year and a half now, so they could have built stuff we don't know about." He tapped the acetate with his pointer indicating the two roof doorways. "That's why the chopper teams have to be so fast—catch 'em before they have a chance to do anything nasty." He paused. "So, where do you want to be, round eyes?"

I pointed at the roof, too. "I've always liked starting at the top," I said.

Tosho gave me a thumbs-up. "You want it, you got it." He machine-gunned some Nippon at his troops, and there was laughter from behind the balaclavas.

Yoshioka clapped me on the shoulder. "You're with me, *Gaijin,*" he said, handing me a suppressed MP5, eight loaded magazines secured in pairs for quick reloading, a fistful of nylon handcuff restraints, and five Def-Tec No. 25 flashbangs. I stuffed everything into the appropriate pockets and pouches of my CQC vest. But I wasn't fully loaded up, yet: Yoshioka pointed to a Go-Bar sitting on the ground. "That's yours, too."

I picked the heavy steel bar up off the asphalt and hefted

it. "Yeah—solid." Was it ever. Go-Bars are thirty-inch-long steel rods with a heavy pry bar on one end, and an adze and pike on the other. There are few doors that can't be induced to open with a little help from these twenty-pound puppies. I adjusted the strap to fit my extra-large *Amerikajin* frame and slung it over my shoulder.

It felt good—reassuring, in the way that two-handed swords and stout-shafted maces felt reassuring to knights about to go into battle. *"Suki-desu.* I like it, Yoshi," I said. "Let's move."

Mister Murphy arrived shortly after takeoff. There were twelve of us crammed into an old Huey UH-1H (actually it was a Bell 212, but they're really quite similar), and the aircraft seemed wobbly and unstable as we lifted off and hovered while the pilot struggled to find the proper trim. Frankly, I prefer heavier craft, like Pave Lows, which can hold a large assault team and its equipment comfortably. But I wasn't overly concerned because our flight time wasn't going to be very long, high, or complex. The assault sequencing was KISS-simple. The ground contingent would smash the front door; we'd fly in just as they were hitting it, our chopper noise covered by the street-level entry and distraction device explosions. The pilot would hover above the roof. We'd fast-rope, hit the rooftop doorways, and swarm down in two groups—clearing hostiles as we went—and meet up with Tosho's shooters somewhere in the middle.

Have I mentioned that Mister Murphy's stowed away on this flight? I have. Good. Have I told you how I knew he was aboard? No? Well, let me explain.

The pilot had just angled the nose down and we'd started what was to be a two-minute flight to insertion. In each hatchway, port and starboard, one of the Kunika shooters readied the coiled sixty-foot fast-ropes and prepositioned the Heli-Vac arms that would allow us to put five men down each rope within six seconds.

Yoshi patted me down while I did the same to him. Every piece of equipment was secure—and exactly where it was supposed to be. I was third man in the starboard stick, with two shooters in front of me to secure the rooftop. Then I'd hit, run to the doorway, pry it open with my Go-Bar, then follow as the number-three man as we made our way downstairs.

I snugged the helmet chin strap, then opened my thigh flap pocket, pulled my gloves out—and saw Mr. Murphy giving me the finger.

What's the prob, you ask?

The prob, bub, is that I was holding a pair of first-class, soft leather-palmed Nomex gloves.

So?

So, Nomex gloves are great for shooting, and since they are fire resistant, they are terrific if you work on an aircraft carrier flight deck, or fly a chopper. They are so form fitting that wearing 'em you can pick coins off a table. Now let me tell you about fast-roping gloves. Fast-roping gloves are made from three- or four-ounce cowhide. They are like a quarter-inch thick, with heavy burn pads on the palms because, when you throw your ass out the hatch, you are moving at about thirty miles an hour as you careen down the rope. That makes for friction. Friction makes for heat. And while Nomex is flame-proof, it ain't heat-proof.

But there was no time to worry about Murphy. The chopper banked sharply to port. Yoshi slapped me on the shoulder. "Ready, Dick—"

I nodded and slapped the shoulder of the man in front of me.

And then we were above the warehouse. Below, I heard the first explosions. The floor plates of the Huey shuddered, Yoshi screamed "Go!," and I threw myself onto the rope.

It was the very sort of descent that makes me know how much I am indeed alive. I came down in a heap. My palms were fucking smoking, my ankle buckled, I smashed my knee, rolled to my left—and got creamed by the next man in the stick, who fell the last three yards because the chopper, relieved of most of its weight, simply rose like a fucking express elevator, leaving a ten-foot gap between the bottom of the fast-rope and the surface of the roof.

No time to waste. I scrambled to my feet and limped to my assigned door, retrieving the Go-Bar as I went.

I assessed as I moved. Solid steel exterior stairwell door, probably a single panic-bar inside. I crammed the thick pry wedge into the jamb just below the steel lock plate and pulled toward me, as if the Go-Bar was an oar and I was the ferryman on the fucking River Styx.

The door separated and opened outward.

I kicked it full ajar—saw a single flight of concrete steps and metal rail leading down to a landing one floor below. I dropped back to rearrange the Go-Bar and grab my MP5. As I did, the point man went in, his subgun at low ready, its combat flashlight probing the stairwell. The number-two man followed, his weapon pointed over the point man's left shoulder.

My turn. Just as I started around the doorframe, the point man was knocked back by a burst of automatic weapons fire. The number-two fired two long bursts down the stairwell to cover us as we grabbed the point man's CQC vest and dragged him out of the line of fire. There was bright red spilling all over his mouth and chin—oxygenated blood coming back up his throat from a bad neck wound. I pulled him around the doorframe and handed him off to someone behind me.

I backed off too, my left hand patting my vest until I found two flashbangs. Extracted them. Grabbed the first pin, pulled it, reached around the stairwell, and tossed it gently—heard it go *bouncie-bouncie-bouncie,* and then repeated. I didn't hear the second flashbang bounce, but then, that was probably because the first one fucking *exploded.* A hundred and seventy-five fucking decibels. Two point four million candlepower.

I looked at number-two man and gestured, Follow me. I

led the way. The Kunika shooter followed two paces behind. Through the door. MP5 in low ready. Scan. Breathe. Scan. Breathe. Then all of a sudden he must have seen something nasty that I'd missed because he screamed *"Fuhatsu!!"*[19] and threw himself backward through the doorway like a fucking circus acrobat. That was when I stopped scanning, looked down, and saw what he had seen: the second Def-Tec. I noted with horror it was sitting intact directly between my two feet. There had been four, five, maybe six seconds since I'd tossed it—and the Def-Tec No. 25 is constructed with a 1.5-second fuse. Obviously, not this one. This one had been put together by Mister Murphysan.

Well, fuck me too much. I flung myself headlong down the stairwell—which is, of course, precisely the instant the goddamn thing exploded, its blast adding to my speed as I hurtled down the stairs. Oh, that hurt. Yes, the Def-Tec No. 25 is a very nasty, even spiteful object when it misfires.

This was not a Good Thing. I reached out and tried to catch the railing, but I couldn't get hold of the fucking thing. Finally caught hold of the rail, flipped like an easy-over egg, and came down on my bad ankle. Well, not quite. I actually landed on my foot. But I was immediately back in the air again because my foot had in fact come down on the cylindrical, heavy-gauge steel casing of the now exploded flashbang. The aforementioned casing had, of course, been aided by Mr. Murphy or one of his fucking relatives, and hence had beat me to the landing. It was like stepping on a fucking roller skate—my foot went out from under me, my legs lifted higher than my goddamn shoulders, and I shot down the next flight of stairs, flailing as I went.

It occurred to me as I was hurtling downward that the fucking Go-Bar on my back would not feel very good if I landed on it. So, borrowing a technique from HALO work, I jerked my shoulders (cracking every one of my goddamn

---

[19]Japanese for "That's a misfire!"

vertebrae in the process) and executed a half-roll. That helped stop my momentum, although I was still carried down onto a landing, where I rolled up against the door in a noisy heap. First things first: I pushed back from the door and pulled what was left of my gas mask off. The damn thing had cracked in two during my fall, and two of its straps had separated. It was useless. Then I reached up and back, and pulled the Go-Bar strap around my neck so I henceforth could carry it sideways—a less hazardous position for Dickie's health and kidneys in general.

Unhampered by my weight, the door to the landing cracked open. I let go the Go-Bar and reached to scoop my HK up. Oops. It is said that Heckler & Koch's MP5 submachine gun is virtually indestructible. The operative word here is *virtually.* As I rolled onto my hands and knees and scrambled for my weapon, I discovered that my fall had bent the goddamn barrel—not much, but enough to render the fucking gun inoperable.

And that was the good news. You want to know about the bad news? It is that my unintentional forward progress had put me two flights of stairs in front of everybody else on my assault team. But don't worry—I wasn't alone. I had company. He was large, and he had a long, long quasi-Samurai ponytail (and ugly horse's ass face to match), and he had me in the fucking sights of his AK-47, which was pointing straight down at me from the doorway.

Remember what I said at the beginning of the chapter about RS? Remember the phrase violence of action? Good. Well, since there was no time to think, I took my useless MP5 by the barrel and batted his weapon. It wasn't a goddamn home run shot, but the stock of my subgun caught the front of his muzzle and foul-tipped it up and away just long enough for me to launch myself at him.

First I hit him with the door—he was standing in the frame—and rocked him back. But not as much as I'd have liked. He brought the folding stock of the AK down on the point of my shoulder, which hurt like hell and knocked me off balance. But he must have liked my company because as

I fell backward, he grabbed my web gear and pulled me out of the stairwell, his free hand raking my face as he yanked.

Well, this fucking Yankee wasn't going home. I slammed the bottom of his chin with the meaty part of my open palm. That rocked him back a giant step. As he reeled, I hit him squarely in the chest with my forearm.

Big mistake. He was wearing body armor. Plate body armor. Hard plate body armor. My whole arm went numb, and he took advantage of the momentary lull to try and smash me across my hard Slovak head. But he telegraphed: I saw the blow coming, reached through the door, lunged up, and grabbed him by the long hairs.

A word of real-world, life-experience caution here. If you have lengthy hair like I do, make it a cardinal rule to wear a balaclava over your ponytail, or a knit cap to keep your dreadlocks under wraps, because they be an inviting target of opportunity for somebody like me who (sorry, Mom) don't fight fair.

I wrapped his ponytail around my hand and pulled hard. His head came crashing down—right onto my raised knee. There was a satisfying *crunch* as his nose broke. (Well, it was satisfying to me, anyway.) I smashed his face down twice more—*whomp, whomp*—to make sure he'd have a hard time breathing from now on.

But the sumbitch wasn't downed yet. He put his shoulder into my gut and pushed me into the doorframe like I was a tackling dummy. I felt my back go all Rice Krispy—that's snap, crackle, and pop. Then his hands came up, grappling for the Go-Bar, which was hanging athwart my chest.

I tried kneeing him in the nuts, but he was having none of that—his arms pressed while his hands searched for the steel Go-Bar rod.

He found it and started to exert pressure, pressing it like a goddamn barbell slowly up my body, moving inexorably toward my neck.

I broke free and used a forearm blow to stagger him back—God but he was a solid motherfucker—but I rocked him just enough to catch the Go-Bar with my left hand and twist it downward. The thumb is the weak link here, and while he was bigger than I and outweighed me by thirty to forty pounds, I was better conditioned, stronger, and—this is the significant factor—more determined.

So I pushed, and I twisted, and I wrestled, and I took the fucking bar away from him. Well, not away, but at least it was I who controlled it—not he.

I jerked the bar vertical, with the pry blade under his chin. He didn't like that at all, which he indicated by slapping the bar forward six inches and smacking me straight in the face with it.

My helmet took the brunt of the blow—it was knocked flying.

But now the sonofabitch only had one hand on the bar.

I torqued it away from him, kneed him in the balls to back him up flat against the wall, reversed the Go-Bar's ends like a fucking baton twirler, held it like a bat, and using every bit of force I could muster, I swung the six-inch spike up, up, up, slipping it under his left armpit just beyond the body armor and slamming it home toward his lung area.

You look dubious out there. Well, bub, lemme tell ya, the spike on a Go-Bar will puncture a steel door, and tangos are much softer targets than steel doors.

The look on his face told me I'd hurt him bad. But he still wanted my ass. Even as he went down, he was clawing my face, pulling my web gear, trying to wrestle the pistol out of my tactical holster. Fuck it—it was time to put him away for good. I yanked out the Go-Bar (oh, he didn't like that at all), reversed it, drew it back, and then slammed him hard upside the head with the steel shaft, splattering brain and bone in a nasty Rorschach pattern on the wall. He capsized, rolled over, and slid onto the deck. Sayonara, asshole.

He wasn't the only one. I just about collapsed from exhaustion just as the "train" of Kunika shooters passed me, moving to clear the stairwell and hallway. There was the sudden pressure of a hand on my shoulder. I knelt, as drained as an empty beer can, trying to catch my breath and slow my pulse. I looked up and saw Yoshioka. His face was tinged with the sort of concern youngsters feel for old farts. "Hey, you okay, Cap?"

"Affirmative," I wheezed, sucking air. I must tell you in all honesty that this sort of exercise is a young man's game, and I am not as young as I used to be. I breathed deep, hoping to stifle the pounding in my brain and chest. "You keep your men moving, Yoshi, I'll catch up with you."

Twelve minutes after entry, Tosho declared the site secure. The op hadn't been a total success, even though the score was Kunika 15, Red Seeds 1. First, the shooter on my assault group who'd been hit in the throat had died—he'd taken a burst right through the carotid artery, and by the time the medics had got to him he'd lost more than half the blood in his body. And another of Tosh's boys was going to spend a couple of months in the hospital with a cast on his leg—he'd been hit twice in the thigh and the bone was badly shattered. Second, there were no survivors. One Red Seed had been taken alive, but he'd died of his wounds within minutes. Two more had committed suicide. They were obviously a determined, committed bunch.

Tosho debriefed his assault team on site. It was good procedure to do while their memories were still fresh, and besides, the area would be free of interlopers for the next few hours while the police brought in investigators and forensics personnel. As the shooters discussed things, talking with their hands like Italians, or fighter pilots, I watched Alixe Joseph make her way through the debris, methodically poking through the rubble, opening crates and boxes, looking for evidence.

I followed suit, digging, probing, searching the detritus, too. Yes, there were nasty things inside those crates—bomblets, weapons, and ammunition, too. There were cellular phones and electronic equipment. There were uniforms, too—Japanese Defense Force uniforms, as well as dozens of sets of the distinctive coveralls used by Tokyo's power company and electric utilities workers. Tosho was going to have his share of headaches over this group, but he'd obviously hurt 'em bad with this hit, because they hadn't had time to divvy the stuff up and hide it in small lots. Tosh had discovered the mother lode.

That may have been great for him, but to be honest, my heart wasn't in my work. I was antsy. I wanted to go back to Washington. There were things to do, important matters had to be attended to. I had Big Brother on my mind. And I wanted to settle the score with the anonymous (but not anonymous for much longer) asshole at the White House who'd ordered that C²CO, Admiral Gray, to commit his Marine guards, which got the McDonald's hostages killed. Besides, my hands were singed, my face was sore, my ankle throbbed, and there wasn't a bottle of Dr. Bombay Sapphire to be found anywhere within two kilometers.

And then, as often happens when you're not really looking, something caught my eye. On a pallet on the far side of the second floor was a rough wood container. Stenciled on the outside was the legend EXPORT—Zelinograd Machine Tools/MVD.

Oh, we've seen that name before, haven't we? That's right—it was aboard the *Nantong Princess,* on the crate that held Russian AK-47 assault rifles. Which brought to mind the fact that the log on the *Nantong Princess* had listed Yokohama as one of the ship's ports of call. I took my Go-Bar and pried the container open. Can you guess what I found inside? If you said *totsugekijin,* which is how Tosho refers to assault rifles, you'd be right on the old yen.

I reached for the pad and pen that were stowed inside my CQC vest. I wanted the serial numbers off these suckers. We'd check to see if they were part of the same shipment we'd scuttled on the *Nantong Princess.* And once I'd finished copying, I'd fine-tooth-comb this whole fucking place to see if there was anything else of significance I'd missed. I've told you this in the past, but it's important enough to repeat: no matter how hard the bad guy tries to cover his tracks, he always leaves some evidence behind.

Well, I wasn't going to leave this warehouse until I'd found a new shard or two to take back to Washington with me. There was a dangerous pattern emerging here, and I wanted to unravel it.

Who the hell is that out there shouting, "What pattern, what pattern?" Wait—I see him. It's that dweeb editor again. He's running down the hallway, waving his goddamn blue pencil around, complaining that I'm making too much of a jump; that it's too soon to talk about patterns.

Yo, ed, since this is a Rogue book, let the Rogue get a few words in edgewise, will ya? You will? Good.

Okay, let's look at what's gone on recently.

- *Item:* The Russkies and the Chinese, habitual and historical adversaries, have recently formed a very public alliance with each other, to the detriment of the United States.
- *Item:* To counteract this new Sino-Russian alliance, United States policy in the Asian region has undergone a disastrous sea change. We seem to be abandoning Japan and the rest of the Pacific Rim, and throwing our support (both overt and covert) to China, offering the United States as an alternative to the Russkies.
- *Item:* This current policy is exactly the one recommended by an ex-State Department official and consultant, who is currently making loads of bucks helping the Chinese put trade deals together. Happenstance? Coincidence? You tell me.
- *Item:* Big Brother, one of America's most state-of-the-art tactical military communications packages, turns up on a Chinese freighter. My quiet inquiries indicate that the U.S. package is there with White House approval. Happenstance? Coincidence? You tell me.
- *Item:* The Chinese are buying Russkie military equipment—paying off the Russkie Ministry of the Interior—and covertly shipping it all over the Pacific Rim. Where is that stuff ending up? Well, from the look of things, some of it ended up right here in the Red Seeds warehouse. And guess what—the *Nantong*

Princess had less than one-third of its cargo still aboard. It had made half a dozen stops before we scuttled it.

- *Rhetorical Question:* how many warehouses from Pusan to Jakarta are currently filled with smuggled Russkie ordnance, courtesy of the Chinese government? And here's another rhetorical question: who were all those weapons and other lethal packages intended for? Tangos? There are enough of 'em around these days. Fifth columnists? That's a possibility, too. Homegrown insurrectionists? There are half a dozen so-called movements of national liberation currently simmering all over the Pacific Rim.
- *Item:* Alixe Joseph and Tosho—both of whom are fluent in Chinese and knowledgeable about Chinese intel ops—had described an increased level of hostile military intelligence and pro-Chinese terrorist activities in Japan after the arrival of Li Chimen to run the Xinhua bureau. Happenstance? Coincidence? You tell me.
- *Item:* Li Chimen, a SpecWarrior-turned-intelligence agent (and bona fide DIA-certified thug), whose previous posts coincide with all the *Nantong Princess*'s ports of call, is currently headed for Washington for a short-term assignment. Happenstance? Coincidence? You tell me.

Now, my old rabbi and mentor, the late warrior CNO Admiral Arleigh Secrest,[20] taught me that intelligence isn't something that you should look at piecemeal. "Base thine actions neither on the factoid nor the infobit, lest ye step in nasty poop on the road to victory," he growled at me. "Seek ye the big picture, examine every small detail by placing it in context. And when ye hast developed a pattern of action,

[20]You can learn why he's the late CNO by reading *Rogue Warrior: Green Team.*

therein shall ye find the answer to your problem—and the path to triumph."[21]

And so, dear editor (and devoted readers), if you will look over the above information carefully, if you will try to see each element as part of a larger whole, then you—like I—will conclude that there is something very . . . hinky going on.

Do we know precisely what that hink is? No—not yet. But I am absolutely certain of two things. First, whatever is going on bodes no good for my country. Second, I am going to find out exactly what *is* wrong, and put a stop to it.

---

[21]No, CNO Secrest didn't really talk like that. I am simply employing a literary device to make you readers hearken back to the Ten Commandments of SpecWar, the teachings of General T'ai Li'ang, and other elements of these *Rogue* books, so that you will see how the Rogue mind works—always free-associating, making connections, and looking for patterns.

Part Two

THE EARTH STRATEGY

Chapter

7

IT WAS SNOWING LIGHTLY AS MY PLANE TOUCHED DOWN AT Andrews Air Force Base just outside Washington. Did you know that a recent federally funded survey indicated that the average driver in the national capital area spends the equivalent of two weeks per year stuck in gridlocked traffic? Have I ever pointed out that whenever it snows, even just a dusting, the normally sluggish Washington road system becomes even slower and more congested? Have I alluded to the fact that despite half a dozen messages left on the Rogue Manor answering machine and at the Alexandria, Virginia, apartment shared by Gator Shepard, Boomerang, and Duck Foot Dewey, I hadn't been able to confirm that anybody would be coming to pick me up? Have I ever told you that when it snows, it is virtually impossible to find a taxi cab?

Well, then perhaps you will be able to calculate the roguish blackness of my mood after forty-nine hours of flight-slash-delay, riding in steerage class—i.e., sleeping on a splintery wood pallet and pissing into a tube—on a Military Air Transport Service priority zero cargo flight. Its Flying Dutchmanlike odyssey took me from Tokyo to

Sydney, Australia, meandered through Hickam Field, Hawaii, stopped for fuel at Nellis AFB just outside Las Vegas, Nevada, and detoured to Montgomery, Alabama, to deliver some C^2 general's personal household belongings, before finally setting down at Andrews right at the height of the evening rush hour.

Now, my forty-nine hours had not exactly been wasted. I'd had a lot to think about as I plucked pallet splinters from the Rogue butt. Before I wheels-uped, I'd made a handshake deal with Alixe Joseph and Tosho. I'd given them the rough outline of my nasty-pattern theory (*sans* the Big Brother stuff of course). They thought it made sense enough to agree to work the problem as if it was a real-world situation, not an intel squirrel's scenario, and to sit-rep me on a regular basis.

Alixe Joseph even gave me a bunch of bon voyage gifts: there was a file containing her eval of Li Chimen, accompanied by English-language news clips and photographs. There was a second file, enumerating the probes that she believed the Chinese had made in Korea, Japan, Singapore, and Indonesia since she'd arrived in the region. From the look of things, they had been concentrating on each nation's various warfare capabilities. In Japan, for example, there had been attempts to recruit agents; there had been probes of Japanese Defense Force installations. Most troubling, there had been a push to obtain materials dealing with Japan's technological infrastructure—its power grids, telephone networks, and transportation and air traffic control networks.

She let me read—but wouldn't give me—a third file. In fact, she cut the code word designator from the top sheet before she even let me see it, but I caught a peek as she snipped (I'm naturally nosey). The result: I learned that all her HUMINT materials bore the compartment label Weather Gable.[22] A very pissed-off Alixe swore me to

[22]Like most American intelligence organizations, DIA uses computers to assign code words. It is done that way to prevent the opposition from coming up with a formula that would allow them to figure out what the files deal with if they can decipher the code word designators.

secrecy on the subject of her compartment designator, and I promised—Warrior's Code honest—not to tell anybody what I'd seen, or what it meant.

Anyway, I scanned those two pages carefully before giving them back. They were dynamite; they bore a few of the latest results of her HUMINT-gathering networks. The Chinese were actively recruiting Koreans, Malays, Filipinos, and Singaporeans, among others. And not just any sort, either. They were looking for disgruntled former cops, bitter, retired soldiers, and other cynical, bored, or just plain crooked security types—the exact same sorts of renegade malcontents that are actively recruited by the outlaw groups that often call themselves militias in the good old U.S. of A.

Alixe Joseph watched the expression on my face as I read her materials. I looked up. "Have you shared any of this with Tosho?"

"Not yet," she said.

"Maybe you'd better, given what we found at the warehouse today."

She considered the suggestion and finally nodded her agreement. "Will do," she said. "In fact, I'll ask him to check the background of the tangos he took down today and see if they fit the pattern." She paused, her hands on her hips. "Look, you're the counterterrorism expert. What do you make of it all?"

What I made of it all was that the Chinese were putting together a series of paramilitary fifth columns, all across the Pacific Rim, and that we'd better watch our butts.

She'd nodded. "That's what I've been trying to hammer home, too. But my memos just seem to disappear into the void back at headquarters."

My look told her what I think of bureaucrats. "Well, *I* think it's a good premise. Stay in touch—let me know what you guys come up with."

* * *

So, during the flight, I'd hunkered over a legal pad and—Hey, hey, hey, what's that ruckus out there? Oh, it's that bleeper-blanking reader again—the one in the dumb-looking worn-backward ball cap, interrupting my train of thought to wonder aloud why I had to take such a long, circuitous flight home when there are at least half a dozen direct and nonstop commercial polar-route flights from Tokyo straight to the States every day.

You want to know why I just didn't jump one of those? It's another good question, despite the dumb ball cap, so I'll explain.

Y'see, it helps to have a passport and other forms of personal identification with you when traveling on commercial flights. In fact, the security personnel at airlines insist on it these days. But I had no passport. Fact of the matter was, I had no IDs at all. Nor money (except for the two twenty-dollar bills that Alixe Joseph kindly pressed into my hand just before I left). Nor anything else, not even a wallet. I didn't even have the correct time: the goddam cheap allegedly waterproof East German dive watch I was wearing had gone *mausetot*[23] shortly after we'd hit the South China Sea.

And where *was* everything you ask? Well, my worldly possessions had all been left behind in a Navy safe on Guam before we'd set off to hunt the *Nantong Princess.* You do not go on a covert mission carrying a fucking passport, an ID card, a Visa, AMEX, or any other sundry items that might serve to identify the origin of your corpse should something untoward happen during said covert mission.

Happy now? Yes? Okay, then back to our narrative. We taxied (and taxied, and taxied) to what had to be the most distant arrival position on the tarmac. Finally, the engines were shut down, the ground crew chocked the wheels and opened the hatch. I clambered down the ladder onto terra

---

[23]That's Kraut for dead as a doornail.

firma, tossed the bird at the Alabama-based flight crew that was performing its postlanding check,[24] and slogged, frigid in my borrowed Kunika lightweight Nomex flying suit, across the slushy macadam. I trudged wearily past the trio of huge, well-illuminated hangars where the presidential aircraft are stored, in the direction of the squat terminal building three hundred yards away. The terminal was barely visible in the freezing drizzle beyond a low chain-link fence. I knew there was a pay phone inside, and I'd try to raise someone to come and get me. If that didn't work I hoped I'd be able to beg, borrow, or steal, and believe me, in my mood all three were equal possibilities, a ride home from a ground staff Samaritan.

As I drew within a hundred yards of the fence, I saw what looked like two yuppie scum sphincters. They were swathed in brightly colored goose down and patterned, knit ski caps—holding a long paper banner. You've seen 'em, those seamless sheets you can print out on a computer to celebrate a birthday or anniversary. Who the fuck are they expecting, I wondered.

The closer I mushed through the slush, the more distinct the letters became to my tired Rogue eyes. The sign read: WASHINGTON WELCOMES DICKHEAD.

And the yuppie scum? Well, holding on to one end of the banner, complete with his trademark wraparound shooting glasses, was the world-class operator I call Stevie Wonder,

---

[24]When I come back in my next life, I'm gonna come back as an Air Farce MATs pilot. That way I can get paid without having to work. There had been five—count 'em, five—changes of air crew over the course of this flight. SEALs perform under incredible physical and mental strain at warp speed for goddam weeks at a time. These guys' shifts could be counted in fucking *minutes*. Shit, the Air Force has better union rules than most fucking commercial airlines. (It is also, incidentally, the only uniformed service that issues regulation umbrellas to its male personnel. God forbid that a drop of water should fall on a pilot's *kop*.)

even though his real name resembles neither Stevie nor Wonder. With his free hand, he was waving my wallet and car keys at me. And on the other end of the banner, swathed in a bright red parka and Oakley baggy surfing shorts, his bare feet in plastic flip-flops, stood Boomerang, an SES (look it up in the Glossary) on his Huckleberry Hound face and a spare down jacket under his arm.

"Yo, schmuck," Wonder bawled in his New Yawk accent, "How many times do I have to tell you? Never stay on the fucking C—that's the goddam local. You gotta change at Forty-second Street for the A train if you want to make any fuckin' time."

I gave each of them a big abrazo. "Good to see you guys."

Wonder looked at my banged-up face. "I see you've been keeping yourself very existential," he said.

Boomerang threw the spare parka over my shoulders and wiggled his bare foot to shake loose some slush that had lodged between his toes. "We better make tracks, Boss Dude. You have a command performance tomorrow at the Chairman's office—zero six-thirty. They've been on the horn all fuckin' day asking WTF you were."

"Merci, trouducs," I grunted gratefully, calling them shits-for-brains, which as you know by now is a term of endearment in Frog Frogspeak. "But if that's the case, why the hell are we still standing here with our fingers up our bung-holes?" Hell, even though I'd been working nonstop on the flight I knew there was still a shitload to do before I'd be locked, loaded, and ready to see the Chairman. I shrugged into the parka and stretched long and hard, all the better to work the cramps, cricks, crimps, and kinks out of my aching joints. Stretching didn't work, of course, and I knew there was gonna be no time for a sauna, or (morer & betterer) a soak in the Rogue Manor hot tub between a pair of warm thighs, either. Oh, doom on Dickie—this was about to become a long, long night.

* * *

I was sitting in the Chairman's anteroom by 0612 the next morning, in pressed dress blues, my French braid tied off neatly with black parachute line, my metal polished and my black shoes spit shined, poring over the current issue of *Navy Times.* Between my knees, one of the waterproof duffel bags I'd used aboard the *Nantong Princess* sat squat and heavy on the polished marble parquet. I'd had exactly seventeen minutes of sleep—the briefest of combat naps. But I was absofucking S&P (look it up in the Glossary): all showered, shaved, and Right Guarded. More to the point, I was fucking *prepared* for making *WAR,* which word, as you should know, is the acronym for We Are Ready.

Now, being ready for WAR is a large part of what being a SEAL is all about. Remember the Rogue Warrior's Fourth Commandment of SpecWar? Let me refresh your memories so you don't have to waste my time turning to the front of the book to find it.

The Fourth Commandment goes, "I shall punish thy bodies because the more thou sweatest in training, the less thou bleedest in battle." Well, that commandment applies to your paper wars in the Pentagon as well as it does to your blood-and-guts struggles on the battlefield. The Warrior is always prepared, always more prepared to do battle than his adversaries. The Warrior also knows that sometimes you can't just out-kill your enemy—you have to out-think him, and you have to out-perform him.

To make these points during training, our Frog tadpoles are pushed way beyond any level of stress they may have encountered in their lives before. They are deprived of sleep but still must be able to think clearly. They are deprived of food but still must be able to operate at their physical peak for days on end. And they are deprived of warmth but they still have to make it all the way through. They learn, often the hard way, that they are a part of a team, platoon, boat crew—a *unit.* And they come to understand that if the *unit* does not succeed, then the *man* most likely will fail, too. But at the core, the center, the nucleus, the root of it all, it is each man alone who must summon up within himself the courage, the stamina, and the pure guts to go on until he has completed his assignment.

Because the lucky tadpoles who survive this anvil of pain, anguish, despair, and agony will, through their suffering, have come upon one of the central epiphanies of Warriordom, which is: You Must Go On. The Warrior does not give up. Ever. No matter how tired, or cold, or fatigued, or stressed, THE WARRIOR WILL COMPLETE HIS MISSION. There is no demand too great, whether physical, psychological, strategic, or tactical. There is no exigency that cannot, and *will not,* be overcome.

That is why when I select men for my teams, I do not necessarily select those who can breeze through the qualification tests like gazelles. I want men like Boomerang—grunt-and-bear-its who, if they fail once, just keep trying and trying and trying until they succeed. *They* are the ones who become the real Warriors because they have been endowed with the hearts, souls, and the boundless, persistent, uncompromising, indefuckingfatigable gritty determination of Warriors.

Thus endeth the lesson.

And so, as tired as I might have been, I worked the same way tadpoles do during Hell Week at BUD/S—which is to say flat out, and balls to the wall. I wasn't alone either. My guys had been going full-tilt boogie since they'd returned, and they'd come up with some nuggets I could use. But I wanted more. So I sent Stevie Wonder to the Navy Yard, where he knew of an Intelink terminal he could, ah, borrow, and had him siphon off as much classified material on our relations with China and Russia as he could lay his pernicious paws on. I rousted Tony Merc out of his warm bed in Oakton, dispatched him to DIA headquarters, and had him print out as many of the agency's reports on current Chinese intel operations as he could be persuaded to give me.

I laid every piece of paper we'd assembled out on the

floor, sorted everything twice, separated thrice, then sifted once. That done, I shuffled the whole package thoroughly, then dealt each "card" one more time.

Thomas E. Crocker, General, United States Army and Chairman of the Joint Chiefs of Staff, walked through the door at 0621, followed by two aides. I knew the first of 'em, a tonsured, straight-leg Mick colonel named O'Grady, whose round, rimless glasses gave him the look of the old-fashioned parish priests I used to altar-boy for in New Brunswick, New Jersey. O'Grady had worked for the Chairman for more than fifteen years. The second aide was new: a woman in her midthirties (and a civilian to boot) dressed in a dark blue pantsuit. I almost double-taked. Although she wasn't wearing the lapel pin common to DOD security, I could see the faint outline of a pistol at waist level. But she wasn't part of any security detail: the Chairman's personal top secret document case was chained to her left wrist.

I stood, saluted, and greeted the Chairman by his first name. "Keeping banker's hours these days, General?"

I was hoping Chairman Crocker would crack the hint of a smile. But he didn't. He didn't introduce me to his new aide, either. He just looked back in the general direction of his retinue and barked, "You folks wait here. I won't be long."

Then he pointed his right index finger at my chest, jerked his thumb over his right shoulder, and intoned First SEAL Roy Boehm's two-word definition of leadership.

"Follow me," he said, abruptly about-facing.

I can take orders from a real leader as well as any man, and the Chairman comes under that category, so I followed General Crocker across the wide second-floor hallway, past the reception area with its flags and Marines in dress blues, to an anonymous doorway secured with a cipher lock. The Chairman blocked my view with his broad shoulders, hunched over the lock, and punched in the combination. The lock opened. Then he turned the doorknob, swung the door wide so that I could muscle the duffel through, and beckoned me to precede him inside.

I went through the door into a SCIF, which stands for Sensitive Compartmented Information Facility. SCIFs are safe rooms—they can't be bugged, either by the opposition, or by a fellow agency that might like to learn what's on your mind when you think you're not being overheard. This was the Chairman's SCIF. It wasn't the only one either: each of the joint chiefs has his own SCIF these days. That should give you some idea about the growth of institutional paranoia here in the Pentagon since the arrival of the Clinton administration.

Chairman Crocker shut the door behind us, then shook it to make sure that it had closed properly. He pointed to one of the half dozen molded plastic chairs that sat adjacent to the three-by-five-foot Formica table, and indicated that I was to Park It.

I Parked It, the duffel between my feet.

He perched on the edge of the table, looking down at me. His expression was not especially friendly. "Remember what I emphasized to you before this most recent exercise began?" he asked. He didn't bother waiting for an answer, so I guessed the question must have been rhetorical. "I told you not to leave any pecker tracks," he said.

He paused just long enough to grab a lungful of air. "Goddammit, Dick, right now my friggin' message pad looks like the friggin' bedsheet from a friggin' California gold rush whorehouse."

He cracked his knuckles and edged closer, staring down at me intently. "Hell has been breaking loose around here over the past couple of days, and it all seems to have to do with you. First, somebody over at the White House called SECDEF's office to complain that you and some idiot from DIA were making loud inquiries about a program that's so fucking classified that even I don't know all the compartments. Then yesterday, somebody else at the White House told NSC adviser Thompson that the reason the hostage rescue at Yokosuka got screwed up was that you'd muscled your way in—and he went and fucking tattled to the fucking president. Result? My goddam butt got boondockered by the CINC before I could set him straight. Then there are all kinds of inquiries coming from the NSC about your being tasked out of this office—which is something that only you, me, SECDEF, and the president are supposed to know about. And as if all of the above wasn't enough, I got blindsided by your old pal Viktor Grinkov, who wants a quiet, off-the-record meet in Rome to talk about the fifty mil we siphoned out of his offshore accounts—and SECDEF says I actually gotta go talk to him. And that's only the beginning—"

I know it is considered rude for those of us who wear mere eagles on our collars to interrupt folks who wear four stars on theirs, but this was one of those times when it was necessary. "General," I said, "I wasn't able to reach you from the *Nantong Princess,* or the *Scorpion* and I certainly wasn't about to leave a message with whoever was picking up your secure phone. And the Grinkov thing's important, I know, but I really think you'd better take a look at a few things I brought back from overseas before you finish reaming me my new asshole."

One of the things I admire about Thomas E. Crocker, General, USA, is that he has never suffered from the HICs—head-in-cement syndrome—that affects so many of our senior officers these days. The man is willing to listen. He may fire your ass when he's heard your side of the story, but you will have had a fair hearing.

The Chairman raised his hands in mock surrender, growled, "Okay, Dick, you have your say, then I'll finish mine," and vacated his perch on the table.

I unzipped the duffel bag, retrieved a handful of manila file folders on which I'd written numbers, and carefully laid six piles of paper out on the table for inspection. Then I unbuttoned my blouse, retrieved two sheets of xerographic bond from my inside pocket, unfolded them one by one, smoothed them out, and placed them on the table under the

Chairman's intent gaze. They were, of course, photocopies of the Big Brother technical manual cover pages.

I watched General Crocker's eyes go wide. "Where the hell—"

"They were in a document safe aboard the *Nantong Princess,"* I interrupted. "So, General, how's about you let me give you the fuckin' show-and-tell that's kept me awake for the last couple of days."

Chapter

8

After just over an hour-long monologue from me, it was his turn. There was no more chastisement, either. I sat back and listened as General Crocker spoke from the half dozen legal-pad sheets of neat handwritten notes he'd made, ticking off the problems and flagging the political minefields as he saw them.

Tick One was that he believed, as I did, that the Chinese *were* on the offensive—indisputably—both on the Pacific Rim and, more ominously, here in the United States. One didn't have to be cleared top secret to know it, either: it was obvious, he said, to anyone who reads newspapers or watches television that Beijing is working hard to expand its political and economic influence.

He went on to point out that there was nothing wrong with that, either. We Americans do the same thing overseas. But, the Chairman added, the Chinese weren't just trying to sell us toys, shoes, diesel engines, and knitted goods. They were buying influence inside the White House and on Capitol Hill. They were infiltrating agents of influence inside our government. And they were trying to penetrate our high-tech and defense industries, much as the old Soviet Union had done during the 1950s, 1960s, 1970s, and 1980s.

And the new Chinese dragon enjoyed some advantages that the old Soviet bear had never had. There were, for example, tens of thousands of Chinese students in American colleges pursuing graduate degrees in everything from nuclear engineering to physics—and the FBI had determined that more than 10 percent of them—some willing, some not—were being used by Chinese intelligence as spies.

China was also America's largest trading partner, which gave it clout in the marketplace, not to mention in the White House. But the administration seemed willing to ignore the fact that Chinese were using their leverage to seek illegal goods and services. There had been half a dozen Silicon Valley employees caught selling restricted information to Chinese agents in the last five months alone. And the Chairman said he knew of at least a dozen cases over the last two years in which Beijing had managed to infiltrate American defense-industry corporations. The companies had been targeted because they built the sorts of missile guidance components the Chinese were still unable to manufacture.

There was also intelligence gathered by DIA's HUMINT project. In contradiction to the CIA's current assessments (assessments that the Chairman noted bitterly were being kept from him by the director of Central Intelligence) DIA's own reports indicated that the Chinese were out there prowling and growling aggressively—covertly supplying weapons to pro-Chinese movements all across the Pacific Rim. His information dovetailed very neatly, he said, with what I'd uncovered on the *Nantong Princess.*

It even made sense. Freelancing—that is, the White House clandestinely pursuing foreign-policy goals without informing the other branches of government—is commonplace. The Clinton administration did it when, with the president's permission, the NSC adviser allowed Iran to sell arms to Bosnia. During the Reagan years, Oliver North freelanced most of the Iran-Contra affair. During George Bush's presidency, he allowed a clandestine counterterrorism program to be freelanced out of the vice president's office.

But all those freelance affairs had two elements in common. One: the man in charge—i.e., the President of the United States—knew about 'em and sanctioned 'em, and, Two: they all worked (more or less) to the U.S.'s advantage.[25] Here, someone had convinced the president to give away our most capable technology, but get nothing in return. Moreover, the Department of Defense and Joint Chiefs had been entirely frozen out of the process.

So, when you added what the Chairman knew and what I'd discovered—the Russian arms, the missiles, and the Big Brother materials—to the fact that one of Beijing's nastiest intel honchos had just been transferred to Washington, it was clear that something pretty nefarious was going on, and someone close to, or perhaps even actually inside the government, was helping Beijing achieve its goals—to the detriment of the United States. Hopefully, Chairman Crocker said, some hint of that would be found in the duffel bags of papers and other goodies I'd brought back from the *Nantong Princess,* all of which he said he'd have translated ASAP.

That brought us to Tick Two, which was that no matter how we—that is to say he and I—may have felt about the situation, we were still MILPERS, or MILitary PERSonnel. And in the United States, MILPERS come under civilian

---

[25]The counterterrorism program during the Bush years bore fruit in April 1997, when Peruvian troops, many of whom had received their initial hostage-rescue training from a team of American experts back in the 1980s, rescued seventy-one of seventy-two hostages from Tupac Amaru terrorists at the Japanese embassy in Lima.

authority. The Jeffersonian bottom line: we don't allow either kings, or juntas, in the U.S. of A. Which meant that we MILPERS aren't allowed to take matters into our own hands, no matter how strongly we believe that someone, probably someone in the executive branch, might well be selling the country out.

No way. We would have to go through channels, which meant reporting what we knew to SECDEF, and letting SECDEF convince the president that he should change course, and turn the matter of who was giving the Chinese aid and comfort over to the Justice Department for investigation.

Which brought us to Tick Three: which was that we couldn't report diddly-squat to anybody right now. Oh, we—that is to say, I, and now the Chairman—had doubts, apprehensions, misgivings, suspicions, and intuitive concerns. But there was no hard evidence of wrongdoing. No obvious traitor. No mole. Ergo, nothing indisputable to take to SECDEF.

Which was followed hard by Tick Four. In order to convince SECDEF of anything, we (that is to say yours truly) would have to obtain said aforementioned hard evidence. Which brought us back to Tick Two: we were military personnel, and we weren't supposed to conduct investigations of the executive branch. (Do you sense a certain circumscriptive quality to General Crocker's recitation? I certainly did.)

Then, having thoroughly ticked himself off, the Chairman proceeded directly to point out the political minefield flags.

Flag One was that no matter what the fucking rules said, I'd probably have to do some sneak-and-peeking of the sort that could end me up deep in PIG SHIT, which is to say, a Penal Institution with Guards and SHiv-Inflicted Tattoos.

That brought us directly to Flag Two. Let me put this flag in Chairman Crocker's words, because he is a four-star general and I think you should be exposed to the way a four-star general talks when he is in a bug-proof room. "Use extreme fucking caution, Dick," is the precise phrase he employed. That made sense: if I created waves; if anyone got wind of what was going on before I obtained any hard evidence of wrongdoing, malfeasance, or other nefarious behavior, we would both be out of jobs. Clandestine military investigation of the government is an act frowned upon these days. Discovery of my activities would bring us directly (Do Not Pass Go; Do Not Collect $200) back to Tick Two and Flag One—and bury us both in PIG SHIT, and you already know what *that* acronym stands for.

Flag Two was followed by flags Three, Four, Five, Six, Seven, Eight, Nine, and Ten. I won't take the time to go into them now, but you should know that for someone who, like the book jacket says, obeys no rules, I was being handed a fucking list of do's and don'ts almost as long as my *szeb.*

Flag Eleven was that I was going to have to distance myself from the Chairman's office for the duration of this little exercise. Now, *that* flag made sense for any number of reasons. What were they, you ask? Well, let me cite just two for now, so we can climb out of this literary narrative section of the book and get back into some fuckin' action.

First, any Navy captain walking in and out of, or phoning in and out of, the Chairman's office on a regular basis draws attention to himself—and attention was something that I didn't want, or need. Second, General Crocker had mentioned that there'd already been discreet inquiries from someone at the NSC regarding my being tasked out of his office. That was Bad Juju. And third, we'd managed to keep the *Nantong Princess* mission a secret so far, and I didn't want to jeopardize a successful mission.

So OPSEC (OPerations SECurity) would be a primary concern. Oh, I don't mind taking risks, but I also don't like my rogue butt compromised. And yet I still had to maintain contact with Chairman Crocker on a regular basis.

Obviously, if all evidence of my rogue persona was going to be exorcised from the office of the Chairman, what we needed was a cutout. I suggested we repeat a system that had worked once before: I'd keep the Chairman sit-repped through a one-star admiral named Kenny Ross, a submariner I'd worked with before who had been detailed to the Chairman's intelligence staff a while back.[26]

That, the Chairman said, was a no-go. It was Ken Ross who had fielded the NSC call about my activities. Whoever it was over at the White House making waves (that's a Navy technical phrase, y'know) knew about the association between Ken, the Chairman, and me.

"I've got a better idea," Chairman Crocker said. At which point he picked up the secure telephone that sat on the conference table and punched in a series of numbers. He didn't identify himself, but simply barked, "Joe, come on over to the SCIF, would you, please?"

Less than half a minute later, I heard the cipher lock on the outside of the door being punched. The door opened, and a young woman walked in, the same one who'd been chained to the Chairman's briefcase. She closed the door behind her, leaned against it to make sure it had sealed properly, then stood at attention. "General?"

Chairman Crocker pointed his right thumb and index finger first in her direction then mine. "Jo—Joanne Montgomery, this is Dick Marcinko. Dick, this is Jo."

I rose and extended my hand. "Hi. Dick Marcinko."

She gave me a strange look as she took my hand with a firm grip and pumped up/down once, formally, in the Eurostyle. "Hi, Dick Marcinko, I'm Joanne Montgomery. We've talked on the telephone."

"Jo's a White House Fellow," the Chairman was saying. But I wasn't listening. Of course I'd heard that voice before—I'd heard it on the fucking secure phone asking me if I wanted to leave a message.

I grinned and got a grin from her in return. And then, with that particular circle closed, I refocused on what Chairman Crocker was saying. He was saying, "Joanne's

[26]You can read about it in *Rogue Warrior: Designation Gold.*

been with me for about six weeks now, functioning as my special assistant. Learning all about the Joint Chiefs."

I know about White House Fellows. The program dates from 1964, and it was designed to nurture future leaders; indeed, General Colin Powell, former U.S. Senator Tim Wirth, and the ex-inspector general of the U.S. Department of Transportation, Mary Schiavo, had all been White House Fellows. Generally, about a baker's dozen are selected each year from more than a thousand applications. Roughly two-thirds come from the private sector. The rest of 'em are midlevel government, both civilian and military. Each fellow gets to serve for a year as a special assistant to a high-level government official.[27]

Joanne Montgomery was one of the government selectees. How did I know that? I knew it because while all White House Fellows must undergo a security clearance, non government people—even fellows—aren't allowed to carry weapons inside federal facilities. And she was packing, remember?

"Where are you from?"

"State—Diplomatic Security Service."

"Joanne was the agent who saved our ambassador to Burundi's bureaucratic butt last year," General Crocker said, exhibiting his usual diplomatic form.

I remembered reading DIA cables at the time. The ambassador had been on a trip up to the Rwandan border to inspect some refugee stations. On his way back to Bujumbu-

[27]Fellows write speeches, help review and draft proposed legislation, answer congressional inquiries, chair meetings, conduct briefings, and otherwise assist high-level government officials. They are assigned to work with senior White House officials, Cabinet secretaries, or other deputies. In the past, Fellows have worked for the Vice President, the White House Chief of Staff, the national security adviser, the Attorney General, and the Director of Central Intelligence. If you're interested, you can find more information about the White House Fellows Program on the Internet at *http://www.whitehouse.gov/WH/WH_Fellows/html.*

ra, the Burundi capital, the two-car motorcade, a lead vehicle and the ambassador's limo, was ambushed about halfway between Ngozi and Muramvya by a group of rebels.

The ambassador's driver—an FN[28]—froze in panic. The DSS agent sitting in the front seat of the car, one J. M. Montgomery to be precise, had swatted the driver out of the way, thrown the vehicle into reverse, executed a tactical maneuver known as a bootlegger's turn, and sped away to safety. The agent's rapid reaction not only saved the ambassador's life, it also allowed the lead car, which held three more DSS agents and the CIA station chief masquerading under political officer cover, to escape unharmed. It was an act of heroism for which the secretary of state had personally awarded the agent the Department's Medal of Valor. "You're Agent J. M. Montgomery."

She nodded. Y'see what preconceptions can do to you. I'd always assumed that Agent J. M. Montgomery was a man. That's because I hadn't followed my own SpecWar Commandment—the one that says "Thou shalt never assume."

---

[28]The official designation is Foreign National. Let me say right here that the logic of allowing an FN inside your embassy where he/she becomes privy to policy decisions and other sensitive matters has never made any sense to me. The reason for having 'em is that most of our diplomats, spooks, and other officials don't speak the fucking language or understand the modus vivendi of the country they've been posted to. And so they need FNs to do their business for 'em—dealing with the natives in the visa section, running interference with the local authorities, helping diplomats get everything from driver's licenses to finding apartments. FNs also work as chauffeurs, cooks, maids and butlers, and maintenance workers. But allowing an FN that kind of proximity to diplomats and that kind of access to the embassy gives foreign intelligence services a real leg up when they want to spy on us. I thought for a long time it was just me who was being paranoid. Then I discovered that the Russians don't allow FNs to work for them. Neither do the Chinese. The Israelis have only a very few—and they segregate 'em. Ditto the French, and the Brits. Does that tell you anything?

And it wasn't the fact that she'd won a medal that impressed me, either. I'm not impressed by medals, not the way they're handing 'em out these days. No, what registered loud and clear is that Agent J. M. Montgomery hadn't had to think—she'd been ready to *act*. She'd obviously prepared for what she was going to do beforehand—and when ye olde *merde* hit the *ventilateur*, she Just Did It. That, friends, is Warrior behavior.

General Crocker pointed toward one of the plastic chairs that ringed the conference table. "Park it, Jo," he said. "We've got a crisis situation here and I need a volunteer for hazardous duty—and I do mean hazardous." He paused and waited for a reaction from her.

The even smile that spread across her face as she sat herself down was both radiant and reassuring. "Can do, sir."

It made more operational sense for me to work out of Rogue Manor, my two hundred acres of snakes and lakes that kind of sidles up to the Marine base at Quantico, than it did for me to sit anywhere at the Pentagon. But before I could do any prowling, growling, sneaking, or peeking, Jo Montgomery and I had to set up our own OPLAN (Operational PLAN), OPSEC, and OPCON—OPerational CONtrol—procedures. It was already close to 1100, and I suggested that we do our plotting over an early lunch. We then spent some minutes negotiating food types.

As you know, I am a snake eater. That means, I will eat anything. Literally. Others are not so easily satiated. So Joanne ruled out Mexican and Ethiopian on aesthetic grounds. I vetoed French because there was nowhere decent close by. She ruled against Vietnamese because she'd eaten Vietnamese twice in the past three days, and Japanese because she said the food was boring. We finally settled on Chinese. It was a happy and unanimous decision because we both picked the same restaurant as our First Choice.

We left the Pentagon separately. I walked to the white,

F-250 pickup that I'd parked in the Pentagon's river entrance lot, threaded my way out, and headed south along the GW Parkway. I passed National Airport, then suddenly shifted lanes, pulled onto the right-hand shoulder, backed up rapidly, and swerved into the airport entrance. I sensed no incongruous movement behind me—except for a guy in a van who'd thrown me the bird when I cut him off. I circled the airport, weaving in and out of the traffic lanes. I drove into the huge parking structure's front entrance, whipped across it, and exited out the back, adjacent to the airport's south entrance. There, I cut across six lanes of traffic and slipped out the back door, ran a red light on Route 1, then pulled off into a quiet residential neighborhood and made a wide, slow, four-block circle while leisurely checking my six.

Then, confident I was not being trailed, I pulled back onto Route 1, drove north, and worked my way back onto the GW Parkway using an excruciatingly complicated series of vehicular maneuvers that involved, among other things, running westbound for three hundred yards on an eastbound exit ramp. (After all, you can never be too safe or too secure, right?) Safe, secure, and solo, I sidled north past Arlington National Cemetery and the Iwo Jima Memorial, slid onto Route 50, took the Rosslyn exit, then slipped up past the CIA's spook house on Fort Meyer Drive, skidded onto Wilson Boulevard, and strung my way through the light traffic until I passed Highland Avenue. Then I turned left, went around the block, came back, drove two blocks, turned left again, and parked well off the corner. I traded my double-breasted uniform coat for a sweater (all the gold braid and ribbons often attract unwanted attention), pulled on a pair of unlined leather gloves, then walked north and west oblivious of the January chill, past a series of one, two, and three-story buildings housing an ethnic cornucopia of stores that ran the gamut from Thai, Cambodian, Peruvian, and Jamaican groceries, to Vietnamese jewelers, Indian tailor shops, Afghani and Pak rug stores, Japanese sushi bars, and Chinese herb dealers.

I hadn't been through the neighborhood in a while, and I didn't like the developments I now saw. What had once been pristine walls now bore the kind of angular, spray-painted gangsta-cool turf-marking graffiti that has become common to urban areas all over the country. The stores, too, showed signs of increased crime: metal grilles behind the plate glass windows told me that the shopkeepers were afraid of smash-and-grab robberies. Almost every store except the groceries had PLEASE RING BELL TO ENTER signs. Another bad omen. I grew up in a neighborhood of small businesses—and small businesses thrive on walk-ins.

I cut through a small, potholed parking lot that sat between a Salvadoran meat market whose boarded-over window was evidence of a recent break-in and a now-closed Italian restaurant and turned into the unpaved alley that would shortcut my route by three-quarters of a block.

I hadn't gotten more than fifty yards—I was, in fact, picking my way through a muddy section of alley between two Dumpster containers, moving v-e-r-y carefully so as not to ruin the perfect spit-shine on my shoes—when the hair on the back of my neck stood up.

There was nothing overt. Nothing had happened—*nothing*. And yet, some primordial instinct buried deep in my subconscious (it was probably located right behind the pussy detector) took over, and my body told me that things were not right.

Oh, I know, you're going to accuse me of macho Warrior psychobabble right now. Well, bub, here's the truth: when you have been in the field for as long as I have and you have had as many close encounters of the fatal kind as I have, you will appreciate the fact that my antennas have been honed by years of nasty, brutal, sometimes painful experience.

Besides, I always carry myself in what might be called condition yellow. That is, I am perpetually alert. I am constantly aware of my surroundings, and I am quite capable, thank you very much, of responding quickly and lethally to perceived threats without providing any indication to my adversaries I'm about to do so.

So, I didn't stop. I didn't hesitate. I didn't do anything to show that I was now aware of any danger. But my body had subtly shifted its attitude—and so had my brain. Without having to think, I'd shifted into condition orange—in weapons terms, I was locked and loaded, but the safety was still engaged.

It came off when a salt-and-pepper team[29] of teenaged assholes stepped out from behind the Dumpster ten yards ahead of me.

TNO—Thug Number One—held out his arm like a traffic cop. "Yo, my man, hold it up." He was dressed in an oversize, baggy quilted cotton tunic, three-sizes-too-large jeans held up by a clothesline belt, and sported the requisite baseball cap. (Worn backward, of course—what *is* it with people these days?) Around his neck hung a pair of the sort of heavy gold chains favored by cocaine-tooting pro football players and/or pimps, and the $150 NBA-style high-top sneakers I have come to think of as mugging moccasins. My friends on the local SWAT team call 'em felony flyers.

I kept moving, my course steady. My left hand had already emerged from my trouser pocket. The spring-loaded collapsible baton I always carry was extended, and it was concealed from view in a reverse grip that shielded it against my arm. Had TNO seen it? Not a chance. I could read him like a fucking primer, and he was too busy already counting the money in my wallet to pay any attention to anything else but my right hip pocket.

The arm extended once again. "Yo—*hey,* my man, I'm talkin' to you—"

TNO did have an irritating manner. But I wasn't going to let it affect me. My pace was still constant; obviously I was

---

[29]That's copspeak for a team of malefactors composed of one white scumbag and one black scumbag, although in today's politically correct (and gastronomically diverse) atmosphere it could mean one white scumbag and one green scumbag, or one white scumbag and one red scumbag, or, well—you get the idea.

lost in thought. No threat. No eye contact. No War Face. I let the distance seep away. Ten yards, nine, eight, seven, and six—*that* was when he began to shrug his quilted jacket to the side so he could reach toward the sloppy waistband of his oversize trousers and withdraw the pistol I just knew he had. Which was precisely when I accelerated, covering the last five yards in about three-quarters of a second, and smacking the shit out of him with my baton.

Oh, TNO wasn't expecting *that*. He was expecting me to pull up. Stop. Let him proceed with this mugging unfuckinghampered.

But that wasn't what happened. What happened was that I *turned*—rolled into a dervish spin like a gold-medal hammer-throw Olympian to give myself an extra measure of deadly, tight-as-a-fucking-spring kinetic energy—my baton unsprung, punched round like a goddam baseball bat from its concealed position, and, using every ounce of power my hand/wrist/arm/shoulder/torso/back/hips/thighs/legs could muster, I—*whaaaaap*—slashed him across the face, opening a deep, nasty-looking laceration that ran from behind his ear right down to the corner of his mouth. Then I reversed my swing and butt-stroked him, smashing the baton's pommel into his zygomatic arch (for those of you who haven't read *Gray's Anatomy* lately, the zygomatic arch is the thin bone at the outer corner of the eye, and let me tell you, it's a painful fucking place to get hit).

The blow sent him spinning to the ground—where, from the sound of it, I broke at least three of his ribs when I scuffed my perfectly spit-shined, steel-toed uniform shoe on his cheap jacket as I roundhouse kicked the stupid sonofabitch into next fucking week.

No time for any more follow-up, however, because TNT—that would be Thug Number Two—had decided that since I was being uncooperative, his assistance would henceforth be required. But like most inexperienced malefactors, he hadn't had a lot of background in the fine art of dealing with unwilling participants in street muggings. So, like his partner in crime, he, too, was now fumbling for his weapon—which, obvious greenhorn that he was, he'd stowed in the deep pocket of his own high-waisted, low-crotched baggy clown pants.

What was this, the fucking gang that couldn't draw straight? I caught him on the tip of his elbow with the baton. Oh, that brought a delightfully anguished expression to his face. Instinctively, he grabbed at the boo-boo. *Whap*—I hit him in the other elbow. He looked at me, his eyes fucking crossed in pain, and dropped to his knees. He looked up at me as if to say WTF?, but I was in no mood to give out answers during this particular little CQC seminar. So instead, I picked him up by the scruff of the neck and the necktie belt on his stone-washed baggies and ran him face first into the corrugated metal of the Dumpster. When I dropped him I saw that he'd lost all his front teeth. *C'est dommage, non?* Right—*non.* Let's just think of it as a Roguish form of attitude adjustment.

I rolled the now-inert TNT over, pulled his pockets inside out, and found a cheap, nickle-plated .25 caliber pistol. The other thug—also out cold and definitely in need of medical attention—had a Smith & Wesson 9mm semiauto. I unloaded both, tossed the rounds in the nearest Dumpster (a Rogue rule of thumb: unless you are in absolute extremis, never—*never*—use other folks' ammo), pocketed the pistols, then retraced my steps to the truck and stuck the 9mm Smith under the front seat.

Has something significant about the above incident occurred to you? It certainly did to me. What is it, you ask? Well, it occurred to me as I made my way back toward the restaurant that this was the first time in six fucking books I've had an altercation that hasn't been interrupted in some devious way by my old nemesis, Mister Murphy, or any of his goddam family. I mean, I didn't head-butt anybody wrong and knock myself out. I didn't smash my own hand into the wall. I didn't trip myself up, go *splat* in the mud, and ruin my clean, pressed uniform. What made all of the above bad news not good news was, one: TNO and TNT were such obvious fucking greenhorns; and, two: nobody, not Wonder, Nasty, or Boomerang; not Tosho, Avi Ben Gal, or Mick Owen; *nobody*—not even that fucking dweeb editor, who delights whenever I smash myself up—was around to watch as things went blankety-blankety-blank-blank-bleeper-blanking *flawlessly*.

I mean, I'd just creamed the shit out of those two in a goddam vacuum. Gentle reader, where oh where's the justice in this world?

That was all on the one hand. On the other hand, I have lately learned how to take "yes" for an answer. And lemme tell ya, a greenhorn sphincter can kill you just as easily as an experienced asshole. It's just a matter of luck and Mister Murphy.

Twelve minutes later—and just over half an hour behind schedule—I marched past the pair of white marble Shao-Li dogs guarding the entrance to the Hunan Number One restaurant. I pushed the door open and let my eyes grow accustomed to the darkness. I'd been coming to this big, anonymous place for more than a decade, and I was still unknown by the staff. I was just another happy, hungry Big Pink Ghost.

The red frocked wallpaper and mirrored back walls, 1950s lava lamps, and genuine imitation Naugahyde upholstery reminded me of the Chinese restaurants of my youth in North Jersey. But that's where the similarities ended. Hunan Number One's cooking was none of your oughie-gooey chopped-up suey, limp-as-a-dead-man's-dick lo-mein, or red dye number three glazed sweet-and-sour pseudo p-p-p-porky pig. Despite its name, Hunan Number One served only top-of-the-line Hong Kong-influenced Cantonese food. Like what? Well, there were your tiny, steamed pork spareribs in delicate black bean sauce. And shrimp wrapped in lotus leaves, then steamed with black beans and fresh ginger slivers. There were fresh clams in black bean sauce. Do you get the idea that they used a lot of black beans here? Well, you're right. But that wasn't the whole story. There was also real duck soup, complete with gelatinous duck feet for Republican political consultants to suck on. There was crispy chicken roasted in a salt shell. And broccoli stems steamed in salty oyster sauce. And camphor-and-tea–smoked roast duck. Like I said, top-of-the-line Cantonese food: simple, and delicious.

The restaurant was already half-filled with early lunchtimers. There was your smattering of Pentagon types in uniform. There were your Arlington pencil pushers from the consulting firms and Beltway bandit offices, and there were your Chinese families, sitting at the big round tables with the lazy Susan servers, out for some good home-style cooking.

Joanne was there already, looking the way a reproachful teacher regards a tardy student as I made my way toward the table. She was sitting off to the left in the rearmost booth, her back up against the back wall. It's hell when two operators have lunch or dinner and there's only one seat whose back is to the wall.

Well, the booth was plenty big for two. But since the back wall had a mirror that allowed me a good view of the room without being too obvious, I stood, hovering like a chopper in admin approach, while I decided where to sit. My behavior brought a knowing smile to her face. "Make you nervous to sit with your back to the window?"

"Bet your ass." I dropped onto the banquette opposite her. "Sorry I'm late—I got held up."

"But you left the office before I did."

"No, I mean I got *held up."* I palmed the .25 caliber automatic, slipped it under the table between us, and dropped it on her lap.

She hadn't expected that. "What the—?"

"I told you, I got *held up."*

Her eyes told me that I'd actually shocked the hell out of her. She laughed out loud, looked down to examine my memento, then slipped the little pistol into her jacket pocket and looked at me with an expression that registered somewhere between respect and incredulity. "Thanks for the souvenir, I guess."

"Not at all." I swiveled and beckoned the closest waiter. *"Fuwuyuan."* Waiter. He was hovering in a matter of seconds. I surveyed the bare table, then ordered a beer. *"Piju, quing,"* I said, asking for a beer and exhausting my conversational Chinese. I looked over at Jo Montgomery. "You want one, too?"

"I don't drink . . . alcohol," she said in a mock Transylvanian accent, pausing the same way Bela Lugosi paused in the movie *Dracula* when he was asked if he wanted a glass of wine.

She peered up at the waiter. *"Ch'ing wo yao beizi ching-cha?"*

"Sheh-sheh," the waiter nodded, obviously impressed, and bustled off.

"What was that all about?"

"I asked him for a cup of green tea, and he said, 'thank you.' "

I was impressed, too. "Where'd you learn your Chinese?"

"From my mother."

"Your *mother?*" Agent J. M. Montgomery looked like the archetypal gringo to me, complete with a soft, quasi-southern accent I couldn't place.

She read my quizzical expression. "My grandparents were missionaries. Momma was actually born in China, in Soochow. Nana and Pop—they were my grandparents—sent her back to live with her sister Odessa in North Carolina just before Pearl Harbor. Don't forget—the Japanese had invaded China long before they attacked us, and things got bad quickly. Momma was only eleven then, but of course she spoke fluent Mandarin. She'd had a Chinese *ama*—that's a kind of nurse—and she'd actually learned Chinese before she'd learned English."

"Did your grandparents make it back after war was declared?"

Her face clouded. "No, Nana and Pop were executed by the Japanese as spies in 1943. I really don't know how Momma made it through that without a lot of psychological damage. She still doesn't talk about it much. But she did survive. She's a strong woman, Dick, very, very strong. Anyway, sometime back then she developed the habit every night before she went to bed of speaking Chinese to herself. I guess it was a way of staying close to her parents. And also, she kept telling herself that one day, she'd go back—see where they'd lived, and where they'd died. So, every single night of her life, Momma has said her prayers in Mandarin. And then she recites something else she knew as a young girl, a phrase, a greeting, something. Over the years, she taught me a few words, too. Just a little bit." She paused long enough to crack an uneven smile. "Enough to get me in trouble."

"Did she ever go back—close the circle?"

"Actually, yes she did, ten years ago. And she took me." She grinned as she remembered. "I got my divorce—and my master's degree from Tufts—the same week. I had six weeks free before I joined State. Momma had made all the arrangements in secret. She really surprised the heck out of me. We were there for eighteen days."

"It must have been wonderful."

Joanne's gray eyes misted slightly. "It was better than wonderful. Because I saw China not as it was—which was gray, and dusty, and filled with people whose faces didn't reflect much happiness at all—but through her eyes. I saw China as it must have been when Momma lived there. She remembered so much, Dick, so many details about places, and the history of the country, and stories about the people she'd known. And all of a sudden I realized what she'd been doing all these years when she spoke her Mandarin every night. She'd been *remembering.* Forcing herself to hold on to things so she'd never ever forget them. Doing serious memory work." She paused and laughed at herself.

I didn't get it. "What's so funny?"

"'Memory work.' Momma's maiden name is Memory. Mary Fay Memory. The Memorys come from south-central North Carolina, south of Fayetteville, north of Laurinburg. That's where I grew up, in a log cabin in the middle of a big pine forest just outside a one-street, three-church town called Wagram."

She paused as the waiter set his tray down and placed a pot of tea and a cup in front of her, and a bottle of Xingtao beer and a water-stained glass in front of me.

When he'd finished, she said, *"Sheh-sheh."* Thank you.

I did the same, adding (in English, of course) that we'd wait to order. I poured my beer, inclined the glass in her direction, and said "Cheers."

She poured steaming tea for herself with a steady hand, lifted the cup, said *"Gombay,"* and drank. "Good tea." She set the cup down. "Okay, Dick, that's enough about me—now it's your turn. How the heck did someone whose French braid is as long as yours end up in General Crocker's SCIF, anyhow?"

We finished three pots of tea, a six-pack of Xingtao, and a baker's dozen plates of dim sum, the Chinese equivalent of Lebanese meze, Spanish *tapas,* or Italian antipasti, by the time we'd exchanged life stories. And I'd been right in my assessment: Jo Montgomery was an operator. Behind the master's degree from the prestigious Fletcher School of Law and Diplomacy, and the fluency in three languages, and the ten years of real-world experience, lay the soul of a Warrior. She was always looking for ways in which to improve her proficiency. Yes, she'd been to the State Department's management leadership seminar and had taken courses at the Foreign Service Institute. But she'd also been to shooting schools from Gunsite to John Shaw's Mid-South Academy. She'd taken classes at Heckler & Koch, and cross-trained with the FBI's Hostage Rescue Team. She'd learned tactical driving at Bill Scott Raceway in West Virginia and the Scotti School in Lakeland, Florida.

Which brought us to what she'd done in Rwanda. I asked a rhetorical question to which I already knew the answer: "What you did was more mental than physical, because you'd prepared yourself—war-gamed, right?"

She slapped her chopsticks onto the plate, reached across the table, and high-fived me. "You are only the second person in the whole world to have ever said that to me," she said. "And you're so darn right."

I wondered aloud who the other was.

"Tony Blauer. A Canadian martial arts instructor I met a couple of years ago when three of us from DSS got sent to his dojo in Montreal. We went to study Chu Fen Do."

You could see by her animation that she'd liked the course. She retrieved her chopsticks, snagged a "potsticker" dumpling, dipped it in salty hot chili sauce, popped it into her mouth, and tried to speak.

Except the hot sauce obviously got in the way because her face grew flushed, and I could see beads of perspiration form on her forehead.

She watched me watch her. "Hey, if you're not sweating, you're not eating, right, Dick?" Without letting me get a word in edgewise (or any other way) she swallowed a quick mouthful of tea to wash the potsticker and hot sauce down, then continued. "Tony's one of those instructors who preaches that technique can only get you so far, that it's attitude that makes the difference in the real world. We use him—so do a lot of law enforcement agencies. State likes what he does because he teaches mental exercise, psychological preparedness, as opposed to strictly physical combat stuff. Face it, Dick, my job isn't like yours. SEALs are supposed to break things and kill people. We're not. We're essentially defensive types. Our mission is to keep our folks alive."

"So what did he do?"

"He made us work hard at being constantly aware of our surroundings. I guess you could call it antenna-honing. He made us go out on the streets and play 'What If' games. What if those three no-goodniks over there attacked us? What if that car was going to scoop up your principal? What if you're on an elevator and a guy grabs you from behind? How would I defend? How would I react? How would I protect? In essence, what he did was teach us to war-game all the time. Real obvious, right? Keep it simple, stupid." She drained her tea and answered her own question. "Right, but there aren't a lot of people who teach like that. So anyway, there I was driving up the road to Bujumbura, and I was war-gaming the whole time. What if there's a roadblock . . . what if the driver freezes . . . what if they have RPGs . . . what if, what if, what if. When it all actually happened, I don't even remember thinking—I just *acted.* I'd done the mental stuff. The physical was easy."

She was right, of course. That's why I always insist on saturation training. By saturation, I mean You Do It until you don't have to think about it—it all just comes naturally. Shooting? You have to hit that three-by-five card b-bang—two shots—whether you are hung out or hung over, hyperventilating, or hypothermic. Chute fucks up and you're HAHOing at twenty-five thousand feet? You have to know what to do. If you guess at it, you're gonna be dead—which won't do Dickie any good on the mission.

Now, having just preached all of the above, let me make another important point. It is that you cannot just Do It and let it go. You have to spend as much time on the mental aspects of Warriordom as you do on the physical. Yes, shooting is a frangible physical skill, and the more you practice the better you will become. But remember what I explained to you a few pages back about visualizing the front sight picture before you shoot? That's the mental part. And you can spend almost as many hours working on it—concentrating, focusing, fixating on that visualization—as you do working on the range itself. When it all comes together, you will know exactly where that sight picture is going to be under any circumstances. In a dark stairwell, going over the rail of a ship, climbing an oil rig—or sight-acquire-firing as you go through thick smoke and your target is only a shadow among many shadows. But you know you will hit him, because you have, one: shot hundreds of thousands of rounds and, two, because you and the weapon have become one physical and mental entity. You become the ultimate weapon—and you cannot fail.

Then, having pretty much exhausted the life-story stuff, we lingered over a last duo of dim sum—spareribs baked in black bean sauce, and steamed broccoli stems stacked neatly as Tuscan cordwood in oyster sauce, and worked out our operational planning. She'd already pored over most of the materials I'd brought to the Chairman's office in the SCIF. She'd read through the reports carefully, committed the photographs to memory, and asked intelligent questions.

So when it came to an OPLAN, things were actually pretty KISS. Whenever I had something to report to the Chairman, I'd page Joanne. She'd call that number within two minutes, and we'd set a rendezvous. If she had to get hold of me, she'd call Rogue Manor and leave a message from Lucy Memory. I'd call her pager, and we'd repeat the process outlined above.

Yes, I know it wasn't very sophisticated. But simplicity is always the best way. Or, as Roy Henry Boehm, Lieutenant Commander, United States Navy and godfather of all SEALs, used to preach in his Zenlike fashion, "Look, asshole, a straight line is always more efficient than a maze when you're trying to get from point A to point B."

What the lieutenant commander means is that the more intricate things get, the more chance Mister Murphy has to insinuate himself into your operation—and the more chance there is that you will screw up. So we kept it simple, stupid, just like Roy would have wanted.

* * *

Our operational planning finished and our life stories told, it was time to go to work. I pulled my wallet out. Joanne already had a twenty in her hand to cover her share. I protested—after all, I make more than she does—but she insisted: we'd go Dutch, or we wouldn't go at all anymore. Sometimes you just have to take "yes" for an answer. I was about to wave a fist above my head to summon the *fuwuyuan* when I saw Joanne's whole body stiffen. I dropped my hand and looked up, into the tinted mirror.

It was like looking into one of those fun house distortions, because what I saw couldn't possibly be for real: a five-by-five in a generic, badly cut, and even worse-fitting gray pinstriped suit. What's a five-by-five you ask? A five-by-five is the SEAL technical term for an S_3FA—that's a short, shit-filled, slovenly, fat asshole. Anyway, this S_3FA was currently waddling into my field of vision, marching splayfoot up the aisle toward our booth. His baggy trousers, which he hitched once, twice, thrice, in the three yards of travel I could follow, cut a belted smile under a humongous belly. His blue button-down shirt was wrinkled, and either *it* was soiled or the mirror was. His tie—askew—was gravy and/or sneeze stained. You pick it. Around his neck was one of those long steel ID chains that look like lamp pulls. The chain looped down, like a monocle sash, and disappeared into the left side of his suit coat—probably buried in his shirt pocket. Clasped in the chubby fingers of his chubby left paw was a Nokia cell phone very much like the one filled with plastic explosive I'd recently used in Lebanon to disassemble a nasty, corrupt, immoral piece of work named Werner Lantos.

With a heavy wheeze the S_3FA dropped two banquettes away, literally inhaled all four glasses of water on the table, belched twice, then mopped his neck with a greasy handkerchief. It may have been thirty-six degrees on the street outside, but even in the Hunan's dirty mirror I could see the perspiration shine on the back of his head.

Then I saw what had made Jo Montgomery react so

strongly. Following the five-by-five and just coming into view in the mirror was a six-foot-plus, long-faced, thin-lipped Chinese man in a dark blue raglan-sleeved cashmere overcoat that came almost to his ankles. The garment's fluid drape and smooth, graceful sweep gave him the sinister look of a malevolent Mandarin as he made his entrance, gliding with the confident, catlike, spare moves of a seasoned point man. Watching him, you just knew that his footsteps would be silent as an apparition's.

As he drew closer I could make out nuances: thick black hair, combed straight back and slightly gray at the temples. Thin mustache. Under the coat he wore a band collar shirt, and his neck showed the kinds of muscling that betray constant and consistent PT. I picked out the details of his face. It was lined and cruel; his eyes were dark and penetrating. Of course Joanne would react—it hadn't been two hours since she'd stared at his picture to commit it to memory. It was Li Chimen.

Chapter

9

I OBSERVED, FASCINATED BY THE SHEER ATHLETIC SUPPLENESS OF the man, as Li effortlessly shrugged out of his coat, punctiliously folded it in half lengthwise, measured the seams and edges to ensure that everything was precise, then punched the armholes, so that the coat could be rolled over onto itself once again without leaving the faintest hint of a crease in the fabric. As he did so, even in the mirror, I could see something sticking out of the deep inside breast pocket of his coat—and the hair on the back of my neck stood up again, the way it always does when something is very, very wrong.

What I saw was the very, very top of a manila folder. But that wasn't what had made all my systems go to battle stations. What made the klaxon horn sound was the fact that even though the mirror was dirty, I could discern the corner of the top of the folder was tabbed in bright visibility orange. Whatever was in that folder was top secret material. And Li Chimen had no business with it.

Then everything disappeared from my line of sight as Li folded the coat crosswise, laid it carefully on the banquette next to him, lowered his body, and slid onto the seat. His face was obscured by the bulk of the S_3FA's broad shoulders and bull neck.

But not before he caught me looking at him.

Instinctively, I wrenched my eyes downward. Oh, fuck me. Oh, doom on Dickie. It's bad tradecraft to get caught peeking at the fucking opposition. It is worse tradecraft to get caught peeking at the fucking opposition and then to tell them, with a gesture so goddamn operatic in scale it could have been performed by Caruso at La Scala, that yes, you have been caught peeking.

Here is a real world lesson. If you are ever out on a surveillance, and the object of that surveillance happens, because of your stupidity or inattention, or simply because Mister Murphy is standing at your side, to catch your eye, do not, I repeat, DO NOT abruptly turn away, shift to avoid eye contact, or modify your behavior by ONE IOTA. You must not hedge, evade, dodge, shuffle, or sidestep in an obvious manner. Because if you do, your opponent will realize that you are attempting to keep tabs on him, your role will be compromised, and you will be out of the game.

Now, what should I have been doing? I should have been war-gaming the situation, not gawking at Li Chimen, mesmerized as it were, by his entrance. I should have been saying to myself, *Okay—if he looks at me, I'm going to maintain eye contact, then slowly, s-l-o-w-l-y, slide back to my conversation with the obviously attractive young woman with whom I am having lunch, so that Li will think that, like any normal folks, I glance up when I perceive activity in the mirror, then, satisfied everything's cool, I go back to my own fucking business.*

Jo looked at me, concerned. "What's up?"

What was up was my fucked. Oh, yes, even the Rogue Warrior fucks up from time to time. I kept my eyes on the table. "I'll tell you later—outside."

She started to react. I stopped her. "Don't, not yet."

Now she really was puzzled. I looked over at her. "Jo—what's happening over there?"

She looked up, innocently inquisitive, as if searching for the waiter (see, *she'd* been war-gaming even if I hadn't. I told you she thinks like a Warrior), but long enough to take a discrete glance over my shoulder and down the room. Then she focused back on me. "The fat guy's turning to look at you." She paused, raised her head a little—as if responding to something amusing I'd said. "Now he's turning back. Shaking his head."

I could hear the dialogue in my mind, playing out like a little movie.

Li Chimen leans forward. He's a pro, and his antennas are always up.

LI: Well, do you know him?

S_3FA: *(Turns. Looks.)* Nope—never seen him before. And believe me, I'd remember a French braid like that. Nice piece of ass he's with, though.

Hey, hey, hey, out there, don't get the wrong idea. That's the S_3FA talking, not me. And it wasn't that Joanne isn't attractive—she is. And under other circumstances, I might have done something about it. But we'd been assigned to work together, and let me give you the Warrior's most basic social code. It is that in a working relationship there can be no room for anything but work. If that tenet is broken, shit will happen, missions will be compromised, and all the juju will be bad.

Moreover, while my desire for pussy is second to no man's, I believe that any officer or noncom—man or woman—who takes advantage of a command situation to get laid is a traitor to the uniform he or she wears, and the tradition of Duty, Honor, and Country for which that uniform stands. No exceptions.

That's why I have always believed in absofuckinglute equal opportunity: do the job and I will like you and respect you. Do not, and I will fuck you over and transfer your ass as far away from my command as it is possible to do. That's how I want to be treated—and it's the way I have always treated those under my command.

Indeed, I'm am proud to say that *I* have always treated everyone alike—let's say this together, shall we—*just . . . like . . . shit.*

Okay, so much for my Roguish social mores. Let's get back to the situation at hand. By purest happenstance we'd been in the right place at the right time, and I'd caught a glimpse of something that I wasn't supposed to see. Maybe Mr. Murphy'd decided to come over to my side for once. Maybe he hated the Chinese. I didn't care. However things had come about, I was going to take advantage of them. That is part of Warriordom—being fluid enough to know when to take "yes" for an answer.

So—we'd been about to split. But there was no way I was going to do that now. I wanted a closer look at Li Chimen, and more to the point, I wanted to know who the S_3FA—the man who'd probably passed Li the top secret folder—was. Of course, I couldn't do both. Not unless they left together.

I looked down at the table surface again so that no one in the room could read my lips and only Joanne could hear what I was saying. "The Chinese guy has a TS doc on him," I mouthed quietly.

That was all I had to say. Jo nodded. "Got it," she said. "We'll stake 'em out."

Jo ordered us another round of tea and beer, we paid the waiter—it is bad tradecraft to get left behind because the opposition has paid its check and you're still waiting for yours—tipped him well, then sat and plotted.

Jo was parked closer than I was. She'd found a spot just down the street. I was at least three to four minutes away—and that was at a dead run. Certainly, I was far enough away to make pursuit impossible if we all left the Hunan at the same time. The answer, of course, was for us to leave as they were in the middle of their meal, then regroup outside.

And if their lunch came to an abrupt halt and they left before we'd had a chance to set up? Well, there is a SEAL technical term for that circumstance. It is: doom on us—we'd be fuckee-fuckeed.

We were too far away to hear Li's conversation. Which was just fine with me, because it meant they were too far away to listen to ours. Just after their entrées were served, Jo and I nodded at each other. She rose. I helped her into her coat—blocking the view so that no hint of pistol betrayed itself as her suit jacket parted—then let her precede me toward the front door. As she passed Li's table, she paused as if to reposition her handbag—*good war-gaming there, Jo*—which let me get a good look at him, and see what else besides food might be sitting on the table.

Li was older than he'd appeared in the mirror—in his mid-fifties, perhaps. But he was lithe and muscular in his expensive Italian suit of ministerial gray, set off by a well-tailored black silk band-necked shirt. He gave me a quick glance but no more, then went back to his conversation. Li spoke in an uncommonly deep voice; his tone was robust, the timbre unique. But no matter how singular his voice may have been, the gist of what he was saying was completely lost on me, because he and the S_3FA were speaking in lapid-fire Chinese. I mean full-tilt boogie Norinco belted 7.63-by-54 machine-gun ammo Chinese.

We pushed through the front door, kept moving until we were past any possible sightline, then stopped. I looked at Jo. "Catch anything?"

She shook her head. "Not really. He was speaking in a dialect I've never heard before."

"Nothing at all?"

She scratched the side of her head. "I mean, I got a couple of words—something, something, something, *quickly*. And then something, something, something *recovery*. Or it may not have been *recovery*, but something else. Fact is, Dick,

I'm not fluent the way Momma is, and don't forget—the Chinese she taught me is Chinese from the 1930s or even before that."

Such are the pitfalls of real life. Unlike all those pogue-Rogue TV movies, where your superheros stumble on the nugget that allows them to save the damsel, wax all the bad guys, save the world for democracy, and do it all in one sixty-minute hour (less sixteen minutes of commercial time), this was real life. And while I may have just laid eyes on the bad guy of our current little melodrama, I had no idea who his companion was, or WTF they were up to—except that secrets were being given away.

My first reaction was to call the Manor and call out the troops. That was impossible, of course—they were more than an hour out of town. So it would be just Jo and me. We set up in an alley that ran perpendicular to Hunan Number One's front door, about 150 yards north of the restaurant. Jo, in her green late-model Volvo with Maryland plates, faced east. I parked my pickup across the street opposite her car, facing west. She would take fat man. I'd follow Li Chimen. We could even stay in touch, as both of our vehicles were equipped with cellular phones that had the all-important hands-free feature. Were our comms secure? Absolutely not. But they were all we had. You generally don't go out to a get-acquainted lunch with secure comms.

We sat, engines idling, for another twenty-five minutes, phones connected. Why did we do that? Because Mr. Murphy was in the neighborhood, and I didn't want him screwing with the connection once we'd started our surveillance.

I could hear classical music playing in Jo's car. I had my radio turned off and spent the time thinking—war-gaming the hunt that was about to begin. Then, as is often the case, our solitude was interrupted by an uninvited guest: the ubiquitous Mister Murphy. (See—I told you he was close by.) First, Joanne's phone went dead. I knew it died because the music stopped. I looked across the street and gestured

WTF. She paid absolutely no attention to me. That was because she was too busy, all hunched over, trying to restart her car. And from the way she was moving I could tell that the Volvo was not responding. Which, of course, was the very instant that a humongous white Cadillac limousine with Washington, D.C., vanity plates that read WODE right-turned off Wilson Boulevard, pulled past the Hunan Number One, then K-turned, and glided to a smooth halt right in front of the pair of white marble Shao-Li dogs.

The right front door opened, and a tall, athletic kid in a double-breasted blue Armani suit that didn't quite hide the well-developed shoulder muscles and pecs pulled himself out, cell phone in his left hand, scanned the street once perfunctorily and, deciding that things were okeydoke, opened the rear right-hand door.

At which point, smooth as any Secret Service or DSS op, Li Chimen and our S_3FA emerged from the Hunan's front door and swept into the car. Kid Armani slammed the rear door closed, disappeared into the front seat, and the limo accelerated, cut across Wilson Boulevard, performed a quick and efficient left turn, and disappeared from view.

I pulled out of the alley into the street, tapping the horn and waving at Jo. I could see her lips moving, telling the car what she thought of it as she ran, handbag flapping, in my direction.

She hit the running board like a pro. I was moving at fifteen miles an hour or so by the time she pulled herself into the cab. "I swear," she said, breathing hard, "I'm going to take the meritorious service bonus that's sitting in my FARA credit union account, march straight to a car dealer, and put it down on a Mountaineer or an Explorer. I've had it with these damn foreign cars."

I recently told you about the quality of traffic flow in the greater Washington, D.C., metropolitan area. Just in case you were speed-reading and are fuzzy about what I said, "abysmal" may be one valid, though understated description. But for once, the sorry state of metrogridlock was working in my favor. I followed the limo's course—and discovered much to my delight that it was stuck in a construction zone traffic funnel just about opposite the Courthouse Metro stop. We were only three blocks behind our target. I cut across two traffic lanes, and threaded the needle between a cement truck and a police car. Indeed, one of the wonderful things about a full-size pickup truck is that you sit way above the other traffic and maneuvering becomes much, much easier, especially when one has, like I do, heavy ram bumpers fore and aft, as well as a huge trailer hitch that extends (just at radiator height on most cars) a full eighteen inches behind the thick stainless steel bumper. I glanced over at Joanne. "And now, *voilà*—the back door." I right-turned onto a side street, then immediately swung left into the wide, empty alley that paralleled the street I'd been on.

At the next intersection I peered left. Traffic was still not moving. So I ran another block in the alley, then left-turned, waited out the Honda ahead of me, then slowly right-turned back onto Wilson.

"Cool moves, Dick." Jo backhanded my shoulder hard enough to leave an impression. "Can I use your phone?"

"Sure."

She picked it up. Squinted. "Is is analog or digital?"

"Digital."

"Good. Mine's analog and anybody can listen in." She punched in a number and pressed the "send" key, waited, then said, "It's Joanne. I need you to check a DC plate for me. Yes, District. A vanity plate: Whiskey, Oscar, Delta, Echo."

We sat in silence as she waited, the receiver pressed to her ear. Then she said, "Thanks. Yeah I miss you, too."

I looked over at her. "Old friend?"

"We worked on Secretary Baker's detail together. He's a terrific guy. Reliable." She smiled. "He runs our training division now. Best of all he has access to the Virginia State Police computer. That car"—she indicated the white limo we now sat half a dozen vehicles behind—"belongs to one Bentley Brendel, Incorporated."

"The five-by-five?" He sure didn't look like any former diplomat or world-class lobbyist. When Alixe Joseph had described what he did and how effective he was, I thought he'd be one of those tall, smooth operators—the kind of 40-longs whose photographs always appear in society magazines with the daughters of venture capitalists on their arms. Well, you've seen this guy—he looks like a fucking fat toad, doesn't he? I mean, we're talking Jabba the Cunt in a bad-fitting suit.

Of course, I've been in the trade long enough to know not to judge by appearances. It's what you do, not what you look like, that is important to me. And what old Bentley had done was to pass a verboten folder to a Chinese intelligence agent. So far as I was concerned, that was enough to justify my tacking his scalp to my lodgepole.

I checked our position. We were far enough away to escape their attention, but close enough to make sure that both our targets were outlined behind the tinted privacy glass. I squinted. They were both present and accounted for. All we had to do now was shadow 'em.

Which didn't present me with much of a problem. I am speaking here, incidentally, in the automotive, not the surveilative, sense. Once clear of the one-lane construction zone, the Caddie proceeded down Wilson, cut right, and swung onto the parkway, cruised onto the Roosevelt Bridge, then meandered up onto E Street and worked its way north on Seventeenth. No problems there. The snag occurred when the limo pulled to the curb outside the Old Executive Office Building just below G Street, Bentley Brendel got out, and discretely patted the left side of his suit coat. Let me halt the action here long enough to tell you a fact of real life and tradecraft. It is that no matter how well we are schooled in the black arts, we often slip up by being human. Watch men as they come out of restaurant booths—they'll pat their wallets to make sure they've not dropped them. Well, here, Bentley was simply doing the same thing. He wanted to make sure he had his little package. So he tapped the folder, folks, giving himself (and me) a sure sign that it was there. The S_3FA pulled *his* bulk through the door, wheelied and waddled south, head lowered against the chill wind, walking quickly along the tall, nineteenth-century wrought iron pickets that guard the Old Executive Office Building. Half a minute later, Li Chimen emerged from the limo and headed north, slouching toward Pennsylvania Avenue.

One can not simply abandon one's vehicle on Seventeenth Street directly outside the Old Executive Office Building. The United States Secret Service Uniform Division, which is tasked with providing security to the OEOB, which is how it's known to us Washington insiders, is shall we say . . . sensitive about such things as car bombs, and hence tends to frown on abandoned vehicles parked anywhere near the OEOB. I use the word *frown* here ironically, because anything that gets abandoned outside the OEOB is generally T&B'd by the Secret Service.

What's T&B'd, you ask? T & B stands for towed away & blowed to the well-known smithereens. Furthermore, I couldn't flash the lights, hit the horn, cut across the oncoming traffic, and park in that no-parking zone I'd spotted on G where the worst they could do was give me a $200 ticket, because flashing of lights and honking of horn make a Roguish spectacle, thus attracting attention to *moi,* which would not help my ongoing practice of professional surveillance tradecraft.

At least Jo could act. "I'll take Bentley," she said. She let the S_3FA pass us, moving in the opposite direction, checked his position in the rearview mirror, and satisfied he was safely past us, cracked the door open.

"Where do we link up?" she asked, one foot on the running board.

"The Hunan," I said. "Eighteen hundred hours. We'll get your car started."

I got an uneven, sheepish grin in return. "Y'know I forgot all about *that* little problem." She hovered on the running board. "Thanks." Then the door slammed shut and she was gone.

I turned my attention back to Li Chimen. He was almost at the corner now. I had a decision to make. If he crossed Pennsylvania Avenue, I'd be stuck way behind him. If he turned right or left he'd be out of sight in a matter of seconds.

There was a momentary pause on the oncoming traffic. I pulled the wheel left, gunned the truck, and cut through the single line of cars, pulled to the curb—wheels on the sidewalk, shut the ignition off, jumped out, flipped the alarm system on, and cantered back around the corner, searching for Li's blue cashmere coat.

It was nowhere to be seen. I dashed to the corner, wheeled, looked around.

I saw him a hundred yards away, gliding down Pennsylvania Avenue, moving parallel with the White House fence, directly across from Lafayette Park.

The light was red but to hell with the traffic. I cut across Seventeenth Street at a run, slowing down as I passed through the antiterrorism barriers that sit at each end of the White House's section of Penn. I jogged past the entrance to the Old Executive Office Building just in time to see Li disappear into the Secret Service gatehouse that sits astride the northwest gate of the White House, directly opposite Jackson Place.

I stopped and watched, my nose pressed to the wrought iron pickets like any twelve-year-old tourist's. Li walked inside the security checkpoint and was immediately passed through. Then he marched up the long, curved black macadam driveway that leads toward the West Wing—the offices that house the vice president, the national security adviser, and the White House chief of staff among others. He disappeared into a doorway of the one-story building that links the West Wing to the White House proper.

Whoa—a fucking Chinese spook gets admitted into

the West Wing of the White House? WTF was going on here?

WTF, I discovered when I met Jo Montgomery at 1800, was that Li Chimen had a press pass. That's right, our adversaries, if they represent a valid journalistic entity (and Li certainly did, as he was the duly accredited Washington bureau chief of Xinhua, the New China News Agency), can get themselves admitted to the White House much more easily than any loyal taxpaying American citizen can. In fact, during the Cold War, all sorts of KGB types meandered in and out on a regular basis because they were bona fide representatives of *Pravda, Izvestia,* Novosti Press Service, Gostelradio, and half a dozen other "official" Soviet news media.

Now, it seemed, Li was doing the same thing. Of course, the press is kept segregated at the White House. I learned that they are confined to the pressroom and cannot wander the halls unaccompanied to seek out sources and do random interviews. Even the fifty-foot trip to bill signing ceremonies in the Rose Garden are closely monitored by the Secret Service and the White House press-office staff. Moreover, since the place is swept for bugs daily, it is not likely that a listening device can be planted during a photo op in the Oval Office. So the fact that Li had a press pass wasn't troubling in the cosmic sense.

No, much more disturbing was the nasty fact Jo developed. Which was, that Bentley Brendel, the selfsame former State Department official and current lobbyist who has been writing all those op-ed pieces in the *Asian Wall Street Journal,* pushing his own brand of China policy, and—as you have seen—passing state secrets to a Chinese spy, also had a White House pass. More significant, so far as I was concerned, was that he held not a permanent pass, but a *T* pass. The *T* stands for *temporary.* It told me that Bentley had not undergone a security clearance to obtain it, even though that *T* pass obviously gave him access to NSC,

DOD, NSA, and other classified materials.[30] Equally disturbing was the fact that the lobbyist had been given a hideaway office on the second floor of the OEOB (that's the Old Executive Office Building, the old War Department building that sits inside the White House complex). I surmised he had a hideaway office not a public one because he wasn't listed in any of the building directories, and his name hadn't been provided to the White House telephone operators. I knew all of this because I'd checked—I called 202-456-1414, which is the White House's main switchboard number, and asked for Mister Bentley Brendel, please. Quoth the White House operator: "I am sorry, sir, but I can find no such person listed in the current telephone book, or any of my addenda."

I also learned that Bentley Brendel met regularly with the NSC adviser, and had access to NSC research on the Pacific Rim. Jo had developed that tidbit from a Secret Service agent she knew named Ty Weaver, a guy she'd first met at the Beltsville, Maryland, range used by both DS—the Department of State's Bureau of Diplomatic Security—and the Secret Service. Anyhow, she'd run into Agent Ty by the southwest gate, which is where she'd followed Brendel.

They caught up with each other and traded shop gossip, and it turned out that he—along with the rest of the Secret Service's PPD, or Presidential Protective Detail, was pissed

[30]You will remember that in the first Clinton administration, more than a hundred of the political appointees working at the White House held temporary passes for more than a year. That was because they had not complied with regulations that require all White House staffers to answer questions about their finances and background (including drug use) in order to obtain an FBI security clearance. Without it, they were denied permanent passes—even though they had access to classified materials. Why did that happen? Well, there were allegations of drug use as well as other . . . irregularities. If you're interested in learning more on the subject, you might try the book *Unlimited Access: An FBI Agent Inside the Clinton White House,* by former G-man Gary Aldrich.

off because "that fat little fuck," which is how Ty referred to Brendel as the S_3FA waddled toward the OEOB, had a *T* pass (which as I have noted means he hadn't gone through his security investigation, remember?).

"So?" Jo had asked, all innocence.

"So," she reported later, "Ty says that even though the pass is temporary, Brendel uses it to bring bunches of off-the-books, late-night visitors into the compound—even into the Oval Office—to demonstrate his access and his influence."

Now that *was* another nasty piece of news. But there was more. "One group was even speakin' freakin' Chinese," Ty'd told her. "They turned out to be military officers."

Jo asked him what happened.

"The detail that was on duty that particular night complained to the SAIC,[31] who went to Porkchop when they were one-on-one and raised a stink," Ty said, using the Secret Service's radio shorthand code for the president. "So the president said he'd check it out. Then, before you know it, Sunburn[32] is bitching at the Secret Service for getting in the middle of policy decisions. He raised holy hell, even showed up at West One[33] and threw a shit fit. He actually threatened to get the SAIC's ass canned.

"So the SAIC went back to Porkchop, and the friggin' president wimped out—whined that day-to-day China policy was Matt Thompson's department, not his. Told my boss that anything this Brendel guy wants, he gets, because that's the way Matt Thompson wants it—and Brendel's been of great service to the country. SAIC told us bottom line is we can't say a damn thing, even if we believe security is being

---

[31]Special Agent In Charge.

[32]All top White House staff have Secret Service radio code names. Sunburn is NSC adviser Matt Thompson's. The First Family's code names all begin with the same letter. These days, the president is code-named Porkchop, the first lady's handle is Pickle, and first daughter is Princess.

[33]West One, for West Wing One, is the Secret Service's White House command center.

compromised. I tell ya, Jo, the freakin' lobbyists own this damn White House and everybody in it."

Let me take the time for a small digression here. Yes, I know that you may think what I've just told you seems far-fetched—i.e., that someone who is probably the paid agent of a foreign government has access to the White House, and to our national security secrets. Well, it has happened before—remember all those contacts with people representing all sorts of foreign interests during the 1996 presidential campaign? Some of those folks actually had government jobs and top secret clearances. Frightening, ain't it?

Okay. I told Jo to pass her infobits to Chairman Crocker, tell him about the orange-tabbed folder I'd caught a glimpse of, and for God's sake stay in touch with Ty. He was a valuable source, so far as I was concerned, a pair of eyes and ears right in the middle of things. I added that if we needed to contact each other she should call me as we'd prearranged. Meanwhile, I'd go to work.

The look on her face told me that she wanted in. But we both knew that was impossible. She was the cutout in this scheme, not one of the operators.

Chapter 10

Two quick points of information. First, the Pentagon's official definition of counterintelligence is: "any activity initiated, or information gathered, in order to prevent, block, obstruct, impede, or restrain any espionage, sabotage, or other intelligence collection efforts performed by (or on behalf of) foreign governments, organizations, or persons." Second, according to the NAVSOF—NAVy Special Operations Forces—doctrine under which I conduct my SEAL business, I am permitted to use deadly force while within CONUS (the CONtinental United States) *if,* when I employ said deadly force, it is, let me quote again: "To protect the security of nuclear weapons, and/or the security of other combat-system sensitive defense technology the loss of which would cause irreparable harm to the National Security of the United States."

Now that you've heard the highfalutin' twenty-dollar words, let me put the gist of the above paragraph in language that you and I can understand. I sat my guys down and told them the clock was ticking and we were after a traitor—and a spy. I added that we were operating in the black, and if we got caught, not only were our careers over, we'd probably be sent to prison. I added that if anyone wanted out because this op might place his whole career in jeopardy, it was okay with me. I don't mind putting my four stripes on the line when I believe the goal is worth it. But it's not my way to force anyone else to do it. I wanted only volunteers—and I'm happy to say that every single one of my merry marauders stepped forward and said, "Daddy, Daddy, please take me!"

The personnel issue decided, I told the men that things would probably get serious in the near term, and because of that, we would all start carrying weapons immediately. That, too, was a career-affecting decision. Navy personnel are not permitted to carry weapons whilst in CONUS except under extraordinary conditions, and then only when approved all the way up the chain of command. Well, since I seemed to be the entire and self-contained chain of command on this little stealth venture, I decided to approve all weapons requests—starting with *moi.*

There was, incidentally, substantial personal significance to this particular command decision, which is why I did not make it lightly. I am, you will remember, a convicted felon. Being such, I am forbidden to possess firearms. But I am also a sworn officer in the United States Navy, and in that official capacity, I can, and I often do, carry whatever kind of weaponry I may need to get the job done. Of course, trying to explain NAVSOF doctrine to some Washington, D.C., Metro cop—i.e., that I was a Navy officer on official duty—if said officer were to catch me dressed in civvies and with a locked, loaded, and suppressed submachine gun, in a city whose weapons laws are the most restrictive in the United States, would be, shall we say, a challenge.

When one is on assignments like this one, one do not carry a letter from the Chairman of the Joint Chiefs of Staff that says, more or less, "Dear Mister Police Officer, please let this nice Roguish fella do what he wants because he works for me." One be out on one's own—and if I got caught, it would be up to me to get myself off the old hook.

Despite a temper tantrum that would have done Maria Callas justice, Wonder would remain out of play for this entire little exercise. His job was to remain stuck at a desk (curled up in an overstuffed chair, actually), doing his homework. They give the chief's exam only once a year in these days of downsizing and forced early retirements, and in his specialty—machinist's mate—less than 8 percent of the candidates are selected. I wanted him to get a goddamn perfect score. If he didn't get one, he'd remain a first-class for another friggin' cycle, or be up-and-outed with no course of appeal.

Nasty Nicky Grundle was going to be out of action, too. His ankle hadn't just been sprained aboard the *Nantong Princess*—it was friggin' broken. The s.o.b. was going to be laid up for a month minimum. That left Gator, Half Pint Harris, Duck Foot Dewey, the Pick, Eddie "Nod" DiCarlo, and Boomerang available. To round out the squad—I like to work with even numbers because then everybody gets a swim buddy, and swim buddies are the two-man nucleus from which all UDT and SEAL activities derive—I made a call down to the amphibious base at Little Creek, where the playful party animal I call the Rodent was marking time at Special Boat Unit Two.

An hour later Rodent (real name Dave in case you keep track of these sorts of things) was heading toward Rogue Manor in his bright red Bronco at what the *PO*-lice usually refer to as a high effing rate of speed. It seemed that he had sixty days of unused annual leave time available, and a very accommodating CO named—well, maybe I'd better leave the CO out of it. There still are a few unit commanders who don't deserve the C^2CO label, and I don't want to fuck up this one's career by saying a proper *merci beaucoup* and letting the world know whom he be.

I broke the troops up into two four-man teams. Half Pint and Pick, Gator and Duck Foot were assigned to Li Chimen. Li had gotten a good look at me and I didn't want to spook the spook—at least not yet. That left Rodent, Boomerang, Nod DiCarlo, and me to cover Bentley Brendel.

Boomerang, who owns a perfectly restored 1978 750-cc Hondamatic rice rocket,[34] volunteered for motorcycle duty. I accepted. Bikes are efficient in city traffic—remember all the trouble I had trying to park my pickup truck on Seventeenth Street? I did—because I now had a $200 ticket as a souvenir of *that* particular excursion.

I sent the guys out on a preliminary foray within hours after I got back to the Manor. I wanted a site survey of Bentley Brendel's offices, which were located in his home, a pair of renovated row houses just off the C&O canal in Georgetown. I wanted other site surveys on Li Chimen's residence—wherever it was—and his office, too.

Boomerang and Rodent sped off in the Rodent's Bronco. Half Pint and the Pick took my F-250, while I hit the computer, logged on to the Internet, and did some serious research on one Bentley Brendel. After six hours I grabbed a combat nap. Then it was back to work. There were a lot of hits about him, and I wanted to read them all. When I finished the public stuff, I accessed some other, more restricted materials. Those, too, proved interesting. You see, despite my Roguish, off-the-cuff wild-man, seat-of-pants hop & pop & shoot & loot persona, I am a very orderly person who does a lot of research before he goes into battle. Don't let the Rogue act fool ya.

By 0940 the next morning, my lethal Leprechauns were back, sipping strong coffee, and delivering the news.

The news, according to Boomerang, who, being senior man, had overseen the target assessments, was that Li Chimen lived by himself in a three-bedroom apartment in one of the high-rise condos near Ballston and worked out of

---

[34]That's biker shorthand for a fast, maneuverable motorcycle of Japanese manufacture. Yes, I know that on the one hand, the Hondamatic 750 weighs about 700 pounds and isn't the fastest, most maneuverable Jap bike on the road. On the other hand, you have never seen Boomerang ride. He handles the effing thing like a goddamn Kawasaki 500.

a Rosslyn, Virginia, office building located not four blocks from the Hunan Number One. That explained why he'd still had the top secret memo in his coat pocket when they'd arrived. He simply hadn't had enough time to read it all before he and Bentley went back to their respective offices.

The Xinhua bureau was a six-room suite with a steel door, cipher locks, and an electronic security system that relayed its signals straight to the Chinese Embassy on upper Connecticut Avenue. Xinhua had three identical BMW sedans parked in the secure garage, nine floors below the offices. The cars were watched by a staffer. The office, too, was manned twenty-four hours a day.

Boomerang's assessment was that we could crack Xinhua's bureau anytime we wanted. Cipher locks, after all, pose no real problems if you've had the right kind of training, which we have had. The problem would be getting in and out without killing whoever was inside.

Problem indeed. There are rules about these sorts of things. The FBI, which handles domestic counterintelligence, tends to frown on SEALs who shoot-and-loot in downtown Arlington, Virginia. I didn't think the Chairman would look kindly on it, either.

Boomerang continued his monologue. "An' I got some good news and some bad news on the five-by-five's place."

The good news, he reported, was that there are only so many ways of coming and going in Georgetown, which limits the target's access and egress to and from his base. In this particular case, our bull's-eye—Bentley—lived on Thomas Jefferson Street, a narrow, one-way northbound street that ran between K and M Streets. "That very selfsame fact," Boomerang said, "is also the bad news, Boss Dude."

Why was that bad news, you ask? Well, it is hard to remain anonymous very long in such confined areas. Oh, we could have used a surveillance van (if we'd actually had one). You've seen 'em on the cop TV shows with their darkened windows and video cameras, parked across from the target's house. And in real life, the FBI even used a stakeout RV to videotape the crooked congressmen they caught taking bribes when they pulled the ABSCAM sting back in the late 1970s.[35] But here's what: unless you're a congressman (most congressmen tend to have less brains than a pet rock), surveillance vans become obvious, especially to anyone with any intelligence background, after only a few days on-site. I mean, if you lived in a nice neighborhood, and suddenly a beat-up panel van started parking directly across from your house every day, wouldn't you get suspicious? Bentley Brendel certainly would, because he was a pro. And because he was a pro, watching him would be more than a chore—it would be real hard work.

Now, as you all know, I am not opposed to hard work. But the more I thought about a static surveillance the more I decided that it was a bad idea.

Why, you ask? Well, first of all there were the numbers. A static surveillance is terrific if you are the FBI, and you have a hundred counterintelligence agents, twenty-five assorted vehicles, plus a chopper or two or even a plane, as well as a bunch of other miscellaneous assets, like C^3—that's Command, Control, and Communications—vans, to put into play. I had four men, and my total assets consisted of three cars, my F-250, Rodent's Bronco, and a rice rocket. Full stop. End of story.

Now, let me state for the record that any four of my guys are equal to any hundred FBI agents, even the heroes of ABSCAM. But that's not the point. Point is, I suddenly realized that my job wasn't to *surveil* Bentley Brendel and Li Chimen—it was to *hock* their *choinik* as my Israeli friend

---

[35]The FBI targeted crooked congressmen with ABSCAM—for AraB SCAM—in 1978. They set up a bogus Saudi sheik in a town house on fashionable W Street Northwest, where they videotaped the congressmen who promised him their votes and influence in return for cash bribes—*baksheesh* in Arabic. Seven congressional *bakshitters* were convicted.

Avi Ben Gal might say, using an old Yiddish phrase that translates loosely to "rattle their teacup."

In other words, I was going to force Bentley and Li to commit themselves before they were ready. That is one of the key distinctions between conventional thinking and unconventional thinking. In conventional warfare, you tend to play out the chess game in the act/react mode.

Here, I was going to provoke my enemy into acting prematurely. And by doing so I would surely destroy him.

The key to this operation was Bentley Brendel. Why? Because he was the inside man, the one with access, influence, money, and clout. When I did my *hock*ing, he'd nudge Li's *choinik* for me—and I could make the two of 'em tumble and smash.

I was just working out how to do my rattling when the phone rang. Now what's the significance of that, you ask—phones ring all the friggin' time, right? Yeah, they do. But this one was the unlisted phone I keep all for myself. Nobody has the number, not Chairman Crocker, not even Stevie Wonder.

I let it ring half a dozen times, then plucked the receiver off the cradle. "Marcinko—"

"Captain Marcinko, this is the White House operator. Please hold for Admiral Prescott of the National Security Council."

Now, those of you who've been through this historical litany before may skip ahead to the italics below if you want. But you new guys, listen up, because as the old chiefs used to say, you will definitely see this material again. Okay, here's the backstory: Rear Admiral (Upper Half) Pinckney Prescott III has been the bane of my existence since I commanded SEAL Team Six and he was the commodore and grandee panjandrum of NAVSPECWARGRUTWO (NAVal SPECial WARfare GRoUp TWO). He's the asshole who once disapproved my request for extra boot laces for my men. Yes, I am serious. He thought they were an extravagance because we tied our boots with knots not bows and cut them off. I tried to explain to Pinky (these were the days when I actually took him seriously) that when you jump out of a plane at thirty-nine thousand feet your boots can separate from your feet if they are not knotted tightly. Pinky, who hates to jump from more than thirty-five hundred feet (and does it only to keep up his SEAL qualification so he can earn his precious hazardous duty pay for jumping), would have none of my argument.

That gives you a sample of the way he thinks. Now, as to his personal history, Pinky the Turd, as I like to call him, is the son and grandson of admirals. Pinky da foist was foisted on the Navy because, as a pseudoaristocrat from a Philadelphia Main Line family *sans* benefit of trust fund, he had to make a living. So they sent him to Annapolis. Little Pinky (that would be Pinky Deuce) followed in his daddy's black shoe steps twenty-five years later, and—as if to prove the Peter Principle once and for all—Pinky III, aka the Turd, Annapolis '72, brought up the rear. Luckily for the nation, Mrs. Pinky the Turd, the former Harriet Lickadick Suckacock of Blue Balls, Pennsylvania, was spayed some years back and hence has whelped no offspring. Anyway, somehow, after Annapolis, Pinky managed to survive BUD/S training and become a SEAL. Well, let's be honest. He wears the same Trident I do. But he's never been in combat. He's never led men from the front. He's never done anything in the military but fight paper wars, which makes him the epitome of the Can't Cunt officer—a lard-assed worthless pencil-dicked pus-nutted shit-for-brains turd-bucket staff puke. Am I making myself like clear yet? Good—then we can get back to the business at hand.

The fucking White House? The fucking National Security Council?

And then it fucking hit me. Pinky had crowed not three months ago that he was about to be appointed to a White House job. I'd dismissed his boast, written it off as hyperbole, which as you may know is also the name of one of the world's most famous Hollywood agents. But he'd been telling truth. Well, fuck me. (And *that,* friends, is precisely what he was about to try to do.)

He dropped the phone just as he came on the line—I could hear the receiver clattering all over the floor, and Pinky, all flustered, whining and bitching and moaning as he tried (and tried) to retrieve it.

Fact: it is hard to sound like an Important Person when you've just flubbed your entrance. But he tried. After all, Pinky is very trying. The only problem is that when P-P-Pinky gets flustered, he t-t-tends to stu-stu-stu-stutter.

"D-D-Dick," he said, sounding more like P-P-Porky fucking Pig than any naval officer ever should, "this is Pinky P-P-Prescott."

In response, I held my receiver out horizontally by its coiled cord and let it bounce onto the slate of my office floor like a fucking yo-yo. Even at that distance I could hear his howl of protest. I bounced it once again for good measure, caught it one-handed, brought it back to speaking position, and growled, "Sorry P-P-Pinky." I wasn't apologizing when I said that—I was simply describing him.

"G-G-Goddammit, Dick, I am an admiral. Don't mock me," the Turd brayed. I could just see him sitting behind his big desk, all pissed off. I do truly like it when Pinky is pissed off.

"Oh, I truly am so sorry, sir," I said, saying the last word slowly and distinctly so Pinky would know I was spelling it with a *c* and a *u.* Then I waited to see what the sonofabitch wanted. I wasn't about to give him any help at all, either.

"You will report to my office first thing in the morning," Pinky said imperiously. "You are causing grave and profound problems for this administration, and I plan to put the brakes to you right now."

Y'know, sometimes, when the fucking lightbulb goes off it can almost blind you. There was like this big flash in front of my eyes—all of a sudden I realized who the fuck had called Admiral Gray in Japan and ordered him to hit the McDonald's with a team that was unprepared.

Do you remember that Tosho told me that the assault had been ordered when Admiral Gray mentioned my name to the person calling from the White House. That remark, which I'd found puzzling at the time, now made perfect sense.

If I had been in the room with Pinky at that point I would have throttled him, consequences be damned. But I wasn't. All I could do was respond audibly, and so I fired a salvo that must have burned the hair off his fucking jug ears. I told him that, so far as I knew, he wasn't a blankety-blanking part of my blanking chain of command. I told him where he could fold his bleeper-blanking order and stuff it where the sun don't shine, *sans* benefit of K-fucking-Y jelly or any other unguentary blanking lubricant.

For some reason, Pinky didn't appreciate my response—not that it mattered one rusty F-word to me whether he did or he didn't. I heard him huff, and puff, and try to catch his breath so he could blow my house down. But as we all know, Pinky is more wuss than wolf. And, more to the point, he is a bully and a coward, and since he was in no position to bully me, he chickened out by kind of hiccoughing twice, stuttering something-something-something about something-something else (it all sounded so indistinct he might have actually put his hand over the mouthpiece to keep me from hearing).

Then he tried to hang up on me. But he dropped the fucking receiver again, which gave me the chance to Boehm him instead, by hanging up first. What's Boehming? Boehming is the present participle of the verb "to Boehm," a verb derived, as you can probably guess, from the last name of that sneaky, malevolent, lethal man o'warsman, Lieutenant Commander Roy Henry Boehm, USN (Ret.), the godfather of all SEALs. Boehming is when you go out and fuck some fucking fucker before the fucking fucker can go out and fuck you.

So, having Boehmed Pinky, I was feeling pretty good about the encounter for the next eight, or perhaps even nine minutes. That was when the other phone on my desk—the one whose number everyone knows—rang. I picked it up and got my own hirsute earful of Thomas Edward Crocker, General, United States Army, and Chairman of the Joint Chiefs of Staff.

"Dick, goddammit to hell—"

"General, you know what I like about you? It's the great sex. You always engage in so much foreplay before you start to fuck with me."

He had to laugh. Which stopped his verbal hyperventillation and calmed him down. But the unruffled gist he delivered was the same as the message he would have administered had he been Roto-Rootering my sphincter at warp speed.

He kept it simple, stupid and simple, declarative. Dick be nice. Do not kill Pinky. Go see him. Find out what he has to say. Keep me informed.

I began to object.

General Crocker was having no objections. "Dammit, Dick, think of it as recon," the Chairman interrupted. "I am juggling a bunch of balls right now and I need to know what's going on over there, because SECDEF and I have been shut out."

"But—"

"Don't give me 'but.' Remember what SEALs did back in Operation Desert Storm. Just before we committed to the attack, they went in quietly from the sea, reconned Kuwait City, and got the lay of the land. They didn't get to kill anybody or break anything. But we learned a hell of a lot from the information they brought out, information that saved a lot of lives. Sometimes you have to come and go and not let on what you're about."

Point taken. I am a merry marauder. I like to maraud, which is a little-used verb meaning to loot, pillage, burn, & plunder.[36] But my natural appetite for such activities must

---

[36]*Maraud,* in case you didn't know, is derived from the Middle French term *un maraud,* which means . . . a *rogue.* Incredible the way these things come together, ain't it?

sometimes take a backseat to the priorities of the mission. And the mission here was to bring back some HUMINT about what was going on inside the National Security Council; to see what damage had been done, and by whom.

"You're right," I said. Of course he was right. To rattle Bentley Brendel's teacup, I'd have to get myself inside the White House. That might have been a problem—until, that is, the Turd summoned me inside the gates.

The Chairman, obviously relieved, started giving me hints about what I should look for. But I wasn't listening. In fact, my mind was racing. Unconventional warfare means doing the unexpected—winning through surprise, and speed, and violence of action. Unconventional warfare means keeping the opposition off balance.

Well, although there was no way I'd tell General Crocker about it, I was about to go on the offensive. And I'd start by yanking on da Turd's leash and seeing where he led me. My instincts told me that the Turd would lead me directly to Bentley Brendel, and from there, it would be a short trip to Li Chimen.

Oops—there was silence on the line. Obviously, the Chairman had stopped talking.

That made it my turn. "I'll get the job done for you, sir," I said obliquely, telling the truth without divulging any of my own Roguish, UNODIR specifics.

"I'm glad to hear you see things my way," the Chairman said. "And Dick?"

"General?"

"Remember—it's the White House. No weapons."

Chapter 11

There is something special about going to the White House. I don't care who you are; I don't care how much of the world you have seen, or what you have experienced. Passing through those gates, walking or driving up that black macadam driveway and entering through the North Portico doors is something very, very extraordinary. It is equally as special to go through the tourist entrance opposite the Treasury Department, or come through one of the five appointments entrances for a meeting in the West Wing, Old Executive Office Building, East Wing, or residence. No wonder: the White House is a heady place—an icon that represents the United States as a nation.

It is a fact that presidents can awe even the most powerful folks in the nation simply by asking them over to the White House for a little tête-à-tête in the Oval Office, a friendly coffee in the basement library, or an overnight in the Lincoln Bedroom. In fact, this current president raised more than $10 million for his last campaign by doing just that.

But even the president's cynical attempts to turn the White House into a money-making bed-and-breakfast cannot dim the place's significance or its message. Sure, the commander in chief may be a schmuck, but sooner or later, said schmuck will be gone. The White House will remain. Why? Because Sixteen Hundred Pennsylvania Avenue is *America*'s house. More than the Capitol, or any other public building in the Washington area, it represents the very core, the hub, the nucleus, of our unique, American form of democracy. Within its heavily guarded, sensor-laden perimeter resides the spiritual energy of Washington and Adams, of Jefferson, and Lincoln, of Eisenhower, and Kennedy (the president who caused SEALs to be created by Roy Boehm back in 1961), and of Roosevelt and Reagan.

I defy you to pass onto the White House grounds without experiencing a huge, patriotic emotional rush. And I believe that holds true whether you are a tourist, a visiting head of state—or a SEAL captain like me, whose sense of Duty, Honor, and Country is stirred deeply whenever I am there.

It doesn't matter who the president is, either. It's the office that you respect—not the man. As First SEAL Roy Boehm told John F. Kennedy when the president summoned Roy to Blair House, "I didn't vote for you, sir—but I'd die for you."

At 0855 the next morning I presented two forms of identification at the very same southwest gate of the White House where Bentley Brendel had led Joanne not twenty-four hours ago—and got sent around the block for my troubles. Seems that these days the southwest gate is only for those august personages who are important enough to hold White House creds. The rest of us mortals have to use the basement entrance of the Old Executive Office Building, which is located on Seventeenth Street, to get to our appointments.

I didn't need the hassle. I'd been up most of the night.

There is a thirteen-hour time differential between Washington and Tokyo, and I'd been on the horn to Alixe Joseph and Tosho, getting intel dumped, sit-repped, and generally *se mettre au courant,* which is how they say brought up to speed in Paris. Since I didn't have any secure phones at the Manor, I'd used the Big Brother equipment. I can report to all you taxpayers out there that it works as well when it's connected to conventional phone lines as it does when you uplink to a satellite. This is one covert program you got your money's worth out of.

Anyhow, what I learned was disturbing. There had been an increase of clandestine Chinese activity all across the Pacific Rim in the past forty-eight hours. Specifically, there had been antigovernment riots in three Korean cities—twelve dead—a power outage in the Indonesian capital of Jakarta, and a general strike in Tokyo.

I already knew that Beijing had recently increased political pressure on Singapore, Indonesia, Japan, and Korea to join it in a pan-Asian trade, defense, and political organization that would be in effect a combination of the G-7 industrial countries and NATO. The Chinese foreign minister had not a month ago visited his counterparts in Tokyo, Jakarta, and Seoul. He'd been rebuffed. So now, they were striking back.

Alixe, who sounded uncharacteristically agitated and preoccupied, said that it was obvious to her that the Chinese weren't going to take *bu*—no—for an answer, and had ratcheted things up a couple of notches. Couple of notches, hell—they were beginning a campaign of covert operations designed to force things their way. "There has been a definite increase in the number of scrambled transmissions coming out of Beijing," Alixe told me. "Something bad is going on."

That comment made my internal warning light (it's the selfsame one that sits behind my pussy detector) go off. "Hold on." I ran for the digital camera, removed the disk, threw it into the computer, brought up the images I'd taken on the *Nantong Princess,* and scanned them into a file, which I then double-encrypted using DIA's basic shareware encryption program. Yes, I have it on all my computers. "I'm faxing you three pages, double encrypted."

"What're the keys?"

"First key are the first five letters of the first word and the last three letters of your two-word compartment. Second key is your favorite brand of shoe—you were wearing 'em when we met."

I heard her laugh heartily. "You're very observant, Dick."

Four minutes later, Alixe said, "I think I know those faces. Let me do some digging. I'll get back to you as soon as I've got something concrete."

Then I told her about Bentley Brendel's White House pass—and his access to classified material. I heard her gasp.

"That is truly disturbing news," she said, not telling me anything I didn't already know. "Look, Dick . . ." She hesitated, as if searching for the right words.

"What's up, Alixe?"

"We're secure, right?"

"Top of the line."

I could hear her take a deep breath. "In the last six hours, three of my best . . . ah, sources, have been eliminated."

Now I understood her unsettled tone. "Who were they? How did it happen?"

"That's not important. What's important is that they weren't connected. Three sources, three cells. They were operating independently of one another." She exhaled in a *whoosh.* "Remember when I told you there are no coincidences in our business?"

"Roger that."

"Well, there's a leak somewhere, Dick, and I can't do anything about it from here."

"I'll keep my eyes open," I said. "But it's way outside my AO."

"I know. But frankly, you're being out of the loop makes you someone I can talk to. You're not connected—perhaps *you* can see the pattern. Maybe I'm too close."

"I'll keep my eyes and ears open," I promised. "Meanwhile, you keep your head down. And call Tosho if you need protection."

The uniformed Secret Service officers behind the desk in the foyer scrutinized my military ID and Pentagon pass, looked me up and down twice, watched v-e-r-y closely as I walked through the metal detector—and when I failed the test, hand-searched me. I surrendered my collapsible baton and the short knife that most folks think is a belt buckle to an agent whose nameplate bore the moniker Moldea, took my receipt for the toys and my visitor's pass, ran the magnetic strip on the back of the pass through the electronic scanner, then proceeded down the narrow corridor toward the stairwell.

Yes, the OEOB has elevators. Good ones, too. But I always prefer to walk. Pinky's office was on the south side of the third floor, we SEALs do our PT wherever we find an opportunity, and walking up four flights of stairs seemed like an opportunity to me.

I—what *is* it? Sorry for the interruption, folks. It's the dweeb editor again, gloating because he says he's caught me in an inconsistency. Four flights of stairs. And Pinky's office is on the third floor. Yeah—but I walked into the basement entrance, remember? Seems to me that the editor had better start reading these manuscripts as closely as you-all do.

Okay. I chugged up the stairs. At the third floor I turned left, then right, walked down a long, marble-floored corridor lined with piles of cardboard Port-A-Files. I saw to my horror that many of them were marked CONFIDENTIAL, or SECRET.

I have spent most of my career doing work that is classified—and most of that work will remain undescribed, because to tell you anything about it would compromise what I did and how I did it. I may be called a Rogue, but lemme tell you, I have a healthy respect for secrets—and I know how to keep 'em. Moreover, I do not like to see secrets splashed all over the front pages of the newspapers.

Yes, I realize that journalists argue that the public has a right to know, and under that right-to-know rubric they often compromise our national security, damage our ability to conduct intelligence and military operations, and impair our relations with our allies. Furthermore, I defy any journalist to show me where in the Constitution, the Founding Fathers talked about the public's *right* to know. Oh, we have a First Amendment, which guarantees freedom of expression. But freedom of expression does not constitute a "right to know." Face it: there is no *right* to know. Now, I do feel that the press has a responsibility to report, educate, and enlighten, so that the electorate can make informed decisions on national policy.

But this business of spilling secrets has caused people I know to die unnecessarily, and operations I have been a part of either to be called off, or fail. So I do not like the wholesale spilling of secrets. Thus, when I see crates of documents marked SECRET sitting unprotected in corridors, stored in Port-A-Files, not document safes, I get worried. It tells me that, so far as the current administration is concerned, protecting secrets is not a priority. Of course, if the current administration was interested in protecting secrets, it wouldn't allow any lobbyists to hold *T* credentials and bring military officers from a potential adversary nation into the White House complex after hours. Thus endeth the sermon.

I threaded my way south, into a third corridor, which, I noted, was being scanned by a series of TV cameras mounted just below the high, ornate ceiling. The doors in this passageway, antique, heavily oiled wood six-paneled doors with ornate brass knobs, each bore the legend ENTER THROUGH 385 on cardboard signs mounted alongside the doorjambs. Below was another strip of cardboard on which sat an arrow, pointing in the direction in which I was proceeding. I marched another ten yards until I saw "385" printed on the cardboard, wheeled left, and turned the knob.

I walked inside a small, narrow office crammed with filing cabinets and document safes. Two old wood desks holding desktop computer terminals sat one opposite the other in the center of the room. The desks looked like they belonged to grad students in the final throes of dissertation writing: each was piled high with miscellaneous memoranda, news clips, books, maps, and other research materials. Power cords and telephone lines ran haphazardly across the threadbare wall-to-wall carpet. A dusty laser printer, wired through a three-position data transfer box, sat atop a two-drawer document safe.

I closed the door behind me. The office was empty except for a late-middle-aged woman behind the rearmost desk, a desk so neat and orderly that it looked out of place in the chaos that surrounded it. She was half-standing so she could see me over the piles of files, miscellaneous boxes, not to mention her own humongous computer screen. She waved at me. "Captain Marcinko?"

I nodded.

She worked her way around the maze of office stuff and took a couple of steps in my direction, her hand extended. "Come on back and wait with me until Admiral Prescott's ready for you. I'm Avenir Reynolds—his assistant."

I extended my own hand. "Nice to meet you Ms. Reynolds."

"Avenir—Avenir, please."

"Sure." I slalomed over the paper berm and desks piled high with bureaucratic detritus toward her desk. I stopped as I caught sight of the aged, creaky-looking straight-back wood chair that sat dead center in front of her schoolmarm's desk. It was so decrepit that it would probably buckle under my weight. "If it's all right with you, I'll stand."

"He might be a while."

"It's okay—I don't mind standing." Of course he'd be a while. Keeping me waiting was SOP for Pinky. He thinks it gets me on edge; knocks me off my timing. But all it really does is give me more of a chance to Boehm him.

Avenir straightened her perfect bun, took a close look at her creaky chair, then looked back at me with a bemused, quasi-motherly expression. "Why not sit at *his* desk and have a nice hot cup of coffee while you're waiting."

Sit at his desk? That meant he wasn't around. Would I like to sit at (read rummage through) Pinky's desk without him in attendance? Hey—does the pope speak fifty-seven languages?

"Why, that would be just terrific," I said, a huge, playfully Roguish smile spreading across my face.

"Good," Avenir said. "This way." She started toward me.

I headed toward the door to my left—the one that led to all the adjoining offices—so she could take me to Pinky's office suite. Instead, she stopped halfway down the narrow office, in front of one of the pair of scarred, timeworn oak bureaucrat's desks. "Here we are," she said, smiling with a civil servant's professional bemusement at the incredulous expression on my face. "Yes, *this* is Admiral Prescott's desk."

As I've just said, the desk was piled high with papers, newspaper clips, photocopies, and messages. A brown paper bag, carelessly torn open, served as a place mat for a half-eaten bagel half schmeared with cream cheese. Next to the bagel that bore Pinky's capped tooth marks was a teacup filled with coffee so dark it looked solid. A circa 1982, four-line push button telephone sat to the left of the teacup, just in front of the fourteen-inch computer screen with the Navy SEALs screen saver going full speed. Pinky's dirty-lensed half-glasses sat carelessly dropped on the smudgy keyboard.

Now, you are probably asking yourselves WTF right now. I mean, Pinky is an admiral, and admirals, one would assume, always get classy quarters in which to work.

You are correct in your assumption. In most places a two-star anything would get a big office and a great view. But then, this was the White House, and the perk of just being able to say where you were calling from when you make phone calls or give out your address is the equivalent of a Pentagon fourth-floor, E-ring office suite, with a view of the river and the Jefferson Memorial, which is precisely what Pinky had given up when he came to work over here.

Avenir pointed to a straight-back oak chair that looked even creakier than her own, stood back, and crossed her arms like a nanny. "Just make yourself comfortable." Now, I wasn't about to rifle Pinky's desk under Avenir's watchful gaze, and almost demurred the sitting bit once again. But when I looked between the bagel and the coffee, southeast of the keyboard and northwest of the two-week-old *Time* magazine, and I saw precisely what was on Pinky's desk, I double-clutched, threw myself into gear, and changed my mind about the chair—and the coffee. All of a sudden I wanted to get as close to that desk as I could.

Fifteen seconds later I was perched precariously in the straight-back chair, exchanging pleasantries and making small talk with Avenir as she produced a delicate bone china teacup and saucer from the neat and orderly credenza that sat behind her neat and orderly old desk, and poured me a healthy dose of overcooked black stuff from a coffee maker so old it must have been bought during the Johnson administration. The Andrew Johnson administration.

From the way she bustled around, smiling coquettishly and burbling, I could see my company made her happy. Pinky probably treated her like a nonperson—sat all day in the same room and never spoke to her except to bray an order, or bitch about a mistake. He tends to act like that with secretaries, assistants, and other low-ranking factotums who don't wear as much gold on their sleeves as he does.

And so, while I sat there, my legs primly crossed at the ankles, chatting with Avenir Reynolds about the weather, and the Navy, and what being a SEAL was all about, I was taking copious mental notes on what I saw on Pinky's desk. From the messy look of things, and the number of requests he'd been tasked to fill, Pinky had been working his scrawny behind off lately.

And most of what he was doing was in the classified area. He'd left a trio of thin orange-tabbed document folders sitting on his desk, fanned out like king-size playing cards. The way the labels were written indicated they'd been sent over from DIA. The code words Weather Gable printed across the orange tabs told me that inside were copies of Alixe Joseph's raw HUMINT reports, printed out on what I call TS/SCI paper.[37] That set off a nasty bunch of bells and whistles. I looked closely at the middle one, which had a crease down its center, betraying the fact that it had been folded then smoothed out. *That* little piggy had been to market.

A yellow Post-It with a line-drawing cartoon of a computer wonk attached to the top folder read: "Pinky, pls get these three rpts back ASAP. My ass is going to be shredded if the boss finds they're gone." The note was initialed "H." I'd find out who the hell H was, because this was exactly the kind of leakage that can (and, in fact, had just) ended with some of Alixe Joseph's agents being eliminated by a bunch of UNPs—unknown nasty parties. Now, I knew how the leakage had occurred. Pinky had given the folder to Bentley. Bentley had passed it to Li Chimen, who'd read it, and handed it back. But Li'd folded it and stuck it in his pocket so he could finish reading it after lunch.

Here is a real-world lesson, folk: careless use of intelligence materials gets people killed. It's happened before. When the Israelis distributed the raw intel reports from

[37]TS/SCI paper, as it's come to be known, is specially formulated so that if it is put in a Xerox or other brand of photocopier, it will not duplicate. It was put into use shortly after the American spy and traitor Jonathan Pollard allowed one of his Israeli control officers to duplicate 360 cubic feet of TS/SCI documents on a copier. Don't ask me how TS/SCI paper works—I don't know. All I know is that it *does* work.

their paid spy, Jonathan Pollard, some of the documents found their way into the hands of the KGB, the old Soviet intelligence apparatus. By carefully analyzing where the raw data had come from, the Sovs were able to track down the sources we had used to collect our intelligence. They neutralized—murdered—those sources, and our intel flow dried up.

Alixe Joseph was working under embassy cover. That may have given her diplomatic protection. But she still wasn't bulletproof. And her field agents—the Japanese, Chinese, Malay, Filipino, or other FNs working in her networks—obviously *they* weren't bulletproof, either.

Pinky had compromised them merely by showing these Weather Gable files to Bentley Brendel. And Bentley? He had signed the agents' death sentences by showing the files—at least one of 'em, maybe all—to Li Chimen.

I was so angry—furious with Pinky for being so fucking stupid, and with Bentley Brendel for being such a fucking traitor—that I had a hard time keeping myself under control. But maintaining control, friends, is what being a Warrior is all about. And so I channeled my anger, transmogrifying it into energy, and determination, and willpower—and I kept my eyes moving.

From reading the contents of the most accessible of the half-dozen or so White House memoranda (all tabbed top secret and each one addressed "TO: RADM P. Prescott III, FROM: BB"), I surmised that Pinky's most recent assignment had been to check out any possible incident that might have taken place recently in the South China Sea, which involved the United States Navy.

How did I surmise that? Because this is how the MIQ (which stands for Memo In Question, and pronounced MEEK) began:

> Pinky—Imperative you track all USN movements over the past fourteen days in two quadrants. The first is bordered by 105 and 110 degrees East Longitude, and 0

and 5 degrees South Latitude; the second is 122 to 124 degrees East Longitude, and 24 and 26 degrees North Latitude, and get results to me soonest.

I'm counting on you to deliver the goods, just like always. Go get 'em, tiger!

I had no idea what Pinky had been looking for in the second area of operations—the one just north of the Tropic of Cancer. But I knew the first one all too well. It is the quadrant that includes the Belitung Straits, which is where my very own SEAL Force Alpha had begun its infiltration route that resulted in the scuttling of the *Nantong Princess.* The sonofabitch was trying to track *me*—except he didn't know that critical infobit.

So, how had Pinky gone about it? Well, from da Turdlike chicken scratches on his note pad and the scrawled telephone numbers and area codes I could make out, he'd done it by calling every one of his Annapolis schoolmates stationed at PACFLT—PACific FLeet—and CINCPACFLT in Hawaii, and asking if they'd picked up any RUMINT about clandestine or covert activities in the South China Sea AO. He hadn't found out anything—and I am pleased to report that he is too stupid about these things to have bothered to check with any other military commands—like, for example, the Air Force—specifically, the Special Operations Command's 353rd Special Operations Group, First SpecOps Squadron, based at Kadena Air Base, Okinawa.

But he had of course used an open line when he'd called his pals—it said so on his phone log sheet. Which meant that every fucking Chinese, Japanese, Russian, Korean, and Australian intel squirrel with access to COMINT, SIGINT, or TECHINT[38] had listened to Pinky's request for information, and started their own snooping.

---

[38]COMmunications INTelligence, SIGnals INTelligence, and TECHnical INTelligence.

Obviously, Pinky's pals had produced for him, although they'd come up dry. There were half a dozen blue-tabbed (Confidential) transmissions from CINCPACFLT headquarters on his desk. I scrunched the chair closer, smiled over at Avenir, kept talking, and began to read as much as I could:

> No USN activities currently reported in any of the specified AOs.

read one.

> No OPLAN in effect for the specified AO during the time frame outlined.

read the second.

> SUBOPS reports USS *Scorpion,* operating outside specified AO, retrieved NAVSOC[39] unit commanded by Captain Richard (NMN) Marcinko, after unspecified training mission.

read the one just below it. I'd have loved to see the fourth, but I'd of had to shuffle the pages around, and I wasn't about to alert Avenir to my activities by being overt. The Chairman had wanted me to supply him with HUMINT about what was going on here at the NSC. And HUMINT he would get: the NSC, it seemed, was trying to spy on the Navy.

Okay—I see you out there. You're asking how I could do all that reading when the pages on the desk were upside down. Well, bub, reading upside down may be a rapidly disappearing art, but it is nonetheless a capability that is important to industrial spies, intelligence officers, journalists, and other assorted snoops—including *moi.*

But I didn't learn it in spy school, or at some black-arts seminar. I was taught how to read upside down and

[39]NAVal Special Operations Component forces.

backward some years ago by an old-time newspaper typesetter and proofreader named Neil Shine, who was in charge of printing up the St. Ladislaus of Hungary newsletter at my parish back in New Brunswick, New Joyzey, when he wasn't setting type for a couple of dozen other publications in the storefront print shop he ran in the neighborhood. See—in the days before computers, they set type in hot lead on Rube Goldberg machines called Linotypes. You read your page proofs in trays of solid lead letters that were cast by the Linotype, then set into rows of lead print. The words were set upside down and backward, so that when the molds formed from them were rolled through the press, everything came out right side up.

Anyway, as a teenager, I worked for Neil Shine for a while—I delivered packages, cleaned up the used lead, helped him remelt it so it could be cast again, and—ultimately—helped him proofread copy. It took him some time, but he managed to inculcate me in the mysteries of reading upside down and backward closely enough to catch typos, misspellings, and punctuation gaffes on the trays of type that lay haphazardly all over the place. It is another instance of learning something that you think has no significance as a kid, only to find that in your later life, it pays off—and pays off well.

Now I can go into an office and sit, talking to you, and all the while, be reading and committing to memory every fucking memo you have on your desk. It is an art that has saved my Slovak butt more than once. And now, perusing as I sipped my overcooked java, pinky extended from the undersize china cup's handle like a fucking society dame, I realized WTF: having been tasked with checking incidents in the South China Sea, and knowing that I had been in the neighborhood, Pinky had set about finding out WTF I had been doing in the same area he'd been tasked to research.

From what I could make out, he wasn't having much luck. They'd even tracked down the *Scorpion*'s CO—a radiogram from Captain Dave Brancato routed through the SUBOPS message center at Pearl Harbor reported where he'd picked me up. But, Dave's message continued, he had no idea where I'd come from, or what I'd been doing, except sitting out of gas and bobbing like a cork for half an hour. That, and we were so foul smelling that they'd had to hose us off before they took us below.

God bless the Chairman for insisting that we exfil as far as possible from where we sank the *Nantong Princess.* We'd been worried about the Chinese—but his planning had saved us from Pinky.

There was a message from CINCPACFLT which confirmed that he had put out a search for me when my presence had been requested by the head of the Japanese National Police's counterterrorism unit.

> Marcinko was located through office of CJCS. The request was routed through CNO. There was no prior contact by Pearl [Harbor] and his reasons for being in the AO described above are unknown.

CINCPACFLT added that his command had dispatched a chopper to retrieve me at such-and-such a position, and a plane to pick me up in Singapore and take me to Tokyo. End of story. And there was an E-mail from Admiral Gray, the base commander at Yokosuka, stating that he had no idea where I'd arrived from—that, in fact, I had not even had the courtesy to check in with him and report my presence on his hallowed territory.

Finally, a curt note from General Crocker's J-2 (Intelligence Staff) admin officer stated that Captain Richard NMN Marcinko had been temporarily assigned to the Intelligence Staff of the Office of the Chairman and that his duties were nobody's fucking business but the Chairman's, so piss off.

Basically, Pinky was drawing a blank so far as I was concerned. That was the good news. The bad news was contained in the smoothed-out but still obvious vertical crease on that Weather Gable folder. The first thing I'd have to do as soon as I got out of here was call Alixe Joseph and tell her that she—and her nets—had been blown to the opposition. No wonder she was losing people. Damn—she'd have to make arrangements to shut everything down quickly, before Li's people rolled them all up—if they hadn't already been.

My planning was interrupted by the intercom on Avenir's desk. It was Pinky, braying, "We are ready for Captain Marcinko now," and she could show me down. The look that flashed on Avenir's face as she listened to him caterwaul betrayed what she really thought of her boss. But she smiled professionally, rose, smoothed her dress from the lap out, in the way that matronly women of a certain generation so often do, then beckoned for me to follow her.

She led me back into the hallway. We marched back to the stairwell, went down one flight, turned left at the landing, then a quick right, and walked down a long, spotless corridor. Avenir stopped in front of a beautiful, well-preserved rock maple paneled door that must have been installed when the OEOB was known as the War Department. There was no sign adjacent to the doorjamb. Avenir reached under the collar of her blouse, retrieved a single key on a long steel chain, slid the chain over her head, put the key in the lock and turned it until the door opened, then dropped the chain and key back over her head.

She opened the door for me then stood back and indicated that I should go inside. "Please, go right on in, Captain," she said, the slightest tinge of loathing in her voice. "They don't like to be kept waiting."

I did as she requested. She gently closed the door behind me from the hallway side. I heard her footfalls tap-tap-tap decrescendo, fading into the distance.

So, this was to be a solo appearance. Well, that was fine with me—you know how I like the limelight, especially when I am filled with rage. I paused and looked around. I was in a small foyer that had an ornate plaster ceiling twelve feet in height. A nineteenth-century oil painting of the *Bonne Homme Richard* sat on the right-hand wall, mounted over a Chippendale side table; a huge photographic vista of the Washington region was hung opposite the oil. Next to the door towered an old-fashioned coat stand and umbrella rack. The rug on the floor was Aubusson, and antique. I'll tell you what: the effing secretary of the navy doesn't have as nice a foyer outside her office.

Straight ahead sat a pair of ornately carved wood doors that must have been nine feet high. I examined the frames. The big hinge pins indicated that the door opened outward, that is to say, in my direction. I took one doorknob with each hand and quietly tested 'em, rotating the doorknobs. They both worked just fine.

I took a deep breath, preparing my body, my mind, and my soul for deadly combat, exactly the same way I would if I'd been about to jump blind into hostile territory from thirty thousand feet. I was about to begin Show Time—and a flawless, deadly performance here was just as important as it had been aboard the *Nantong Princess.*

But here, I didn't need any cues written in Chinese characters on the hirsute palms of my hands. I didn't need suppressed weapons or assault knives strapped to my CQC vest. My anger at what was being done to the Nation was my motivation, and I'd brought the most deadly offensive weapon I know to this encounter—*moi.*

And, no—I didn't plan to take any prisoners here, either.

I twisted the polished handles, waited for the latches to clear, then swung the big doors outward toward me.

(*Enter the Rogue, upstage center.*)

I froze in the doorway for effect—and to focus on the threat. That was a mistake: I was almost overcome by the view. I looked, transfixed, across the huge, ornately furnished office, behind the antique leather-topped mahogany partners desk, to the five eight-foot-high-by-three-feet-wide windows, beyond which the North Portico of White House and its grounds lay in well-manicured splendor. To my left was an Empire-style sofa, covered in red, green, and blue vertical striped upholstery. The sofa was flanked by two leather club chairs, and the grouping was completed by a Queen Anne coffee table. Arrayed behind the desk were the flags of the United States of America, and the deep blue, gold-fringed standard bearing the presidential seal. Some hideaway office, huh?

I refocused my attention. Pinky the Turd was sitting at attention in the club chair facing the windows, twisted around like a corkscrew, looking wonderfully, delightfully (to me, at least) ill at ease. Behind him, sitting regally at the partner's desk, wedged tightly—even uncomfortably—in the high-backed, Supergrade, black leather and mahogany judge's chair because of his girth, was the S_3FA, aka Mister Five-by-Five, aka Bentley Brendel. He recognized me and my French braid at once from the Hunan Number One. His eyes went wide, then as quickly as he could counterreact, he fought back his emotions and neutralized his expression. But not before I saw what he'd done. Yeah—I'd caught him in bad tradecraft just the way Li Chimen had caught me.

And his attempt to conceal passed me the same sort of unintentional message I'd given Li. You see, there was no reason for him to hide the fact that, by happenstance, we'd run across each other in a restaurant. Except, of course, if he had something to hide. Like, for example, the folder he'd passed to Li Chimen.

His response noted and filed away, I finished my scan. Standing to my right and just behind Bentley's chair was the same baby-faced security boy who'd picked him up at the Hunan Number One yesterday. Kid Armani was wearing another seventeen-hundred-dollar suit—this one an Oxford gray with pinstripes. His White House pass had a big *V* on it—which told me he wasn't a Fed, but a rent-a-cop. That meant he wasn't packing heat—or any other weapons, either, because (being a visitor) he'd had to go through the same metal detectors I had. That information, too, was noted and filed.

So much for the tableau bit. Time to go to work—after all, lives were at stake. I stepped through the doors, swinging them closed as I did so, and peered over toward Pinky.

I am pleased to report that he looked dreadful. Since Pinky never works out, his uniforms have always hung loose on his wimpy, skimpy frame. At the White House, the uniform of the day is civvies. And as bad as Pinky looks in uniform, he looks worse in a suit. First of all, the sonofabitch is cheap, so he tends to buy his clothes at Filene's, or at one of those rubber-stamp factory outlet stores that line Interstate 95 between Washington and the North Carolina border. Second, since Pinky seldom wears civvies, his suits don't fit very well either.

As the Turd scrambled to his feet, I saw that he was even more badly attired than usual. He may have been wearing the sort of blue pinstripes favored by NSC staffers, but since the cheap suit was more polyester than wool, it hung on him like a goddam plastic shower curtain. You could actually see where the trousers hanger had left rude indentations in the cuffs of his pants. The jacket sleeves were so long they hung way beyond his hairless knuckles. There was a full half inch of air between his off-off-white shirt collar and the skin of his scrawny neck. His tie looked like a reject from one of the gauntlet of pushcart vendors on Connecticut Avenue who sell the clip-ons favored by bartenders and off-duty Metro cops. Believe me, it wasn't a very pretty picture—something that brought newfound joy to my Roguish heart.

Oh, and there was more: his hair, which tends to cowlick when he's tense, was standing straight up in a full Dagwood. A second cowlick, on the far right side of his head, protruded obliquely, as if he'd stuck his finger in an electric socket. That told me he was under severe stress. And from the awkward, stilted, downright uncomfortable look of things, all the stress was being administered by Bentley Brendel himself.

The fat man leveraged himself out of the big chair and came around the huge desk, waddling in my direction, his huge thighs chafing, his left hand rubbing the sparse hair on his balding head as he moved. He was working in his shirtsleeves—a well-worn white Oxford button-down shirt to be precise. He wore the same gravy-stained tie he'd sported at Hunan Number One. His light gray pinstriped trousers, which had been cut to give him four or five inches of spare room at the waist, whose baggy cuffs hung three inches above the shoelaces on his well-worn, down-at-the-heels brown cap-toes, were held up by a pair of cheap red elastic clip-on suspenders.

The whole combination resulted in a bizarre, absurd, even ludicrously cartoonish Homer Simpson look. In fact, compared to Bentley Brendel, Pinky the Turd's sorry sartorial résumé looked like Beau fucking Brummel's.

But I'll tell you what: this Bentley had the silver-cloud voice of a fucking Rolls-Royce salesman. It was a voice you just knew made *money;* the same come-and-get-it-while-you-can timbre as fucking game show announcers, auction house shills, or fly-by-night tent preachers. "Bentley Brendel, special consultant to the president for National Security Affairs and Diplomacy," he oozed.

Then his demeanor—and the timbre of his voice—changed. The smoothness disappeared, replaced by nasty, ugly, aggressive reverberations. "And it disturbs me that I've been hearing an awful lot of troubling things about *you,* lately, *Dick,"* he snorted, extending his trotter vaguely in my direction.

Chapter 12

HE CAME TOWARD ME MOVING QUICKLY FOR A MAN OF HIS weight. No way was I going to let him take the offensive. I closed the distance between us and took his hand in a firm—and by that I mean *f-i-r-m*—read viselike—grip. His eyes betrayed the considerable pain I was causing him, but otherwise he covered himself pretty well. Since I wasn't especially glad to meet him, I said, "Dick Marcinko—I've read some of your op-ed pieces and I disagree with 'em." Then I let go.

Kid Armani stood, his arms crossed like a fucking statue, missing the whole thing. I glanced over at Pinky. He knew me—and what I'm capable of. From the look on his face I thought he was going to piss on himself.

Brendel snatched his wounded hand away, turned, and scooted back to his desk, where he dropped into his high-backed chair and peered imperiously at me. "Take a seat, *Dick,*" he said, his voice completely drained of any pretext of courtesy. "Admiral Prescott and I have a series of questions for you that will have to be answered."

Oh, did he indeed? "Thanks, but I'll stand, *Bent*ley."

Now, you're probably asking why I started our relationship off the way I did, instead of playing along, then sandbagging him later. Two reasons. The first is because I didn't have any goddam time to waste—I wanted to get back to the Manor and alert Alixe Joseph about the leak to Li. Second, it would have done me no good at all to delay the inevitable. Not tactically; not strategically—and not plot-wise, either. Remember, I was here to rattle his teacup, not look good.

Besides, tadpole, always remember the words of that great Chinese tactician General T'ai Li'ang, who wrote in 374 B.C., *"Always treat the enemy as if he is the enemy, because the enemy will invariably treat you that way."*

Makes sense, doesn't it. Take this current situation. Bentley Brendel knows exactly who I am—or at least he thinks he does. He's already talked to Pinky about me. And if he is as good as I think he is, he's realized that Pinky is a schmuck, and he's done some outside research as well. Which means he already knows that I don't much care for guys like him.

So to ensure that I, not he, controlled the situation, I proceeded by following the Rogue's way of doing business—dominating the situation from the get-go. The pain I'd just caused him defined our relationship—which was antagonistic. It told him that *Ich versucht den Lebensnerv zu treffen*—which is how I go for the jugular in Deutschland.

General Li'ang doesn't make sense to me, Master Marcinkosan. What about Sun Tzu? Sun Tzu wrote that deception is the key to victory. And General Li Chung, the eighth-century war master who told his disciples, "Feint left, move right; feint right, move left. Hint advance, then maneuver rearward; hint retreat—then advance and decimate."

What's your point, tadpole? Sun Tzu doesn't dismiss direct action—*if* the timing is right. Neither does Li Chung. Besides, General Li'ang isn't ruling out deception as a course of action—he is simply telling you that you should always treat an enemy like an enemy, whether you deceive him or not. And besides, in this particular case, as I've just explained, deception wouldn't help at all.

Why? Because I'd studied this guy. Despite the slovenly appearance, he was a diplomat—and an effective one, judging from everything I'd read. And what did that mean? If experience was any teacher (and it is a great teacher, believe me), it meant that he was a talented negotiator. And diplomats have found that when you are negotiating, you are not taking action—*versucht den Lebensnerv zu treffen*—you're responding to the latest set of positions.

But I wasn't here to negotiate. I was here to make him act precipitously—to go against everything he had ever been taught and learned during his long diplomatic career. To do that, I had to stun the sonofabitch—rock him harder than he'd ever been rocked before. And I wasn't going to do it by playing nicey-nicey. So I put my war face on. It was time to do battle with this fat fuck and roll him like an ugly dumpling.

Brendel looked over at me. "As you will, *Dick.*" He gestured somewhere in Pinky's general direction, as if to cue him. "Admiral Prescott . . ."

Pinky cleared his throat. I could see his Adam's apple bobbing up and down. "There's a p-problem," he began cautiously.

"Well, t-tell me about it—maybe I can help," I said, his obvious discomfort making me smile.

Pinky's face flushed. "D-Dammit, Dick, don't *do* that." He fought to regain whatever composure he thought he might have had. "Look, Dick," he began, struggling to keep his stutter under control, "we are currently in the midst of some very delicate negotiations with the C-C-Chinese, and—"

Brendel's short pudgy fingers slapped the surface of his desk. "This administration's dealings with the Chinese, whatever they may be, are not within Captain Marcinko's purview, Admiral." The fat man glared in my direction. "There have been some disturbing military-originated developments in the past few weeks; developments that are not in America's interest." Brendel turned to face me directly. "I know that you work directly for the Chairman of the Joint Chiefs of Staff," he said. "And in that capacity, you must know that the Chairman has opposed the administration's China policy whenever and wherever he has had the opportunity to do so."

I said nothing.

Brendel's tone sharpened. "The Chairman is wrong. He may be a good soldier, but he is no politician. And it is politics, not military science, that must govern our relationship with China."

Now, my friends, I knew, and you should, too, that this S_3FA is JPW—just plain wrong. Without a tough military policy, potential adversaries like China will run roughshod over us. Remember Colonel Art "Bull" Simon's advice about nationhood. But I wasn't about to say anything—yet. I was still here to learn what this broad-beamed butt-fuck was all about.

Bentley's silver tones rolled on. As they did, something on the credenza behind the S_3FA caught my eye. It was an ornately designed antique silver-hinged double-picture frame. On one side, sat the full-frame image of Major General Zhu Linfan—Li Chimen's boss. It was warmly inscribed *To Bentley Brendel, who has done so much to bring our nations together.* On the other side, sat a sheet of velum. Printed on its ivory surface in elaborate calligraphy, were the following lines:

All warfare is deception.
So when strong, display weakness;
When weak, feign strength.
If your target is nearby,
Make it appear to be distant.
Only thus will you achieve your objectives.

I knew those lines. They were from Sun Tzu's seminal book on strategy, *The Art of War*—and they were the same words of advice I had taken to heart many times over the course of my career.

I shifted my focus back to the five-by-five. "That is why," Brendel was saying, his voice growing louder and more insistent, "we want to know where you have been, and what you have been doing on the Chairman's behalf."

"Now, why would you want to know that?" I asked rhetorically.

"That is not for you to know," he answered imperiously. "This administration does not answer to the military—it is the other way around."

"Do you speak for the administration?"

He smiled self-contentedly. "I do."

It was time for the old Rogue wake-up call. My eyes locked on the S_3FA's. "I'd like to see you produce that in writing, you fat fuck."

Guess who blinked—and it wasn't me. "I do not have to show you anything," Bentley Brendel finally said, his teeth clenched.

"Oh, it's not that you won't show me anything—it's that you *can't* show me anything." I pointed toward the walls of the S_3FA's office. "You know what's not hanging here?" I asked rhetorically. Bentley Brendel gave me a blank look. So did Pinky.

"There is no fucking presidential commission on the wall," I said, directing my comment to Pinky, watching his eyes grow wide.

Now, it is a fact that each and every assistant and special assistant to the president has on his/her/its wall a large sheet of velum, on which, in fancy calligraphy, is printed said appointee's presidential commission. That's the document that makes the appointee official.

But Bentley didn't have a presidential commission. All he had was his fucking fancy art, and his impressive collection of photographs, and the goddamn quote from Sun Tzu.

I jerked my thumb toward the wall. "Bentley," I said, "you don't fucking have a piece of paper. You're here, but you're off the books." I paused. "You don't even have a fucking security clearance."

Now that remark surprised the hell out of Pinky. Because Pinky da Turd, *le grand zero*[40] that he is, knows how the system works. Pinky understands there must always be a piece of paper to show exactly where one fits within the chain of command. Pinky knows that *sans* a security clearance, there can be no access to sensitive materials. Indeed, if anyone understands the concepts of chain of command, and written, stamped, and approved security clearances, to the bureaucratic cross of a *t* and the pen-pushing dot of an *i*, it is Pinckney Prescott III, Rear Admiral (Upper Half), United States Navy, staff officer, bureaucrat, and professional apparatchik.

"A word to the wise, Pinky," I said. "If this special consultant can't produce a current TS/SCI, I wouldn't be showing him anything more than the daily newspaper clips—because if it gets out that you've been sharing DOD's operational secrets with him—and believe me, Pinky, I'm gonna look into that matter very, very closely—I don't see any promotions in your future."

Judging from the panicked look and white pallor on Pinky's face, I'd just put him between ye olde rock and ye olde harde place. Not my problem. He'd fucked things up. Now it was payback time.

From the comic book, my-top-is-about-to-blow look that was roiling across Bentley Brendel's kisser, I'd knocked that motherfucker back a pace or two, too. Time for another jolt.

I tossed my thumb in Brendel's direction. "Hey, Pinky, guess who he had lunch with yesterday." I didn't wait for an answer. "The top Chinese spook here in Washington. Name: Li Chimen. Rep: nasty. Maybe you should go back to your office and check out the name with your pals at DIA."

Pinky peered over at me with a blank expression on his

---

[40]That's how they say zee beeg asshole in *française*.

face. I guess I hadn't been clear enough, or specific enough, or maybe I was talking too fast. Whatever the case, he wasn't picking up his cues. Well—I'd get back to him in a minute. I looked over at Brendel. "You clear your meeting with Li with Buzzard's Point,[41] *Bent*ley?"

I didn't wait for the S_3FA to respond. "And, by the way, what was in the orange-tab folder you gave Li?"

Brendel looked at me with murder in his eyes. "I gave him no such thing," he said evenly.

Itsy-bitsy problem here, folks. First, I'd seen the evidence—the folder in Li's pocket, and the creased folder on Pinky's desk. Second, no matter how controlled his tone or modulated his voice, his eyes—murder look and all—gave him away. Recent psychological experiments at two universities and the National Institute of Health here in Washington have proved that micromomentary shifts in eye focus—that's a fancy way of saying REMs, or rapid eye movements—often indicate mendacity. Let me put that in SEAL technical language: liars are prone to being shifty-eyed assholes. And this asshole was definitely shifty-eyed. He was giving off lots of REMs as his pupils darted quickly side to side, and up and down.

Since I was in an EEO frame of mind—which means as you know that I will treat everyone just like shit—I looked back toward Pinky and let him have a second salvo, too: a barrage that would get his scrawny behind out of the office so I could have a few words in private with this corrupt, overweight asshole.

I faced Pinky and spoke slowly. "If I were you I'd go back to your office and start checking documents," I said. "See whether or not one of those orange-tab folders—the very one you gave old Bentley here yesterday morning—is creased. Because that's what I saw in Li Chimen's pocket." I

[41]Buzzard's Point is the location of the FBI's Washington Field Office and the headquarters for all FBI counterintelligence activities in the nation's capital.

watched as every fucking bit of color drained from the Turd's face. "Pinky, I think you have been passing TS/SCI information to someone who doesn't have a clearance—something that might make your pal over at DIA, Mister H, awfully nervous."

"Holy c-c-c-cow," Pinky stuttered. One thing about the Turd is that you don't have to tell him something bad twice *if* you are speaking slowly, and *if* your lips are moving distinctly, and *if* his whole fucking career is on the line.

The Turd lurched to his feet, wrenched himself toward the double doors with all the grace of a Krameresque pirouette, struggled with the knobs until he finally got the doors open, and careened out of Brendel's office, a panicked, primal squeal coming from deep in his throat.

I walked to the doors and closed them. That left Bentley, Kid Armani, and me. So far as I was concerned, it was about to be serious *choinik-hocking* time.

I crossed back to the desk, put my palms on the smooth leather, taking just enough time to read the number on his private line and commit it to memory, and leaned toward Brendel. "You're dirty," I said.

Brendel flicked a finger in my direction. Kid Armani came around the big chair toward me, his iron-pumping arms coming up into play. I didn't wait—my right arm snapped out and I caught the youngster in a viselike grip, my right thumb and forefinger crushing his throat and larynx, my arm lifting him half an inch off the floor. *Surprise,* asshole—don't fuck with SEALs.

I drew him close. His eyes were bugging. His face was turning blue. "Sonny," I stage-whispered, "it is time for you to take a hike." I squeezed just a tad tighter. "Got that?"

His head moved up/down, up/down.

"Good." I released my grip just in time to see Bentley reaching for the phone. I swatted his pudgy hand away and pulled the receiver cord out. The S_3FA started to protest. I reached across the desk and smacked him across the face. "You're garbage," I said as he howled in protest.

He put a fat hand up to his cheek. "You'll pay for that."

He pushed his big chair backward to stay beyond my reach. I started to move toward him when I sensed something behind me.

It was Kid Armani, trying to get back into it. He'd heard me, but he just hadn't listened. I tell ya—kids these days, they just don't listen. I feinted left with my eyes—his eyes followed. I jigged right with my body—his body followed. That's when I caught him *slam* with a sucker punch that lifted him six inches off the floor. He came down in a heap and didn't move.

I turned back to Bentley. "Worse, you're a liar." I came around the desk, crowded him up against the window and hit him again, across the face, half a dozen times. Not hard enough to hurt him—but more than hard enough to provoke him. Go ahead—check your psychology books: you will see that folks like Bentley dislike physicality of most any sort—especially when they are the ones getting pummeled.

"This is how I deal with liars, Bentley," I said as I struck him. He tried to wriggle free, but he couldn't because I'd trapped his legs between my own. He struggled, but he couldn't do a fucking thing—I towered above him, slapping his face at will with both my open palms.

Finally, I stopped. I scowled down at him. He cringed and hid behind his hands. I saw fresh circles of sweat as he ducked behind raised arms to ward me off in case I resumed my assault. I stepped back and sat on the edge of his desk.

"This is Chairman Crocker's doing," he wheezed. "You work for him—I know that. He is trying to scuttle our China policy. He sent you here." Brendel looked up at me with undisguised hatred. "I will see both of you in hell for what you've done," he said.

I returned the gaze. "Chairman Crocker didn't send me, *Bent*ley. I came here on my own. But I'm more than willing to bet that you get sent to hell a long time before we do."

I rose, turned my back, and moved upstage, stepping deliberately over Kid Armani's inert form, walking slow as a fucking bullfighter who's just scored a clean kill. I gave

Bentley my back as I strode toward the double doors. I opened them, then turned slowly toward the seething lobbyist. "You'd better get a lot more careful, *Bent*ley," I said as I eased the doors of his hideaway closed, "because I know you're a fucking traitor and I'm gonna be watching you very, very closely. Until, that is, I decide to kill you."

Now that I have a moment as I'm making my way back to Pinky's office, let me explain what has just happened. Many years ago, when Roy Boehm, the godfather of all SEALs, was in Vietnam, he was forbidden by the can't-cunt four-striper to whom he ostensibly reported to engage the enemy in battle. "You are here to advise, and to train, and to observe," he was told. "So advise, train, and observe—but under no circumstances are you to engage the enemy."

If you believe that Roy would ever pass up an opportunity to engage the enemy, I have some oceanfront property to sell you. It is located on the beach just outside Mesa, Arizona.

So, how did Roy solve his problem? He simply took his advisees so far out into the boondocks that they ended up way behind Viet Cong lines. Then he arrayed them up in an ambush position. Then he had one of his men make enough noise to attract the enemy's attention. At which point the VC attacked, giving Roy the opportunity to strike back hard and kill 'em. Moreover, when he got back to headquarters, he could truthfully report that while, yes, he had engaged the enemy, he had done so only because his men had been "overrun" by Mister Victor Charlie, and they'd had to fight their way out.

Well, I was about to use the same tactic here. But first, I had Pinky da Turd to deal with.

Pinky was down on his hands and knees as I came through the door of his office, his ass wriggling like a dog's as he searched frantically for something on the frayed rug under his desk. Avenir was nowhere to be seen.

"Lose something, Pinky?"

He reacted to the sound of my voice, and startled, jumped up and cracked his head on the desk hard enough to send him back onto the floor.

He came back up cautiously, his eyes wide. His mouth was a mask of fear. His voice crescendoed into a panicked moan. *"Dick—I didn't know.* I didn't know. He's the one I've been reporting to. He has a big office. The NSC adviser's always calling him—*I didn't know."*

The sorry fact of the matter is that he probably didn't know. Pinky is not an evil man—evil in the sense that he would betray his country. Unprincipled? Sure. Machiavellian? Of course. Unscrupulous? You bet. Scheming and manipulative? *Bien sur.* But not in the traitorous way. All Pinky ever thinks about is getting himself another star. That's probably what got him into trouble in the first place. Bentley had played da Turd for the fool he is. He'd probably been too busy kissing Bentley Brendel's huge ass to check the guy out.

But I wasn't about to let him off the hook. "Who the fuck is 'H'?"

"Who?" Pinky pulled himself to his feet and dropped into the chair behind his desk.

"Mister *H*—the asshole who sent you these." I tapped the Weather Gable files with my index finger.

"I can't tell you, Dick—he'd absolutely kill me. It was done as a personal favor."

I advanced on the desk, put both hands on it, and leaned into Pinky's quivering face. "You'd better worry more about me killing you than him," I said. "You've already compromised a lot of work—not to mention a whole bunch of lives—and if you don't get with the goddamn program and help me with the motherfucking damage control, I'm gonna disassemble you piece by fucking piece."

He looked up at me and saw I was deadly serious. Then he buried his face in his hands and gave up the name. Just as I'd thought, it was one of his fucking Annapolis mafia. Don't they learn anything there besides how to cheat on tests, assault female middies, and deal drugs?

Sure—they're taught it's all right to leak the nation's secrets—under certain conditions. Condition One is to make sure the person to whom you're leaking is a fellow member of the Naval Academy ring-knocker's club. There is no Condition Two.

I stood over Pinky like an impatient headmaster while he laboriously typed out a memo to the file, spilling his guts, single-spaced, onto a thick page of White House memorandum velum. Yes—that's *typed.* I had him use a typewriter because I didn't want to leave any electronic fingerprints where Bentley Brendel—or anyone else—could get their hands on 'em. It took him three tries—and too much fucking time—to get the words just the way I wanted 'em composed. I shredded the drafts. Then I photocopied the finished page and had him sign and date each copy. Then I slipped them both into my suitcoat pocket.

The sight of his career disappearing into my 46 long really panicked him. "But what about *me,"* Pinky whined.

I looked down at the sorry sonofabitch for whom I wasn't sorry at all. "'What about you?' *Fuck* you, Pinky. You're dog meat."

Chapter 13

It was snowing lightly when I got back to the Manor, just after 1300 hours. There was a message from Alixe Joseph to check my computer for an encrypted file. "I hope the information helps," her voice told me. "Use the same numbers that you gave me, Dick. Talk to you soon. Sayonara."

I turned the machine on, decrypted the file, and read. First, Alixe had identified the pictures I'd sent her. Seems that I'd killed two of Beijing's top electronic warfare specialists—a pair of one-star generals, both American educated. I scratched behind my beard. What the hell they'd been doing on the *Nantong Princess* I had no idea. I read on. The situation, Alixe wrote, was getting hotter in Japan, Korea, Indonesia, Singapore, and the Philippines. *"Dick—if I had to bet, I'd say all these areas are feints to keep us off balance."*

Her point of view made sense to me—remember if you will the Sun Tzu quote in Bentley's office. In fact, so far as the Chinese are concerned, deception is a central element of warfare. General Chun Li is the tactician who wrote three books of verse about deception more than two thousand years ago. Sun Tzu's earliest (and mostly forgotten) work, *The First Principle of Victory,* is a short polemic on the subject of deceit.

I assembled the troops and put us on a war footing. I called the Chairman's office to give Jo a sit-rep to pass on. It wasn't all going to be good news, either. On the one hand, the memo I'd wrung out of Pinky gave us the leverage we'd need to take my findings to SECDEF—and, I hoped, get Bentley Brendel's big, broad, bad butt tossed out of the White House and straight into a Justice Department investigation. On the other hand, everything was still pretty circumstantial, and I had the unpleasant intuition that SECDEF wasn't going to act on it until we'd made our case airtight.

Whatever I believed was moot: the Chairman was out of town for the afternoon, giving at West Point what the morning papers had described as "a major policy address about America's military readiness." I asked to be patched through. But the factotum who answered the phone in the Chairman's office refused. I wasn't on General Crocker's list, he said.

"Then please connect me to Joanne Montgomery."

A pause. Then: "I am sorry, sir, but you are not on Miss Montgomery's list, either."

Of course I wasn't. When we'd made our OPSEC plan, we'd kept me off to keep me stealthy. I dialed Joanne's pager number. I waited five, six, seven minutes. There was no response. Frustrated, I sent Boomerang, Nod, and the Rodent into town along with three of the Big Brother components. They'd tune in to Bentley's offices at the OEOB and the Georgetown town house, and see what they could learn, now that he'd been properly spooked. I dispatched Duck Foot, Half Pint, and Pick to Rosslyn with some more of our electronic goodies to get a handle on Li Chimen's activities. Then I used the scrambler phone module to get on the horn to Tokyo and contact Alixe Joseph at the secure receiver at her apartment.

No luck there, either. I switched phones and dialed her pager number, then Joanne's again. When I didn't hear back from either one in fifteen minutes I called AMEMB[42] Tokyo. The switchboard operator rang Alixe's office. There was no answer. I left a message for her to call me as soon as possible.

I was a little concerned. Belay that. I was very concerned. So I woke Tosho up and (we were on one of the Manor's regular—i.e., nonsecure—lines), filled him in as best I could *in re* the last six hours' developments. It didn't take much until he started connecting the right dots—he is, after all, a perceptive asshole with a Notre Dame degree. He told me he'd do what he could, starting immediately.

I was about to dial the Chairman's office again when Duck Foot called. He started to tell me something, then the signal faded, dissolved into static, and the phone went dead. I hung up.

Thirty seconds later the phone rang again and I plucked the receiver from its cradle. "Yo?"

"Li's on his way to Dulles," Duck Foot reported. "He jumped a cab outside his office. Traveling light—just a carry-on and a briefcase. We're six cars behind him on the Dulles access road. What do you want us to do?"

"Stay on his tail," I told him. "Let me know what he does—where he goes."

"Roger-roger, Skipper."

Six minutes later the phone rang again.

"Yo, Boss Dude—it be Boomerang."

"Dica."

"The S_3FA's grabbed the shuttle to New York. Should we go with him?"

"Negative." I wanted everybody to stay close by for the time being. "Just make sure he gets on the plane."

"Ten-four."

I dialed Joanne's pager number again. This time, she

---

[42]AMerican EMBassy.

called back within ninety seconds. "Sorry about the delay. I got your pages but I couldn't get to a phone."

"I have to see the Chairman—now."

"We're still at West Point. A reception at the superintendent's quarters."

"As soon as you get back, then."

"Hold on, Dick." She put her hand over the receiver. I heard muffled words. Then Jo came back on line. "The Chairman says that we should follow the procedure he set up for us."

There are times for procedure—and there are times to ACT. This was one of the latter. "Jo—I gotta see him."

The tone of my voice must have convinced her. She cupped her hand over the mouthpiece. Ten seconds later she said, "Meet us at Andrews at sixteen thirty. We can talk in the car on the drive to the Chairman's residence."

"I'm on my way."

1725. I was waiting on the tarmac as the Chairman's Gulfstream taxied to a halt in the thickening snow. I'd trucked in with Gator, who'd left more than an hour earlier for Fort Meyer, which is where the Chairman's residence is located. He'd pick me up there. While I waited, I called the Manor. There was a message from Duck Foot. Li had caught an ANA flight to Tokyo. He'd done some checking and discovered it connected with a flight to Beijing.

The hatch opened, the stairs dropped, and General Crocker's sinewy, wide-receiver's frame was framed by the craft's narrow doorway. He paused, his eyes searching until he found me. Then he called "Dick" and waved me over.

I jogged toward the plane, reached out and shook his hand as he bounded down the stairs. "Glad to see you, General." He looked tired. Exhausted, in fact. "How was the flight?"

"How was the flight? The flight was goddamn miserable, was how the flight was," he growled, as if he was talking to himself. "Turbulence all the way—I'm lucky there was no coffee. If they'd had any coffee, I'd be wearing it. Then goddamn C-SPAN carried my speech live, so I guess I'm in hot water with the White House again. Probably a whole damn passel of reporters already calling my house asking when I'm going to resign. Then we had a damn weather hold that kept us circling for"—he checked the big stainless steel chronometer on his left wrist—"almost an hour. And tomorrow I have to leave for that"—he caught himself—"damn meeting across the pond—plus the trip to NATO South they tacked onto it—at zero dark hundred, although why the hell they—" He stopped muttering to himself in midcomplaint and refocused his attention. "Sorry to have kept *you* waiting, Dick."

The Chairman's big midnight blue Cadillac limo slid to a gentle halt just in front of us, and the driver, whose blue blazer's breast pocket bore the Chairman's seal, came around and opened the right rear door. I started to stand aside, but General Crocker put his hand on my shoulder and pushed me in first. I took the left side of the big, wide seat. Then he stood back so Joanne could clamber inside.

She shrugged. "It's okay—I'll ride shotgun." She opened the right-hand door and settled herself in. Finally, the Chairman pulled himself through the door, dropped into the right rear, took a sheaf of document folders from the driver, and switched on the reading light as the door closed.

He pulled on a pair of half-framed reading glasses and scanned the folders quickly, shuffling them as he perused. By the time we cleared the main gate at Andrews, he'd stuffed the reading glasses back in his shirt pocket, and the folders were sitting next to his right thigh.

Joanne shifted in her seat belt, swiveling so that her arms came over the seatback and she could hear better. General Crocker looked over at me with an expression that could only be called intense, pointed his thumb and index finger in my direction in his trademark Colt .45 gesture, and said, "Okay, we're all yours. What's so urgent?"

I fired for effect from the very first round. Between the drive and the flight delay, I'd had plenty of time to put my thoughts together, and I wasn't about to waste the Chairman's time. But before I tell you what I told him, there is one ancillary infobit you should recall.

What is it, you ask?

Well, as Alixe Joseph explained earlier—and you *were* paying rapt attention, weren't you?—you will remember that Chinese intel ops are traditionally very broad, but not very deep. By that, I mean, they may send five thousand students overseas for intelligence-gathering purposes. Each student has only a small bit of responsibility. Kind of like using eight thousand people to dig a twelve-mile trench. Each digger shovels only the ground in front of him or her. That kind of way of getting the job done is prevalent in totalitarian societies, which resemble a pyramid: an excess of cannon fodder at the bottom, and a few well-fed, rich, self-important key players at the top.

So, while the Chinese may employ hundreds of thousands of agents on the info-digging front, the collation of those many spadefuls of information—and their refinement from rough intel ore to golden intelligence—takes place back in Beijing.

In fact, because of the way the Chinese system works, nothing ever takes place that hasn't been dictated by Beijing Central—Er Bu headquarters—a seven-story building that sits opposite a park on Huangsi Road, about five kliks from Tiananmen Square.

Big deal, you say. Knowing how the Chinese intel system operates is all very well and good—but it doesn't help because you still don't know when Beijing is going to act.

Not so. Remember that framed quotation in Bentley Brendel's hideaway office? I do—and I believed that Zhu Linfan did, too. And those lines of Sun Tzu's were the key to this tactical problem.

Let's look at the big picture. Let's examine the Chinese game plan.

- *Item:* there were all those Chinese-sponsored political donations during the last presidential campaign.
- *Item:* there was all that pressure on American trade—

all those former secretaries of state, whose law firms, consulting businesses, and corporations did billions of dollars' worth of business in China.

- *Item:* there was the misguided political belief—amplified by such agents of influence as Bentley Brendel—that by currying favor with the Chinese we could lure them away from any alliance with the Russkies.

That was the overt stuff. Then there was the covert.

- *Item:* the use of students, journalists, visitors, and others as intelligence operatives.
- *Item:* the leaks of classified materials provided by Bentley Brendel and perhaps others in positions of power.
- *Item:* there were all those tango cells that Alixe Joseph had identified—cells of disaffected former military types, prepositioned from Pusan to Jakarta. And what did each of those tango-enriched locations have in common?

The common factor was Li Chimen, Er Bu's Number One Son, who'd visited each and every one of the target areas in the short period before the well-known *merde* hit the well-known *ventillateur.* Li's most recent assignment had been Washington—and now he'd skipped. My guess was that he was returning to the Er Bu nest in Beijing. And if that proved to be true, then the Chinese were about to act.

"Okay," Chairman Crocker said, "let's say for the moment that I accept your reasoning. The question is where." He turned toward me. "If CIA knows anything, it certainly isn't saying anything." His face took on an expression of distaste. "They froze us out a long time ago. Now, I sent all your materials to DIA—but they haven't been able to make sense of 'em, at least not yet. So, what do you have to say, Dick?"

The answer, I told him, lay in Sun Tzu's words of wisdom; the words I'd seen in Bentley Brendel's office:

If your target is nearby,
Make it appear to be distant.
Only thus will you achieve your objectives.

I was convinced that the Chinese were engaged in an artful feinting spell right now; a ruse that would conceal their true objective. What that objective was, I hadn't yet figured out. But I believed it wasn't Japan, Korea, Indonesia, or Singapore that we had to worry about. That was where the activity was going on—so, we had to look elsewhere.

What targets of opportunity did that leave? It left Russia. Unlikely. Despite the new alliance between Moscow and Beijing, Russia hadn't pulled its troops off the Manchurian border—more than a million men were still poised on China's border. Moreover, even given the current state of Ivan unrest, the Russkies were still capable of inflicting massive damage all across China if war broke out. They had the nukes, the air force, and the troops. So far as I was concerned, that ruled out the Russkies.

There was Vietnam. The Paracel Islands, near which there may be a huge untapped oil field, are claimed by Vietnam. But the Chinese already controlled the Paracels. That ruled out a Chinese move against Vietnam. Why fix something that ain't broke?

Which left only one viable target so far as I was concerned: Taiwan.

If you will go back with me to the *Nantong Princess,* you will recall that the missiles that surprised me were not the ones that the Paks had bought. They were the ground-launched Cruise missiles with conventional warheads. At the time, I had put 'em out of my mind. I should not have.

I took a map of the South China Sea out of my briefcase. On it, I had circled Taipei as ground zero, and drawn a radius of five hundred miles around the nationalist capital. "I think the Chinese are going to hit Taiwan from somewhere in that area, and I think they're going to do it soon," I told the Chairman.

"But they could hit Taiwan from the mainland easily enough," General Crocker said. "Why go to the trouble?"

"Because it gives them deniability," I insisted. "Or at least it did before . . ." I flicked my eyes toward the back of the driver's head. "Y'know—when I went overseas recently."

"Deniability?"

"That's why they had the suitcases—the ones I brought back." I wanted to say more, but I wasn't about to here or now. I'd finish my monologue in the den of General Crocker's house, where I could speak without being overheard. I knew that Big Brother would have given the Chinese the capability of mounting a stealth attack against Taiwan.

General Crocker nodded, rubbed at his face, and peered out into the darkness as the big car steered gently through light traffic, around the cloverleaf leading to the I-395 expressway, which in turn would take us across the Fourteenth Street Bridge and the GW parkway. "Look—without going any further, I think you have enough circumstantial stuff for me to brief SECDEF. And I'll order CID to take a real hard look at that Li Chimen guy and Bentley Brendel, too."

"Too late, General," I said. "Remember: Li skipped. My guys were following him. He caught an ANA direct to Tokyo at 1700. Used an official Chinese government passport when he went through the gate, too." I paused. "And Bentley Brendel caught a shuttle to New York City. I don't know what he's up to, but I'd bet he was about to take the well-known powder."

The Chairman interrupted. "So, you think—"

"I think that they're going to do whatever they're going to do pretty soon now. I think—"

"Dick—" Joanne interrupted.

I looked up and saw a concerned expression on her face. "What's up, Jo?"

"Look, maybe I'm being paranoid, but I think we've picked up a tail."

I leaned forward. "Why?"

"Same pair of headlights have been following us all the way from the main gate at Andrews."

The Chairman frowned. "Are you sure? It's snowing like hell."

"They're halogens," Joanne said. "They have this bluish tint. They stand out—and besides, the traffic's been real light."

I swiveled and peered out the rear window. "Beemer—about a hundred fifty yards back?"

Joanne nodded. "Yup."

I was instinctively troubled that it was a Beemer following us, but for the life of me I couldn't figure out why. No matter—I reached forward and tapped the driver's shoulder. "What's your name, soldier?"

"Crawford, sir. First Sergeant Billy Crawford—they call me Rommel."

"Rommel?"

"'Cause I drive this here tank of a car like the freakin' Afrika Corps barreling through the freakin' Sahara Desert, sir."

"You E&E qualified, Rommel?"

"Roger that, sir."

I reached over and secured General Crocker's seat belt. He started to protest, but I was having none of it. One of the things you don't want is bodies flying all around the interior of a car while you're attempting to evade and/or escape a nasty situation.

I tapped the driver's shoulder again. "Rommel—are there any arms aboard?"

"Negatory, sir—we're not allowed to draw weapons these days."

Of course they're not. In these politically correct times, military personnel spend more time in sensitivity training than they do on the range. Guards at the entrances to most military installations are not allowed to carry loaded magazines in their weapons. And God forbid that the Chairman's Army driver stows a 9mm or a shotgun in the car. Oh, heaven forfend. Weapons are a manifestation of the sort of incipiently aggressive behavior that might be misunderstood by the panty-waist touchie-feelie generation X-ers over in the White House as aggressive, tough, warlike . . . perhaps even *military,* and therefore completely unacceptable.

The Chairman leaned forward. "Maybe you should call Washington Metro and let them handle this."

Joanne gave her boss an Are you out of your mind? look. "No way—I'm gonna call the Park Police." She plucked the mobile phone from its cradle and dialed, then turned toward the Chairman to explain. "Metro's response time can be as long as half an hour—we never call on 'em. Besides, we're already on the approach to the Fourteenth Street Bridge. Park Police has jurisdiction from here until we get inside Fort Meyer, General."

I rapped the back of First Sergeant Billy Crawford's headrest with my knuckles. "Just keep it nice and steady so we don't spook anybody. But Rommel, you keep your fucking eyes open, okay."

He looked up into the rearview mirror so he could see my face and nodded energetically. "Ja*wohl*—yes, sir, Captain."

The concern on Joanne's face lifted momentarily. "I've got the op center on line." She identified herself as a DS agent and gave her ID code, then quickly described our situation, route, speed, ID'd the car she thought was trailing us, then rang off. Quickly, she dialed a second number. "I'd better let DOD police know what's up, too."

As she dialed, I tapped her shoulder. "You carrying?"

She patted the purse at her feet. That made two pistols in the car.

The big Caddie slowed briefly as the driver started to make his turn onto the northbound George Washington Parkway. "Yo, Sergeant—"

"Sir?"

"Go south, then backtrack onto one-ten. Let's see if this guy really is following us."

Rommel accelerated and veered onto the southbound exit, then hung a quick right that took us back the way we'd come. But instead of crossing the bridge again, he swung sharply onto a narrow access road that would take us alongside the Pentagon's north parking lot, north toward Memorial Bridge, swing west just past the Iwo Jima Memorial, and head straight into the back gate of Fort Meyer.

The Beemer stayed with us through the first turn, then it dropped way back. I strained to see through the rear window, but I'd lost sight of it. There was only the curtain of white, and the darkness beyond the glow of our own head and tail lights.

I like to know where my enemy is. "Slow down, Rommel. Let's see if he shows up."

Crawford braked, and I unbuckled my seatbelt, turned and peered through the rear window glass. Nada. Then, as we came out of the turn, I could pick out the familiar bluish lights above and behind us on the cloverleaf. "They dropped back."

Joanne tossed me a quizzical look. "Strange."

"Maybe not." I pointed at the Pentagon, all lit up and looking beautiful in the snow. "Maybe because we were getting too close to home, now."

She swiveled and faced front again, scanning the road ahead of us. "I hope so."

Rommel came out of the tight turn, and—carefully, because there were obvious ice patches on this little stretch of road—checked his six, then eased onto the single, narrow northbound lane. On one side of us lay the huge Pentagon parking lot. On our right, the shoulder dropped away precipitously. Just below the snow-covered gravel, the land descended into a shallow gully through which ran a small, winding creek that emptied into the Potomac somewhere north of National Airport.

The fucking van came from nowhere. I mean *nowhere.* It

was a dark van anyway, and it was running without any lights, and it must have been idling in the Pentagon lot access road, because that's the only direction we weren't paying attention to.

He closed in a flash and hit the Caddie in the left-hand rear quarter panel—*whaaaam!* From the impact he must have been doing about fifty. I knew what he was doing. He was trying to ram us over the shoulder and knock us into the creek.

Sergeant Billy Crawford aka Rommel *did* have E&E training. Instead of panicking—jamming on his brakes—he accelerated. He fishtailed like crazy for about a hundred yards as he applied steady pressure to the gas pedal. Then the big Caddie found its footing, and Rommel muscled his way into the opposite lane, our metal grating against their metal.

The van man didn't like that at all. The sonofabitch backed off, then came at us again—*whaaaam*—into the rear bumper. The impact threw me across the width of the Caddie, bounced me over General Crocker, and smashed me into the door header face first, opening a nasty cut at the corner of my right eye.

I fought my way back, seeing fuzzy stars as I tried to shift my body across the wide seat. As I scrambled, my peripheral vision—bleary though it was—picked up movement behind us. Y'know, when things like this happen, they always seem to happen in slo-motion. First, I sensed something happening behind the van's windshield. Then, as my brain synapses started to work properly, I saw the shotgun barrel come over the van's dashboard.

I screamed "Motherfucking gun—" yanked the Chairman out of his seat belt, rolled him onto the floor, and threw my body over his just as the van window exploded outward, the Caddie's rear window exploded inward, and we were all showered with hot glass fragments.

"Oh, shit goddam it—" Rommel Crawford screamed, his left hand grabbing at the back of his neck, "I'm hit, I'm hit—"

"I've got the wheel, I've got the wheel." That was Joanne's voice, loud and clear, from wherever she was hunkered in the front seat.

I looked up long enough to see a curtain of blood running down the back of Rommel's neck. Then the van smashed the bumper again. The impact was hard enough to make my teeth hurt.

We were losing speed. You can't lose speed—but if you do, you'd better make the tango stand off. I raised myself off the floor enough to clear my P-7 from its holster, stuck my nose up, and looked back over the trunk.

The van was accelerating again—six yards and closing. I popped up. Saw two faces in the jagged frame that had been the windshield—round-faced, fucking targets with knit caps and ballistic glasses. Van Man One and Van Man Two. I tried like hell to find my fucking front sight and squeezed off two two-round bursts—ba-*bang*, ba-*bang*—and nearly deafened myself in the process. It may be busy here, but let me impart to you a morsel of SpecWar trivia anyway: shooting a pistol in an enclosed space is hard on the old Rogue eardrums.

Hard—but necessary, because even though I hadn't killed the sonsofbitches my shooting forced them to drop back a few precious yards. I snuck a peek and saw Van Man One hunch over the wheel and start coming up on us again. I rolled onto the seat to give myself a more stable platform and, kneeling, double-tapped twice more.

No, I *didn't* hit them this time, either.

Look, despite what you have seen in all those Hollywood movies and TV shows, it is hard to shoot from one moving vehicle into another with any precision, especially when you're in pursuit, or being pursued. There's lots of motion, there's lots of vibration, and it is nigh on impossible to get a decent sight picture. Not to mention the fact that the folks in the other vehicle are also shooting at you. All of the above tends to make the process difficult. It is even more difficult if you are armed with only a pistol. Indeed, that's why shotguns and submachine guns are the most effective weapons during car chases—with them, you can spray and pray, and if you're lucky, some of your shots will find a goddam target.

I rolled out of sight and reloaded. There was one round in the pipe, eight in the new mag, and eight in the mag sitting in my windbreaker pocket.

That's seventeen rounds, folks. Not enough for this kind of exercise.

Another fucking shotgun round came through what was left of our rear window. I heard Joanne scream, "God-dammit!"

I had to put these motherfuckers on the defensive. "Sergeant—can you drive okay?"

Rommel's voice was real shaky, but the kid came through: "Yeah—yeah. Sure I can."

"Put the goddam pedal to the metal, son—get us fifty feet of clearance, then brake like hell—make 'em hit us dead center—our rear bumper."

I pounded the back of the seat with my fist. "Joanne—you stay with the Chairman. No matter what, you stay with him."

She was obviously speaking through clenched teeth. "Got it—"

I could tell from the way he was moving under my legs that General Crocker didn't like being out of the action. But he had no choice. He was the fucking protectee—and things were gonna stay that way.

"Rommel—okay—hit it *now.* Get the fucking lead out!"

I raised myself high enough to shoot twice. We'd progressed past the Pentagon now and were coming up fast on the Memorial Bridge turnoff. Crawford must have stood on the fucking gas pedal because the big Caddie reared up on its hind legs and took off.

Van man followed—gaining on us, gaining on us, gaining on us, gaining on us. I screamed, "NOW—hit the fucking brakes NOW!"

God bless all sergeants. The goddam limo swerved,

fishtailed, then straightened out—just as the fucking van closed on us.

It was Van Man who panicked. He must have been going sixty-five when he hit his brakes—and one of the fucking icy spots on the road at the same time. The goddam van swerved, whipped around, caught itself on the low pavement edge, flipped twice, and rolled into the gully on its roof.

"Brake, brake, brake." I was reaching for the door handle even before Rommel managed to get the big car stopped. I yanked and pushed. The fucking thing was stuck. I yanked and pushed harder. Nothing.

"Shit—" I rolled my shoulder into the door. Nothing moved.

Well, fuck it. The goddam car was going to need body work anyway. I shoved the P-7 into my belt, lay on my back, raised my legs, and kicked the fucking window out. Then I pushed myself through—ripping something or other on a shard of glass stuck in the frame.

I slammed my fist twice on the roof of the Caddie. "Rommel—get this fucking car the fuck outta here—I'll catch up with you." The Chairman would be safe back at Fort Meyer, in a protective cocoon of DOD police and MPs.

I waited for Rommel to move. As soon as he'd started to pull away and the big car disappeared into the snowfall, I retrieved my pistol from my waistband and started across two lanes of snow-covered pavement toward the shoulder where the van had disappeared. I wanted those motherfuckers. I wanted 'em bad.

So bad that I didn't see the asshole in the Jeep Cherokee who, determined to Keep Going No Matter What, nearly smacked my Slovak butt into next week as he drove past, eyes fixed straight ahead in an "I don't wanna know what that mean-looking individual with the French braid and the gun is doing on the parkway" expression, at a steady forty.

I crested the shoulder. I was facing the Potomac, which lay about three hundred yards beyond and below the roadway. The van had skidded from my right to my left, hit the low curb, then—from the look of the ragged track it had gouged out of the earth—it had flipped and rolled, the momentum carrying it into a grove of saplings that bordered the stream some sixty yards from where I stood.

The fucking thing was smoking. Two of the wheels were still turning. The impact had popped the passenger side door open. I saw no movement inside.

I started over the crest toward it, hit an icy patch in the darkness, and tumbled ass over teakettle, pitching and bouncing like a fucking pachinko ball as I caromed off trees, and rocks, and who-knows-what-the-fuck-else. I came to rest upside down about fifteen feet from the van. I straightened my legs and rolled over onto hands and knees, checking myself from the ankles up for bruised and-maybe-even-broken bones. The quick verdict: I was sore as hell—and I'd probably get a lot sorer before too long—but there was nothing broken.

In the kind of panicked flash you get when you wake yourself up from a nightmare all sweaty, I suddenly realized that I'd been checking myself with both hands. You want to know what the significance of that was?

Okay—if I was using both hands, then where the fuck was my pistol? It had been knocked out of my hand when I'd tripped. I felt the ground around me. Nothing.

Onto hands and knees again, feverish fingers probing the snow all around me. Where the hell was the goddam weapon. This is why they put lanyard loops on pistols such as the P-7, which are intended for military and police use. It is a no-no to lose your weapon. But lanyards are not your typical SEAL equipment—although I sure wished I had one right now. But wishing wasn't getting the job done, so I kept crawling, moving in rough circles, retracing the random path I'd followed when I'd ass-over-teakettled from the road.

I searched about ten yards of hillside when I realized I was wasting everybody's fucking time—especially mine. I regrouped and patted myself down to see what I had on me. Not much. The folding knife I habitually hook on my trouser pocket had disappeared. I'd left the collapsible baton back at the Manor. I wasn't carrying my favorite sap—a flat, black leather job filled with six ounces of bird shot. The only blip on my radar was the Gerber Multi-Plier that sat on my belt adjacent to what was left of my right kidney.

I retrieved it. The Multi-Plier is a handy little pocket tool whose hollow steel handles encase a pliers, a file, two screwdrivers, a church key and—more to the point here, two blades—a traditional pocketknife, and a blunt-tipped serrated blade. I selected the serrated blade, then dropped the pliers, locking the handles so the fucking thing wouldn't collapse and cut me off at the knuckles.

Gingerly, now, I worked my way up to the van in a careful approach. Came up from the rear as stealthy as a crafty fucking dacoit. Put my ear to the back door panel. Heard nothing—no breathing, no moans, no scratching.

So I crept forward in the dark, moving slowly toward the wide-open passenger door. Tried to catch signs of movement by using the rearview mirror, which had been twisted grotesquely by the impact.

But it was impossible to see anything inside the van's black interior from my angle. Maybe they'd both been tossed into the rear by the impact and the ensuing rocking-and-rolling. But maybe *ils font le mort*—which is how they play possum in le Frog-speak, and were waiting to gig me before I could gig them.

No time to take chances. I backed off so I could circle wide, then come in from the opposite side. No sense walking into a trap.

I crept to my left, and worked my way along a narrow line of saplings to the bank of the creek, dropped down, broke through the ice crust, and sloshed into the knee-deep water.

Was it cold? You bet. But so what. I didn't have to like it—I just fucking had to do it. Besides, the white heat of my rage over these two assholes who'd nearly killed the Chairman was more than enough to equalize things. Yard by yard I worked my way back, moving southward—downstream, toward the crushed, smoking vehicle.

Thirty feet from it I saw something in the darkness. Cautiously, I moved closer. Pulled myself out of the creek and up onto the snowy bank. Ten feet away lay one of the van men. He—what was left of him—was sprawled facedown on the ground, arms and legs akimbo. I drew closer to make sure he was dead.

Was he ever. His skull had cracked like the well-known melon from impaction against a large and sharp rock. His blood and brains formed a nasty Rorschach in the snow.

I rolled him over and patted him down for ID—or anything else I could get my hands on. He wasn't carrying a fucking thing. No wallet. No keys. No ID. No labels in his clothes. Nada. *Klum. Blee.*[43] I checked him for a watch. He wasn't wearing one. But he did have a tattoo on the back of his hand: a dragon intertwined with an anchor. The artwork looked vaguely familiar but my woozy brain couldn't place it.

I dropped his arm when I heard sirens in the distance. That was a fucking welcome sound. I could use the cavalry right now to help sort things out. I started back, toward the van. I hadn't gotten two yards when the hair on the back of my neck stood up. I stopped. I held my breath. And then, that same basic, instinctive, visceral intuition that has kept me alive all these years grabbed me by the goddam figurative lapels and tossed my hirsute ass three feet to the right—*now.*

I tucked and rolled—just as a fucking nasty ninja in a knit cap came hurtling past me, the long tire iron in his hand whistling past my Roguish right ear.

He was moving like a fucking bull in a ring—it was all

---

[43] *Klum* is nada in Hebrew. *Blee* means *sans* in Hebrew. Avi Ben Gal taught me those words.

charge; no cunning, just raw, naked, kinetic energy. The sonofabitch wanted me *dead.*

Yeah, well get in line, chum—so do a lot of others. *Ole!* My roll took me out of reach, and Van Man's momentum carried him past me, right toward the creek. I tried to play picador and stick him with the blade as his muscular back slammed past me. I missed. But I wasn't about to wait for him to charge again. I went after the motherfucker before he could turn and whip that big piece of steel anywhere near me.

I caught him still on the fly—hit him with my shoulder and smacked him hard into a big tree. He turned, grunted, wriggled out of my grasp, and brought the tire iron around, its angled knob striking at my head. I deflected it with my right forearm—I saw the damn thing coming and reacted in time to blunt the main force of his swing.

I said the main force. But not the whole force.

Let's use another sports metaphor. Van Man had tried for a home run—but all he got was a bunt.

However, I don't think I have to tell you that even a bunt hurts like hell when it connects with the radius bone. There's no padding anywhere to cushion the blow. I saw dots and stars in front of my eyes. I went numb from my shoulder to my cuticles.

But that wasn't the bad news. The bad news was that the shock of tire iron on forearm made me drop my Multi-Plier into the creek.

Oh, shit. Oh, doom on Dickie. Do not pass "GO." Do not collect the two hundred fucking dollars. Take Mister Murphy by the hand and proceed directly back to square one.

My friends, I must tell you truth and say you sooth: I *hate* fucking square one.

So, I wrenched myself free and grabbed at the hand holding the tire iron with both of my huge paws before he could swing it again. He tried to knee me in the balls, but he missed—I'd already worked my way inside and he couldn't muster his leg properly. Now that I had both hands on the tire iron, I used it for leverage. Remember, I'm the fella who presses 450 pounds, 155 times, every morning rain, snow, sleet, or sunshine, at Rogue Manor's outdoor weight pile.

This felt like the 152nd fucking rep. Every part of my body burned. But slowly, inexorably, I worked the shaft up, and around, adjacent to his left temple. His eyes shifted when he saw what I was doing, and there was a look of panic as he realized that he couldn't stop me. I popped him twice—a quick & dirty *wham-wham*—upside the head.

Now *he* was the motherfucker seeing dots and stars.

But Van Man was a wiry little asshole. He clawed at my face, smacked the meaty part of his palm into my nose—geezus, that *smarted*—then grabbed for the iron so he could return the nasty favor I'd just done him.

This was going on too long. I wrapped him up; took the tire iron and raised it high—out of his grasp—and while he struggled and flailed for it, I brought it down—hard—between his shoulders, directly at the spot where his neck joined his spine.

That stunned him just long enough for me to careen us both to the right, and tumble us down into the creek.

Now here is some more sooth. I am a SEAL. I can survive very nicely, thank you very much, in the cold and the wet. He wasn't—and couldn't.

We spun into the water. Yes it was scrotum-shriveling frigid. But I was white hot enough to stay fucking warm and toasty while I hoped he'd freeze up—both literally and figuratively. I popped him with the tire iron, which loosened his grasp on the fucking thing. Then I took him in a headlock and rolled us both underwater.

Oh, he didn't like that. But instead of struggling like most folks—which is exactly what I wanted him to do because he'd lose his air and die—he worked at me methodically, his fists and legs punching in that rapid Spetsnaz-like syncopation of two hundred blows a minute, fought his way to the surface, caught a quick breath, came back with more energy than I thought he had left, wound up, and slammed me hard in the solar plexus with his elbow.

That took my breath away—and knocked us both back up onto the scrubby, frozen bank.

Now he grabbed the initiative—swung around, made a spear of his hand, and chopped at my throat with it. It was a glancing blow, but it caught my Adam's apple and it hurt like hell. Then he rolled on top of me and squeezed at my throat with both his hands. I came up between his arms, broke the hold, and swatted him across the ears.

I must tell you that it did very little to improve my situation. Van Man was better then I'd anticipated. We grappled for advantage—neither of us was able to get it, either. Then he hit me with a shoulder like I was a tackling dummy. But not in the direction I'd have expected: the motherfucker was trying to slide me back down, down, down, into the cold creek.

Geezus—*he was trying to get me underwater.*

My left hand still held the tire iron. I used it like a riding crop and hit him on the outside of his leg—right at the knee joint.

That brought him up short. He whispered a sweet nothing in my ear—while trying to remove it from my head with his teeth.

But it gave me an opening. I brought the iron up, around, and over the top of him. His hands tried for it once more—wrestling and twisting desperately. He got one hand on it, but I wasn't about to give up control. Then I held him close, and, screaming, we rolled off the bank.

I grabbed a breath just as we dropped under the water's surface again. In the blackness and the cold I was able to wrest the tire iron out of his grasp, and work it into my right hand. We surfaced. I pushed off—my legs kicked free of the slippery sonofabitch—and I thrust the tire iron backward, swinging it like a club, catching him in the mouth.

He never stopped. Just spat teeth and came at me again, his face a bloody, determined mask. I never give up ground—or water—so I lunged at him—cutting the distance between us; making it impossible for him to take the offensive. He drew back—feinted to his left. But I was watching his eyes, not just his body, and I didn't buy it—which meant that instead of swatting where he wasn't, I was able to whip the tire iron around and smack his lower right arm with all my strength. I heard the brittle *snap* that told me I'd shattered both of the bones halfway between elbow and wrist.

Oh, *that* brought him up short. But it didn't stop him. He charged again, his wounded right arm hanging useless while he flailed toward my face with his left claw. I put the pointed end of the tire iron between us like a bayonet. Then, as he drew within half a yard, I brought my arm back, and body-punching like a goddam steam engine piston at full throttle, I screamed, *"Yaaaaah!"* and impaled the nasty little motherfucker on the tire iron's wide, chisel point.

He screamed, too—although it came out like a fucking gurgle—as I worked the steel shaft into his body cavity about two inches below his sternum, and lifted him up, up, up. Now his ass belonged to *me*. My war face was the last thing this asshole would ever see.

Oh, but Van Man was a wiry little fuck, and he tried to pull the shaft out of his body, but he had only one good arm, and besides, I outweighed him by eighty or ninety pounds. I held him away from me, thrust him back, and down, and pitched him into the creek. He started to come back. I gigged him with the point of the tire iron again—then used every ounce of my energy to pin him to the bottom. I stood on him, pressing on the tire iron's head, holding him firmly underwater until all the life went out of him and he stopped struggling.

My whole body was shaking. I sank to my knees, threw up what seemed like a gallon of creek water, reached down and grabbed Van Man's corpse, struggled toward the bank in a desperate half-crawl, pulled myself up as far as I could manage, and collapsed facedown, dry-heaving my guts into the snow. I could feel myself getting hypothermic—losing control of my body; slipping into a drowsiness that could kill me if I didn't keep moving. So I kept going. I rolled Van Man over and began to search him. Like his partner, he carried no ID, no labels, no nothing—except the same fucking tattoo on the back of his hand.

As the hypothermia washed over me and I began really losing it, I had the kind of epiphany reserved for the dying: I realized where I'd seen the goddam dragon and anchor tattoos before. They were on the *zhongdui* corpses when we'd taken down the *Nantong Princess*. Then everything went black.

I don't have any idea how long I lay there, but the next time I remember anything I know I heard sirens. I cracked my eyes open. Suddenly I was aware that there were lots of flashing lights in the neighborhood. But I was still too fucking tired to pay any real notice.

Then a bunch of hands grabbed at me roughly and rolled me over. Lights shone in my face. I was patted down and handcuffed, then dragged by my arms up to the roadway and pushed into the rear of a DOD police car. I wasn't about to protest—they had no idea who was a good guy and who wasn't, and I'd have done the same thing in their place.

Indeed, they pulled me out, took the handcuffs off, and wrapped me in a blanket after they got a good look at my ID card. I gave the cops as accurate a sit-rep as I could, adding that I'd lost my duty pistol, and that when they found it, could they send it over to the Chairman's office. Then I asked to be driven to Fort Meyer—Quarters Six. The Chairman's residence. The OIC made a quick phone call, nodded in the affirmative to a grizzled sergeant, and I was handed off to a DOD security officer.

He, a two-striper in dark foul weather gear, helped me clamber into his vehicle. He climbed in, started the car, and turned the heater fan up full blast. I sat next to him, shivering. He flipped the interior lights on and with professional detachment peered into my face. "Geezus," he pronounced, "what fucking meat grinder have you been through?"

I gave him a playfully Roguish look. "Y'know, I could tell you," I said through chattering teeth, "but then I'd have to kill you, too."

Two and two began to equal four pretty quickly. Joanne called her contact at Park Police and learned that a unit had stopped a Beemer belonging to Xinhua in the vicinity of the Pentagon six minutes after she'd placed her call to them. Two occupants. No reason to hold 'em—and they were let loose. The wrecked van had been stolen earlier in the day—about one and a half hours after my meeting with Bentley Brendel. The deceased occupants were Chinese—Chinese *sans* IDs. It would take forever to check 'em out—*if* they could even been checked out at all. Except: I knew that they, like Li, were *zhongdui.*

That was why Van Man had tried to pull me underwater. He'd been as comfortable there as I. He just hadn't been as good at his job as I'd been at mine.

I asked General Crocker if there was any way we could check Bentley Brendel's phone logs without making waves. The Chairman gave me an upturned thumb—and called in a big chit from an old colleague. He secure-dialed the colonel who ran WHCA (the White House Communications Agency) and had him check the phone logs. There had been a call from the Old Executive Office Building to Xinhua's Arlington offices three minutes after I'd left Bentley Brendel's hideaway suite. It had lasted two and a half minutes.

But Li Chimen was on his way to Tokyo—and even Tosho couldn't even shake him down when he arrived because he was traveling on an official passport and had to be treated as if he was a diplomat. Even so, I put in a call to Tosho. I wanted to see whether he'd found Alixe Joseph—and I wanted him to have a heads-up *in re* the matter of Li Chimen. I tried him without any luck at Kunika headquarters. When I dialed his home, the phone rang twenty times and I hung up.

Okay—the next question was spelled *B-e-n-t-l-e-y*. Joanne called Ty Weaver, her Secret Service agent pal, and gave him a heads-up about the five-by-five. He put her on hold while he called the FBI to secure Bentley's office, then came back on line and said he'd get on the horn to a fella named Forbes, an old contact of his at the Customs Service in New York.

Six minutes after Ty Weaver hung up, Special Agent in Charge Forbes was on the phone. Joanne sit-repped him in simple declarative sentences, and as soon as she was finished, Forbes put the word out through his airline network to locate one fugitive S_3FA yclept Bentley Brendel. It didn't take him long to discover that the SIQ—that's S_3FA in question—had caught an Air France flight from New York to Paris. Smart move on his part: we couldn't call the flight back because it was sovereign and French once it had left the runway at Kennedy.

I put Tony Merc on the case. Merc's friends at AMEMB[44] in the City of Light traced Brendel to a connecting flight out of De Gaulle Two. Destination: Beijing. Bentley was on the run, too. I guess I *had* rattled his fucking teacup.

I sit-repped everything I knew to Chairman Crocker. He rubbed at his twenty-two hundred shadow with a broad hand, and nodded. "That fits," he said cryptically, then disappeared into his study to use his private comms unit and brief SECDEF.

On the domestic front, there was good news and bad news. Let's deal with the upside first. It turned out that Rommel Crawford hadn't been hurt too severely. He'd absorbed a glass frag in the neck, and he'd be sore as hell because they'd cut and stitched him to get the fucking glass shard out. But he'd be okay. Not-so-good news was that Joanne had taken a trio of shotgun pellets in the upper arm. The medic's diagnosis: wound trauma and minor nerve

[44]Remember, that's the acronym for AMerican EMBassy.

damage. She wouldn't be lifting any weights, shooting any pistols one-handed, or even working on a computer much for the next month or so. But she didn't complain—and she insisted on staying on the job.

Meanwhile, it was important to keep the lid on while my men and I did as much digging as we could. The Chairman's limo had disappeared long before any TV camera crews showed up. So, after that short and secure conversation with SECDEF, the Chairman's office put out a short press release stating he'd been involved in a minor, weather-related traffic accident on the way home from Andrews. He was unscathed, the release said, and would maintain his schedule.

Which meant leaving for NATO at 0930 the next morning, with a private stopover in Rome—the schedule said he was paying a courtesy call on the ambassador, but in point of fact Rome was where he'd meet with Viktor Grinkov. Which brings me to the bad news, which I received at 2335, sitting in an overstuffed club chair in the formal living room of Quarters Six.[45]

I was wearing a borrowed set of coveralls and a pair of half-a-size-small, two-widths-too-narrow boondockers, and well into my third Doctor Bombay Sapphire on the rocks, which meant that I was almost warm and able to feel my fingertips, when General Crocker interrupted my recuperation. "Dick—I want you and your men with me when I leave tomorrow for my meeting with Viktor Grinkov. There is a lot at stake here—more than you might understand right now. Frankly, I don't trust him. He's damn mad about the fifty million we took,[46] and I'd feel a lot safer if you and your people were watching my six for me."

---

[45]Quarters Six, a huge red brick house that sits on Grant Drive in the center of Fort Meyer, is the official residence of the Chairman of the Joint Chiefs of Staff.

[46]I've mentioned this sluiced money before. It belongs to the Russian Minister of the Interior, Viktor Grinkov. I took it from him. To see how I did that, you'll have to read *Rogue Warrior: Designation Gold,* which has recently been released in paperback.

I had a hundred reasons why that wasn't a good idea. Like the fact that I was making palpable progress here in Washington—and that if I should be going anyplace it should be to Tokyo, to work with Tosho and Alixe Joseph on cracking the Chinese operation that was, I was convinced, about to break wide open somewhere near Taiwan.

But none of my hundred reasons outranked General Crocker's four stars. He even put his "request" to me in words I understand perfectly: "Dick—you do not have to like this assignment. You just have to do it."

And I *was* willing to do it, not like it—until Tony Mercaldi called for the second time in two hours.

I took his call in the Chairman's study. I hoped he had more news on Bentley Brendel. But he didn't. He was edgy. Nervous. He hemmed and he hawed until finally I broke in. "Merc—just spill it, okay? WTF—Did mister five-by-five disappear altogether?"

"Dick—" He stopped cold again. There was an uncomfortable, tormented quality to this performance, which was very unlike Merc. I did not like the way things were going at all.

"Merc?"

"Yeah?"

"You're covering something. I've known you long enough to know." I paused. "C'mon—spill."

I heard him swallow and breathe in. "Alixe Joseph is dead—she was shot to death six hours ago."

I was standing when he said it. I sat down—hard. No time for feeling. I'd grieve later, in private. Right now, I wanted the facts so I could run with 'em—and obliterate the motherfuckers who'd murdered Alixe. "How, Merc. How?"

"Like I said, shot. It was staged to look like a Yakuza hit, but we know better."

"Where?"

"Right outside her apartment. She had the keys in her hand. She was hit from close range in the back of the head. Three shots from a twenty-two, from what I've been told." He took another deep breath. "It's still pretty sketchy."

"Who?" I wanted to know. I wanted to go find 'em.

Merc sighed. "We're still working on that—assembling the reports."

That's the thing about fucking intel squirrels. They are always assembling, or distilling, or refining, or processing. But they're never fucking *acting*. Well, a DIA officer had been killed—and it was time to go to war. "Fuck, Merc, get off your ass." I was pissed. I was angry. I wanted somebody's fucking head on a pike. "Goddammit, Tony—she was vulnerable. Her nets were being rolled up by Li Chimen's goons. She told me that—and she told it to you, too. But from what I can see you guys did nothing to protect her."

"Hey—come off it, Dick." Merc's tone was vehement. "That's a load of bullshit. First of all, she knew the risks. She was a professional—like you, and like me. Second, we beefed up her security as much as was feasible—given her mission. But she was a goddam HUMINT officer—not some computer analyst. HUMINT officers can't work from inside a friggin' cocoon. She had to move. Get around—*operate.* You know that as well as I do. But we did what we could."

He stopped long enough to catch his breath. "Look—Dick, we did some things. I'm not about to tell you what on an open line. But we are making progress on this. Do me a favor. Cool down. Call me back later—on equipment we can talk on—and I'll fill you in. I promise." The phone went dead in my hand.

I wandered back into the living room. General Crocker took one look at my face and shifted gears. "Dick, what's wrong?" The tone of his voice was evidence of the concern he was feeling.

I told him what was wrong—and why my men and I had to go to Tokyo, not Rome. There was a murder to solve. There were bad guys to eliminate. There was—

That's as far as I got. The general was having none of it. His face grew red. He rose and pointed me toward a chair. I sat. He stood over me. There would be no goddam

UNODIR operations, he said—none whatsoever. We were scheduled to wheels-up for Rome at 0930. Sharp. And my blanking men and I would blanking be there. No blankety-blanking excuses. I would coordinate with the motherblanking RSO[47] in Rome. His name was Olshaker. Olshaker was up to blankety-blanking speed about the meeting, although he had no blanking idea what it was all about.

General Crocker's language was like a slap across the face. I'd never heard him talk like that before. On he went, sounding like a grizzled DI barking at a wet-behind-the-balls recruit. No bleeper-blanking missed plane. None of my blankity-blank-blank bleeper-blanking Rogue blanking behavior. This was a goddam command blanking performance, he growled—and *he* was the blanking one in bleeper-blanking *command*.

You do not argue with generals. Not when they're talking like that. I saluted, and gave him an "aye-aye, sir." But I must tell you that my heart wasn't in it.

---

[47]Regional Security Officer.

Chapter 14

ROME WAS COLD AND WET WHEN WE TOUCHED DOWN AT *zero zero e un quarto*—which is 0 dark hundred in anybody's language. Most flights arrive at Rome's big international airport at Fiumicino and take the autostrada directly into La Bella Roma. For better security—always keep the bad guys guessing—we changed the flight plan over Genoa, notified AMEMB Rome by secure comms, and flew into the smaller airport at Ciampino, sixteen miles southwest of the city.

Despite the weather, the hour, and the last-minute shift of plan, the American ambassador, the DCM, and the embassy's chief military attaché were all waiting like pensioners at the bottom of the rolling stairway as the plane's hatch was popped open. It was proper protocol to Welcome The Chairman, and they were going to follow protocol no matter what the hour—or the weather. I peeked through a window and saw that each principal had his own soaking-wet, pinstripe-suited FS[48] factotum holding a huge umbrella to

[48]Foreign Service.

keep said principal's consequential self dry. I tell you, when you live your life as a junior-grade, still-wet-behind-the-demarche diplomat, it ain't just a job, friends—it's a fucking adventure.

While the Chairman strode out the front door and played the PE role—that stands for proper emissary—I dropped out of a rear hatch directly into a puddle and squished my way toward the five embassy limos parked on the tarmac.

As I strolled over, a tall, thin prematurely gray dude in a double-breasted 44 extra long with a dark microfiber raincoat thrown over his shoulders in zee Continental style, pulled himself out of the shotgun seat in the first Caddie. He hunched his shoulders against the insistent drizzle, ambled in front of the hood, looked me up, looked me down, then smiled and extended his arm. "You must be the Dick Marcinko look-alike they promised would be traveling with the Chairman. I'm Olshaker, the RSO."

"*Ciao,* Olshaker, *molto piacere*—nice to meet you." I took his hand and shook it. "What's the drill?"

He pointed toward the last three cars in line. "Those are yours. Serviced 'em yesterday in our own shop, and they haven't been out of our sight since, so I don't think there are any bombs aboard. They've got partial armor—reinforced windows and door panels, but nothing underneath. I'll show you where the panels are, so if you have to shoot through the doors you can do it without the rounds coming back on you. You've got two sets of radios per car. One of them's a dual-channel, it goes car-to-car, and direct to the embassy ops center. Plus, there's a cellular."

"*Va bene.*" I wasn't about to say anything, but I'd brought two sets of radios with me, too—and those were the ones we'd be using. There's an old sailor's creed that goes, Never piss into the wind, never eat at a place called Mom's, and never, never, never use another man's comms—unless you want the sonofabitch to listen in to what you are saying.

But you had to admit, he was thorough, was Olshaker the

RSO. I put on a grateful face. "I can work with that. Drivers?"

"Yup," Olshaker said, dryly. "Three. One for each car." He cracked the hint of a smile. "And even though I know you Navy guys like to do your own driving, I'm gonna saddle you with my DS jockeys, because unless you're all named Tuzzolino or LaBrusciano, and they speaka the Italian with a Romano accent, I figure we know the city better than you do—especially if you have to haul some real heavy ass at high speeds through these narrow damn streets."

Well, that made sense, too—I didn't want any FN drivers handling the Chairman's car, and I knew that DS—that's shorthand for the State Department's Bureau of Diplomatic Security—runs its personnel through a twice yearly defensive driving course. *"Benissimo,* Olshaker—terrific."

He pointed his long jaw toward the aircraft, where my guys were offloading. "You need any help with your stuff?"

And let him see exactly what I was carrying? No fucking way. "Hell, no—I've got seven horny youngsters who've been cooped up for the last nine and a half hours with nothing to do but clean weapons and sharpen knives. They need to burn off some excess energy or they're gonna kill something right here."

Olshaker nodded. "Well—if there's anything else you need . . ."

"There any pussy handy?"

"Not close enough to do either of us any good." He'd never even blinked. I liked this asshole.

"Then I'd like to get sit-repped."

He rubbed his face. "Not a whole lot to say. Russkies came in yesterday—delegation of three: Grinkov and two military types. Probably special forces from the way they were built and moved—all wearing civvies. They flew in on Alitalia, so they're obviously trying to travel in mufti."

So Viktor was traveling light. Only two bodyguards—probably former Spetsnaz Alpha Unit types who currently worked for the Ministry of the Interior in OMON, the

MOI's SWAT team. Well, I'd come up against 'em recently, and they were second-rate. "That's manageable."

"Not really." Olshaker's face went grim. "They were followed by a second security team—of forty. We're talking goons, man, real goons." He noted the concern on my face. "They came in on Aeroflot, nine hours after Grinkov—as if we wouldn't notice." He shook his head. "How damn stupid do they think we are? Anyway, they brought a lot of shit with 'em—automatic weapons mostly."

"Are they looking to hit us?"

"My gut tells me, yeah. I'd say a hit from motor scooters—like the old Red Brigades used to do. They weren't staking out your hotel as of twenty-three hundred hours, which tells me they aren't gonna try something frontal. But I'd be real careful moving around town."

For 'not a whole lot to say,' Olshaker was giving me a real earful. "Anything else I should know?"

"Not much—the three Russkateers spent today in the Via Condotti buying up half the friggin' city, according to the Langley gumshoes who were shadowing 'em. Where they get their dough I have no idea—but they sure do spend like it's going out of style."

"Where are they staying?"

"Grinkov and his two pals have a big suite that takes up the whole top floor of the Grand Palace—it's the place that looks like a friggin' Sicilian wedding cake. Sits between the Piazza della Repubblica and the Piazza San Bernardo—near the main railroad station."

"Goons, too?"

"No friggin' way. Not at three million two hundred fifty thousand lire[49] a night. No—the goons are all six to a room at the cat house—that's what we call the Hotel Katty, which is about five blocks from the Grand, and about one-eighth the price."

"What about our Italian brethren?"

---

[49]Two thousand bucks, more or less, these days.

"SISMI?"

"Yeah, that'll do for a start." Yes, I see your flapping hand out there, wondering WTF. *Si,* I will explain. SISMI (pronounced *seize me,* and rhyming with *please me, tease me,* and *greeze me*), is an Italian acronym that translates into full-length English as the Service for Information and Military Security. It oversees all of the political, military, and economic intel ops for the Italian government. It also handles counterintelligence and assumed the counterterrorism portfolio about five years ago. SISMI operates out of the Ministry of Defense on the Via Twenty September.

You *what?* You want to know how many people work for SISMI? What are you, trying to give me a fucking test to see whether I'm as up-to-date on this shit as the publicity releases claim I am?

Okay—fuck you back: according to the most recent classified CIA analysis, SISMI has about three thousand full-time employees, plus an equal number of agents, snitches, informers, and other assorted scuzzballs. They are scattered throughout Italy, Europe, the Middle East, and North Africa. Happy now? Can I get back to the fuckin' action now? Oh, I *can?* Well, *fuuuuck* you.

Olshaker nodded in the *affirmativo.* "Yeah—they were on-scene when Viktor arrived, so I guess they're on his case, too. Probably bugged the hotel room by now. But SISMI's going to stay hands-off when shit hits fan. The Russkies are about to close a big deal with Fiat to build car plants, and the Italians don't wanna rocka da boat."

If they'd bugged the Russkies, they'd probably bugged our rooms, too. The Italians like to do that sort of thing—it makes 'em feel Machiavellian. Did it matter? Not really. I'd come prepared. I slapped Olshaker across the back. "Well—what about getting this sideshow on the well-known *strada.* The meet is scheduled for zero ten hundred tomorrow." I glanced down at the big-watch-little cock timepiece on my thick, hairy wrist. "Sorry, that's ten hundred *oggi*—today."

Olshaker gave me a double thumbs-up, turned, and hand-signaled two of his Caddies to move toward the pile of boxes my guys had piled near the plane's aft hatchway. "Stow your gear and we'll roll the wagons," he said. "You're headed for the Grand Flora."

He pulled a sheet of paper out of his pocket and unfolded it to reveal a well-drawn map of Rome's center. The one-way streets were all marked clearly; the best routes had been highlighted in bright yellow. "Usually, they put you Pentagon folks up at the Ambasciatori"—he put a long index finger on the paper—"because it's right across from the embassy. But"—he slid his finger north an inch and a half—"we've moved you up the Via Veneto to the Flora. It's a smaller place—it's also got a nice driveway we can get a car up to. The entire building is illuminated all night because it sits right opposite the Borghese Gardens and the old Roman city wall. Besides, we can cover the Flora more easily because it has only two ways in—the front door and the service entrance—and two ways out."

He folded the map and handed it to me, then turned ninety degrees and pointed through the misty rain. "See over there? That's four *carabinieri* cars. They'll be running interference for you guys on the drive into the city."

"What about you?"

He perused my meat-grindered face and abraded knuckles. "Hey, from what I hear, you can take care of yourself pretty good. Me, I'm gonna run the boss and the DCM back in my cars. Then I'm going back to my flat, and grab a warm shower and some hot pussy. I got me a long-haired dictionary waiting there—she's got a real nice set of vowels, too—and I want to improve my vocabulary tonight."

"Well fuck you very much, Olshaker—I want your life."

0028. We pulled off of the tarmac and threaded our way through the airport, flanked by the quartet of Alfa Romeo sedans (each of them containing a trio of *vigilantes*—submachine-gun toting, *Carabinieri Nazionale* tactical officers in black combat fatigues and a dour driver), and motorcaded north, east, then north again. Soon we'd shifted from the airport road onto the Appian Way, our blue flashers illuminating the gates of the stone quarries, brick factories, and tourist restaurants that currently line the two-thousand-year-old route.

We came into the city southeast of the Forum, then took a circuitous course that more or less followed the old city wall, until the Alfas dropped back and allowed our limo to pull into a narrow driveway on the top of the Via Veneto, just opposite the Borghese Gardens and the *muro antiqua*—the old Roman wall. Heeey . . . *ecco:* the Grand Flora. Across the wide street, just closing for the night, was Harry's Bar. Also across the street were two Alfa sedans, each occupied by a pair of well-turned-out SISMI greezemes, trying to look inconspicuous. Yeah—right. Somebody should tell 'em that (a) smoking is bad for you; and, (b) if you do smoke, it is hard to look inconspicuous if you drop a dozen or so butts right outside the window of your car. It's like a fucking sign that says, "Yo—look at me—I'm on a stakeout!"

0112. I got the Chairman tucked into his second-floor, front-of-the-hotel, two-room suite and left Gator and Half Pint (and their suppressed MP5-PDWs) in the living room, and Nod DiCarlo and Rodent (and *their* suppressed MP5-PDWs), in the bedroom to baby-sit. Yes—that was correct. *In* the Chairman's bedroom.

Oh, General Crocker protested. Oh, he bitched. He wanted my guys down in the lobby or out in the hallway—just like the three pairs of young, energetic DS agents Olshaker had assigned to augment our SEAL security force. And did he try to countermand my order? Hey, do I have a big dick? But I would have none of it. He'd commanded me to protect him—and I'd do it. But I'd do it (let's all sing this together just like Ol' Blue Eyes, shall we?) *m-y-y-y w-a-a-a-y.*

0121. We turned out all the lights in our four rooms, made a big and noisy show of going beddy-bye—just in case anybody happened to be listening to the SISMI transmitters we'd discovered by using our Big Brother equipment. I'd disabled the pair in Chairman Crocker's suite, but left the single mikes in our rooms alone. So, yeah, as that old *briccone,*[50] Machiavelli, might have said about the Flora, *I muri hanno orecchi*—da walls hava da ears. Then, as prearranged during the long flight from Andrews, we quietly changed into our work clothes in the dark.

Work clothes, you ask?

Yeah. Basic black—*senza*[51] benefit of pearls. BDUs, which as you know stands for those oxymoronic Battle Dress Uniforms I like so much. Soft nylon ropes. Carabiners. Rubber-soled climbing shoes. Suppressed sterile[52] handguns and a pair of MP5SD's. Sharp knives with blackened blades. FLIR[53] enhanced night-vision devices. My pocket-size digital camera. Nondescript, crushable hats stuffed into pockets. All to be hidden under the dark nylon raincoats that we'd tied around our waists for the time being.

0134. We used our secure radios to coordinate our exit. I pressed my transmit button four times—*stic, stic, stic, stic*—and received three double-*stics* in return. Everybody was ready to move.

Our rooms—which adjoined one another—bracketed the Chairman's suite. The tall, narrow windows, *con vista sul parco*—with a view of the Borghese Gardens—faced the hotel's northern side. We were directly opposite the old Roman wall, just east of the Porta Pinciana. Below my window ran the Via Campania.

Stic-stic. With lights extinguished and secure radio earpiece securely stuffed in my hairy Slovak ear, I turned the cremorne bolt, cracked the French-door window of my

---

[50]A *briccone* is a guinea Rogue.

[51]Without.

[52]Untraceable. In this case, we were carrying suppressed Tokorevs I'd picked up in Moscow, and a pair of Czech CZs.

[53]Forward Looking Infra Red.

room, and crept out onto the narrow balcony. Slowly. Deliberately. Without making any silhouette. I peered through the wrought iron railing. The street below was deserted. I raised my head until I could sweep the street left/right, right/left with my night-vision monocular.

Nada. No traffic. No pedestrians. No SISMI baby-sitters either. I double-clicked. Although I didn't hear anything, I knew that three other French windows were cracking open.

I counted to twenty, then began my move. Tonight I was point man. First, I tested the rail—I've had the perverse pleasure of these things giving way in the past—then after I found it stable, I eased myself over the wrought iron, stretched out full length, and plunged noiselessly, dropping two meters onto the floor of the next balcony below, landing on the balls of my feet. I hunkered down, caught my breath, and waited.

No reaction—on the street, in the park, or from the room inside. I pressed my transmit button twice. *Stic-stic.* As I glanced up, five bodies rolled over the rail, hung, and dropped, one by one, soundlessly, to the balcony on which I crouched. I waited for three thumbs-up. I got two—and a big hairy bird from Boomerang.

Okay—one more once. Over the rail. Down to the next balcony. Stop, look, listen. I clicked my transmitter—let's do it all again.

Avanti! Duck Foot dropped silently, his landing was a modified tumbler's tuck-and roll. Boomerang came down, light as a fucking Nureyev jeté. The Pick came down hard—he landed with a grunt (and got as nasty a surfer's look from Boomerang as if he'd wiped out). I waited. We hadn't called attention to ourselves, so it was Over The Rail time again. I tested the rail—it was solid, Jack—and rolled over the top. This was the big one—ten feet at least to the pavement below. I stretched myself out full length, and was just about to let go and drop onto the sidewalk, when I heard *Stic-stic-stic-stic-stic* in my ear.

I froze, my big Frog feet dangling three meters above the pavement. I risked a look groundward. Geezus fucking Christ—a goddam creature out of a Fellini movie (or a Bonnard painting) hove into view.

And what was it, you ask?

From where I was hanging, it looked like a little Italian *fungo*—that's a mushroom. By that I mean a short, squatty guy, complete with a huge, flowing cape and a big, floppy fedora with a wide brim. He stopped dead in the water right below where I hung, and the *figlio d'un cane*—that's a guinea sonofabitch—stood there and lit a fucking cigarette. Didn't he know that smoking could be bad for his health? Especially if I landed on him and broke his fucking neck.

I shifted my attention to more pressing matters. Like the fact that my hands were coming loose from the railing. This was not a Good Thing. Time to regroup. I used the rail like a pull-up bar, and—my fingertips leaving fucking impressions in the goddam paint—I hauled myself up, up, up three, four, five, six, seven painful inches. It is hard enough to do fingertip pull-ups when you are programmed to do 'em. When you haven't set your body attitude properly, they become nigh on impossible. My damn muscles were on fire. The sinews in my arms were so tight I could hear 'em popping. I grit my teeth—I'd have loved to grunt and groan right then but I couldn't allow myself to make any fucking noise—and raised myself another four inches. It was barely enough to allow my left knee to hit the balcony lip, gain a fraction of traction, and take my hundred-plus kilos of body weight off my fingertips. More or less stable now, I clenched the rail with my left hand, slipped my right arm over the top like a grappling hook, and held on, rivulets of sweat running from my face down through mustache and beard, trickling down my neck and cascading into my black BDUs.

Finally, after an eternity—Rome is the eternal city after all—he moved on, sauntering away into the darkness. I released my grip, lowered my body, and dropped like a fucking stone onto the concrete—a move that did not do a lot of good for my already tender ankle and previously banged-up knee. This was turning quickly into a very existential sort of night.

0139. We shrugged into our raincoats to cover our assault gear, pulled on our hats, then followed the Roman wall for some seven blocks. There, I signaled a right turn onto a narrow side street. I pulled a map from my thigh pocket, unfolded it, shone a red-lensed light on the heavy, water-proofed surface, and diagrammed the routes I wanted everyone to take to our final assembly point.

Plans made, we broke into three groups so as to attract zero attention. I proceeded down a winding thoroughfare lined with narrow, five- and six-story houses that held stores on the ground level and apartments above. Duck Foot and Boomerang turned left, threaded their way through a small piazza, and disappeared into the night. Pick reversed course, heading back the way he'd come.

Nineteen minutes later, we had reassembled on the small piazza a block and a half from the rear entrance of the Grand Palace hotel that I'd pointed out on the map. Now, I see you out there. You're asking WTF we're doing right now.

My friends, the answer is simple. I was about to Boehm ol' Viktor Grinkov before he could Boehm Chairman Crocker. And yes, I realize that the general had forbidden me to UNODIR while we were in Rome. He wanted me to handle his security—and nothing else. Well, to my way of thinking, that's what I was doing right now. Viktor had brought forty tough Ivans with him. They were no doubtski about it shoot-and-looters from OMON.[54] Maybe they'd ambush us on the way to the meet; maybe they'd hit us somewhere else. But I knew, because I'd had recent hands-on experience with these folks, that they were planning something nasty. By preempting Viktor's goons, I was simply doing my job—*i.e.,* protecting the Chairman's valuable butt.

---

[54]The acronym for *Otdel Militsii Osobovo Naznacheniya,* or Special Purpose Militia Detachment, a SWAT team that is run by the Russian Ministry of the Interior.

0207. We moved on the Grand Palace. The hotel dated from the thirties—indeed, it had once been Mussolini's favorite stashing grounds for his mistresses. Unlike many others of the same general period—like the Flora, where we were staying—the Grand Palace hadn't been built in the style of a classic Italian palazzo. Instead, it had been designed in the pseudo-Roman style common to Fascist Italy. Which meant it was a big, ugly box, seven floors in height, with an absurd mélange of rococo trim that included gargoyles, quasi-Corinthian columns, and even a flying buttress or two. There is an architectural technical term for this sort of design. It is: abominable.

But I wasn't concerned with aesthetics tonight. Y'see, I look at things differently than you do. You see a repulsively designed building with gargoyles and columns and go "yuck." I see all those loathsome protrusions, ugly protuberances, and odious projections as keep-it-simple-stupid ways to get in, do my job, and get out, without leaving any telltale signs that I've come a-calling.

0209. I gave Boomerang my night-vision monocular and ran him around the block—the piazza, actually—to do a site survey and target assessment. The kid's a quick worker: he was back in eight minutes with a detailed sit-rep. The SIQ—Suite In Question—was located dead center below the hotel's ornate marquee, seven floors above the sidewalk. The suite had eight windows, five of them humongous double-hung jobs and three narrow casements, all facing the piazza. Two of the big windows, right dead center, were cracked open. So far as surveillance and security were concerned, Boomerang had picked out three cars of watchers—he didn't know who they were—on the piazza. There were half a dozen loiterers in the hotel lobby. And he'd taken a look up at the roof and caught the hint of a cigarette's glow up there. The opposition—and I considered everyone but me and my guys in that category—was definitely present and accounted.

0221. I checked my watch as we began our move in and didn't like what either the big hand or the little hand told me. It was already getting late—which means it was moving toward early morning. Hotels tend to start getting busy very early in the day. No—I don't mean the guests. I mean the employees. The kitchen help, housekeepers, and other factotums generally arrive between 0400 and 0500. That didn't give us much time.

We made our approach from the rear of the hotel, working our way past the empty—and more significantly, unlit—loading dock. A pair of cast-iron drainpipes next to one of the three service entrances led from street level to a small balcony about thirty feet above the sidewalk. From there, I saw that we could climb from window ledge to window ledge, making our way like urban mountaineers, up to the roof.

I tested the pipe—it was solid—took off my raincoat, and tied it securely around my waist. I looked up. Thirty fucking feet is a long fucking climb.

Hey, don't snicker at me. I mean, have *you* ever tried to climb a thirty-foot drainpipe? My suggestion is: don't. It is a nasty and painful activity. There is very little to do except hold on as tightly as possible, and muscle your way up by sheer will and determination, using every molecule of your upper body strength and every ounce of power you can summon in your thighs.

When I ran SEAL Team Six and Red Cell, I expected my shooters to be able to shinny up caving ladders, ropes, and drainpipes. We worked daily to develop our upper body strength. We still do. But since those days, my Roguish body has taken its fair share of dings, dents, nicks, and notches. And—I know you find this hard to believe—I don't climb those caving ladders, ropes, and drainpipes with the same exuberant abandon I did just four or five years ago. Especially when I've just been suspended by my cuticles from a fucking wrought iron railing.

But then, I didn't have to like it—I just had to do it. And since I have always practiced First SEAL Roy Boehm's two-word definition of leadership—FOLLOW ME!—I reached as high as I could, got a good grip on the pipe, wrapped my legs tightly, sprang up—and slammed the shit out of my previously dinged, dented, nicked, and notched left knee as I smacked it hard into the stone wall.

Oh, my friends, that hurt. But I wasn't about to let a goddam guinea drainpipe spoil my evening of fun & games. I just kept going. Didn't look down, didn't look up. Just hugged, and pulled, and hugged, and pulled, and fucking inch by fucking inch I fucking crawled up the fucking pipe.

I'd soaked clean through my damp BDUs by the time I came even with the dark stone of the balcony rail. As I strained to make my final assault, I was taken up and pulled in by lots of strong hands. Wheezing, I caught my breath and looked up to see that, in the time it had taken me to muscle my way up, the rest of my team had scampered upside the other drainpipe and were waiting for me.

"Maybe next time you might consider the elevator, Skipper," Duck Foot said helpfully.

That was something I really needed to hear right now. I pulled myself to my feet. "Fuuuuck you, you wet-behind-the-balls cockbreaths—that was just the beginning. Now let's see how you youngsters do on the serious stuff."

Duck Foot removed his hat and performed a neat little jump-and-bow flourish that would have done a commedia dell'arte performer proud. "*Prego,* Skipper—after you, *per favore, Signore* Beeg Deek."

Chapter 15

0248. I POKED MY BROAD SLOVAK BEAK THROUGH THE FOUR-inch crenellations that saw-toothed the top of the Grand Palace's roofline and took a quick look-see. Yes, I hurt. Yes, I was sore. And cold—and wet from the SEAL-strength sweat that had three floors ago soaked through all my clothes. But I'd done what I'd had to do: I'd brought us up a long, arduous, clandestine route without disturbing anybody—including the infamous *Signor* Murphy who, I hoped, had taken an overdose of sleeping pills tonight.

I paused, then scanned the rooftop using the night-vision monocular I pulled from my top right BDU blouse pocket. Half a dozen yard-square air vents jutted into the night air like squatty monoliths. In the center, the fire stairs housing rose like a miniature saltbox house, the front of its sharply angled top sat nine or ten feet above the tar-and-metal surface of the roof; the rear end dropped down to perhaps three and a half feet. A huge spool, the kind that's used to transport the thickest kinds of electrical cables, sat on its side about halfway to the farthest corner of the roof.

Other miscellaneous detritus—several piles of construction and maintenance equipment—were scattered randomly on the rooftop. A quartet of television antennas completed the bleak landscape. And, *ecco*—there was the rooftop security force. There were three of them up here tonight: a trio of tired Russkies. The Ivan closest to me looked to be almost asleep. His head kept bobbing up and down. It would nod toward his chest, then jerk fitfully up again as he lolled, his back against the fire door, a suppressed Bizon submachine gun—which is how I knew they were Russkies—cradled in his arms.

From where Ivan had situated himself, I knew what he was thinking. He'd assumed that no one could get onto the roof without coming through the fire door—and his body provided the burglar alarm. Well, he'd never read the old Rogue commandment: "Thou shalt never assume."

The other two, in short leather coats, but *senza* hats, were over on the far side of the roof, some twenty-five yards away. Through the green night vision, I saw hot dots of cigarette ends dangling from their lips. They slapped at themselves to keep warm as they shifted their weight in the same shuffle-footed manner centurions, castle guards, doughboys, constables, Secret Service agents, gatekeepers, and other similar security types through the ages have always shifted from one leg to another as they stand lonely watch on cold, dark nights.

One of the sentries turned and pointed down toward the piazza, his arm extending through one of the big, cutout letters of the hotel's marquee sign. The other one followed his gaze, nodding with the same sort of deliberate head/neck movement as one sees with cattle. As they stood, their backs to me, I could make out pistol butts jammed into the center, rear, of their trouser waistbands. Suppressed Bizon submachine guns hung idly from their shoulders. I ratcheted up the power of my monocular and looked at the fire indicators. The guns were on SAFE. I panned up, down, and side to side and saw no radios or other communication devices. Oh, these Russkie pusskie assholes were about to be *mine.*

Not that it was their fault. Let me take a couple of seconds here to tell you a little known fact of the Warrior's life: standing watch is hard. Being a sentry is tough. It is easy to get bored. It is easy to succumb to drowsiness and nod off. It is easy to lose your concentration and your focus.

But the true Warrior *forces* himself to remain alert. The true Warrior fights apathy, ennui, monotony, and inertia with every ounce of his strength—and he remains wakeful, vigilant, heedful, and wary. The lesson here, tadpoles, is that the Warrior never gives in to weakness—whether it is mental, physical, or emotional weakness. The Warrior always remains strong—and so, while the wannabes flunk lunch, the Warrior WILL NOT FAIL.

Now, I am happy to report that most of those who stand watch when my SEALs and I are out-and-about, prowling & growling, sneaking & peeking, or snooping & pooping, are not Warriors. They are wannabes—average Joes, or Paolos, or Ivans, or Rafiqs. You get the picture. They grow weary. They bore easily. And so, in those solitary, lonely, desolate hours between midnight and dawn, they lower their defenses. They give in to their weaknesses. They lose their edge. And that, my friends, is precisely when I attack out of the dark, bringing death and devastation, mayhem and destruction.

I let my body drop below the roofline, catching myself on the eight-inch-wide, finely scalloped decorative shelf four feet below the crenelated roof. I half turned, and hand-signaled to Boomerang, who stood tiptoe on the top of a window frame, six feet under my size ten-and-a-half boots. Like Gaul, the message was divided into three parts. One: there were three unfriendlies up there. Two: I'd deal with 'em. Three: pass the information on. He returned my signal with an upturned thumb. Boomerang reached over his left shoulder, extracted the suppressed MP5SD with ACOG[55]

[55]Advanced Combat Optical Gunsight.

night-enhanced sight he'd stowed in the scabbard on his back, and carefully handed it up to me. I took it, clipped it to the lanyard that hung around my neck, then unclipped Boomerang's own safety line from the gun and let it fall away.

I glanced down. My guys were strung out over two floors, looking like black-clad Spider-man imitations as they clung to window ledges and frames, gargoyles, and other outcroppings. Tactically, this was not a Good Thing. Remember when we stormed the *Nantong Princess?* I told you about the AV—the Area of Vulnerability—during a SpecWar operation. If you don't remember, then go back to the beginning of the fucking book and read it all over again, because you need to understand this shit. To nutshell the situation, we were currently too widely dispersed to achieve the kind of violence of action necessary to bring off the mission. We were vulnerable. And it was up to Dickie to makee-makee all better. To put it in Roguish literary terms, Since I was the tip of the spear right now, I'd have to do all the impaling.

Show Time. I pulled my balaclava down over my face, flipped the safety to its semiauto position, held the weapon in my right hand, and leveraged myself back up so that I was crouching just below the roofline.

Carefully, so as not to make a silhouette, I edged up, up, up, ever so slowly, and peered through the crenellations once again. The far-side Ivans hadn't moved. Neither had the closest target, who was still in pseudosiesta by the doorway.

Moving cautiously but decisively, I raised myself up high enough to bring the weapon over the edge of the roof without making a sound. Then I stood, crouched, with my weight on the cold stone lip, brought the MP5 up to my shoulder, and held it tightly.

The sight picture was perfect—the reticle shone bright red in the darkness; my point of aim was directly on the left eye of the snoozing sentry twelve yards away.

I pulled the weapon tighter. Got myself a perfect cheek mold. My finger eased onto the trigger and I began to take up the tiny bit of slack I knew was there. The balance was just as it should be. I inhaled, then partially exhaled, held myself and my weapon steady as the well-known rock, and s-q-e-e-z-e-d off a single shot.

The only sound was the MP5's hammer dropping—and the thud of the motherfucking round as it whacked past my target and hit the fucking metal door with a *clang* much louder than Big Ben's peal—at least that's the way it sounded to me. The somnolent, snoozy Russkie sonofabitch had snored, jerked his head just as I'd pulled the trigger—and I'd missed him entirely.

But now he *was* awake—jolted into battle-stations alertness, bringing the Bizon up, sniffing like a watchdog and scanning the horizon. He began to rise—and as he did, he saw my silhouette, and I saw him see me and react.

It didn't take him but about a third of a second or so to do all of what I've just described above. But there is a phenomenon that often occurs during incidents such as these. It is called tachypsychia, which is a fifty-dollar word that means you appear to see everything going on around you in slow motion. The FBI, which has always had trouble with big-money words, calls it "visual slowdown." But no matter which term you use, it all comes down to the same thing: it is as if time freezes. Tachypsychia often occurs in conjunction with two other psychic phenomena during gun fights, hostage rescue assaults, and other spec-ops. The first (and most dangerous) is tunnel vision. If you do not see the threat, you will get yourself—and your teammates—killed. The second, much less dangerous, is known as auditory exclusion. Simply put, it means that your hearing often shuts down during the extreme conditions.

Now, I have taught myself to counteract tunnel vision by remembering two things. First, I breathe regularly no matter what else is happening. Second, I always keep my eyes scanning left/right, right/left, constantly searching for threats.

And so, as time slowed down inside my brain, I saw the Russkie see me; saw him as he struggled to bring the muzzle of the Bizon down and across, more or less in my direction. And because I'd kept my breathing steady and my eyes moving, I also saw that the other two Ivans had turned toward the sound, and one was fumbling with his subgun while the other was reaching around the back of his trousers for his pistol.

My brain may have been in slo-mo. My body wasn't about to waste a millisecond. I snapped the fire selector of the MP5 down to full auto and squeezed off a six-shot burst, catching the closest Ivan in b-belly, c-chest and f-face. It wasn't the neat one-shot, one-kill sniper shooting I'd been prepared to do—but it knocked the sumbitch down and kept him there.

That left the other pair. I raised the muzzle and scanned with the ACOG. They'd disappeared. I murmured "shit" into the lip mike to keep my guys sit-repped about the latest developments, rolled over the ledge, and scuttled to the first of the air vents, some three yards northeast of where I'd come over the top. I worked my way around the yard-square device, then moved to my left, so I could cut off any flanking move the opposition might try.

I'd just taken cover behind a second air shaft when I heard the *thwock* of a body hitting something solid behind me. I swiveled, bringing the MP5 up threatward, when Boomerang's voice hissed in my earpiece, "Yo, Boss Dude—I'm white six and ready to rumble."

"I'm green eight," I responded. "We got two targets—somewhere in black or red I think, and moving this way."

Gibberish, you say? Not at all. Boomerang was telling me that he'd come over the top and was at the rear center of the roof—behind me and to my right. I'd told him where I was, and where I believed the missing Ivans to be. The shorthand terminology comes from something called the Colour Clock Code, which is an assault tool invented by SAS 22 Regiment—the Limey counterterrorist unit currently run by my Welsh shipmate and fellow shoot-and-looter Colonel Mick

Owen. The CCC has been adapted by most hostage rescue units, as well as SpecWarriors all over the world.

I'm a little busy here, but to give you a quick pic, the target area is divided into four quadrants: front one is white, then left quadrant is green; top quadrant is black, and right quadrant is red. Center black is twelve o'clock; center white is six, center green is nine, and center red is three.

"Going red," Boomerang said. That meant he was moving to my right.

"Flanking green," I answered. I moved forward, my MP5 in low ready, scanning and breathing. I'd gone about six feet when I heard Duck Foot quack, "White six going green."

He was coming up behind me. I checked my position relative to the roof—I'd progressed about a quarter of the way to the marquee. I whispered "green eight" into my lip mike and kept going. Another six feet and I heard The Pick's voice: "White six going red."

There is a lesson to be learned here. The lesson is simple: during an op, concentrate on your job—not on anyone else's. I was listening to my men as they arrived. I should have been scanning and breathing—because Pick's last syllable hadn't cleared my earpiece when the fucking air vent next to my face exploded.

I rolled right, then left, then scrambled forward eight or nine yards, launched myself airward, and tumbled over the top of the big wooden cable spool. As I took off, a round shattered the heel of my boot. *Doom on Dickie.* I tucked and rolled, my shoulder slamming off the edge of the rough wood spool, knocking it back and to the side.

The MP5 came out of my hands—and nearly knocked me cold as the lanyard jerked it rudely, the butt end swiveled, followed the lanyard's lead, and slapped the shit out of the upside of my much mistreated haid as I came down in a fucking arms and legs akimbo heap.

Let me rephrase the last portion of that ungrammatical, one-sentence paragraph, so that it is more precise. Came down in a fucking arms and legs akimbo heap—right on top of one of the fucking Ivans.

At least I knocked the wind out of him—and sent the pistol beyond his reach—when I did my crashing. But the interruption didn't distract him for long. He recovered, then started to flail the way Russkies are taught to flail—two hundred blows a minute is what a passing grade during Spetsnaz Alpha Team training requires. This cockbreath must have graduated Phi Beta fucking Kappa by the way he kept it up—slamming and swatting and gouging and clawing while we rolled between the spool and the outer wall like a couple of arcade-game pinballs.

My life was made somewhat more difficult by the MP5, which kept getting in the way as I tried to wrest the advantage from him. Well, what's life without a challenge every now and then. I grabbed the Ivan by the neck and slammed him into the ground. He kneed me in the balls (if he'd connected properly I'd be telling you this as a coloratura). I responded by gouging his eyes. That slowed him down—if only marginally—as he struggled to get his hands on my MP5, and I tried to move him toward the silenced pistol that lay just about a yard beyond my reach.

I say "struggled" because he kept up the fucking Alpha exercises *sans* stoppage. Oh, that playing the punching bag routine gets tiresome. Finally, I was able to wrap my arms and legs around him and smother the blows, while using my elbows, knees, and teeth to do some in-close damage. Yeah—teeth. So far as I was concerned, he didn't really need both his ears.

We rolled left, then right, then left again—back inside the big wood spool, where it was harder for him to maneuver. Why harder, you ask? Because he was on the inside—which left him less room. I jammed him back against the core—I outweighed the sumbitch and was able to muscle him—then, as I held him in place, I reached down into my boot top, retrieved the Gerber stiletto from its sheath, brought it up, and stabbed toward his solar plexus.

He realized what was happening—and he rolled, tossed, and scrambled like a mad motherfucker. One of his hands found my knife arm and grabbed on to it, deflecting my aim. I fought back, stabbed as hard as I could—and buried the fucking blade in the wood.

Now *he* grabbed for it—both hands on my knife arm; his legs flailing, a series of guttural imprecations that no doubt expressed sarcasm about my parentage coming from his throat as we wrestled in the confined space. In the absurd way that things come to your mind when you are in extremis, it occurred to me as we lay there, fighting for our lives, that this guy really needed to use some fucking mouthwash—badly.

Then Mister Murphy actually did something unexpected. He played with somebody else's karma for a change. The goddam MP5's suppressor came into the picture again. Before it smacked me, I was able to grab it with my left hand and, using it very much like my collapsible baton, I slapped Ivan the Terrible Breath *whap-whap, whap-whap,* across the face with it.

Which brought him up short. The muzzle of the suppressor cut him across the eyes, and his hands loosened on my knife arm—didn't entirely free me, but his two-handed grip released just enough to give me some fucking wriggle room. I bit his wrist—that made him let go—then wrenched the blade out of the wood, brought it back, *slammed* it up between us, and—quick, before Mister Murphy could screw with me again—jammed it up-up-up into the right side of Ivan's neck, smashing the dagger's point and quarter-inch-thick double-edged blade through sinew and muscle until I found his carotid artery.

I pushed the fucking knife home, worked the blade around as best I could, then brought the blade down and cut at a ninety-degree angle—parallel to Ivan's jawbone. That got him. The sonofabitch gurgled and thrashed. I held his head down with a forearm, my full weight on his body until he stopped moving. Then I pushed back, rolled off him, and crawled out of the spool. I rolled over and lay on my back, my chest heaving, my lungs burning, and my extremities completely numb. I closed my eyes, and counted to twenty to repress the hyperventilation that was pushing my heartbeat and breathing way into the triple digits—and yeah, if the other Ivan was going to kill me, so fucking be it. I was JPE—just plain exhausted.

I sensed someone approach. I opened my eyes—even my fucking eyelids hurt when I raised 'em—and looked up.

Boomerang's long face appeared over me upside down. "It's all clear, Boss Dude—we're ready to move—that is, if *you* are," he said in a voice untinged by any hint of exertion, but so heavy with irony that if I'd had the strength I would have throttled the wonderful motherfucker then and there.

Gentle reader, there are some times when I hate youth—its energy, its vitality, its . . . youth. And this was one of 'em. I rolled onto my hands and knees, then pulled myself to my feet. Boomerang, Pick, Duck Foot, and Half Pint watched solicitously as I plucked a pair of three-inch-long splinters from the meaty part of my right hand, then pulled another two inches of nasty wood from the side of my left knee.

"You assholes have got to be the world's most outstanding bunch of motherfucking cocksucking no-load shit-for-brained pencil-dicked pus-nutted sphincter-lipped world-class bunghole cockbreaths," I said, my voice displaying the kind of affectionate spirit that told 'em just how much I really do love 'em. I knelt and wiped the blade and grip of my Gerber on the dead Ivan's trouser leg, then replaced the knife in its sheath. "So, now that we've enjoyed the preliminaries, and I've told you how I really feel, let's stop standing around like a bunch of pussy-ass can't cunts and get our real work done already."

See, the thing that makes being a SEAL different from being any other SpecWarrior is that SEALs really do believe that getting there is more than half the fun. I mean—look at us. We'd fucking climbed the outside of a goddam eight-story building, killed us a trio of nasty Russkies, and we hadn't really begun our evening's work yet.

0312. I lowered myself down three yards of soft climbing rope, just under the hotel marquee, parallel to the living room of Viktor's top-floor suite. Carefully, I pulled myself close to the window frame and peered inside. The lights were off—although I saw illumination under two of the three doors leading to the bedrooms.

I swept the room with my night vision. There was no one lurking. And so, moving cautiously, I pendulummed right, then left, then right again, hooked the windowsill with my toe, and pulled myself around until I could raise the window, and slip through.

Stealthy as a fucking panther I dropped onto the Oriental carpet. I released the rope so Duck Foot could make his descent and proceeded into the huge room, my eyes growing accustomed to the darkness. Behind me, Duck Foot dropped onto the carpet. He moved to my left and took a defensive stance, suppressed MP5 up and ready. Right behind him, Boomerang slid through the window.

0314. We moved on the lighted bedrooms first. I stood to the side and allowed Pick to check the door handles, which he did using my FLIR-enhanced night-vision monocular. Neither was locked. We split into two groups. I waited until we were set—then went *stik-stik* into my radio.

Boomerang and Pick opened the doors simultaneously, and Duck Foot and I charged into the target rooms. I went in low, my suppressed pistol ready. Only the bedside lamp was on. Across the room, a big, fat, pusskie-eating Russkie tried to scramble from underneath a lithe, dark-haired hooker (yes, I can report that she was a real brunette), who I could see had been working hard but without results on his long, limp Ivan dickski.

It wasn't Viktor. No matter: I was on him before he could react—swatted him across the temple with the butt of the pistol and knocked him cold. Before the hooker could scream, Boomerang'd clamped a gloved hand over her mouth, and I'd looked her in the eye and raised my left index finger to my lips in the universal sign for *silenzio.*

She nodded vigorously. Boomerang held her steady while I bound her—and the Ivan—with duct tape. No sense in taking chances. We covered them with the blanket, turned out the lights, and moved on.

0317. Duck Foot was already back in the living room, his gloved hand giving me a downturned thumb. I shrugged. "Empty," he mouthed.

That was not good news. The last thing I needed right now was for some fucking partied-out Russkie general to show up, accompanied by who-knows-who.

I hand-signaled Pick to wedge the suite's door. It wouldn't stop a determined assault, but it would slow 'em down and give us some advance warning. Then I turned my attention to the remaining bedroom door.

Since the door opened inward, we stacked outside on the doorknob side. Pick stood opposite me, clear of the door so his feet couldn't be seen underneath. His hand moved toward the knob, grasped it, and tested. He looked at me and nodded once, up/down. It worked.

0318. I waited. Duck Foot's hand was on Boomerang's left shoulder; Boomerang's left hand rested on mine. I felt a solid squeeze, which meant they were ready. I nodded once at Pick, who turned the knob and opened the door.

Except it didn't open. Pick pushed again. He used his shoulder. Nada. The motherfucker'd been locked from the inside.

Goddammit—Pick had examined the other two doors. But he hadn't checked this one out. We were fucked. We'd made noise. For all I knew Viktor was on the fucking phone to his OMON shooters, or the hotel desk, or both. I pushed Pick out of the way, stood back, and kicked the door with the flat of my foot, just below the ornate brass knob.

The latch and frame shattered cleanly—just one *crack* of splintering wood, and I went in, pistol at low ready, my mini assault light up and on. Boomerang was right behind me; Duck Foot on his tail.

I lit Viktor up with the bright, narrow beam. He stopped what he'd been doing and looked in my direction, his pale, flabby arm flew toward his face to cover his eyes from the piercing brightness of my light. He screamed something unintelligible and tried to cover himself and his young playmate with the bedclothes.

Frankly, I was shocked—*shocked*—at what I saw. Y'know, there is a Latin medical technical term for what I'd just caught Viktor doing. But since I'm not a doctor and neither are most of you, I'll use, ah, layman's language. To put it plainly, I had interrupted Viktor as he was in the midst of sucking some serious cock.

Shocked or not, I wasn't about to waste my time—or his. I was on him before he could react. Swatted him down and slapped him upside the head with the butt of my pistol to keep him quiet. His bedmate, who was in far better condition than Viktor, tried to put up a fight. But he was no match for my guys, who had him wrapped up like Tutankhamen's fucking mummy in less time than you can say eighteenth dynasty.

We pulled the drapes closed, then turned on the bedroom lights.

I bound Viktor's arms and ankles, ran a loop of tape around his mouth to keep him quiet, then propped him up atop his big bed. Boomerang, who I must tell you looks very menacing when he's wearing his balaclava, did the same for Viktor's playmate.

There was something familiar about the guy. I pulled a chair over to the foot of the bed. Turned it around so I could put my arms over the rail and sat astride it. Looked closely. He was a tall, rangy, muscular asshole, whose cruel eyes still tried to intimidate even though he'd been rendered harmless. I never forget cruel eyes—and I'd seen this guy's baby browns somewhere before. It took me about thirty seconds to figure it out—after I spotted the key to his identity on the bedside table. A solid gold Rolex President-model watch lay there. The fucking things probably weigh half a pound or more.

I gave Viktor's playmate a Roguish grin and tapped him on the big toe with the same silenced Tokorev pistol I'd taken off one of his men in Moscow. "Colonel Rolex—how's it goin'?" I'd met this bona fide prick in Russia, not six months before, when he'd tried to wax my ass. He was an OMON colonel. He was a big-time OMON hatchet man. He had ties to the Russian Mafiya. And now, I'd just discovered much to my delight that he was also Viktor's main squeeze—make that main suck.

I didn't wait for a reply—Colonel Rolex was gagged in any case—but turned my attention to Viktor.

Now, it can get cold in Rome during the winter. Even so, Italian architecture has never utilized much insulation during construction. The reason is that, while there may be occasional frigid spells, winter in central and southern Italy is generally pretty temperate. And hence, buildings—whether they are apartments, office buildings, or five-star hotels—tend to get downright chilly at night. But you couldn't tell that from Viktor. Vik sat there, sweating buckets, his little Russkie dik shriveled into never-never land. I gave him a critical once-over. Shit—the motherfucker had bigger tits than my first three girlfriends back in Lansford, Pennsylvania, combined.

I pulled my balaclava off and shook my French braid out. "Yo, Viktor—remember me?"

He rolled his eyes away and remained silent.

"You wanted to talk to General Crocker about your money, right?"

The *szeb* just sat there and sweat.

"Well, Viktor, he's not here. I am. So let's you and me do some *zapodlo.*"[56]

His eyes told me that he wasn't in the right frame of mind to do beez-i-ness.

"Okay—don't say I never asked." Hey—I wasn't about

[56]*Zapodlo* is Russian Mafiya slang for business. It's a word that Viktor understands all too well.

to waste my time trying to convince him one way or the other. I pulled the digital camera out of its padded fanny pack, made sure that I hadn't broken it during the night's exertions, flipped the strobe to automatic, then snapped half a dozen images of Viktor and his pal sitting there with his tits and their plumbing hanging out. "Maybe we could sell these to *Pravda.* What about *Novosti*—is *Novosti* still in business, Viktor? Or maybe *Time,* or *Newsweek*—or one of the German tabloids. The fucking Krauts wouldn't bother to mask your poor excuse for a dick, y'know. Or maybe your beloved president would like to see 'em—I'd bet mine would."

That got the motherfucker's attention. He went crazy behind the gag, throwing himself around the bed like a fucking organ-grinder's monkey.

I handed the camera off to Duck Foot. "So, does this mean you want to deal, Vik?"

Now, you may think that I'm being a little heavy-handed here. I mean, I was about to blackmail the sonofabitch—and blackmail isn't generally considered your everyday dignified, well-mannered, genteel sort of behavior. Of course, I'm not your everyday dignified, well-mannered, genteel sort of Rogue, either.

And don't be so fucking squeamish out there. You've read the stuff in the front of these books. You know that there are no rules when it comes to making war. You know that I'll fucking win any way I can. And so far as I was concerned, I was at war with Viktor—and the sooner I was finished with him, the sooner I could move against Li Chimen and Bentley Brendel.

Let me add something else here. War is not a nice thing. It is not neat. It is dangerous. It is bloody. The powers that be keep testifying up on Capitol Hill about how we will make meticulous, orderly, prim and proper war in the next century. They talk about smart weapons and battlefield electronics; about nonlethal munitions that confuse the enemy and thus defeat him. Hey—let me tell you something. That testimony, well intentioned as it may be, is all so much horse puckey so far as I am concerned. Sure, the weapons and the technogoodies will get more sophisticated. Just like laser-guided missiles, and stealth aircraft, and the fucking arsenal ship that they're talking so much about these days, and on-the-ground, real-time C^4IFTW materials like Big Brother.

But war will always come down to the grunt in the field, or the SEAL in the water, doing his nasty, messy, lethal job. War will always come down to one simple premise: kill your enemy before he kills you. And no "nice" technology, or "smart" weapon will do the job as well or efficiently as a man with a gun—or his bare hands, if that's what it takes.

It is my unshakable belief that our wars will always be decided by the ability of one man being able to kill another man, face-to-face. It is also my strong belief that when you kill enough of the other guy, you'll destroy his will to fight. When the will to fight is broken, his leaders will capitulate—and you will have won. But the foundation of all war is killing—and tonight, Viktor understood that he was the dead meat.

0323. Boomerang and the Pick moved Colonel Rolex to his own room so that Viktor and I could speak in private. Meanwhile, Duck Foot did his CI[57] number on Viktor's room—and flagged a pair of listening devices. I made sure that Viktor saw them. When he indicated that he had, I turned on the clock radio that sat by his bedside, found a station that played rock-and-roll, and turned the volume loud enough to mask our voices.

Then I sat on the edge of the bed, reached over, and pulled the tape off of Viktor's face. Oh—sorry. That must have hurt, because I took some skin with it.

No, I didn't bother covering him up. I kept him sitting there, nervous, sweating, and cold, with his limp-as-a-corpse's-dick pecker hanging out in plain sight. It's an old psychological warfare game that works well during interro-

[57]Counterintelligence.

gation. Most folks become real ill at ease when their plumbing's exposed. I was happy to see that Viktor was one of those folks.

Now, I had three goals to achieve tonight. The first was to make sure Viktor understood that General Crocker was off-limits to OMON—or anybody else that Viktor might hire to wax the Chairman's four-starred behind. Second, I needed information. Remember, if you will, back to the *Nantong Princess.* When we'd boarded it, we'd discovered a cache of arms masquerading as machine tools, all labeled EXPORT—Zelinograd Machine Tools/MVD.

Remember I told you that "MVD" stood for Russia's Ministry of the Interior?

Well, Viktor ran the fucking MVD, and I wanted to know what the hell he was doing selling all those weapons to the Chinese, when the Chinese had more than enough weapons to sell on their own. Matter of fact, I wanted to know everything Viktor knew about the fucking Chinese and their current politico-economic-military strategy.

And third, I wanted to make sure that Viktor and I would enjoy . . . (Hold on a sec. Enjoy is probably not quite the correct word. I don't think Viktor enjoyed a single aspect of *moi.* Something which, under the circumstances, is quite understandable. Therefore, let me rephrase.)

Okay. And third, I wanted to make sure that Viktor and I would *sustain* a continuing relationship over the next few years. Frankly, I don't have many top-level sources of information in the former Soviet Union. Oh, I've met my share of ex-KGB gumshoes, killed my full bag limit of ex-Spetsnaz shooters, and spent more time negotiating with retired GRU colonels than I care to remember. But I lack regular rations of firsthand, top-quality information. The kind that someone at Viktor's level could deliver—if he could be persuaded to do so.

Now to be honest, I'd come a-calling tonight with a dual purpose. My primary goal was to dissuade Viktor from trying anything untoward with Chairman Crocker. But I had a second objective in mind as well. I figured that I could save General Crocker some work, and do some good for the country, by buying Viktor's assistance. After all, I had access to something he wanted: the fifty million simoleans (less what we'd spent on the *Nantong Princess* op) I'd siphoned from his Swiss and other offshore bank accounts. And I had actually been willing to let him have his money back—small chunk by small chunk—in return for the right kind of Grade-A information.

But that quid pro quo shit wouldn't be necessary any more. I had Viktor by the S&Cs—which as you can probably guess stands for short-and-curlies. Literally. See, your typical Russkie tends to be somewhat homophobic. Ergo, male-on-male cocksucking, rimming, and butt fucking are activities that most Ivans just don't cotton to. So Viktor would have a hell of a time explaining away the digital pictures in my camera—even though I hadn't actually caught him in flagrante delicto, which as you probably know is an old SEAL synonym for flagrant sphincter licking.

Just to be sure that he understood the situation, I snapped half a dozen more frames—good quality pictures of him sitting in the bed, trussed up like a porker ready for the oven. Then, like the SEAL Mafiosi I am, I sat on the edge of the bed, looked Viktor in the eyes, and stage-whispered the kind of *bricconesco* offer he simply couldn't refuse, right into his P-P-Porking the P-P-Prick ear.

Chapter 16

0623. We pulled out way before first light. At 0456 I coitus interruptus'd Mark Olshaker (it sounded to me like I'd caught him in the middle of the idiom "to fuck the brains out of" with his long-haired dictionary). I let him catch his breath, then arranged for a security detail to replace my men *immediatamente.* He wheezed, groaned, then rolled out of the sack (all the while describing my choice of timing in a series of ornate, extravagant, and thoroughly unprintable Italian terms), checked his laptop and his emergency call-up sheet, and told me he could assemble an eight-agent crew of top-rated shooters to be on site by 0600. That was perfect—it even gave me about half an hour of Murphy time.

Next, I rapped quietly but insistently at Joanne's door until she answered groggily, handed her two sealed envelopes to give to the Chairman, and told her we were leaving. That remark certainly helped cut through the painkillers and wake her up enough to start lobbing questions in my direction. But I wasn't about to answer any of 'em. Frankly, the less she knew about my plans, the better for us all.

My first note to the Chairman was pretty KISS, too. It explained to General Crocker that his meeting with Viktor had been canceled, and that I'd update him on all the details back in Washington. Meanwhile, I wrote, I'd completed the assignment he'd given me—*i.e.,* securing his butt during this leg of the trip. And so, as I considered my job in Rome concluded, I had other priorities to see to—like dealing with whoever had murdered Alixe Joseph. So unless otherwise directed, *sayonara,* General, I'll see you back at the Pentagon in a few days.

Yes, it was an abrupt, brusque, curt note. Some might even have found it impertinent. But it did the job. And since I am not looking to receive an admiral's stars—my captain's scars still look damn fine to me—I don't mind sometimes cutting a corner or two (or three or all four) in the bedside manner department.

The second message was neither short nor abrupt. It was a memo that detailed my thoughts about what the Chinese were up to, based on the intel materials I'd seen from the *Nantong Princess,* and the information I'd been able to gather, assemble, and analyze over the past few days—including some pearls of wisdom I'd gathered from Viktor earlier. I suggested that the Chairman might like to speak directly—but securely—with his counterparts in Korea, Indonesia, Singapore, and the Philippines, so they could crack down on the Chinese networks that Li Chimen had built. I added that I believed that time was crucial, as Li's clock—actually, it was more of a time bomb than a Mickey Mouse watch—was ticking away.

I closed by telling the Chairman that I was acting in what I believed were the best interests of my country—and that I'd take whatever lumps might come my way when I got back to Washington. But I emphasized that those lumps were to be mine alone—my men were to be considered blameless.

Good News/Bad News department: the good news was that we had valid diplomatic passports, which would help us to travel with the two lockboxes of lethal equipment we'd brought with us from Washington. The bad news is that when you carry diplomatic passports and boxes of weapons, ammunition, and explosives, you need visas from the countries to which you are going.

I called Tosho, pulled him out of a meditative, postworkout sauna, a nefarious offense for which he called me a larger and more grotesque variety of unprintable things than Olshaker had. (Small sociological point: Olshaker's and Tosho's different reactions really tell you volumes about the way diverse cultures function, don't they?) Anyway, Tosho arranged for us to be vetted at the Rome airport by Japanese consular officials. He kept me on hold while he worked his magic. After eight minutes of silence, he came back on line. We would fly JAL from Fiumicino. Unfortunately the only flight he could get us all aboard was a GG—remember, that's a local train—which had stopovers in Riyadh and Delhi. Bottom line: it would be a minimum of twenty-two hours before we'd wheels down at Tokyo. But those twenty-two hours would at least be spent flying first-class—something that would give my men a chance to grab a series of long, restorative combat naps between sessions of sushi and Ichiban, and games of saki-to-the-stewardess. The long flight would also give me time to come up with an OPLAN.

Because, y'see, although I was certain that the Chinese were about to attempt some form of offensive, and I was convinced that their strike would be directed at Taiwan, I still wasn't certain about which direction it would come from. They were about to act. But where? I believed the answer to that quandary was to be found at the start of this story. Yes—at the very start. Every molecule of my instinct, every element of my operational experience, told me that the solution lay at the beginning of my current odyssey. We'd discovered the answer aboard the *Nantong Princess*—we just hadn't known what to look for at the time. The *Nantong Princess* was the linchpin of Li Chimen's little exercise.

And so, while my men slept and played, I worked. I scoured DIA's translations of the materials I'd brought back with me to see what Tony Merc's people might have missed. I cross-checked Viktor's political insights about the Chinese with materials I'd been able to get my hands on. Then I went back and pored over every one of my own notes. I reconnoitered the maps and charts; I double-checked the intel reports, and reassessed the target assessments. I reread all of the files I'd brought with me. And after sixteen hours, groggy from lack of sleep, I was no further along than I had been in Rome.

Part of it was Alixe Joseph. The white heat anger I'd felt at her murder still gnawed at my guts. But you cannot allow such things to sway you, or you will not focus properly on the threats you have to counter and the problems you have to solve. Oh, there is a positive way to use rage—I'd used my rage constructively after one of my SEAL Team Six plankowners, Cherry Enders, was killed taking down LC Strawhouse's oil rig in *Task Force Blue.* His death kept me going when my own resolve began to waver. And I'd used rage to help give me the drive to find those responsible for the murder of my godson Adam in *Designation Gold* and take my revenge on them all.

But here, I realized that I was pushing the edge of the emotional envelope. I wanted Li Chimen and Bentley Brendel—but I had no way to get my hands on them. They were in Beijing. And so I sat, goggle-eyed and burnt out, thirty-nine thousand feet above the Arabian Sea, trying to make head &/or tail of the *Nantong Princess*'s ship's log, and its messy navigation charts.

Nothing made fucking sense anymore. We were sitting here, captives of time and space. In five and a half hours we'd arrive in Japan—and I hadn't the foggiest fucking idea what I was going to do there. Frustrated, confused, angry, and punchy, I locked everything away in my huge briefcase.

I ordered an Ichiban beer. The word means number one

in Japanese. Ichibans come in tall, twenty-two-ounce bottles. I watched as the obi'd stewardess poured it out into my proffered glass (we were in first class, after all). When she'd finished, I didn't just gulp it down. Instead, in pseudo-Japanese fashion, I passed the glass under my nose, smelling the hops and the malt, appreciating the perfect shape of the foamy head, and allowed my fingers to savor the coolness of the glass—as if I were participating in a classic tea ceremony. Then, I drank slowly, *feeling* the beer as I swallowed it, letting the liquid release my tension and give me energy.

I pressed the recline button. My seat slid back and the leg rest raised itself. I lay supine, the cold glass of beer in my hand, and let my mind drift off and free-associate. It is a truth: sometimes, *not* thinking produces more valuable results than thinking.

Oh, I see you, snickering among yourselves, pooh-poohing the above two paragraphs.

Well, tadpoles, listen and learn about the real world. When I was still a wet-behind-the-flippers Warrior, Roy Boehm, the godfather of all SEALs, took me aside and whispered (growled and croaked, actually) some sooth into my shell-like Slovak ear.

Quoth Roy: "I am fuckin' convinced that there are times when the fuckin' Warrior simply cannot fuckin' deal with fuckin' problems in the Western way, by which I mean, taking a heads-on, literal, straightforward approach to military problem solving. No, Dick—what you sometimes gotta do is take the Oriental approach. Use the discipline of Mindfulness. Let everything be everything, and in equal degrees of being."

Oh, I hear you: *Master Marcinkosan is engaging in Asian psychobabble. Master Marcinkosan is trying to lay some new and inscrutable form of strange Oriental manure on us.*

Listen up, tadpoles. Roy Boehm went through fucking BUD/S *twice.* The second time he did it he was *forty-two* fucking years old. Let me tell you something: you will fucking pay **attention** and **respect** to anybody who has the brass balls to go through BUD/S at the age of forty-two, because it's more than any of you can do.

More to the point, the philosophical nucleus of what Roy told me makes perfect sense to anyone who has devoted his entire adult life, as Roy did, and as I have, to the art of making war. And even *more* to the point: Roy's advice has made me a better Warrior; it has allowed me to kill vast numbers of my own enemies efficiently and mercilessly, just the way it helped Roy kill vast numbers of *his* own enemies, efficiently and mercilessly.

In retrospect, Roy managed to teach us tadpoles a great deal about the Asian mind, despite our recalcitrance at the time. He knew the region. He'd delivered weapons to Filipino guerillas during WWII. He'd been to China back in the late 1940s; his first tour in Vietnam came while President John F. Kennedy was still alive. And Roy was—still is—an inquisitive little Frog. And so, by the time he decided to take me under his flipper he'd studied it all: Taoism, Confucianism, Buddhism. He'd read so much Sun Tzu, Ssu-Ma, Fudo, Huang Shih-Kung, T'ai Li'ang, and Wu Tzu that he'd begun to sound as fucking inscrutable as they were, sitting like a fucking BWB—that's a Buddha with beer—going on and on about concepts such as "endless interaction" and "mindfulness." We, of course, were young, foolish, and resisted his advice. He sometimes had to pound it into us—literally. "Physical inculcation" is what he called it. We referred to it as mucho fucking pain.

But the simple fact is, the sort of Asian thinking Roy preached really works if (a) you study hard, and (b) you let it just wash over you. So just S^2—that's sit the fuck down and shut the fuck up in case you don't feel like going to the Glossary—and learn something.

Okay, let's start with what Roy calls "that heads-on, literal approach," which is common here in the West. The Army's Field Manual 100-5, *Blueprint for the AirLand*

Battle, states the Principles of War in nine simple terms.[58] They are a valuable resource, so let me quote them to you.

1. *Objective.* Direct every military operation toward a clearly defined, decisive, and attainable objective.
2. *Offensive.* Seize, retain, and exploit the initiative.
3. *Mass.* Concentrate minimum essential combat power to secondary efforts.
4. *Economy of Force.* Allocate minimum essential combat power to secondary efforts.
5. *Maneuver.* Place the enemy in a position of disadvantage through flexible application of combat power.
6. *Unity of Command.* For every objective, ensure unity of command under one responsible commander.
7. *Security.* Never permit the enemy to acquire an unexpected advantage.
8. *Surprise.* Strike the enemy at a time or place, or in a manner, for which he is unprepared.
9. *Simplicity.* Prepare clear, uncomplicated plans and clear, concise orders to ensure thorough understanding.

There is nothing wrong with these principles—in fact, some of them come very close to paralleling the Ten Commandments of SpecWar. But the very codification under the important-sounding rubric Principles of War has the potential to make them restrictive, confining, and limited so far as I am concerned.

Here is a second Western example. All SEAL missions are currently divided into seven phases. There is premission,

---

[58]The original *Principles of War* were first published by the U.S. Army in 1921. They are derived from the work of British Major General J.F.C. Fuller, who developed a similar set for the Brits during WWI. It was General Fuller, incidentally, who first formalized the concept of KISS—Keep It Simple Stupid.

insertion, infiltration, actions at the objective, exfiltration, extraction, and postmission. Each of those seven steps is broken down and analyzed; moreover, each one is currently diagrammed and flowcharted. Today, statistical analyses of virtually every mission are generated by computer, allowing holographic simulations to be run by the senior mission planners before a single SEAL is permitted to go anywhere or do anything. The formulations derived are precise and meticulous. They are conscientious, and explicit—just like the Principles of War. But they, like those nine principles, also can be restricting.

Here is a third example. The SpecOps theory of relative superiority (you should remember it because I told you it was important to do so earlier in the book, and I'm not going to take the time to restate it here) was created in a way that allows it to be diagrammed on a chart. In point of fact, flowcharts, graphs, computer-generated models, and statistical-type diagrams have become a large part of what SpecWar is all about these days.

But, as Roy told me so many, many times, things cannot, and—more important—*should not,* always be diagrammed, programmed, graphed, charted, or codified. Sometimes, he insisted, things must just be *felt;* sometimes they must simply be *sensed.*

Listen, for example, to how the great swordsman Fudo described the tactics of winning in his 1648 seminal work, *The Sword.* Fudo wrote:

> Some teachers insist that in combat, your eyes must focus on your enemy's sword in order for you to succeed in killing him. Others say no—follow your opponent's hands and you will prevail. Still others teach you to watch your opponent's eyes, or his face; to focus on his hips, or his feet. All of these are wrong. What you must do is to sense your opponent in much the same way the archer senses the flight of the arrow before the arrow is loosed, or the painter senses the stroke of his brush,

before the bristles touch the paper. The true archer does not have to *see* the center of the target; he can sense it perfectly in his mind. The great painter does not have to use a compass in order to draw a perfect circle. That perfect circle already exists—a vision inside his head. What they do is to translate their visions to the target and the paper. In the same way, you must never fix your eyes on any one thing, but must perceive the whole world around you as you engage in battle. If you fight in a manner that is consistent with that all-encompassing vision—adjusting, compensating, and harmonizing as you do combat—you will never fail.

I remember the day Roy first read that passage to me. He finished, slapped his empty beer can down on the kitchen counter, grinned at me (he has big white teeth, and he has always looked a little bit like Freddie, the malevolent, Dixie-cupped, dynamite-holding, cigar-chomping UDT Frog mascot when he grins), put his big, wide nose right up to my big, wide nose, and growled, "Now, try to diagram *those* fucking tactics, you asshole."

And so I reclined the seatback, closed my eyes, and replayed everything that had taken place aboard the *Nantong Princess.* Played it all like a fucking videotape, in my mind. Occasionally, I stopped the tape and reran a section. I played things in reverse. I shuffled events. I looked at the problem as if it was a holograph—examining it from top, bottom, and side-to-side. Then I free-associated—let my mind play games until I forced myself to recall every morsel, pseudofactoid, and partial infobit of picayune, inconsequential, and meaningless intelligence I'd absorbed since we'd taken down the *Nantong Princess.*

Yes, friends, despite the fact that I love to hop & pop & shoot & loot, a great part of Warriordom is mental, not physical. And the mental part is just as demanding—if not more so—than the physical.

After two and a half hours of Ichiban and free association, I unlocked my briefcase, pored over the contents, and extracted three items: a page from the *Nantong Princess*'s ship's log, the ship's chart of the South China Sea, and my notes from a conversation with Alixe Joseph. I looked them all over carefully and saw on those sheets the information I had been looking for, but previously had been unable to detect. All of it was right there in front of me. And it was so fucking simple that I had to be right.

Part Three

THE FIRE STRATEGY

Chapter 17

TOSHO AND A SHORT, BESPECTACLED JAPANESE IMMIGRATION official whose shiny black sharkskin three-button suit with all three buttons buttoned, white long-pointed collar shirt, and narrow black silk tie gave him the look of a type-casting Nisei William Mollis agent, were standing on the mobile platform as it wheeled up to the 747's fuselage. Tosho looked exhausted. He stood off to the side, his arms crossed, his foot tapping impatiently, his face grim.

He gave me a cursory abrazo and my guys an off-handed *Kon-nichi-wa* before he led us all down a steel stairway onto the tarmac, toward a pair of black Ford Broncos with smoked-glass windows and lots of radio antennas. The plane's huge cargo hatches were already open—and our luggage and the three big equipment lockers we'd brought with us were being unloaded from their own container, which sat separate from the others. "I had your stuff specially tagged in Rome—easier and faster that way," Tosho explained abruptly. I watched as the immigration man took our passports, laid them out on the hood of one of the Broncos, peered through his thick-rimmed glasses at each picture and, satisfied that us was us, inserted small sheets of paper atop our visas, stamped every sheet neatly, restacked the documents in the order he'd received them, and returned each with a polite bow.

I'd seen the same thing done once before. In the days before there was any sort of Middle East peace, the Israelis used to slip a sheet of paper into my passport and stamp it, instead of leaving a permanent mark inside my passport. That way, when I traveled to such places as Saudi, or Kuwait, Oman, or Algeria, those countries, still in a technical state of war with Israel, would accept my passport.

Puzzled, I accepted my passport and lowered my head to return the official's courtesy. *"Domo arigato*—thank you."

Immigration Man bowed even lower. *"Doo-itashimashite*—you're very welcome."

We took the expressway back into the city, crawling the last twenty kliks or so through exhaust-heavy glidlock. Tokyo traffic was even worse than I'd remembered—it made Washington in the snow look good. Tosho drove in silence, his jaw clenched, looking like some kind of Japanese bulldog. He habitually played country music on the Bronco's cassette deck, singing along volubly with Garth Brooks, or Mary Chapin Carpenter. Today, there was nothing but silence. I wondered what was bothering him but knew enough to leave him alone when he was in one of his solitary black-brack moods.

Our two-vehicle caravan made its way along the Tokyo Expressway Number 1, exited just above Yurakucho Station, threaded through traffic behind the Imperial Hotel, took a turn onto Uchi Sai Wai-Cho, and finally came up behind the Nippon Press Center. Half a block on, Tosho veered into a narrow alley and pressed a button on the Bronco's overhead console. Fifty yards in front of us, a huge, reinforced steel vehicle barrier painted yellow and black lowered itself into the ground. I peered up through the windshield and made out multiple surveillance cameras on mechanical gimbals. We bumped across the lowered steel barrier. Tosho stopped far enough beyond it to allow the second Bronco to clear, then tapped his siren and flashed his lights twice. The antiterrorist device raised itself with a loud, hollow *clung,* after which, a pair of massive metal doors sixty feet beyond our front crash bumper retracted, allowing the two Broncos entry into the huge, multilevel garage taking up the first two floors of the windowless, six-story building that I knew served as Kunika's headquarters.

We parked the vehicles and locked them. Tosho led the way, chugging up four flights of stairs at a constant double time, never breathing hard. He quick-marched us past a trio of security checkpoints, returning the guards' salutes with hasty waves of his hand, and wheeled into a long corridor off of which dozens of Kunika officers worked in cramped cubicles that looked to be a lot smaller than the hot tub back at Rogue Manor—not that I'd had the chance to enjoy that or any of the Manor's other amenities, lately.

He swung left at the corridor's dead end, opened the door to what looked to be a small conference room, beckoned for us to enter, then when we'd all done so, he closed the door with the back of his broad shoulders and turned the deadbolt lock.

Now that ve vere alone, Tosh looked over at me—and the look wasn't especially friendly. "What the fuck, Dick?"

What the fuck indeed, gentle reader? Do I have such an ineffable effect on people that they habitually tend to greet me in loving terms and affable sobriquets?

I looked back at Tosho. "What the fuck what the fuck, Tosh. I have no damn idea at all what you're so fucking steamed about."

Tosho withdrew a sheet of paper from the inside pocket of his jacket. "Try this," he said, handing it to me.

I looked. I read. It was a confidential fax to the head of Kunika from the chief American defense attaché in Japan, and written at the behest of the Chairman of the Joint Chiefs of Staff, requesting assistance in finding and detaining one Captain Richard No Middle Initial Marcinko and seven of his enlisted men, who, the fax continued, were currently engaged in the commission of an unauthorized action with regard to the recent death of an American Embassy official, and hence presumed to be somewhere in the area of the Japanese capital.

"Guess who got the assignment," Tosho said. "And when Boss-san finds out I'm the one who let you into the country, I'm gonna be toast."

"I don't plan to be here long," I said. "Maybe he won't find out."

"He finds out everything," Tosho said. "That's why he's Boss-san."

All of a sudden, Kunika headquarters didn't seem the best place to be. "So why bring us here, Tosh?"

"To be honest, it's the one place nobody'll be looking for you. As you can see, the Americans think you're here to shake the city up trying to find whoever killed Alixe. DIA's got gumshoes staking out her place—and a few other locations, too."

Actually, I had a pretty good idea who'd killed Alixe Joseph—had her killed is a more accurate description—and he wasn't within a thousand miles of Tokyo. Which is what I told Tosho.

"You mean Li Chimen," Tosho said. "Yeah—I think he's dirty, too. But he came through on a diplomatic passport and we couldn't touch him. The sonofabitch is back in Beijing."

"I think he's already out—or close to it, and without his diplomatic creds," I said.

That got Tosho's attention. "Out? Where, in Tokyo?"

"Not quite," I said. "South of Tokyo. I'm about to check it out and take him down." I wriggled my eyebrows in Tosho's direction. "You speak Chinese. I happen to have an opening for somebody who speaks Chinese. So—you wanna come along for the ride?"

For the first time since we'd arrived, I got a warm smile and an eager grin. "Hey, *Gaijin-san,* I'm supposed to 'find and detain,' ain't I? I guess that means I have to keep you in rine-of-sight until I put you on the prane for Washington. If that means I gotta deal in some second-rate, third-world language like Chinese for a while, so be it."

Now I see a bunch of you folks out there, scratching your heads, and starting to ask all those reader-type questions that always seem to start 'What the . . .' and 'How the . . .' Don't worry—you're not the only ones. My favorite dweeb editor's just stabbed out his cigarette and started to reach for the ol' blue pencil, because he thinks he's caught me in a string of inconsistencies. Okay, I'll take the time to elucidate here and now, because once we get going in the next action sequence, things aren't gonna let up until the very end of the book, and I don't think I'm going to have much time to stop for these literary asides and 'splain things to you.

- *Item:* I know where Li is going to strike. He is going to strike in the Senkaku Islands. How do I know that? I know it because the Senkakus are noted on the ship's charts I took off the *Nantong Princess.* Now, there is no reason for them to be noted on said charts—unless the ship was going to stop there. But why would the *Nantong Princess* stop at the Senkakus? After all, we all know that the Senkakus are uninhabited islands—and there are no port facilities.

The reason the *Nantong Princess* was going to stop at the Senkakus was to offload cargo.

Offload what, you ask? Missiles, friends. Missiles. And two electronic-warfare officers. And Big Brother.

- *Item:* There were half a dozen French-made GLCMs[59] aboard the *Nantong Princess*—but no launchers.

---

[59]Ground-Launched Cruise Missiles.

That told me the Chinese had already prepositioned the launchers.

- *Item:* The cruise missiles aboard the *Nantong Princess* had been stored in watertight containers. That told me they'd be dropped over the side as the ship passed the island and stored underwater until it was time to launch. Then they'd be brought up and deployed. But since I'd scuttled the *Nantong Princess,* the Chinese were going to have to bring missiles with them when they came.

I'd tossed another lench into the plot as well when I'd wasted that pair of one-stars aboard the *Nantong Princess.* The ossifers I'd killed were Li Chimen's EW—electronic warfare—officers. They were the guys who would have run Big Brother.

That was another major piece of the puzzle now in place. Big Brother was one of the keys to this plan. I'd spent my time worrying about how the Chinese had gotten their hands on the system. What I should have been doing was trying to figure out how the fuck they'd use it—where it fit into Li Chimen's plan.

Well, by letting my mind wander in that ineffable, enigmatic, inscrutable, abstract, Zen fashion just as Roy had taught me to, I had done just that. Big Brother was an extremely versatile system. It was, in fact, fully capable of functioning within the three capabilities our Pentagon planners have given to electronic warfare. Does that sound like incomprehensible bureaucratic Navyspeak? Let me illustrate what I mean in language you can understand, given our current scenario.

- Big Brother could initiate EA—an electronic attack—which would degrade and destroy Taiwan's capabilities to resist a missile attack.
- Big Brother could provide EP—electronic protection—which would neutralize and thwart all Taiwanese capability to retaliate against Li and his missiles.

- And Big Brother could provide ES—electronic warfare support—by enabling Li to listen in to the Taiwanese command-and-control communications networks and silence them at will.

But I had scuttled the *Nantong Princess* and its cargo of cruise missiles, and, even more significantly, absquatulated with his Big Brother system. That had to have made Li's OPLAN a lot more complicated. It also opened up his AV—that Area of Vulnerability, which exists during the first, precarious stages of all SpecOps. And when it did, when Mister Murphy-san was doing his worst to crusterfuck Li Chimen, I'd be waiting—to take advantage of the situation.

Okay, okay—I hear you. You want to know how I'm so sure that Li will be on-scene. That's easy. It is because I know that Li Chimen tends to be a micromanager. And how do I know it? I know it because he has never, so far as I can see, delegated any important job to anyone else. He set up his own ops in Singapore, Jakarta, Hong Kong, and Tokyo by going there himself and supervising. And when someone—Alixe Joseph—started nipping at his heels in Tokyo, he went straight to Washington to find out who it was—and neutralize the threat. So, now that the well-known *merde* was about to hit the well-known *ventilateur,* I knew Li would want to keep his dirty hands on the switch.

And if all of that isn't enough for you, try this: Li Chimen is a SpecWarrior officer; a Chinese SEAL. A shooter. Like me, he leads from the front. No, friends—Li Chimen will be on the scene.

And so will I—I have a score to settle with the cock-breath.

Chapter 18

As you know, I've always believed that getting there—wherever *there* might be—is more than half the fun . . . not to mention more than half the pain. The fun (and pain) I was currently contemplating would consist of somehow moving ourselves and our equipment about a thousand miles south of Tokyo, then dropping onto a rocky, uninhabited island, and setting up an ambush that would annihilate Li Chimen and his forces—and do all of it without alerting the Japanese, the Americans, or the Chinese to our plan. Hey—piece of tofu, right?

Absofucking*rutely*.

But first, we had to achieve that first thousand-mile leg. How to do it? We'd steal a plane. I contemplated hot-wiring a commercial jet at Narita, but discarded the idea as impractical. First of all, boosting a commercial jetliner would attract unwanted attention. Second, someone—read *moi*—would end up having to pay for the damn thing. And even though these books have made me several dump trucksful of money, I still have a problem shelling out the kind of petty cash that JAL or ANA's lawyers would demand for one of their 727s or DC-9s.

That left the military—to be precise, the United States Air Farce. Now, stealing an airplane from the USAF is actually much easier than you might think. There are no ignition keys to worry about, and the sky cops who are in charge of security at most Air Force installations spend more time reading girlie magazines or surfing on the Internet than they do actually watching all those billions of dollars' worth of equipment sitting idle on the tarmac. To be honest, the toughest part of stealing from the Air Force is making sure that you have adequate fuel—*and* that you can get your hands on it. The Air Force takes more precautions with its gas pumps than it does with its aircraft. They generally put locks on their gas pumps—which is more than they do for their airplanes.

So, with evening coming upon us quickly, I was ready to head straight for the nearest Air Force base, when Tosho, who had been scanning the radio, came up with a better idea. "Let's go south right now," he said. "They're looking for you from Akita to Kobe—a real full-court press. Why push our luck?"

I was delighted to hear Tosh include himself in my little group of merry, marauding miscreants. "South? Atsugi? Yokosuka? Where?"

"Actually, I was thinking about Okinawa. There are what—thirty or so U.S. bases there—lots of places to borrow a plane. It's more than halfway to the Senkakus—which means we can take something smaller than a C-5." He pointed toward my crotch. "Despite what you may imagine, *Dick*, sometimes smaller is better—because that way we attract less attention, *Gaijin-san.*"

I have always liked the way Tosho thinks, and I told him so in Roguish style.

He responded by extending his thick middle finger in my direction. "You're always Ichiban with me, too, Dickhead."

I rapped my scarred knuckles on his desk. "So—how do

you propose we get to Okinawa without attracting attention?"

"Aren't you the one who's always talking about 'Keep-It-Simple-Stupid'?" he asked. He didn't wait for me to answer him. "So, I'm gonna keep it simple. I'm planning to fly commercial," Tosho said. "Want to come along?"

Sure I did. But there were all sorts of people out there looking for us. I posed Tosh a simple question: how do you get nine armed and dangerous fugitives aboard a commercial flight?

He gave me such a simple answer that he sounded like Roy Boehm: "Easy, Dick: you go as nine armed and dangerous . . . policemen."

Sound puzzling? It's not—it's as KISS as Tosho said it would be. How? Well, Okinawa—and some 160 smaller islands—are all a part of Japan's forty-seventh prefecture, which gave Tosh all the operational authority he needed. He picked up the phone and dialed one of the three interisland airlines. He identified himself, asked for the government service desk, and then proceeded to rattle machine-gun Japanese into the phone. Six minutes later, he turned to me, a big, wide grin on his face and an upraised thumb on his right hand.

"I told 'em I have a training team that has to scramble immediately. We're booked on a flight at nineteen hundred," he said. "Now—lemme get on the horn to Okinawa and make sure we'll have the right kind of transportation waiting at Naha."

1858. We drove three big black Kunika Broncos right onto the tarmac, unloaded under the gaze of the ground crew—not to mention the passengers, their noses pressed to the windows—and humped our equipment up the steel steps of the rolling gate and through the hatch into the DC-10's first-class section. Tosho did all the talking. The rest of us, in black SWAT coveralls, thigh-holsters and Glocks, web equipment, balaclavas, Bolle goggles, Nomex gloves, and kilos of Velcro, did all the schlepping. Yeah, we probably looked like a bunch of exceptionally un-Japanese Japanese—but as long as we kept our *gaijin* mouths shut, no one would be able to prove anything one way or the other.

1909. Our crates, cases, and bags were seat-belted securely into twelve aisle seats. We took window seats and strapped ourselves in just as the wheel chocks were yanked and the tug began to push the plane back from the gate.

1939. We reached cruising altitude thirty-two thousand feet over O Shima island. According to the schedule, we had ninety-six minutes until touchdown. Tosho shooed the stews—oops, sorry, please excuse the political incorrectness—*the flight attendants* out of first class—an act that earned him dirty looks from Boomerang, Rodent, Gator, Duck Foot, Nod, and the Pick, and a "you're number two-thirds with me" gesture from Half Pint. Then, curtains closed, he waved his index finger in the classic circle the wagons move and said, "Okay, gents, time to change clothes—let's all get civilian."

2115. We sat patiently—curtains still closed—until the plane had emptied out and the flight crew and stews had disembarked. Then we picked up our gear and trundled it down the portable stairs and into a pair of waiting Nissan vans.

I looked them over in the airport's amber sodium light. Perfect. The vans had seen better days—they looked like well-used family transportation. Lots of small dings and scratches, but well maintained and clean. One was tan, the other maroon.

If you want to stay anonymous, friends, don't be driving some kind of transportation that makes you stand out in traffic. Cops, MPs, and other sundry law enforcement types tend to notice flashy cars the way hunters see deer in the forest. They don't see the whole deer—just a flash of white tail or a movement that shouldn't be there. Same principle applies here. Drive a red Testarossa or a fancy gold Jeep Cherokee Laredo with mirror-tinted windows, or a Bronco brimming with radio antennas and it'll catch a cop's eye not because he's looking for that specific car, but because it stands out in the normal traffic flow.

We stowed the goods. Tosho clambered into the driver's seat of the tan van. I rode shotgun. Duck Foot, Half Pint, and the Pick rode with us. Boomerang took the wheel of the maroon van, with Nod at shotgun, and Rodent and Gator squeezed into his backseat. Tosho turned the engine over and gunned it a couple of times. Running with only our parking lights on, we convoyed across the tarmac, paralleled the main taxiway, and exited the two-meter chain-link perimeter fence through the gate that led to the airport's fuel farm.

When we'd cleared, Tosho pulled onto the shoulder and turned toward me. "Okay, Cisco—I got us this fuckin' far. Now it's your turn. What's next?"

That was a good question. Frankly, I had no idea what was next. I mean, we were here to steal a plane from the military. So that meant heading for an air base. Uncle Sam's Misguided Children had one at Camp Butler—which is headquarters for III MEF, or the Third Marine Expeditionary Force. But Marines tend to be possessive about their aircraft. They actually do mount decent security. The Air Farce, on the other hand . . .

I looked at Tosho. "Go north, Pancho," I said. "Head for Kadena."

2321. We skirted Naha with its congested streets and all-night tourist bars, and drove north on a multilane freeway running parallel to the coastline, passing klik after klik of the USG—U.S. Government—issue razor-wire fence that denotes military installations, interspersed with knots of fast-food restaurants, pachinko parlors, used-car lots, and beer halls. Even this close to midnight, the road was chockablock full of traffic moving from pachinko parlor to beer hall to McDonald's. Tosh eased into a garishly lighted gas station just outside Kozo, a town from which you can just about spit—and hit the razor wire secured to the top of Kadena's perimeter fence line. I looked inside. The convenience shop was filled with late-night shoppers buying Orion beer and Baggies of Japanese snacks.

I'd come up with a plan, which I shared with the guys. The drill would be simple: we'd abandon the vans in town, break onto the base through the fence line—we're talking miles and miles of fence line and there are lots of places to sneak through it without attracting attention—take whatever we could lay our hands on, fill it with fuel, and haul butt. The Pick would get us off the ground,[60] then fly us over the target. When we were ready to go out the hatch, he'd turn the plane due east so it would run out of fuel over the open sea, secure the controls, and we'd all HALO onto the island.

I swiveled toward Pick. "What do you think—they've got a bunch of Hercules here that're always ready to go. C-9s too—for all the damn CODELs[61] they get."

"I-ee," Tosho grunted. "Stay away from the big stuff. Too complicated. You'll need a tug to move the damn thing—and most of the 130s are probably on a working flight line."

Pick wrinkled his nose and shook his head, too. "Negatory. Tosh is right: smaller's better, Skipper. Finding enough fuel for a fuckin' C-130 or a C-9's gonna give us problems—not to mention towing it over to the damn fuel farm without attracting every sky cop in the area. I think we should look for a C-12. It's got the range and it doesn't have a very big signature."

I know when to take "yes" for an answer—so I did. Besides, the Japs ran E-2C ELINT flights over the Senkakus—and I didn't want any stray pups sniffing at our sphincters. Yeah—so long as we're not talking about my cock, smaller might be better. I turned to Tosho and pointed

---

[60]As we demonstrated in *Rogue Warrior: Red Cell,* Piccolo Mead can fly anything from a C-130 to a fucking Buckeye powered parachute.

[61]CONgressional DELegations.

toward the road that led to the air base. "Hey, Pancho, let's go shopping."

We'd just turned onto the road when it hit me. "Whoa—stop—hold it up." I smacked Tosho on the left arm hard enough to make him wince.

He brought the van to a screeching halt so quickly that Boomerang nearly rear-ended us. "Now, what is it, Dick—"

"You have phone change?"

Tosho snaked around in his seat belt until he was able to work his hand into his right trouser pocket and wiggle his fingers.

I watched the crotch of his pants dance. "Are you playing with yourself or getting me the goddam phone change?"

Tosho shot me a knowing look. "Both, asshole." He extracted a handful of coins and handed me six of them. "These should do." He looked at me quizzically. "So, what's up?"

I opened the van door and eased out into the cool night air. "I'll let you know in a few minutes—if things work out."

I was back in eight minutes. Tosh looked at me inquisitively. "What's up?" he asked.

"We wait here."

Six minutes later a mirror-waxed, black vintage Corvette coupe wheeled up to the gas station and pulled in front of the van I was sitting in. Lieutenant Colonel Arch Kielly, dressed in pressed coveralls, hoisted himself out of the cockpit and sauntered over, a shit-eating grin on his face. He wore mirror-polished boondockers and gold-rimmed, tinted glasses that shaded his dark, killer's eyes. The yellow, 353rd Special Operations Group unit patch with its winged black-and-blue panther stood out against the sage green, flame-retardant material of his coveralls.

"Long time no see, you asshole," he said, his arms extended wide so he could give me a *fuerte* abrazo.[62]

---

[62]That's how Cubans hug one another.

I jumped out of the van and hugged him back. "Fuck you, too, Arch. Thanks for coming."

I made introductions. Well—sorta. He already knew my guys, so I gave Arch a thumbnail on Tosho. The pilot was obviously impressed. And I explained to Tosh that Arch and I knew each other from a previous mission we'd both been a part of. Arch picked up the cue flawlessly. "Just think of me as your government-approved taxi driver," he explained.

Then Arch turned to me. "So, what was so fuckin' important that you couldn't come over to the house, drink a case of cold Orions, and explain it there?" he asked.

When I told him in general terms what I needed, he leaned back against my van, arms crossed. His eyes went wide. "Shit, Dick, when I say 'call on me anytime for anything you need,' you really do take it literally, don't you?"

"Hey—what are friends for, if not to ruin each other's careers." Now, I may have been flippant just then; the situation, however, was anything but—and that's what I told Arch.

"It's that important?" Arch scratched his broad chin.

I shook my head. "It is, Arch." I gave him a quick sit-rep about Li Chimen and Bentley Brendel. I provided a timetable, and related what I believed to be the consequences of inaction. Arch looked as if he'd heard it all before. Then I told him about the murder of Alixe Joseph.

Arch's expression grew intense and the color drained from his face. "I had a friend who was in the same kind of trade," he said. "I knew him as Brian Williams—although we both knew that wasn't his real name but a professional alias, just like Alixe Joseph wasn't your friend's real name. Anyway, we'd been to the War College together, and afterward, well, we ended up working on the same real tight-hold joint project—you know the kind of thing I'm talking about. I was back in the States. Brian, he was out there all by himself. No backup. No protection. Bottom line: he was betrayed—and he was killed. And it's always outraged me that the people in charge forbade me to do anything to avenge him, or go after the scumbags who had him killed—although we all had a pretty good idea who they were at the time." He paused and stood there, remembering. His cobra's eyes went misty. "He was *alone,* Dick. He died alone—and in very great pain."

I understood only too well what was going on, so I let him take his time. "You know," he finally said, his voice heavy with emotion, "people like Brian, or your friend Alixe Joseph, they're the real heroes—the ones the late director of central intelligence Bill Colby once referred to as the gray men of intelligence gathering. I mean, Dick—you and I, we can draw weapons, and we can go out and use 'em on the bad guys. Oh, sure—we may put ourselves in harm's way. But we're given the means to defend ourselves and kill our enemies before they kill us. The ROEs[63] under which Alixe operated didn't allow her to use anything like the stuff we can put our hands on. No guns. No missiles. She had to work out in the open. Undefended. She was vulnerable." He paused, overcome with emotion, and bit his lower lip. Then, after a few seconds, he continued. His voice was low, but its tone was resolute. "Look, if this scumbag Li was the one who had her killed, then I'm in—all the way. Anything I can do to help you put these cocksuckers in the ground, I'll do—pedal to the metal."

0012. We followed Arch onto Kadena—letting him precede us by six or eight cars so that the guard at the gate wouldn't link his Corvette with our vans. Yes, we just drove onto the base. I stowed Tosho on the floor, and the rest of us round-eyed devils rolled our windows down and waved at the bereted guards as we cruised past. The technique had worked during my days at Red Cell—and it still works now. It distressed me to see that some lessons don't ever get learned. I also noticed that the guards' pistols had no magazines in their butts; the M-16s stowed inside the gatehouse were unloaded, too. Neither do others.

---

[63]Rules Of Engagement.

We parked the vans in the darkest corner of the BOQ parking lot[64], and changed back into our basic black outfits once more. I knew there are so many transients at a base the size of Kadena, that the sky cops hardly ever take notice of new vehicles. So we had at least twenty-four hours before anybody would ask WTF. Just to be on the safe side, Gator extracted the slingshot and Baggie of ball bearings he habitually carried in his fanny pack, and shot out the three closest security lights.

Arch cruised by, his headlights out, gave our location a critical once-over, and me a thumbs-up. Then Pick jumped into the 'Vette and took off with him. They would recon the plane, get charts, and check on fuel. Before they left, Arch handed me a map of the base from his glove compartment. Using it, I sent Boomerang, Nod DiCarlo, and Half Pint Harris to the rigger's loft to cumshaw us our parachutes from the sport-jumping club's locker. Gator, Rodent, and Duck Foot were dispatched to find enough webbing to secure our gear for a jump. And Tosho and I stayed behind to load magazines, and guard the equipment.

0019. Mister Murphy paid a visit, in the person of an Okinawan rent-a-cop.

I saw him coming before he saw us, and shoved Tosho onto the floor of the van. "Shhhh—"

The rent-a-cop Took Notice. He turned in our direction and marched toward the van. He was a wizened little guy in a bad-fitting uniform. A huge flashlight hung off his belt, and a time clock weighed down his left shoulder. He extracted the flashlight, brought it up, and shone it at the van.

I stepped out, closed the door, and moved in front of him to block his view. *"Kon-ban-wa."* Good evening.

He looked past me, bowed slightly at the waist, and painted me with his light. *"Ohayo gozi-masu."* Good *morning.* He went on tiptoe so he could look inside the van.

---

[64]Bachelor Officer's Quarters.

He was a nosy little guy with a creased, round face and a gray, wispy mustache. He walked up to me, looked me up, looked me down, looked me side-to-side, and finally peered right up and into my face. His mustache twitched like antennae. Slowly, he drew his tongue across his lower lip, letting it come to rest in the far right corner. *"Amerikajin,"* he finally said.

"Hai," I answered. Yes. "Captain."

He bowed. *"Kon-nichi-wa."* Greetings. He paused. He perused me again. I think it was the full beard and French braid that caught his attention. "ID paper please?" he asked.

His accent was so thickly Japanese that I could literally shrug the question off, my arms opened wide in the universal gesture for, I don't understand what the fuck you're saying.

He repeated the question. I had two choices right now. I could show him something, in which case he might go running off and ask someone about the *Amerikajin* with the French braid and it would be doom on Dick time, which as you know is the way of telling you in Vietnamese that I'd be fuckee-fuckeed. Or I could jump his bones, tape him up, and leave him where he'd be found in a couple of hours—and I'd be long gone. I knew that he couldn't be allowed to see Tosho—or the rest of my merry band of murdering marauders. Most of all, I couldn't let him learn about Arch Kielly, who was due back any minute, now.

So, I started to reach into my back trouser pocket, as if to withdraw my wallet. Instead, my left arm whipped around to knock the flashlight out of his hand and wrap the old guy up.

Except that by the time my big Slovak fist arrived at the spot where he'd been holding the flashlight, it grabbed a handful of air. Simultaneously, my arm was pulled forward, my body was yanked off balance, flipped like the proverbial flapjack, and I came down—hard—wham on my back on the fucking macadam of the BOQ parking lot. Who was this guy—the fucking star of those *Karate Kid* movies?

I rolled over onto my hands and knees, and groaned. The old watchman stood there, waiting, his face as impassive as an Oriental Sphinx. He waited until I'd pulled myself to my feet, bowed slightly from the waist—never taking his eyes off of me—and repeated his request: "ID paper, please."

I brushed myself off. Okay—so he knew Okinawan karate, or judo, or whatever the martial art flavor of the island happened to be. But guess what—I know that stuff, too. So I feinted left and watched as Old Guy watched me. I feinted right and watched. I saw where his eyes were moving, and I knew what I had to do. No, my response didn't include killing. I didn't want to hurt him, after all—just put him down long enough for me to bind and gag and stow him, so we could get on with the night's work.

Time was a-wasting. I feinted again—then, my feinting spells over, I went for his legs. Here's a fact: take a man down onto the ground and grapple with him, and all those wonderful holds and throws and kicks and the other sophisticated third-degree black-belt techniques he's mastered at the dojo are just about useless.

I dove, stretched out like a cornerback reaching out to shoestring tackle a wide receiver with the ball. But the sonofabitch stepped aside like a toreador and—*ole!*—as my body shot by him, he tapped me on the back of the neck with the butt of his flashlight. Not enough to do any real damage. But quite enough to let me know that if he'd wanted to, he could have broken my Roguish neck.

Once again, he stepped back and bowed. "ID paper, please."

What could I do? I bowed—keeping him in focus all the time while he did the same to me—and reached for my wallet. Which was when Tosho, moving like the real-life ninja he is, caught the old guy from behind, buckled his knees, and fell on him, his bulk pinning the watchman to the ground. The two of them rolled around like kids on a fucking playground, with Tosho stage-whispering—desperation creeping into his voice—"Stop the sidewalk superintendent shit and Get The Fucking Duct Tape, Dick—"

0032. I'd just finished stowing the night watchman in a phone booth sixty yards from the BOQ when my rigger's loft cumshaw crew returned with long faces. They'd found enough altimeters, wrist compasses, and miscellaneous web gear for all of us. But we were two MC-5 chutes short—MC-5s are the seven-cell Paraflite RAPS—Ram Air Parachute Systems—that we SEALs (as well as Recon Marines and Army Special Forces) normally use for HALO or HAHO operations. There were a bunch of MC3s—the old, round chutes that are used in static-line drops. But they'd rejected 'em and instead rooted around until they'd found a tandem—an old, military nine-cell Vector, to be precise, which had obviously seen more than its fair share of use. I examined the damn thing and wondered aloud if it had even one more hop in it—especially a blind jump in which the air conditions, ground conditions, sea conditions, and potential hostile conditions were all unknown.

Boomerang hefted the big, dark pack. "No prob—I'll jump this thing with Nod here, Boss Dude," he said, thumping Ed DiCarlo on the shoulder. "It's so cool."

"Cool, hell—I *hate* it when we jump tandem," Nod complained. "You gotta understand, Skipper, he's impossible. Always trying to fucking backseat drive. 'Steer right.' 'Steer left.' 'Flare now, brake now.' I swear, he's worse than my wife."

0047. Arch Kielly and Piccolo Mead drove up in a regulation USAF Hummer with a truck body on it. They jumped out and Arch began tossing our stuff into the boxy rear of the vehicle. "C'mon, c'mon." Arch's tone was urgent. "I found the plane—a C-12 just like you wanted. C'mon—get your stuff packed and we'll drive over. You guys can stow your gear while I locate a fuel truck."

Hey, maybe Mister Murphy had finally gone to sleep for a few hours. The C-12 is small enough so that we wouldn't need an APU—that's one of those four-wheeled, electric-driven auxiliary power units you see running around airports—to jump-start its dual Pratt & Whitneys. Arch could flip the switches, play with the chokes and throttles—in other words, do whatever magic that pilots do—and we'd be on our way. It was great news, and I burbled with enthusiasm. "Where is it? How long until we get there? What's the configuration? Where's the nearest runway?"

Arch interrupted his packing long enough to point vaguely over his shoulder into the darkness. "It's that-a-way some, just past the chop shop." He resumed stowing goodies, pausing long enough to look at me standing there, asking questions. "C'mon, Dick—get the lead out. What the hell difference does it make what where when why how? We have a plane. So, let's just get this fucking gear put away ASAP and get our asses over to the fucking thing."

He had a point. Warriors do not ask superfluous questions or burble like five-year-olds. Warriors do the job. I buttoned lip and started stowing.

Chapter 19

0053. We jammed ourselves into the Hummer like clowns in one of those half-pint circus cars (to be totally honest, a bizarre, even outré similarity could probably be argued, given the absurdity of our current situation). Arch hit the ignition switch, the diesel gurgled to life, and, *sans* headlights but *avec* running lights, we chugged across Kadena like a squat tug cutting through a harbor. We passed some of the administration buildings, drove behind some huge stowage facilities, and skirted the humongous hangars and maintenance sheds. In the distance I could make out red landing lights and blue-lighted taxiways, as well as the dim lights in the "cab"—the air base's main control tower. Every few minutes, we could hear the roar of jet thrusters reversing as a plane came in to land, or the high-decibel sounds as a fighter took off into the moonless night sky with afterburners on full.

But Arch kept us well away from the active portion of the base. He drove slowly so as not to attract attention, easing past the darkened warehouses, stowage sheds, and outbuildings. He cut across the road maintenance facility with its dump trucks and graders, and skirted the recycling collection area, making his way around Kadena's seemingly endless perimeter, until—after what I thought was an interminable trip—we came upon the VIP terminal, approaching on a little-used service road that came up on the terminal's blind side.

We swung wide past the darkened structure and stopped, bathed in soft orange light from the sodium lamps on twenty-foot poles. Arch got out, opened a double-wide gate, pulled the Hummer onto the tarmac, and then rolled the four-foot-high chain-link fence closed behind him. He cut the engine and the lights, jumped out, did a little courtier's bow—the kind you see in the sorts of Tyrone Power/Linda Darnell movies they tend to show on AMC—and pointed to a half dozen aircraft in a neat line, chocked directly behind the low, neutrally painted building, and facing toward us. "Your transportation waits without, my liege," Arch pronounced.

It was too good an opportunity to pass up. "Without what?" I asked.

Arch's face went elastic. "Hey—I thought this was action-adventure, not Abbott and Costello."

0105. Gator used his slingshot to extinguish the three closest security lights, which allowed us to work in semidarkness. First, we changed clothes once again, back into the black SWAT stuff Tosho had given us. We strapped on our web gear and our side arms, our CQC tactical vests, thigh pouches, and other sundry lethal items. Then it was time to pack the aircraft.

I took my flashlight and peered inside. The plane had been configured as VIP transport. My beam illuminated six plush reclining chairs, a walnut wood desk console, a galley, with full bar—and very little damn space for our pile of lethal goodies. Doom on Dickie—fuckee-fuckee me. We were going to have to reconfigure the damn cabin before we could load out. I turned toward Arch. "You carrying a wrench with you tonight?"

Arch went through the Hummer's toolbox, then shook his head. "Negatory."

"Anybody else?"

The silence was absolutely deafening. I sighed and reached for the Gerber Multi-Plier on my belt—fuck! It was gone! I was going to have very existential fingers before the night was over.

0135. We began to load our gear a full thirty minutes behind the schedule I kept in my brain. Even with the seats and desk console removed, it was going to be a tight fit.

We were delayed even more when Arch reported that he couldn't find a topped-off fuel truck that was unlocked. The pilot took Duck Foot—and Duck Foot's set of lock picks—with him and disappeared into the night on foot. By the time they drove back, it was another quarter hour we should have been airborne.

Now, you may be wondering just why I was so intent on getting going quickly. First of all, since we were borrowing an aircraft, it would be easier to stay out of sight in the dark. Second, if by some chance Li Chimen and his crew had beaten us to the Senkakus, we'd have an easier time with them—and they a harder time with us—if we hit at night. But from the way things were progressing, it was gonna be light—or almost light—by the time we jumped. And third, the more time we took now, the less time Arch would have to get the plane back to Kadena unnoticed.

0154. Arch topped off the tanks and sealed 'em. He pulled the crib sheet out of the document folder and ran the preflight check with Pick. Then he did a solo walk around, pulling the wheel chocks as he did.

0157. He settled into the left-hand seat and adjusted for back and forth and side to side and up and down and pitch and yaw and whatever the fuck pilots adjust their seats for, until he was comfortable. I scrambled forward and watched as he and Pick played with the switches and dials, talking that fucking pilot-talk that nobody ever understands or makes sense of. I guess they were satisfied with themselves, because Arch's head turned, and he said, "Good evening, ladies and gentlemen. My name is Arch Kielly and I'll be your pilot tonight. We'll be following a southerly route over the beautiful South China Sea—"

Impolite though it might have been, I interrupted. "Yo, Arch." I didn't need a monologue—I needed to get our asses in the air, and that's what I told him.

"What's your point?" Arch got himself comfortable, and hit what he had to—and the port engine grumbled, growled, and snarled into life. When Arch was happy with what he heard, he kicked the starboard engine in, watched as his revs climbed, adjusted the prop pitch to just where he wanted it, then eased off the brakes and started a slow roll.

"Okay, gents, we're on our way," he said, stating the obvious. He steered us away from the VIP apron. We began to pick up a little bit of speed as we taxied off into the darkness.

I realized what Arch was going to do. The C-12 may not be a STOL—Short TakeOff and Landing—aircraft. But it can hustle its airframe skyward pretty damn quickly. So Arch was going to roll us out to a deserted taxiway at the very edge of the field, and sneak us right into the sky before anybody noticed.

Except he didn't do that at all. In fact, he flipped on what had to be every single one of the C-12's running lights, as well as its taxi/landing headlights. And he wasn't heading anywhere near the perimeter, but taking us directly toward the long line of red, orange, and blue lights that I knew designated Kadena's main taxiways and active runways.

One minor, niggling question occurred to me. It was this: how the fuck did Arch think he was gonna use a fucking runway? Hey, Kadena has multiple active runways. To use them, you've gotta get cleared by the control tower, especially since the air base is operational twenty-four hours a day, and if you just fucking go for it there is a very good chance that you will get yourself creamed by an F-15, or an F-16, or a C-5B, or—well, you get the idea.

But so far as I knew—and this knowledge was based on my own firsthand experience—it is generally hard to get clearance from a control tower when you are stealing the fucking aircraft. Being an inquisitive kind of Rogue, I posed that question to Arch.

"Hey, Dick, go back and close the drapes," he said by way of an answer. Who the fuck had he studied Q&A with, Roy Henry Boehm?

Puzzled, I stood up and turned to do as I was asked. Without warning, Arch gunned the engines, increasing our speed. He fucking knocked me clean off my feet. I careened back into the cabin, smashed snout first into one of the Big Brother suitcases, bounced off the adjacent bulkhead, then reversed course and landed in a heap at Boomerang's feet.

His long face peered down at me. "Awesome English, Boss Dude. What do they call that—a massé shot?"

"Fuck you, cockbreath." I found my footing, and my handkerchief, and blew fresh blood from my throbbing nose. What was it with Arch? Did he like to play STR—Smack the Rogue—every time we fuckin' flew together?

My eyes still teary from the blow my nose had sustained, I peeked through the porthole. We were moving past a series of hangars well illuminated by the warm, orange-tinged light of sodium lamps. A pair of black, stealth-painted C-130s sat outside one of the hangars, guarded by half-a-dozen dark-uniformed individuals with automatic weapons.

"Hey, fellas, that's where we keep the plane you rode in," Arch shouted toward the rear, oblivious of my newfound pain.

I stowed the hankie and continued into the fuselage. "Let's close the fuckin' drapes," I barked.

Drapes? Well, actually they were more like opaque curtains. But each window had a pair, stretched between two horizontal rods. That way, the VIPs could nap on the way to their destination. I slid curtains across the first of the four pairs of round windows, and watched as Gator and Rodent pulled the rest shut.

I headed back toward the cockpit. "Done, Arch," I said.

"Now, will you please keep the fucking speed stable and answer the fucking question?"

"Pick—get the hell off the flight deck until we're airborne," Arch replied by way of an answer. "And Dick—you keep out of sight, too."

He didn't wait for a reply. Instead he plucked the pilot's headset from its rest, slipped the cups over his ears, adjusted the microphone to sit just below his lower lip, and turned the comms system on.

I hunkered down well below the window line and behind the cockpit doorway and watched as he played with the radio dials and the keypad, punching in a series of frequencies. When he'd done that, he hit his transmit button. "Tower—Beech Two-Two-Three-One-Lima."

Tower—WTF?

"Repeat—Tower. This is Beech Two-Two-Three-One-Lima, Lieutenant Colonel Kielly, requesting taxi and takeoff clearance for a nonscheduled night navigation and evasion exercise."

There was a fifteen-second pause as Arch waited for an answer. "That's KILO, INDIA, ECHO, LIMA, LIMA, YANKEE," he replied, using the phonetic alphabet to spell his name. "Three fifty-three special ops wing. Yes—that's right. I'm nonscheduled. I have to work out a specialized approach for something upcoming." He grinned vaguely in my direction. "I think they bought it," he said excitedly. He clapped a hand to his ear so he could listen more easily. "Affirmative, tower." Another pause. Arch nodded positively. "Sure thing. Can do."

He dropped our ground speed and veered the C-12 gently to the left. "Confirm: Taxiway Tango-Papa-One-Six to Runway Romeo Three-Three. Hold and wait for flight path and takeoff clearance." He paused. "Affirmative. Thank you, tower."

He waited another thirty seconds, then hit the transmit button again. "Tower, Beech Two-Two-Three-One-Lima." He paused. "Affirmative. Mission profile has me turning the squawk off after I'm feet wet. Yes—affirmative: I will fire up the squawk prior to final approach, ETA three hours."

The C-12 coasted along the taxiway, its headlamps probing the darkness. Arch gave the plane some additional throttle as he approached the runway we'd been assigned. He turned the aircraft perpendicular to the runway and braked, bringing us to a full stop. He looked out over the wings to make sure his flaps were in the correct position, did a final cockpit check, then turned toward me. "We're ready to go," he reported.

Arch's attention was diverted by the radio. "Affirmative, tower," he barked. "Beech Two-Two-Three-One-Lima standing by." Arch turned toward where I was crouched in the cockpit doorway. "We have to wait for a pair of planes coming in—a flight of F-16s, I think."

From out of the black, an F-16 roared in front of us at an altitude of fifty feet, its engine screaming. Arch tapped his headset. "Say again, tower—say again." He lifted his head in my direction. "I can't hear worth shit with that engine noise."

The second fighter roared in. Arch was shaking his head, as if there'd been a malfunction. But obviously, nothing was wrong because he didn't wait for further clearance but jammed the throttles and bounced the C-12 forward, almost smacking me into the doorjamb as he did so.

"Hang on." Arch gunned the aircraft, launching it crudely and rudely to the right. The props were at full pitch, and we lurched down the runway, fishtailing a little bit for the first two hundred yards until Arch could steady the plane.

He was gaining speed when the runway lights went dead on either side of us. "I think somebody in the cab[65] just realized I'm not cleared to be flying this here plane tonight," Arch shouted. "Well—they're too fuckin' late, right?"

He checked the airspeed and, happy with what he saw,

[65]Remember—that's the main air-traffic control facility.

eased back on the wheel. We slipped into the night sky. "Say again, tower, say again," he said into his lip mike. "Sorry—say again, tower—I can't read you. I'm going radio silence now. I'll catch you on the flip side." He swiveled toward me and grinned. "Yeah—right."

We were climbing steeply now, banking into the darkness. Arch retracted his gear, trimmed his flaps, then waved Pick up from the rear and pointed him toward the right-hand cockpit seat. "You get yourself settled in," Arch said. "I'll hand it over to you once we're clear of Kadena airspace and I've put this thing where they won't be able to find us." Pick dropped into the copilot's chair and locked the armrest down. "Hang on," Arch growled, "I'm about to see just how much punishment this airframe can take."

He banked sharply left, then right, as he continued to climb steeply. Then he heeled over to my left, and kicked the fucking plane into a balls-to-the-wall dive.

My gut knotted, just like it does every time I ride a fucking state-of-the-art roller coaster, and I slammed Arch on the shoulder. "Fuckin' A, Arch—great!" I braced myself against the cockpit door and watched the altimeter roll backward as we roared groundward. I could see whitecaps through the front windshield.

Arch whipped the nose around, and we leveled off at two hundred and fifty feet. "Fun, huh?" he asked. He didn't wait for an answer. "Okay—we're feet wet," he continued—but heading northwest. "Now—let's start the disappearing act."

He hit the squawk switch, which killed the IFF—Identification, Friend or Foe[66]—transmitter.

---

[66]IFF uses electromagnetic transmissions—pulses—to which similar equipment carried by friendly forces automatically responds. IFF keeps you from shooting down your own (or allied) aircraft. Some aircraft have an IFF/PI, which is an IFF with a Personal Identifier, so that a specific aircraft—SECDEF's, for example, or Air Force One—can be distinguished.

"Now they'll have trouble spotting us." Arch played with the radio frequency buttons, and listened to what was going on. "Even so, they're scrambling something to come after us," he reported glumly.

So much for leaving Mister Murphy on the ground. But we weren't without resources of our own. "Boomerang," I shouted, "weren't you the asshole who wanted to try out the radar-defeating module in that suitcase we brought with us?"

0244. Enveloped by Big Brother's electronic shield, we were invisible. Don't ask me how the fucking thing works because I don't know. All I do know is that I was able to listen in to the pilots of the F-16s that had been sent to find us and escort us home, and the kind of language they used wasn't even fit for *this* fucking book. This damn equipment was *good.* We flew on in total darkness—no exterior lights, no interiors either. Pick kept our altitude at two hundred feet, plus or minus fifty, holding the C-12 steady above the mild chop below.

Back in the cabin, we parceled out the equipment by Braille and secured everything so it was jumpable. You cannot jump holding on to a three-hundred-pound steel crate, for example. And so the explosives, claymore mines, minigrenades, and other goodies I'd brought all the way from Washington via Rome got repacked in ballistic nylon bags and Velcro'd to our CQC load-supporting SEAL combat vests, or H-harnessed inside combat packs or aviators' kit bags. The guys looked like Michelin men by the time they were all suited up and ready. I played jumpmaster, checking each man's toggles and straps; making sure that the Velcro tabs were tight, and that all pouches would remain closed during our jump. It is hell when you're upside down in the air and you see all your ammo fall out.

Arch Kielly squinted at the shadows as we set up for the jump. "It has occurred to me," he said, "to ask how the fuck you guys are ever going to get back once this little exercise is over."

"Arch, if I knew that I'd tell you," I said. I hadn't gotten that far in my planning yet.

He shrugged. "Maybe I should come and get you."

It was a wonderful gesture. But it was impractical, and I told Arch so. He was going to have a hell of a time explaining what he'd done—and I didn't want to make things any worse for him than they already were.

"I guess you're right," he said grudgingly, sounding disappointed. He headed back toward the cockpit and the controls so Pick could douse his face with cammo cream and get his gear on.

0252. Pick and I were the last ones to make ready. I undid all the straps on his RAPS then let him shrug into the harness container. I held it steady as he pulled it high onto his back, threading the chest strap around his jumpsuit. Then he fastened his leg straps, pulling each one tight and securing the loose ends. As I held his pack in place, he adjusted his main lift webbing straps and tightened the horizontal adjusters. He stood straight, threaded the waistband through its buckle, and cinched it as tight as he could. He jumped up and down—that was hard for Pick because he's a tall sonofabitch and his head barely cleared the C-12's bulkhead—and, happy with the way the chute rode, stowed all the excess webbing so it wouldn't flap around during decent. Satisfied, he gave me a thumbs-up. I checked him once again—stuffing a loose web end I discovered into his waistband, then pronounced him good to go.

Pick held my chute for me while I strapped myself into it. Once it was secured, it was time to load up. Now, we SEALs are normally issued combat packs—either medium or large, depending on the mission requirements—which come with sets of webbing specifically designed to be attached to your front, or to your rear. The packs positions allow you freedom during your freefall so that you can maneuver your body and not kill yourself. We, however, were jumping with cumshawed equipment. That meant we had no combat packs. Instead, we had an unlikely assortment of ballistic nylon duffels, helmet bags, and carryalls with which we'd have to make do.

We would also be hampered by the sheer amount of equipment we'd be jumping with. Listen up—this is important. The Ram Air parachute has a more or less constant speed. By that I mean you travel at twenty-five to thirty miles per hour during descent. But that descent rate is calculated on a maximum load of 360 pounds of suspended weight.

Okay, let's run tonight's numbers. I'm a big s.o.b., somewhere in the 220 range. My MP5 and its eight loaded forty-round mags, plus my USP pistol and its six loaded fifteen-round magazines, come to about twenty-seven pounds. That's almost 250. My jumpsuit, vest, boots, belt, web gear, first aid fanny pack, and other assorted accoutrements add another twenty-seven pounds, eight ounces. That brings us up to 275. The parachute system—the RAM chute, reserve, and the packs, cables, and straps that come with 'em—weigh just over forty pounds. That's 315. Then there are the miscellaneous goods—ranging from two one-quart canteens, knives, and ropes to bolt cutters—that weigh about fifteen, sixteen, maybe even seventeen pounds per man. That takes us into the 325–326-pound range. Each of the Big Brother suitcases weighs seventy-five pounds. And our claymores, explosives, detonators, grenades, and other goodies added a total of 350 more pounds to the total. That's 500 more pounds of weight to be divided among eight chutes—62½ pounds each. The weight of the bags we were going to carry everything in added another fifteen pounds to the total—two pounds per chute. That's more than thirty pounds above the limit for which the chutes are designed.

Thirty pounds is not a lot of weight, you say. I'll tell you what: *you* carry a fucking thirty-pound sack of potatoes around for a few days and then tell me if you've changed your mind. And it's a shitload of weight when you're jumping. Combine thirty pounds of excess weight and an old, worn chute (or one that's been partially destroyed by saltwater landings) and the opening shock can destroy a cell or two. Result: you burn in. Or, if the chute has a malfunction and you've got to cut away and deploy your reserve chute—and you're well below the five-thousand-foot safety altitude—that thirty pounds can make a big difference then, too. But we would jump with the additional weight because tonight we had no choice.

That's another element of tonight's jump: the difference between training and balls-to-the-wall combat. Training jumps have safety officers on site; they always use lots of flares to mark your landing zone; there's constant monitoring of the ground wind speed. (According to the latest training manuals, "peacetime ground wind training limits will not exceed eighteen knots.")

Tonight, I had NFI—no fucking idea—what the ground level wind speed was. And frankly, I didn't care either, because we'd jump no matter what the velocity might be. Ocean chop? It didn't matter. The only thing that mattered was getting down and killing as many of the enemy as could be done. We had the murder of an American intelligence officer to avenge. And we had the Nation's security to protect. So no matter what the price was, I'd pay it. I'd pay it so that we would not fail.

0301. Arch turned on the radar and the plane's GPS system long enough for us to get a fix on our target. We were approaching from the north; our ETA was seventeen minutes. "Hang on—I'm climbing to ten thou for the release," Arch called out. The nose of the aircraft rose sharply, and the pitch of the props changed.

Tosh eased his way forward. Together, we used the Big Brother scanner to check for radio transmissions from the biggest of the islands—the only one with sufficient land mass to plant missiles. There was nothing emanating from the island. That was a piece of good news: it meant that we'd be arriving before Li Chimen. Tosh took the scanner, stowed it in the improvised combat pack that hung between his legs, and made his way aft. He was jumping third in this stick.

Boomerang signaled that we were still clear of surveillance. I gave him an upturned thumb. He would monitor until the last minute, then switch off the Big Brother module and stow it just before he and Nod jumped their tandem chute.

0313. I worked my way up and down, checking everyone's gear one last time, securing errant straps and making sure that all the flaps and seals were closed tight. As I checked, I peered into each of my men's faces. Their skin was dark with cammo cream, but all of their eyes were bright, and their War Face expressions were resolute. They'd come to play—and to win. There was no mistaking it.

Now let me digress for just a couple of minutes here to tell you a few things that are very, very important to me. First—and most significant—there is something euphoric about commanding such men as these Warriors. It is a thing that fewer and fewer officers ever get the chance to do, these politically correct days when manager-officers flourish and warrior-officers are shunned.

But, when you come to the old bottom line, isn't *war* what the military is supposed to be all about? So far as I am concerned, the military is not about getting money for college, or learning a trade, or getting an education, or feeling good about yourself. Those may all be peripheral aspects of being in the military, but they're not what the military is about. And here comes Point Number Two: which is, that at its core, being a sailor, or being a soldier, or being a Marine, is about being a warrior. It is about *MAKING WAR*. It is about Duty, Honor, Country. It is about breaking things and killing people. It is about spit and polish. It is about blood and sweat. It is about training, and discipline, and the sort of internal fortitude—the old guys like Ev Barrett and Roy Boehm call it GRIT—that keeps you going when your body and your mind want to lie down, roll over, and quit.

The folks in charge today—all too many of 'em—seem to have forgotten what the military is all about. They spend their time designing new sorts of missions; missions that make our sailors and soldiers and Marines into cops, or tree huggers, or social workers. Shit—our military spends more money these days on fucking recycling and environmental fucking protection than it does on goddamn bullets. So the fucking grunts may be perfectly accomplished when it comes to stacking old fucking newspapers in bins, and sticking plastic fucking bottles in the right colored containers, but they haven't learned how to fucking shoot straight, or clear a jam in their fucking rifle under battlefield conditions, or bring down an enemy tank with a LAAW, because there's no money for live ammo and realistic training anymore.

So let me tell you something, friends: we don't need any more fucking bureaucrats, or any more fucking apparatchik systems analysts, running our military (as has been the case with all too many of our recent Chairmen of the Joint Chiefs of Staff). We need kick-ass officers. Real leaders. Men like Tom Crocker, who is a Warrior in the tradition of Grant, Sherman, Pershing, and Patton; Nimitz, Halsey, Stilwell, and "Chesty" Puller—all officers whose men would follow 'em to hell. Those true American heroes, blooded by battle, their mettle forged on the anvil of war, were all willing to take chances—and risk lives—in pursuit of victory and defense of democracy. It is a hard thing to give an order that you know will result in casualties. But that is what being an officer is all about. It is about taking charge. It is about being responsible. And there is another thing, too: being an officer is about living Roy Boehm's two-word definition of leadership. Being an officer is about the words "Follow Me!"

And so, as I looked in my men's eyes, I realized that I was, once again, being given the greatest gift any officer can ever receive. I was being given the rare opportunity, the sacred responsibility, of leading Warriors into battle. There is no more fulfilling feeling a man can ever have. Thus endeth the sermon.

Chapter 20

0317. Ten thousand five hundred feet. Arch slowed the airspeed to just over a hundred knots. Then he turned on his systems. He scanned his screens and peered at the GPS readout. "Good luck," he said. He extended a gloved hand in my direction.

I took it with a firm grip. "Thanks for everything, Arch. You know . . ." I struggled for the right words. This Warrior had put his career on the line for me and my men.

He turned and looked at me. "Hey—forget it. You'd do the same for me, asshole, right?"

No doubt about that. "A^3, Arch—anyplace, anytime, anywhere." I released his hand, struggled aft, and hooked myself into the last of my gear. Then I cracked the hatch and stowed it securely. The wind screaming past the aircraft was deafening. I adjusted my goggles, stood in the hatchway and looked down, the slipstream slapping at my face. Ahead and below I could make out the narrow chain of islands in the darkness. I stood to the side, so that Gator and Rodent, my first two jumpers, could stand ready in the door, and peered forward into the darkened cockpit. Arch held a flashlight in his right hand, its beam pointed vaguely in our direction. When he extinguished it, we'd go out the door.

The beam went out. I slapped Gator's back and he threw himself through the hatch. Rodent followed. Then Tosh, Duck Foot, Pick, and Half Pint. Boomerang and Nod waddled up to the hatchway in their big tandem rig—and stuck halfway through it. Their equipment had wedged tight in the hatchway and wouldn't move.

There was more—I saw that one of the equipment bag straps had come loose and wrapped itself around the hatch hinge plate. I reached under my chute waist strap, extracted my Spyderco folder from its horizontal belt pouch and sliced through the strap. Then I took hold of the ballistic nylon bag that was causing the logjam and shoved against it, using every ounce of my body weight to get the fucking thing moving. When it finally pulled free—and went out into the slipstream—it yanked Boomerang and Nod right with it. They disappeared into the void with a fast-fading "Hoo-YAAA!"

Time to go—I threw Arch a salute, followed it with the hairy bird, and jumped last.

I never saw the aircraft disappear—I was too centered on the jump itself. I went through the hatch and jumped, swiveling as my feet cleared, to position myself groundward. My body was in what I like to call "the hump"—back arched, arms and legs akimbo. I fell six hundred feet like that, my arms and legs extended, knees bent, my feet higher than my shoulders—a perfect example of what they call "the stable free-fall position" in the ops manuals.

It was perfect until the strap holding the improvised combat pack between my legs decided to separate and the pack came loose, yanking my legs around and skewing my body. Thus altered, my aerodynamics were unfavorably transmogrified and detrimentally metamorphosed in a negative manner. That's the Navyspeak way of saying that the fucking pack threw my big Slovak butt into a nasty, upside down, right-hand spin—the kind of spin that makes jet fighter pilots puke.

I reached down to resecure the broken strap. Big mistake. Did you know that extending the arms in an uneven manner during free fall will cause the parachutist to execute a turn? Well—you know it now, and so did I. I'd extended both arms to reach toward my combat pack. I was now spinning so unevenly that my eyes began to roll back into my head. This was an HFS—one hard fucking spin—which is a maneuver they don't teach at jump school. Belay that. I'd gone way past "spin." I was all the way to "corkscrew." Put all your emphasis on the last syllable, please.

This was not a good thing. From here on, I was vulnerable for a rough-and-tumble time—which was something I didn't need. Moreover, all this pitch-and-yaw shit was not doing my brain any good. It was like being inside a fucking tumble dryer.

Time to makee-makee better. I brought my arms back to what's known as the "Delta" position—arms about a foot from my sides, palms down—like a swept-wing fighter. That stabilized me out of the spin—which left me only the nasty loose pack to deal with. Look, Ma—no hands: I used my thighs to work at the combat pack, worming it with my knees until I had it centered once more. And they think they know fucking spin control at the White House.

Woozy, I checked my altimeter and compass. GNBN.[67] The GN was that I was stable again. BN: my current heading was 165 degrees from where I should have been going. Of course, where I should have been going was a guesstimate. Oh, there is a formula to calculate the HARP—or High Altitude Release Point—for HALO missions. To do this, you take the aircraft speed, the average wind velocity at jump altitude, the average wind velocity and direction at each two-thousand-foot interval from the exit to the opening altitude, factor in the forward throw as

---

[67]If you're too dense to figure this one out, you can look it up in the Glossary.

you exit the aircraft, and the free-fall drift, and *voilà:* the HARP you will need to land on the proverbial dime. Believe me—the textbooks say it's all mathematically precise and can be worked out to within a few centimeters. Yeah—well I know better. In a vacuum, things might go as planned. But you don't jump in a vacuum.

Tonight, for example, there was no information about the wind speed after we left the plane. No poop about its direction, either. To use the technical language of parachuting, we didn't know fuck all. And so, we'd have to feel our way down—use our intuition; our instinct—based on the experience of the thousands of jumps that each of us had made over the years. That's why I have always insisted on saturation training. The more experience you have, the more you know, the easier it will be to take evasive action when Mister Murphy sticks his ugly face into your business.

I turned my head and shoulders slightly to the right to execute what's known as a slow body turn. As I drifted left, I kept an eye on my compass until I'd hit my original bearing. I was back on track. Where I was in relation to the rest of my group I had no idea—but at least I was heading toward the Senkaku chain, and not toward the China coast.

The altimeter read 4500. Yes, I know that in the ops manuals that's five hundred feet below the MCA, or minimum clearance altitude, for air training operations. But this was the real thing, not some training exercise, and we would pull at 2500 feet above the island.

3100 feet. I could see waves breaking against the craggy shoreline. This was going to be a very chancy fucking landing.

2700 feet. I reached for the big rip cord handle. It wasn't there. Oh, it was definitely Doom-on-Dickie time.

With my right hand, I reached up, tried to locate the rip cord housing, and felt for the cable—which should have been protruding—and felt, and felt, and felt. Nada. Nothing. Bupkis. I started to barrel roll—fuck me—and brought my left arm up to counter my right. That kept me stable. If, that is, you believe that falling toward the earth at a rate of a 180 feet a second is a "stable" activity.

2400 feet. I found the cable end and worked my thumb and index fingers around it. Except that I was wearing gloves. And when you're wearing gloves it's hard to grasp hold of the inch-long end a fucking eighth-inch-diameter steel cable in the best of conditions, and this was not the best of fucking conditions but the worst of fucking conditions because I was free-falling at a high goddamn rate of speed while strapped to a shitload of equipment—and I didn't want to make myself any more unstable than I already was.

1900 feet. I worked my fingers up past the swage balls, along the cable end, as feverishly as any fucking freshman ever fingered pussy—except this goddamn cable was slipperier than a slurpee, hormonal, sixteen-year-old cheerleader humping in heat in the back of a van. But I kept at it, pushing the rip cord housing aside as I did.

1680 feet. I *felt* it. Oooh—it felt good, too. I wrapped the cable once around my index finger—which gave me some fucking purchase. And then I pulled—HARD. Nothing happened.

1500 feet—and the ground moving up real, real fast. I pulled HARD again.

1200 feet. The fucking chute deployed—breaking my free fall by standing me upright as the big Ram Air slammed open above my head. It was like—wham! My velocity dropped from 180 feet per second to zero. My head snapped back almost breaking my neck; my eyes bugged from the pressure the straps were placing on me. And yes, friends, all of that kinetic energy of Dickie and every single ounce of his equipment being brought up short, was centered on the triple-reinforced canvas strap that cut right across my right nut. It was all excruciatingly existential enough to make me cross-eyed for a few seconds.

But only a few seconds. There was stuff to be done. I checked to make sure all the cells of the chute had deployed properly. They had. I grabbed the toggles and steered right, then left—and moved as I wanted to. I brought the toggles to shoulder level and applied half brakes. My descent speed and angle changed, just the way they should. Okay—the controls were working. I couldn't quite see the ground, so I checked my altimeter. Four hundred feet and descending at a rate of nineteen feet a second—faster than I might have liked—but then I was carrying a lot of excess weight. The wind was at my back, and I toggled left so that I could fly my downwind leg, then come back into the wind for my final approach and landing.

300 feet. I knew I was awfully low for this downwind leg, but some things can't be helped. I unsecured and lowered my combat pack and the supplemental equipment bags so that my landing would be softer—hitting the ground still strapped to all that equipment is not good for the jumper's health. I felt to see that my weapons were stowed tight and right. They were.

180 feet. Shit—I hadn't paid attention to my position and I'd drifted much farther offshore than I should have been. I craned my neck. The breakers were more than half a mile to my rear and off to my right, now—and I was being carried offshore at thirty-five, maybe even forty miles per hour.

Why was this happening? It was happening because I hadn't been paying attention and been caught in what's known as a land breeze.

See, during the day, coastal land warms faster than coastal water, and the air above the land rises. The cooler air above the water takes its place, with the result that you get what's known as an onshore breeze. At night, the reverse takes place. The coastal land mass is cooler than the water—and the breezes move offshore. I'd been caught in one of these nighttime thermals.

This was real bad juju. I pulled hard on the control toggles to bring the chute around and come into the wind. RNT—Rule Number Two—of parachuting (it is right up there with Rule Number One, which, as you can probably figure out is always remember to pull the fucking rip cord) goes: always land into the fucking wind. Yes, I know that the dust jacket of this book says that as the Rogue Warrior I obey no rules. But there are a few rules that even Rogue Frogs like I have to obey—unless, that is, we want to croak prematurely.

No fucking way. I yanked on the steering toggle with all my weight. The airfoil reacted—dipping its outer edge into a tight turn. Tight turns are dangerous—especially at the altitude at which I found myself, which was so low that I thought my combat pack was going to catch the water and, acting like a fucking sea anchor, drag me under.

I released the toggles. The airfoil lip caught a big breath of air—and I was lifted up, up, up—two fifty, three hundred, three fifty, four hundred feet.

Now I saw breakers directly ahead of me, perhaps a quarter mile away. I steered toward the shoreline, looking for other parachutes as I descended. None were in sight.

135 feet. Since things were going altogether too well, Mister Murphy decided to fuck with me. One second, I was coming in as smoothly as a goddamn 747 on computer-assisted final approach. The next, I was slapped upside the haid by a nasty patch of wind shear and dropped sixty feet in about a second and a half. All the fucking bells and whistles went off at once. It was like fucking klaxons. The chute stalled, collapsed, and I dropped the last thirty-five feet, feet first, into the water, like a boulder rolled off a bridge.

I barely had time to grab a breath before I was dragged under. The shock was fucking explosive—water is hard when you hit it. My goggles were torn off, my body was ensnared by the nylon lines. Above, the dark parachute shroud descended to entwine and entomb me.

There was no time to think—only act. My right hand clawed at the quick-release toggles on my chute harness and I shrugged out of it and kicked away as best I could, hampered by the equipment packs whose long straps were wrapped around my legs.

My left hand reached for the automatic inflation valve on

my UDT combat vest. I yanked it—and felt an upward surge as the compressed gas was released, the vest inflated, and I was borne surfaceward.

I popped the choppy surface, snorted water like a fucking humpback, rolled onto my back, and sucked big, welcome lungsful of cool air. I looked around to get my bearings. I was about three hundred yards offshore. The vest would keep me afloat. Now all I had to do was pull in that hundredweight of soggy equipment, heave to, and swim. Yes, I am being ironic right now, in case you were wondering.

0332. I pulled myself out of the breakers, deflated my UDT vest, retrieved my combat pack and equipment bags from the surf, shouldered them as best I could, and staggered across the short span of rocky shoreline. I'd been carrying more than a hundred pounds of baggage. Now, everything I had—including my clothes—had been soaked through, increasing the load by what felt like 100 percent but in fact was probably only 50 percent.

And, oh, have I mentioned that it was cold and getting colder? Yes, I know it's the South China Sea. And I know we were just north of the Tropic of Cancer. But the water temperature was only about seventy degrees—and seventy degrees gets cold after a while if you do not have thermal protection—which I didn't. More to the point, the night air was about fifty-six, and from what I could tell there was a ten- to fifteen-mile-an-hour wind blowing across the island. The Roguish bottom line is that I was getting cold, fast. And there was nothing to do about it except keep going.

0340. I'd humped my baggage a hundred yards inland, when I heard something off to my right. I dropped to the ground, released my gear, withdrew the USP from its ballistic thigh holster, and moved forward, staying low and moving silently.

I heard the sound again and stopped. Withdrew my night-vision monocle from its pocket on my CQC vest, stretched out, and scanned. Twenty yards away, his head just as visible over the crest of a low, rocky ridge as it would have been in the midday sun, Half Pint was working feverishly at something. I retrieved my gear and moved in his direction.

When I got closer I saw that he was working on Piccolo Mead, who was lying on his back, his face contorted in pain. Half Pint looked up. "Yo, Skipper—asshole here decided to break his ankle on a rock." He worked on the Pick's left leg, handling it gingerly as he wrapped tape around an improvised set of splints and secured them. Half Pint turned back to his swim buddy. "You probably did this on purpose—thought we didn't have enough tactical problems already, right?"

"You got it," Pick said through clenched teeth. "Hey, Skipper, you have any morphine—if I had morphine I think I could walk once asshole here gets me bound and splinted." He sucked air sharply as Half Pint gently lifted the injured leg and wrapped surgical tape under the arch of his foot. "Oooh, that smarts." Pick shifted his shoulders. "Nurse Ratchett here says he doesn't have any. I think he likes it when I'm in pain."

I felt behind my back to the first-aid pouch that hung above my kidneys, unlatched it, pulled one of the half-dozen Syrettes out, and placed it into Pick's hand. "Go for it," I said. "But don't get a habit, huh?"

I closed the first-aid pouch. "You guys see anybody else?"

Half Pint nodded. "Gator came down over there." He pointed to the south. "And I think Boomerang and Nod did, too."

"Rodent? Tosho? Duck Foot?"

"Oh, we're all present and accounted for—although how we're still alive amazes me." Tosho's deep voice came from my left. He limped into view, followed by the five missing SEALs. "I think we have to talk about your choice of landing sites, Dick. Did anyone ever tell you you're a shitty jumpmaster?"

0410. We split into two squads and recced the island well before first light. It didn't take long—even though this was the only island in the chain large enough from which to launch an attack, it was less than a mile in length, and only six hundred yards or so in width. There were no structures—except for a single burnt-out shack with a wood flagpole lying out front, located on the island's highest point. Vegetation was limited to scrub brush, thistle, sea grass, and the sorts of dwarf trees that thrive in salt air and bad soil environments.

The place was uninhabited, although there were signs—well camouflaged signs but signs nonetheless—that someone had been snooping and pooping recently. All footprints had been obliterated by dragged branches. Wheel tracks had been raked out, then dealt with in a similar fashion. But Duck Foot, the Eastern Shore deer hunter that he is, was able to discern 'em all. I put him on the scent. It didn't take long for him to discover that the tracks led to a series of caches. One cache contained weapons. Another held marine communications equipment—the same sorts of waterproof radios that SEALs use. A third—a cave just off the landward, or southwestern, end of the island, held an eight-meter, rigid inflatable boat—very similar to the one we'd dropped to chase down the *Nantong Princess*—on a wheeled utility trailer. An outboard motor sat on an adjacent pallet, a pair of fifty-gallon drums of gasoline, a siphon, and five fuel bladders on the ground nearby. Now I knew how Li planned to make his getaway.

At 0535 we struck real pay dirt. Duck Foot led me toward a large cave just inshore of the island's southernmost coast. It had been covered with radar-defeating stealth netting. Inside, sat two mobile GLCM launchers. Country of origin: France. You remember about GLCMs. The acronym stands for Ground-Launched Cruise Missiles. I'd discovered six French GLCMs onboard the *Nantong Princess.*

Okay. Now we had everything but the supporting cast—e.g., the bad guys. Which presented me with a certain tactical dilemma, to wit: where the fuck were Li and his people going to land? I mean, we had a whole damn island to cover—and nine people to do the job. Sure, we could booby-trap the arms and comms caches, and disable the launchers. But if we allowed the bad guys to come ashore unimpeded, they could overwhelm us by sheer force of numbers. It would take 'em a lot of time, and cost 'em a lot of KIAs. But in the end, they'd overrun us. And then? Then they'd replace the equipment and procede with their mission, delayed but not deterred.

Unless, that is, we could stop 'em as they came ashore. Remember the principles of SpecOps—AV and RS and all that shit? Well, if we hit Li—hard—just as he and his men were most vulnerable, then we could keep them from achieving relative superiority. We would win—and they would fail.

And when were they most vulnerable?

Just as they were coming ashore is when. But where the fuck would they do that? I assembled the troops and outlined the problem. We sat down Indian-style in a circle. I drew a rough map of the island on the ground, setting pebbles to represent the caches and caves of equipment we'd found.

"What story does this picture tell us—if it does in fact tell us a story?" I asked. I waited for a response—but no one spoke.

Finally, Duck Foot's hand went up. He skewed his face up and pulled on his lower lip. "The pattern seems to be random, Skipper. I don't think it tells us much of anything." He paused and tugged at his lip again. Then he continued. "But the tracks I found—I think *they* speak loud and clear. The tracks tell me that Li Chimen brought everything inland from the same place," he said. He took his K-Bar and inserted it where I'd outlined the island's southern tip. "There," he said definitively. "That's where they're gonna land."

Tosho's round face turned toward Duck Foot. "How are you so certain?"

"Two things. One is that the beach there is all gravel and stone—no sand. So they leave fewer tracks coming out of the water, and those they do leave are easier to disguise." He looked at Tosho. "Didn't you tell us that your people fly

E-2C aircraft regularly over the island to make sure the Chinese haven't pulled any stunts?"

Tosho nodded. "Two Hawkeye flights a day—zero seven hundred, and fifteen hundred. Regular as clockwork."

"Well—the thermal gear on a Hawkeye can't pick up anything on stone." Duck Foot shook his head. "And the aircraft doesn't have infrared capability—it can't track." Duck Foot pursed his lips and set his bulldog jaw. "Nope—that's the way they came."

Rodent interrupted his shipmate. "What was your second point, Ducks?"

"That was the clincher. The track leading from the south coast was the most disturbed one. It was the only track used over and over—the signs were obvious."

Gator snorted. "Obvious? To who? Shit, Ducks, I didn't see anything—not a broken bush or a single fuckin' footprint."

Duck Foot grinned. "Maybe you weren't looking in the right places, city boy."

I looked at Duck Foot and marveled. There are some things that you can teach a man—and there are others that you can't. Duck Foot Dewey was a hunter. He'd been out in the woods since the age of four or five. And the basic tracking skills he'd learned in the woods and marshes of Maryland's Eastern Shore as a kid would keep us all alive here in the fucking South China Sea today. "You've convinced me," I said. I looked around. "So what are we waiting for, assholes—let's get to work."

0642. Tosho translated the Japanese Defense Force E-2C pilot's transmissions, while I tracked the Hawkeye on my Big Brother miniradar. The plane was getting close enough to make me nervous. I put my fingers in my mouth and blew a shrill whistle. "Everybody get your asses under cover—the Hawkeye's due overhead in ten minutes, and I don't want us fucking up in case he's early."

"Early, shmerly." Tosho continued working on the series of detonators he'd assigned himself to wire. "We Japanese are very punctual people. You heard him on the radio, and that little black box of yours plotted his position to within a hundred yards. He said he won't be here until oh-seven-hundred—and he won't. We still have a few minutes."

"C'mon, Tosh—move."

"Look, Mister Dickhead, I know about time. Timeliness is next to Godliness. That's what they taught us at Notre Dame."

"I thought it was cleanliness that was next to Godliness."

"Well, they taught us that, too." His extended middle finger told me I was still *Ichiban* with him.

"Look," I said, "maybe they'll come on time, maybe they'll be late. But I don't want Mister Murphysan screwing with my karma today," I said. "We're getting under fucking cover—*now.*"

1000. The inland booby traps were all set. Duck Foot and Rodent set one series at the arms cache—just in case Li's people made it that far. Gator, Half Pint, and Pick—who hurt like hell but was damned if he was gonna miss any of the fun—disabled the missile launchers so subtly that the Chinese wouldn't realize it until they'd locked, loaded—and hit the "launch" button. Then, just for good measure, Pick booby-trapped the comms. While he played, Nod DiCarlo, Boomerang, Tosho, and I laid out the (blood) red carpet with which we'd greet Li Chimen when he arrived.

Now, when you are setting up an ambush, there are four benchmarks that you must always try to satisfy. First, you want to locate your ambush in a place that will force your enemy into a fatal funnel—a killing zone. Second, you must be able to position your own force so that it enjoys several overlapping fields of fire. Third, you must be able to withdraw quickly and effectively—so that, for example, if the enemy calls for artillery or air support you can haul your butt outta there pronto, Tonto. And fourth, you want to be able to make your ambush site look as if no one has ever so much as disturbed a single twig, so the enemy will walk right in.

Now, as we all know, nothing is ever perfect. The southern end of the island was wide and flat. It was going to be hard to create the sort of fatal funnel you can create on narrow jungle trails, in urban alleyways, or twisted riverine settings. I improvised by setting a series of camouflaged Claymores at each side of the natural landing zone. They would keep Li's force—which was probably going to be much larger than my nine-man contingent—from getting around the sides and flanking us.

We did enjoy good fields of fire. That was because we controlled the high ground. Well, relatively high ground—we were perhaps twenty feet above sea level. We dug our positions out and camouflaged 'em.

It was good—but not good enough. I needed an additional element—something that would really bottle Li up.

I was problem-solving when Boomerang ambled up, holding one of the Big Brother black boxes.

"Whatcha got?"

"Radio transmission override, Boss Dude."

"So, nu?"

He shook the box under my nose and gave me the sort of bemused look computer wonks reserve for folks like me who can't tell the difference between a RAM and a ROM. "*Override,* Boss Dude," he repeated, moving his lips s-l-o-w-l-y and enunciating each syl-la-ble, as if he were speaking to an idiot. When he saw I still didn't get it, he sighed, shook his head, and said, "I can make a detonator out of this, Boss Dude. We use one of the Chinese radios. Wire it with some C-4. Then I use this little widget, set the frequency here"—he showed me where—"and then, when I turn the radio on, the circuits close, the C-4 goes *boom,* and we stir-fry some Chinese."

"Sounds like the same thing we've already got with the Claymores," I said.

"But I'm talkin' *underwater,* here, Boss Dude," Boomerang said. "I can plant the C4 underwater—cut 'em off as they land."

He is a devious child, isn't he? "Do it."

* * *

1134. Tosho, who was monitoring the Big Brother radio equipment, waved me over to the command post he'd dug. He removed his headphones. "There's definitely something going on out there," he said.

"Close?"

"From what this thing tells me, yeah—close. It started out real faint. But over the last half hour, it's been getting stronger. Not constant—but it's like *there,* y'know? Sounds like encrypted stuff. UHF."

I had a pretty good guess what he was listening to. It's the sort of stuff that gets sent from a sub, which is what I told Tosh.

"That would explain the signal strength," he said.

I looked at him. "But no voice transmissions yet?"

He shook his head. "I haven't heard anything yet."

"Keep listening." I started to move off. "Hey, Tosh—"

"Yeah?"

"Can that thing really gauge distance?"

"Yeah, it sure can." He flashed a smile. "You *Amerikajins* are getting real good at this hi-tech samurai stuff."

I bowed low in the classic style. *"Domo arrigato."* Thanks a lot.

He returned the gesture. *"Doo-itashi-mashite."* You're welcome. Then he fitted the headset over the top of his head, adjusted the earcups, and started playing with the digital controls on his black box.

I turned and jogged across the crest of the stone-covered rise down to the water's edge. Boomerang was sixty yards out, facedown in ten feet of water. He had strung his C4 across a fifty-yard stretch of the bottom, burying each charge carefully, then concealing the line between the charges. I shouted at him. He surfaced, trod water, and shook himself like a dog to take the seawater out of his long hair.

"Yo, Boss Dude—"

"How's it coming?"

"I'm done, but I'd like another five, maybe ten minutes. I wanna make double sure my tracks are invisible."

"Yo—*gaijin*—" I turned. Tosho was standing atop the rise, waving his arms. I jogged back up toward where he was standing.

"They're awful fucking close, Dick." He looked down at his equipment. "I'd say five, maybe six miles offshore."

Shit—given the quality of optics these days, a sub's scope could just about pick us out moving on the beach at that distance.

Ready or not, here they come. I turned and hand-signaled to circle the wagons.

Boomerang tread water, his hands on his hips, immobile.

"Boomerang—move."

"But I ain't quite done yet, Boss Dude," he called.

"Oh yes you is." Even at more than a hundred feet, Boomerang could tell from my expression that I wasn't making a request but giving an order. Abruptly, he stroked for the shoreline.

I put two fingers in my mouth and shrill-whistled. The rest of the troops came-a-running. "Company's coming," I said.

Chapter 21

1955. WE SPENT THE REST OF THE DAY WAITING—WITHOUT ANY sign whatsoever of Li's approach. Now, there's some significance to this. When you are laid up in your ambush position, there's no movement allowed. No coffee break to stretch the aching muscles and crack the joints and generally get limber. Hell—there's no coffee, either. You have to remain motionless, right where you have dug yourself in. You stay coiled to spring—ready to GO.

Now, achieving this kind of passive yet kinetically active balance is much harder than it sounds. Just remaining in one position for a long time can be difficult—hey, hey, hey—you out there. Yeah—the one with the dumb expression who just said "bullshit." *You* go out in the woods, or to a park, and secrete yourself for six to seven hours, motionless, your face, neck, and hands darkened by greasy cammo creme, your BDUs soaked by sweat and piss. Then come back and tell me how easy it was.

Because it is not easy. And there was more. I have told you that these islands were uninhabited. That is not precisely true. What I meant is that there were no *humans* here.

But there were more than the fair share of polydactyl creatures, most of the creepy, creepie-crawlie variety, many of them equipped with sharp mandibles and nasty stingers, and the uncanny ability to make life extremely uncomfortable.

And then there were the gnats. Kamikaze gnats. Big, brown, persistent, tenacious, aggressive, blood-sucking critters. The kinds of gnats that get inside your ears and bite you just past the point where you can work a finger up to dislodge 'em. The kinds of gnats that fly into your eye, bury themselves just under your lower eyelid, and squirm around until you are almost blinded.

Last but certainly not least, there was the small but significant matter of drinking water—or, more to the point, the lack thereof. We'd been exercising our bodies. Between the jump, the landing, and the work ashore, we'd been sweating like crazy. But we'd brought only two canteens of water per man: sixty-four ounces. That's not a lot when you have been engaging in strenuous activity, or operating under stressful conditions. It's not a lot when you've been held in one position for almost a full day, and the sun is beating down on your back, and you're dressed in black. A man can go without food for a week if he has to. But water is a definite life-or-death factor in warfare—and we didn't have enough to last more than another few hours.

It occurred to me as I was lying there, that if Li got suspicious—as I might under similar conditions—he could sit offshore for a day or two, checking on things from afar. If he did that, we'd be up the well-known creek *sans* paddle—or anything else—by the time he decided to come ashore.

The evening E-2C had long since come and gone—and we hadn't given ourselves away. Indeed, even though we were packing radios, earpieces, and lip mikes, I'd ordered radio silence—and double-checked to make sure that everyone's receiver had been turned off. I wasn't going to give our existence away by allowing someone with monitoring equipment to listen in as we chatted among ourselves, or leaked signals.

2003. I wanted to know whether there'd been any sign at all that Li and his *zhongdui* were on the move. So I eased from my position and crabbed around to the well-camouflaged position sixty yards below the ridgeline where we'd put our Big Brother equipment.

Tosho and Gator were in charge of monitoring. My hands asked if they'd heard anything lately. I got a negatory head shake from Tosho and a downturned thumb from Gator in response. They weren't picking up anything. Well, they weren't alone: the SpecWar radar that sits inside my head may have been going round and round, but there was nothing on the screen there, either.

I crawled back to my post and scanned the horizon. Nada. I passed Boomerang, who lay prone behind the mound of rock and earth that would protect him from any thermal scanning emanating from the water. He was observing the waterline through the ACOG sight on his MP5. He paused long enough to give me a dirty look. He'd wanted to finish his underwater booby traps, I hadn't let him, and he was still sore at me. Well, I was right and he was wrong. Just because Li hadn't come ashore back then, and still wasn't giving off any signals, didn't mean he wasn't in the neighborhood, prowling and growling.

2109. It was dark, it was quiet—and it had grown comfortable. A dangerous time for Warriors. The kamikaze gnats had returned to base for the night. The air currents had moved offshore, sweeping the day's heat away. And the last-quarter moon shone through partial clouds onto the water's surface, providing us with just enough light to enjoy the wave patterns as they broke gently on the offshore reef.

We lay in our ambush positions in pairs, strung out over sixty yards in a crescent that gave us effective, crossed fields of fire, concealed atop the uneven, scrub-covered ridge some seventy yards above the water. The gentle lapping of the water against the rocky beach was soothing, lulling me and the men into a quiet state of relaxation. This was not good. The white noise and quiet sapped our ability to concentrate on the possible dangers out there. Being uncomfortable—just like pain—can be a good thing: it keeps your senses primed; keeps your body and your mind sharp.

Even though I knew what was happening, by 2110 or so, my eyelids got tremendously heavy, and the thought of grabbing a combat nap was very, very inviting. And then, I don't know what it was—a subtle change in the air currents, or a motion in the water so slight that it was almost (but not quite) imperceptible, but something tripped the sensor wire inside my brain and the fucking klaxon horn screwed in position just below the bullshit detector went off. No—I didn't react outwardly. But even without any discernable movement, I went from passive alert to battle stations in a millisecond.

Then, the hair on the back of my neck stood up. I don't know where this instinctive reaction to danger first came from, friends—but it is a regular, palpable sensation that has kept me alive for years. When the hair on the back of my neck stands up, I know that something or someone that wants to do me damage is close by.

I moved oh, so s-l-o-w-l-y, lowering my head a millimeter at a time until I'd cleared well below the ridgeline. I swiveled to my left and clenched my right hand into a fist, then stuck my thumb out and pointed it toward the ground, silent-signaling "enemy suspected." Six yards away, I saw Duck Foot's eyes move in my direction—the moonlight catching the whites of his eyes. His blackened face bobbed up and down, and he turned and repeated the signal to the Pick, who lay six yards to his left. Pick would relay the signal to Half Pint, who controlled the leftmost field of fire. Then I turned to my right and repeated the sign, passing the word to Nod, who passed it to Boomerang, who passed it on to Rodent, who'd pass it to Tosho and Gator.

2111. I eased my way back up to the ridgeline. Pulled my night-vision FLIR[68] monocular from its pouch and let it

[68]That's Forward-Looking InfraRed, in case you didn't remember.

drift left/right/left across the surface of the water. Then I repeated my action, panning slowly, letting my eye grow accustomed to the green-lit fluorescence.

Once again, the hair on the back of my neck stood straight up. *There was something going on out there that was out of the ordinary.* I screwed my eye tighter into the monocular, concentrated, and—goddamn it—lost whatever it was.

Fuck me. That was my fault. Remember your basics from Hunting 101? I certainly hadn't. When you're in the woods stalking deer, you almost never see a deer in its entirety. What you see is a piece of something that catches your eye—a furry ear caught against the vibrant green of a holly bush, or a hint of that flicking white tail, moving in front of the rough bark of a locust tree, or the rapid movement of the deer's head as it senses a predator. The accomplished hunter sees these flashing signs because he is not tunneling. Oh, his vision is like a cone—but it is narrow at his eye, and grows wider and wider as he surveys the forest around him. The neophyte looks at things in precisely the opposite way: his cone is wide at the eye, and it narrows down the farther away it gets.

That's what I'd done here—I'd tried to focus closely on what I thought I'd seen—and I lost it all.

I pulled my eye away from the monocular, rubbed at it, and then tried again. I panned across the water's surface, letting my eye pick up what naturally attracted it.

There—there they were. Something was working against the wave pattern out there. I used the range finder. They were just over 250 yards from shore and coming closer, closer, closer—the infrared painting 'em like a school of fish moving close to the surface as it shifts direction in the currents. I'm not talking about anything big, friends. It was just a touch, a trace, a trifle; only the slightest insinuation of contrapuntal motion out there—the merest *flick* of the deer's tail—but it was fucking contrapuntal motion nonetheless, and I fucking saw it.

I panned again. Now that I'd caught the hint of movement, it was easier for me to pick it up. Yes—one, two, three swimmers, stroking so quietly that they weren't making any ripples, moving just under the surface of the water. They were obviously wearing rebreathers so as not to leave any telltale bubbles. But they couldn't escape the FLIR's half-mile range—or my man hunter's eye. I dropped behind the ridge and my hands relayed what I'd seen. *Stay down,* I told my guys. *Don't let them catch us with thermal imagers or infrared.*

Did I know they had that kind of equipment with 'em? Nope. But I did know that, given the proliferation of technogoodies, even your basic Hizballah terror cell can buy over-the-counter night-vision devices, hand-held GPS monitors, and secure comms. That being the case, why shouldn't I believe that *zhongdui* shooters should-could-would have 'em too? Answer: never underestimate your enemy.

I picked the targets up again. Now they were less than a hundred yards out—stroking steadily toward the shoreline. I used every molecule of my consciousness to pan the night—vision monocular back out where they'd come from—but couldn't pick up on anything. My instinct told me that this was the advance party—and that once they'd secured the beachhead, Li and the rest of the troops would follow.

So, we had to let 'em come ashore. That was fine by me. I hand-signaled orders up and down the line and received affirmative responses.

2119. The waiting is bad enough when there's nothing going on. When you know your enemy is out there, moving inexorably in your direction, I don't care how many times you have gone to war; I don't care how many men you have killed. It is always the same: your breath goes shallow. Your blood pressure and your heartbeat accelerate. There is a slightly oily, queasy feeling in the pit of your gut. Even though your bladder's empty and you couldn't get a straight pin upside your sphincter, you all of a sudden feel the need to take a piss and a dump.

2121. The trio of swimmers stopped about fifty yards

offshore, in waist-deep water. I could see 'em plainly in my night vision now. They dropped their masks around their necks; eased the rebreather hoses from around their necks and secured 'em; squatted to remove their fins, and secured them one by one at the rear of the UDT-type vests. Then they lay back in the water, retrieved their weapons, and checked 'em out.

I studied the men we were about to kill, totally absorbed by what I was seeing. It was like watching a mirror image of ourselves coming ashore in a potentially hostile environment. We have operated against terrorists of various stripe; against Russkie special forces, Libyan Army units, and the Iraqi Republican Guard. But never before against a maritime unit like the *zhongdui.* I could tell by the way they moved that these guys were good. The *zhongdui* we'd gone against on the *Nantong Princess* were second-raters—these guys were *operators.*

Slowly, covering one another, they moved out of the water and up onto the shore. Point man had night vision held to his eyes. He scanned the rocky beach in front of him, searching for any sign of hostiles. Then his vision shifted, rose toward the ridgeline where we were hidden. I held my breath—kept myself absolutely motionless—and watched as he watched me. The temptation to move my eyes as he moved his was absolute—but I fought it. I was going to give this sonofabitch *nothing.*

His night vision dropped to his chest, he retrieved his submachine gun, and the trio moved off stealthily along the beach, toward the path leading to the cave that held the missile launching equipment. They were here to check it out—then they'd call the landing party in.

Of course—Li had to bring the fucking missiles with him tonight. I'd made it necessary when I'd sunk the *Nantong Princess.*

I came off the ridge and silent-signaled my intentions, first to the left, then to the right. When I got confirmation that I'd been received and understood, I removed my CQC vest and web gear, my boots and my socks, keeping only my suppressed MP5—on which I fastened the FLIR—and my knife. Then I worked my way down the inland slope, making my way at flank speed toward the eastern coast—toward the cave concealing the launchers. Tosho, similarly equipped but wearing boots, slipped into my wake.

2131. We got there first—and we got there silently. That's why I'd taken my boots and socks off. The soles of my feet are tougher than the fucking Vibram they're using on boondockers these days. So I run through the woods faster barefoot than you can in boots. But that's not why I do it. My feet are like sensors. I can probe for trip wires and other booby traps more effectively with my ten-and-a-half-triple-E feet than I can with a couple of hundred thousand dollars' worth of newfangled electronic countermeasures gadgetry. So when I need to move, really *move,* I prefer to go the old-fashioned way: barefoot.

And, having stubbed the Rogue toes only once or twice on the way, I'd picked out a trail that allowed us to move fast—but not make any noise. We approached from above the cave's mouth—setting ourselves so we'd be impossible to pick up if the *zhongdui* swept the area surrounding the orifice with their imaging equipment.

2141. I heard the slightest hint of movement below my position and to my left. My body tensed as the trio of *zhongdui* came closer. I had to really work to hear 'em at all—they *were* good—until they came to the camouflage netting. We'd fucked with it so that it rustled more than anybody'd want—and gave their position away.

I waited until the rustling stopped—which meant they'd gone inside to inspect the launchers—then, inch by inch, I began my move.

To my right, Tosho mirrored me.

The pace was excruciatingly slow. My big toe probed the ground. When I felt confident, the ball of my foot followed. Then the arch; then the heel. Sixty seconds to move less than a yard—and I wanted to cover another six yards before these assholes emerged.

There was nothing to do but keep moving. And that's

what I did—my whole body turned into an early-warning system. I put another yard behind me. And a third. In two more feet I'd be in a good position to "cut the pie" of the cave mouth—which meant I'd finally enjoy a decent field of fire. Which is precisely when Mister Murphy stuck his own bare foot onstage. First, I stubbed my big toe on a loose rock and sent it skittering and clattering. Then Mister Murphy booted me in the ass and sent me sprawling down the last eight feet of hillside.

Oh, fuck. Oh, doom on Dickie. I clutched my MP5 to my chest, tucked my shoulder, and rolled as I fell, so as not to hit face first.

I needn't have worried—because halfway down, Mister Murphy flipped me over, and I landed flat on my back, which under other circumstances might have knocked the wind out of me. Tonight, however, there was no chance for that—because as I hit, half a dozen rounds kicked the ground two feet from my right thigh. No gunfire sound, either—just *phhht-phhht-phhht* as they struck the hard earth.

Fuuuck you, whoever you are!—I sprayed-and-prayed the cave mouth while trying to focus on where the hell the threat was coming from—it was just a tad dark, you recall—and received a second barrage from my left.

Yeah—but this time I saw his supressor flash. *He was outside.* This was Mister RSG—the rear-security guy. I rolled away from him, came up looking through the FLIR sight. Found him—he was wedged behind a boulder, his position hampered by his bulky CQC vest and other equipment. I fired a three-shot burst in his direction to keep him off balance. Came up onto my feet. Took cover at the opposite edge of the cave mouth. Was about to draw down on him when I heard the welcome sound of a body collapsing on the ground. Stuck my MP5 around the mouth of the cave and saw RSG facedown—and Tosho's upraised thumb extended for me to see.

One down. That was the good news. The bad news was

that *Zhongdui Er* and *Zhongdui San*—that's how they say *zhongdui*s two and three back in Beijing—were primed to repel boarders—and if I'd been them, I'd have been on the radio at the first sign of commotion.

No time to waste—and no one but me to do the dirty work. I rolled under the cammo netting and into the pitch black cave. Hugged the side wall. Brought the MP5 up so I could see through the FLIR. Swept side to side. Three yards from where I crouched, two heavy four-by-four stowage crates provided meager cover. I crabbed behind the first of 'em, poked my night vision out and panned. Thirty feet in front of me, the missile launchers stood, low and skeletal on their fat pneumatic tires. Behind them, the big crates of auxiliary equipment glowed green against the green phosphor of the lens.

The infra red picked up a white-hot spot at ground level next to the rearmost, right-hand crate. The lens of my night vision picked up the nasty beam as it shot past my head. Fuck—*Zhongdui Er* was trying to laser me. I pulled back—if he hit me in the face with the fucking thing he'd burn my corneas like *cuchifritos.* DOD issues antilaser goggles to all its combat forces these days—including me. But mine were safely stowed, fifteen thousand miles away, back in the duty locker at Rogue Manor. BFH[69] they were, sitting there.

I rolled to my left—the second crate providing cover. Sucked ground and stuck the business end of the MP5 far enough out to get a sight picture. The angle was bad. From where I lay, no way could I hit *Zhongdui Er*—unless he just about stood straight up like one of the fucking paper pop-up targets we use when we borrow the FBI's kill house at Quantico.

Sometimes, as Doc Tremblay says, *entiymah feeshmok*—which is Cairene for the fact that I sometimes have fartbean brains.

---

[69]Big fucking help.

Why do I say that? I say it because we fucking train for this exact fucking scenario. In total darkness. Using the same goddamn equipment I currently had on my Roguish person. Except I hadn't been war-gaming, or thinking, or what the fuck. I'd just been flailing along.

I mean, this was as simple as assembling a Port-A-File.

Fold along the dotted lines to reveal Tab A. I tucked back out of sight and retrieved my knife.

Depress scored portion of cardboard to reveal Slot B. I resumed my prone position and got a sight picture.

Insert Tab A into Slot B. I threw the knife at the left-hand wall.

Like fucking clockwork, *Zhongdui Er* and his laser-equipped subgun and *Zhongdui San* and his semiauto pistol popped up—both exposing head and shoulders, thank you very much. *Zhongdui Er* was right where the crosshairs of my FLIR were zeroed. I stitched him with a three-round burst, and he dropped faster than the automated targets at Quantico. Deader, too. I pulled left, which is where the second commando had shown himself—but there was no sign of him.

Okay—*Er* down, *yi* to go. And no time to waste.

I rolled back to my right, came around the crate, and charged, using my night vision to make my way in the blackness.

The sonofabitch was hunkered down behind the rearmost crate—fumbling in his CQC vest. Fumbling for what I didn't know—but I wasn't about to let him get his hands on whatever it may have been. I charged. He fired wildly down the cave. That did him more harm than good. The muzzle flashes fucking blinded him, and now he shot twice again into the stone roof of the cave. He was still trying to recover when I let go three three-round bursts to make him keep his head down.

He did exactly as I hoped. I vaulted the first of the missile launchers, skirted the second, worked my way around the first crate, and came up five feet behind him.

April fool, motherfucker. I caught him in my sight looking the wrong fucking way—and squeezed the trigger.

There was a very ominous click as the MP5's hammer fell on an empty chamber and he turned toward me, his pistol pointed at my chest. Yes, I see you out there waving your hand, screaming that the MP5 bolt locks back whenever the magazine expends its last round. You are correct. But sometimes even the MP5 misbehaves. Maybe it was all that saltwater. Maybe it was the fact that I hadn't cleaned the fucking thing since before we'd left for Rome. Maybe it was the fact that suppressed weapons need more TLC than your normal submachine gun. I didn't know the reason—and I didn't fucking care. What I did know was that the goddamn gun was no use to me now, and I don't have time to stand here fucking explaining things to you.

Zhongdui San had his War Face on. I could see it through the night-vision sight. I dropped and rolled against the back wall of the cave just as he fired five rapid shots in my direction. My eyes shut reactively and I went into a ball—hoping to absorb only one or two of the rounds that had to impact. He kept shooting—sharp stone shards cut at my head and neck.

Then the gunfire stopped—and he'd fucking missed me. The old Rogue reflexes had come through for me once again. I listened as best I could (my ears were ring-a-ding-ringing from the at-close-range explosions). But through the reverbs I still managed to pick out the hollow sound of a mag dropping onto the ground. Shit—the sonofabitch was reloading.

No fucking way. I shot forward and tackled him around the knees, my subgun clattering to the uneven stone surface of the cave as it danced clumsily on its sling. The MP5's hot suppressor muzzle slapped the side of my face—I felt heat through my beard, but that didn't stop me from body-slamming the *zhongdui* as hard as I could. Then the sling separated and the HK fell away.

I found his gun hand, rolled him to my left, and smashed

weapon and hand on the cave floor. He grunted and tried to bring the gun back across my face. I fought him off and—*"uh"*—slammed his hand back into the ground again. The pistol dislodged and went skittering off in the blackness.

But *Zhongdui San* wasn't giving up. He rolled away, scrambling like a fucking tadpole out of water. I grabbed at his legs. He smashed one of his soft-soled boots into my face hard enough to jar my teeth. I found his ankle and twisted it 180 degrees to starboard. He screamed but kicked again. The blow glanced off my forehead. I saw stars and lost my grip on him.

He came straight for me, his shoulder found my solar plexus, and, grunting, I was knocked backward. He kept at me—our hands grappling, groping, probing for weakness. Then I felt him shift—his right hand shook free of my left, and he turned away slightly as we battled for advantage.

Instinctively, I knew WTF was happening. *The sonofabitch was going for his knife.*

I hate knives. I hate using them as weapons because no matter how good you are, how proficient, how deadly, you will almost always get cut in a knife fight. But I had no choice. I reached for the big Cold Steel blade on my belt—and came up empty. It was gone. I'd used it—tossed it away to draw fire. Fuck me—I guess I could try to beat the sonofabitch to death with my dick—he'd suffer the blunt-instrument trauma known as death by friendly weapon.

Fuck—this was no time for black humor. I wrestled with him in the darkness, feeling for where his hands were going. His left hand had my right hand tied up, and we played fucking fiddly-fingers as we struggled for dominance. He was a wiry little finger-fiddler—and he *was* little, built like many SEALs, who are short and small-framed. But those pint-size SEALs will outlast most five-gallon Rangers when it comes to endurance. And this *zhongdui* may have been small, but he was wiry, and strong for his size. Shit—he was strong for *my* size.

His right hand—knife hand—was behind him. I worked my way down from his shoulder and tried to find it and break a finger or two before things got serious—or dangerous. But I could tell from his position that he'd already drawn whatever kind of knife he had from its sheath, and his wrist was turning, turning, turning, so that he could get the business end of the fucking thing pointed in the direction of my vitals.

Now, let me pause here just long enough to remind you of something I said earlier: when you are rolling around like this on the ground all those fancy moves you've learned in the dojo don't do you fuck-all. This ground fighting shit is down and dirty. Like the Rogue's Tenth Commandment, there are no rules.

I broke my right arm free and smashed his cheek with my elbow. I shattered a bone. I heard it go—and he reacted. But my blow hadn't been effective because he didn't stop working his right arm around—I could feel the point of the fucking knife bite into my left hip. It penetrated and nicked the bone—which sent a spasm of white-hot pain from my leg to my shoulder.

I fought him off, my teeth gritted to keep from screaming. Balled my right hand into a fist, kneed just enough clearance between us so that I could strike across my body, then—*"Fuuuuck* you"—brought my right fist down like a fifteen-pound sledgehammer on his left clavicle.

The shoulder bone snapped—and reactively, he released his grip on the knife, which fell away. I didn't chase after it—and I didn't allow him any recovery time, either. All I could think of was killing the sonofabitch—and doing it soon. I used my bulk to wrap him up, slam him onto his back, and then I leaned into him—my forearm crushing his throat—and pressed with every fucking ounce of fucking energy I could fucking muster until I fucking crushed his fucking Adam's apple and shut off his fucking air. When he stopped struggling, I took his head in my hands and twisted until I'd broken his neck—hey, hey, hey, don't be so fucking queasy. You don't want the opposition reviving and coming after you when you think they've been neutralized. This *zhongdui* s.o.b. wasn't gonna be able to do that.

I rolled off his corpse and worked my hands around, trying to find my MP5, and *Zhongdui San*'s pistol and knife.

A blinding beam of light penetrated the cave's blackness. "Yo, Dick." Tosho's voice came from behind the light.

I tried to pull myself to my knees—and rolled over onto my back instead. My fucking hip hurt like hell. "Over here, Tosh."

He came through the cave gingerly, examining the *zhongdui* to make sure they were dead before he got to me. Then he looked me over—including the blood on my BDUs. "Nicked you, huh?"

"Yeah—but not too bad I think."

"Lemme look." He pulled and poked and un-Velcro'd until he exposed the wound. "At least he didn't nick an artery," Tosho said, his expression tinged with concern. "Hey, guess what—the guy outside wasn't carrying any comms." He directed his light at the two corpses. "And these two don't seem to have any radios, either."

He swung the light around to catch me probing the wound on my hip, slapped my hands away, and before I could react, jabbed me with a tetanus Syrette he'd plucked from his first-aid fanny pack. He retrieved a second Syrette. "Novocaine. That'll keep you on your feet for a while."

I shook my head. "I can do without it—want to stay sharp."

Tosho shrugged. "Up to you, bub."

"You know how much I like fucking pain—how alive it makes me feel." I pulled myself to my knees, then stood up, tentatively shifting my weight onto my injured leg. Oh, yes, fuck, it *hurt*—but that pain would give me an edge. It would remind me why we were here: to avenge Alixe Joseph's murder and checkmate Li Chimen.

But my *will,* not the pain, had to dominate the situation. I focused my whole being on the problem, allowing my body to absorb the pain and diminish its intensity and its hold on me. The weaker the pain grew—the more my mind was able to control it—the stronger I became. When I had conquered it, I was able to stand tall and straight. I rolled my neck and shoulders, working the kinks out. I shifted my web gear around until it was comfortably balanced, then adjusted my BDUs until they were shipshape, too.

It was time to go back to work. "They weren't carrying radios?"

"Nope." Tosho helped me sling the MP5. "But the *zhongdui* outside was carrying these." He pulled an olive drab plastic container holding two foot-long IR lightsticks from his BDU pocket. "That's how they were going to signal the rest of the troops to come in."

I nodded. Then I gave the plastic a second look. "Lemme see that again."

I took hold and examined it in the beam of Tosho's flashlight. "Fuck me."

"What's up?"

"This is American—U.S. Government issue." This didn't make sense. "Lemme see the light."

I took Tosho's flashlight and examined the first of the two *zhongdui* corpses in the cave. It didn't take long for me to see WTF. "Holy shit—"

"What did you find?"

"Something *you* overlooked, Sher-rock."

Tosho approached. "So, nu, Doctor *Rot*son?"

"Look at their uniforms—their equipment."

Tosho nudged the corpse with his toe. Then he saw what I'd seen. "Holy shit indeed." He knelt and started a closer examination. "These guys aren't wearing Chinese equipment."

"Bingo," I said. I fingered *Zhongdui San*'s CQC vest. "This vest is the same one the Royal Marines use." I pointed at the pistol the dead Chinese had carried. "Beretta—a model 92. U.S. Army issue." I rolled the corpse over. "French fins and mask; German web gear." I paused. Let's look at the other two.

It didn't take us long to discover that *Zhongdui Yi* and *Zhongdui Er* were as multilaterally equipped as *Zhongdui San* had been.

Does that tell you anything, gentle reader? It tells me volumes. Remember how I'd outfitted my men when we'd set out to scuttle the *Nantong Princess?* That's right—I'd equipped us with gear that didn't read "This Equipment Belongs to United States Naval Special Warfare Personnel" in bright neon lights. I'd provided my nasty SEAL strike force with the same model British CQC vest these *zhongdui* swimmers had on. We'd carried vintage East German ammo—they were using Czech. We'd worn French wet suits, and Israeli Kevlar helmets. They wore Italian wet suits, hadn't bothered with helmets, but they carried Japanese knives. None of the weapons I'd seen so far—Italian pistols; Belgian submachine guns—had any visible serial numbers.

Well, the main reason to use such sanitized equipment is to confuse the opposition during a covert operation. If you get waxed and your body is discovered, the use of untraceable or varied equipment makes your country of origin much harder to determine. So, when I operate in the black, I never carry USGI,[70] or even American-made equipment, even though that's what I prefer. I mean, I like the Royal Marine CQC vest. It's okay. But the one made by Blackhawk Industries of Virginia Beach is better, more durable, and it weighs less. It was designed by SEALs for SEALs. I could go on, but I think you get the picture.

Okay—fast-forward to the present. Here are three *zhongdui* commandos. They're not wearing the regulation Chinese-issue equipment in which they normally operate (remember, I saw what they normally carry aboard the *Nantong Princess*), but a jumble of foreign-manufactured stuff.

I rolled the corpse closest to me and started working my way through its pockets. "Check for IDs," I told Tosho. "I'm willing to bet you a hundred bucks we won't find anything on these guys—not even a dog tag."

---

[70]U.S. Government Issue.

Six minutes later, I was absofuckinglutely certain that Li was running an off-the-books operation. Oh, perhaps it had been sanctioned by the Chinese government—or one faction of the government. Maybe Li had been unleashed by Major General Zhu Linfan in the same way I'd been turned loose against the *Nantong Princess* by Chairman Crocker. Maybe he'd even been given the green light by Defense Minister Chi himself.

But no matter who'd approved this little operation, I knew in my Roguish heart that Li was operating covertly tonight. The thought made me smile—because if he and his crew disappeared at sea, no one was going to make any diplomatic waves over the vanishing act. Not even one tiny ripple.

Show time. I turned toward Tosho and shook the package of IR lightsticks in his direction. "Well, *I* think it's all clear—don't you?"

Tosho's War Face dissolved into a malevolent grin. "I think it's rock-and-roll-out-the-red-carpet time for Mister Li," he said.

Chapter 22

2235. I'D STOOD ATOP THE RIDGELINE, PARTIALLY OBSCURED BY vegetation, twisted the IR lightsticks, and activated 'em. Tosho'd held one high above his head; I'd held the other. We stood there like fucking Statues of Liberty for three to four minutes. Then we'd planted them high enough on the ridge so they'd be visible guideposts for the incoming force, and got to work.

2252. My FLIR was trained out to sea in the general direction the trio of *zhongdui* had come from. The night-vision unit—it's built by Texas Instruments just in case you wanted to know and order one—has a range of just over a thousand yards—more than six-tenths of a mile—although it can pick up only a man-size target eight hundred yards out.

I didn't have to worry about man-size targets—I spotted the RIBs coming at us as they churned into the FLIR's range. Four of 'em, traveling slowly, inexorably, toward the point of shore that dead-centered between the IR light-sticks.

Tosho was back on the Big Brother equipment. I looked

over toward his position and shrugged, arms out, palms up. "Anything?"

He shook his head negatively. "Either they're maintaining radio silence, or they're not carrying."

I thought about SFA's approach to the *Nantong Princess.* We'd had radios, but I'd made sure they were turned off, too.

Back to the ridgeline. I'd reminded the guys to stay low, below the prying IR that Li was carrying. I'd do all the spotting through my FLIR.

I peeked through the tube and used the range finder. The RIBs were six hundred yards out now—moving clumsily as they tried to maintain a straight line through the crosscurrents and riptides that sent the RIBs skewing off course. Progress wasn't made any easier by the weight each boat was carrying: one cruise missile, and one-two-three-four-five-six-seven men. Twenty-eight of the opposition in all. I could handle those odds. I set the FLIR down. The high clouds had blown out to sea. The sliver of moon provided minimal light and I could make the boats out with my naked eye now.

"What's the range, Boss Dude?" Boomerang hunkered with his hands on the improvised radio detonator.

"Five hundred yards and closing."

He grinned at me. "Cool."

2259. I waited until the boats were just athwart the explosives to give Boomerang the go-ahead.

He was actually giggling as he flipped the switch on the Big Brother black box and the C-4 exploded, kicking water and sand and rock fifteen yards into the air. The detonation was fucking textbook. It caught two of the four RIBs square under their keels. The boats cracked in two and folded like cardboard under the weight of the missiles. The second pair of RIBs were tossed rudely shoreward by the explosions—sending most of the *zhongdui* inside flailing into the churning surf.

I let loose with a series of full-auto three-shot bursts into the floundering *zhongdui* shooters. I hit one, two, three, as quickly and efficiently as if I'd been on a sporting clays range. Hey—what were my guys waiting for, an invitation? "C'mon assholes." Now the rest of the men followed my example, catching the survivors in a murderous cross fire.

But things weren't completely one-sided. The Chinese returned fire—from the water and from the boats. It was haphazard, but a stray round can kill you as easily as a well-placed shot if you're in the wrong spot at the wrong time.

But it was we, not they, who controlled the situation. We'd caught them at the most exposed segment of their insertion—the precise instant when their AV (Area of Vulnerability) was most pronounced. And we were currently taking full advantage of the situation.

I watched through my FLIR as Tosho caught one of the two remaining RIBs broadside and loosed a stream of 9mm into it. He killed one pair of Chinese shooters outright. The surviving *zhongdui* rolled into the water, firing wildly as they went. The second RIB, still untouched, tried to escape our killing zone by heading toward the safety of the rougher but less dangerous shoreline, two hundred or so yards off to my right. I fired at the RIB, hoping to hit the outboard engine and bring the fucking thing to a stop.

After one three-shot burst, the MP5 jammed. "Fuck." I racked, tapped, reloaded, and slapped the bolt forward. Nada. I dropped the mag and exchanged it for a new one, then racked the round out of the chamber and let the bolt fall once more. I looked up, found a knot of targets charging onto the beach, and squeezed the trigger.

Click. Nothing. The fucking gun was not being helpful. Maybe I'd bent something during the fight in the cave. Maybe it was overheated, or dirty—sand and grit are not beneficial to the internal working parts of the MP5. Whatever the case, it wasn't doing me any good now. I transitioned, easing the subgun to the ground, retrieved my USP, sighted just above the heads of the struggling *zhongdui,* and fired. I caught one, knocking him backward into the water. It was a lucky shot—but I didn't give a damn: it had put the s.o.b. *down.*

Fuck—one of the downed *zhongdui's* shipmates swept the ridgeline with machine-gun fire, kicking up huge shards of earth and rock as the belt-fed weapon spat rounds at us.

A rock fragment tore past my cheek and sliced the lobe of my left ear. "Shit." I peeked over the top of the ridge. The survivors were forming a skirmish line—disciplined firing coming at us now—and charging the beach. We'd cut their number by almost half. But that wasn't good enough. They were heading for the weakest side of our position—and if we weren't careful, they'd be able to work their way around our right flank. I ducked as the machine gun stitched our position again.

"Fire the mines," I shouted off to my right, where Rodent hunkered, the small electric detonator for the starboard-side Claymores secured next to him. He was stretched over the top of the ridge, firing down at the beach. "Rodent—*Rodent*—hit the fucking switch *now!*"

Finally I caught his attention and received an upturned thumb. He rolled toward the detonator, shouted, "Fire in the hole," and turned the fat knob.

I ducked and waited for the concussion. Nothing.

I stuck my nose over the ridgeline—and saw the RIB beach itself and the Chinese in it head for cover, firing to give their shipmates still in the water a chance to make it ashore.

"Rodent—fire the fucking thing."

He worked the mechanism again and again, then threw it down in disgust. "It's dead, Skipper—damn thing won't work."

Of course not. The fucking thing had probably had its wiring reversed by Mister Murphy when we weren't looking.

I grabbed my useless MP5 only so I could use the FLIR night sight. Peered through it and saw six, seven, eight, nine, ten Chinese shooters heading for cover, firing at our positions as they charged up the beach toward cover. In the lead, I picked out a tall, lithe figure firing a chunky Styr assault rifle one-handed. It was Li Chimen. He had a smaller, stocky *zhongdui* by the web gear. He was dragging the poor sonofabitch, whose feet were kicking uselessly, as he was hauled across the rocky beach, toward the flank of the low ridge on which we'd dug ourselves in.

I lowered the MP5, brought up my pistol, and squeezed off half a dozen rounds in Li's direction, but all I managed to do was kick up dirt. After all, I was shooting more than 150 yards away—and I was doing it with open sights, in the dark. Without the IR sight, it's hard to shoot effectively at night. You are rendered almost sightless by your own muzzle flash—and the enemy's. Your eyes lose all night vision and you're effectively firing blind.

I picked up the MP5 and caught him again in the FLIR just as he disappeared into the underbrush and rocks, out of my line of sight. He was shouting back toward the beach, trying to rally his troops.

Well, they wouldn't get rallied for very long if I had anything to say about it. I wanted this motherfucker's head on my own personal pike. Pistol in hand I rolled off the ridge top, lunging toward the track that would take me down the back way to cut Li off at the pass. As I went by Pick, he rolled over onto his side and lofted his MP5 in my direction. "Skipper—take this."

"Thanks." I grabbed the weapon, pulled the bolt back, and checked it on the fly, and inserted a fresh mag from the pouch on my left thigh. I patted myself as I loped downhill. I still had two full MP5 mags. One was in the gun. I dropped the USP's almost-empty magazine and pulled a full one from my belt. I had five more—seventy-five rounds. In the pouches of my CQC vest I also carried half a dozen of the mini frag grenades I'd developed some years back. I figured I had enough ordnance to do Li in. And if I ran out, I'd gnaw through the motherfucker's carotid artery if I had to. I'd do anything I had to, to put him down.

I scooted down the hill and zigzagged through a field of large, rough boulders interspersed with tough, thorny bushes, working my way southeast like a broken-field runner. But I wasn't single-minded—wasn't without my early warning system. I hadn't gone more than a couple of hundred yards when I sensed rapid movement behind me. I dropped into the shadows between two boulders, cut behind one and took a different path, going back the way I'd come.[71] I waited until the footsteps passed me, then stepped out, MP5 raised and ready to do nasty business. Nod and Boomerang stopped their forward motion and turned toward me.

I dropped the MP5's muzzle. "What goes?"

"See—" Nod started to explain, but Boomerang cut him off.

"Yo, Boss Dude—just thought we'd tag along. Like, we don't want you having all the fun."

I put a palm on Nod's shoulder. "That right?"

Nod nodded, his head bobbing up and down slowly. "Yup."

I shrugged. "Suit yourselves, assholes." That's what I said as I turned and resumed the pace. But in my heart, I rejoiced to have these two Warriors with me. They had chosen to follow me; they had chosen to risk their lives with me. What greater tribute can an officer receive from his men than to be followed by them?

2307. We worked our way back parallel to the main trail that Duck Foot had identified, but keeping eight to ten yards off. I didn't want to run into any of the opposition in a head-to-head confrontation. I took point—and the right-hand field of fire. Boomerang's 44 long frame followed six yards behind me, his weapon scanning the left side of the trail. Six yards behind him, Nod moved stealthily, his weapon's muzzle scanning left/right. I moved quickly—perhaps faster than I should have—but we had a lot of

---

[71]What I was doing, of course, was following one of the precepts set down in 1759 by Major Roger Rogers, whose Rangers were America's first SpecWarriors. Rogers' Standing Order Number Seventeen goes as follows: "If somebody's trailing you, make circle, come back onto your own tracks, and ambush the folks that aim to ambush you."

ground to cover if we were going to cut these assholes off before they were able to mount a counterambush. We hadn't gone more than three hundred yards when I heard a series of sounds crescendo off to my starboard side. The opposition was close by—and getting closer by the second.

No time to prepare. I silent-signaled "enemy ahead," pointed in the direction they were approaching from, then dropped. Behind me, Nod and Boomerang also disappeared.

The hair on the back of my neck stood up. Now I heard soft footfalls in the darkness as the *zhongdui* came closer. The point man came by, moving carefully, no more than eight to ten yards away. He drew opposite to where I lay, and stopped, as if sniffing the air. I slowed my heartbeat and breathing. Incredibly, I could actually smell the *zhongdui*—he gave off a scent redolent of garlic and onions.

Roy Boehm used to say that when he operated in Vietnam, he always knew where Mister Charlie was, because Mister Victor Charlie used *nuoc mam,* a sauce made of fermented fish heads, on his food. "I could smell the fuckin' enemy," Roy used to say.

Here and now I experienced what he'd been telling me. Point Man moved on. After a twenty-second hiatus, other *zhongdui* followed—precisely how many there were I had no way of knowing, but by counting (or trying to count) footsteps, I guesstimated eight or nine. Things grew quiet once again. We lay in our position for what seemed like an hour but was no more than a minute. And then—incredibly—I heard two voices coming along the same track the *zhongdui* had just passed. As they drew closer, I realized they were arguing, in sotto voce. They were speaking Chinese, so I couldn't understand what the hell they were saying. But one was obviously plaintive—whiny and complaining—while the other was taut, tense, tight, and angry. I'd only heard that forceful voice once before—but its deep tone and uncharacteristically rich timbre had stayed rooted in my brain. That voice belonged to Li Chimen.

There was a sharp exclamation from the angry voice—and then silence. The whiner started to say something. He was interrupted by the unmistakable sound of palm slapping against cheek, and the same angry exclamation, stage-whispered. You didn't have to have a degree in Chinese—I certainly don't—to understand that Li's warrior instincts had kicked in, he'd sensed our presence, and he wanted noise discipline RIGHT NOW.

There was the single muffled sound of something hitting the ground, about six yards off to my left. Then things went absofucking silent.

There are any number of elements here that could be classified as GFs—goatfuck factors. Nod, Boomerang, and I were spread out in a single-file line. We hadn't had enough time to set ourselves into an ambush position—that is to say, facing the enemy in a way that allowed us intersecting fields of fire. We were strung out over somewhere between ten and thirty yards—I had no idea precisely what the spacing was—and we'd allowed the main enemy force to pass us by.

And then, in one of those wonderful Warrior epiphanies, I saw in my mind's eye the framed verse in Bentley Brendel's White House office. You remember it. *What?* You say you don't remember? You'd better take a fucking course in reading retention before the next novel's published. Okay—here it is:

All warfare is deception.
So when strong, display weakness;
When weak, feign strength.
If your target is nearby,
Make it appear to be distant.
Only thus will you achieve your objectives.

Lying on my side, I e-a-s-e-d two of my minifrags out of their pocket, quietly pulled the pins out of the spoons, and lofted the fucking things as hard as I could. I sent one out as far behind Li's position as I could throw it; I tossed the other in the direction the *zhongdui* had taken, hoping to land it near the middle of the group.

The first explosion obviously caught the *zhongdui* by surprise. I knew it because one of 'em panicked: he abandoned all pretense of fire discipline and unleashed his whole fucking magazine at once. Tracer cut overhead from way off to my right.

Doom on you, *zhongdui.* You just told Boomerang and Nod precisely where you are. I heard more grenades, followed by the unmistakable chatter of MP5s, and knew that my pair of merry, murdering marauders were on the case. These *zhongdui* were about to become *zhong*chop-suey.

The second explosion—maybe a second and a half after the first—surprised Li Chimen. I knew that because he tucked and rolled in my direction.

Bad move, Li. Now I knew exactly where he was. I slid the MP5 onto my back, came up, slithered to my left, and caught him from behind, my arm around his neck, the crook of my right elbow shutting off his air, while my left hand tried to hold him in place.

It wasn't gonna happen. Li rolled just far enough to give himself some space—he didn't need much—at which time he used the muzzle of his Styr to hit me hard in the solar plexus.

Yes, I have a rippling washboard tummy because I do my hundreds of sit-ups every single day. But rippling washboard or not, you take a full-tilt boogie hard-ass poke in the solar plexus with the steel muzzle of an assault rifle and I guar-on-tee that it will feel just like you have been hit with a cold chisel driven by a fucking fifteen-pound sledge. Given the physics of the situation, my body doubled over, my arm came loose, and my elbow released his neck. I felt that fucking poke all the way to my eyelashes. Li wriggled away, reversed course, turned to faced me from a distance of six feet—and then realized precisely who the Rogue round-eyes was.

His face became a mask of rage. He bellowed an unintelligible imprecation and fumbled for the Styr.

Bad move. I was on him before his finger could even deal with the safety. I knocked the weapon up into his face. He brought his arm around and slapped it away. I tried to twist the gun—wrap the sling around his throat and use it like a garotte, but the fucking thing was too short. Then the sling unhooked itself from the butt end. I grabbed the Styr and twisted it out of Li's hands by the muzzle and swung it like a fucking baseball bat, slamming him upside the head and shoulders with it.

I connected once or twice, but the Styr is an unwieldy weapon—it's got that goddamn bullpup stock—which makes it easy to shoot, but as a kickass butt-stroker it is a goddamn POS. Finally I slammed the fucking thing onto a rock and shattered it—wasn't gonna give Li the opportunity to use it on me.

He regrouped, backing off slightly.

Another bad move, Mr. Li. Never give up any of your territory, or this fucking Rogue will move into it.

I pressed forward, crowding him. I didn't say a fucking thing—I let my eyes and my War Face do the talking. His hand dropped toward the tactical holster on his right thigh. I feinted with my hands, and as he reacted, kicked him in the left thigh.

It brought him up short—but not short enough. He was still fumbling for the pistol. I tackled him, knocking him backward into a scruffy tree. The fucking tree was dead—it just went *over*—and we tumbled with it, rolling and grappling for position as we did. We were face-to-face—nose to nose. I tried to bite his ear, but he elbowed me away. He clawed at my eyes. I drew back and buried my teeth in his neck. He tried to pull my left ear off. I grabbed his right hand with my left, brought my right hand up and separated the fingers until I had just one—the middle one—then bent it back until it broke.

That got his fucking attention. He roared like a Spielberg

dinosaur. But the sonofabitch didn't give up—he gritted his way through the pain, managed to extract his body from my grasp, caught me with a nasty shot to the ribs, and slammed the base of his palm toward my jaw.

I deflected the blow and struck back with the edge of my hand. My target was the portion of his neck just below his left ear and above his carotid artery. But Li's body wasn't being cooperative—he moved as I swung from the shoulder. The edge of my hand made contact—with the very solid trunk of a tree.

Oh, that smarted. Belay that. It fucking hurt. But there was no time to think about dings because Li was coming back at me—a dervishlike kick that brought his long, muscular leg up and around, and his heel moving toward my face at a tremendous rate of speed.

Since the perception of time has slowed here—it always does during combat—let me explain what's about to happen. Blows such as kicks can be turned against the enemy by using the principle of turning force. Simply put, by changing the direction of the blow, it can be not only deflected, but also turned to your advantage, because you will force your enemy out of position and leave him vulnerable.

Yes I was hurting. Yes I was in pain—and my injured hip wasn't helping much—but that, friends, is when all that training you've gone through over the years pays for itself. All the pain of BUD/S. All the dings from saturation jumps; the hypothermia from cold-water swims and long, frigid nights out in the boondocks, getting rained and snowed on. All the workouts. And the range time. All of those things are what make Warriors able to keep going when others do not. And when you combine the ability to keep going with white-hot rage, the combination makes you unbeatable. YOU WILL NOT FAIL.

And so, pain or no pain, I moved past his linear kick and, as his leg went past me, I smashed the back of his calf with my fist as hard as I could. The blow cramped him—and he went down. I dove at him and hit hard before he could recover—an elbow to the chin followed by a knee to the balls designed to make a eunuch out of him. But he deflected my knee and tried to roll out from under me.

I was having none of it. It was time to put this sucker away for good. My left forearm came down hard on his throat, cutting off his air. My right reached for the USP in my tactical holster.

Li realized what I was doing—and he fought back, desperately trying to counterattack. He clawed and bit and kneed and struck—but I had him and I wasn't about to let go. The pistol came out of the holster. He grabbed at it with his left hand, but it was no use. I brought the fucking muzzle up, up, up, until I wedged it under his armpit. Funny thing about that—it's real hard to dislodge the muzzle of a gun from under your arm without giving the shooter ample time to squeeze off a couple of rounds.

Oh, we were struggling. Oh, we were going at it full tilt boogie rock-and-roll hoochie-koo. But when he felt the gun's ineffable presence up in his armpit, his eyes went wide.

He was mine—he knew it and I knew it. "They're rolling up your networks," I told him, my voice even and low. I kept full pressure on his throat. "Korea, Indonesia, the Philippines, Singapore—they'll all be shut down." I leaned down toward him so he could see my face up close and personal. "They're going to disappear—the same way I made the *Nantong Princess* disappear. But that's not why I'm here."

I let him see my War Face—let him see it good. "Those *zhongdui* you sent to kill Chairman Crocker—they're dead." I cut off more of his air supply. "But that's not why I'm here, either."

I pressed down harder on his neck. "No, I'm here because you had a friend of mine murdered. Had her killed because she was effective."

He tried to spit at me, but he couldn't summon any breath, and the saliva bubbled uselessly between his lips.

"And y'know what they say—do the crime, do the time." I adjusted the USP's muzzle—didn't want to shoot myself in the forearm, after all. "It's time to pay, Li—time for you to pay in full."

He really started to struggle now.

My finger tightened on the trigger. The trigger on the USP's Variant One has about a twelve-pound pull in double-action mode. That's not a lot for me.

"Sayonara, Li." I squeezed off a round.

It must have hurt. His eyes went wide—then glazed over as he struggled. Blood, bright in the faint moonlight, bubbled in his mouth. He kicked and screamed and fought. But it was a death throe—I'd hit him where it would kill him.

Just to make sure, I pulled my forearm back, raised the muzzle of the pistol, and squeezed off two more rounds. The first blew his jaw away. The second took a big chunk of skull when it exited.

I pulled myself off his corpse and struggled to my feet. I was one tired sonofabitch. I started to holster my weapon—but heard movement behind me. Brought the USP up. Its front night sight squarely center-massed on a short figure in black combat gear.

"Geezus—don't shoot." Bentley Brendel waddled toward me, his hands raised in surrender.

He came forward slowly. Looked down at Li's corpse. "Thank God," he said. "You got him."

I said nothing.

"I'll be able to straighten things out as soon as we're back in Washington," he said.

"You're not going back to Washington, *Bent*ley," I said.

He began to lower his arms. The muzzle of my pistol told him to keep things exactly as they were.

"What—"

"Alixe Joseph," I said. "You betrayed her. You betrayed our country."

He shook his head. "No—it wasn't me—"

I closed the eight feet that separated us and slapped him across the face with my pistol. The front sight drew blood. "You're a liar, Bentley." I slapped him again, drawing more. "Worse, you're a traitor." I paused. "I hate traitors."

He started to say something—but I wasn't in the mood to listen. I kicked him and he went down. He rolled onto his hands and knees, scrambling to put some distance between us. He turned toward me, his round porker's face contorted with rage. Struggled to retrieve his pistol from its holster.

Now, I'd actually considered—in passing—bringing the sonofabitch back alive. But then I remembered what my old colleague Colonel Charlie Beckwith used to preach. "Kill 'em all," Charlie said, "and let God sort it out."

Good advice. Advice to live by—and die by. And so I double-tapped Bentley in the head. He went down like the pile of shit he was.

I holstered my weapon and walked over to check the bodies. I knew they weren't carrying anything, but as the old chiefs taught me, never assume anything. In the distance, I heard only the sporadic firing of MP5s—and I knew that my Warriors had prevailed once again. I sat down on the cool ground, put my head in my hands, and worked to slow my heartbeat. It had been one long, fucking day.

0244. We blew the undamaged cruise missiles but left the *zhongdui* bodies where they lay. That would give the Japanese E-2C overflight something big to report later in the morning—and tell the Chinese, who monitored every bit of radio traffic in the region, that they'd fucked up, too. By 0300 we'd rolled the eight-meter boat into the surf, floated it off the trailer, and packed what was left of our gear. We took the *zongduis'* water and some of their weapons. Gator and Rodent had filled all five fuel bladders—more than enough to take us back to Okinawa.

0335. I stowed the last of the Big Brother suitcases, then ran a quick circuit to check the situation on the island. Boomerang and Duck Foot set explosive charges in the caves. I counted heads to make sure we were all accounted for and shooed everyone out to the boat. We helped Pick over the side, easing him into the scuppers. Finally, I made my way into the water and pulled myself over the gunwale.

Nod started the engine. Tosho checked the Magellan GPS screen, punched in a set of coordinates, and set our course for Okinawa. Nod gave us some throttle, and we cut through the rising tide and headed out to sea.

I lay back in the scuppers, bone tired. I watched my men as they re-created the evening's events, their hands moving like pilots describing combat.

By the time we'd lost sight of land, the breeze picked up and the seas became following. On the eastern horizon, the first glimmer of dawn started to rise out of the sea—a hint of vibrant color painting the dark sky. I let my head loll back onto the gunwale, and felt the water's motion; allowed myself to respond to its incredible strength and power. I felt a sailor's sense of absolute belonging. What is perfection, you ask? Perfection is being here—on the ocean, out of sight of land—with my Warriors.

But it was also time to move on. To go home. After all, there was Pinky's retirement to plan.

Glossary

A²: Aforementioned Asshole.
A³: Anytime, Anyplace, Anywhere.
Admiral's Gestapo: what the secretary of defense's office calls the Naval Investigative Services Command (See **SHIT-FOR-BRAINS).**
AK-47: 7.63 X 39 Kalashnikov automatic rifle. The most common assault weapon in the world.
AVCNO: Assistant Vice Chief of Naval Operations.

BAW: Big Asshole Windbag.
BDUs: Battle Dress Uniforms. Now that's an oxymoron if I ever heard one.
BFH: Big Fucking Help.
BOHICA: Bend Over—Here It Comes Again!
Boomer: nuclear-powered missile submarine.
Briccone: (Italian) Rogue.
BTDT: Been There, Done That.
BUPERS: Naval BUreau of PERSonnel.

C-130: Lockheed's ubiquitous Hercules.

C-141: Lockheed's ubiquitous StarLifter aircraft, soon to be mothballed.

C-4: plastic explosive. You can mold it like clay. You can even use it to light your fires. Just don't stamp on it.

C²CO: Can't Cunt Commanding Officer. Too many of these in Navy SpecWar today. They won't support their men or take chances because they're afraid it'll ruin their chances for promotion.

C⁴IFTW: Command, Control, Communications, Computers, and Intelligence for the Warrior.

CALOW: Coastal And Limited-Objective Warfare. Very fashionable acronym at the Pentagon in these days of increased low-intensity conflict.

Cannon Fodder: See **FNG.**

Christians in Action: SpecWar slang for the Central Intelligence Agency.

CINC: Commander-IN-Chief

CINCLANT: Commander-IN-Chief, AtLANtic.

CINCLANTFLT: Commander-IN-Chief, AtLANTic FLeeT.

CINCUSNAVEUR: Commander-IN-Chief, U.S. NAVal forces, EURope.

CLIQ: Combination Lock In Question.

clusterfuck: See **FUBAR.**

CNO: Chief of Naval Operations.

Cockbreath: SEAL term of endearment used for those who only pay lip service.

CONUS: CONtinental United States.

CRACKERS: CRiminal hACKERS—cyberpunk tangos.

CQC: Close Quarters Combat—i.e., killing that's up close and personal.

CQC6: Ernest Emerson's Titanium-framed Close Quarters Combat folding knife favored by Marcinko SEALs. It is currently licensed to Benchmade Knives and available commercially.

CT: CounterTerrorism.

DADT: Don't Ask, Don't Tell.
DEA: Drug Enforcement Agency.
DEFCON: DEFense CONdition.
DEVGRP: Naval Special Warfare DEVelopment GRouP. Current U.S. Navy designation for SEAL Team Six.
detasheet: olive drab, 10-by-20-inch flexible PETN-based plastic explosive used as a cutting or breaching charge.
DIA: Defense Intelligence Agency. Spook heaven based in Arlington, Virginia.
Dickhead: Stevie Wonder's nickname for Marcinko.
Diplo-dink: no-load cookie-pushing diplomat.
DIPSEC: DIPlomatic SECurity.
Dipshit: can't cunt pencil-dicked asshole.
Dirtbag: the look Marcinko favors for his Team guys.
Do-ma-nhieu: (Vietnamese) Go fuck yourself (See **DOOM ON YOU**).
Doom on you: American version of Vietnamese for "go fuck yourself."
Dweeb: no-load shit-for-brains geeky asshole, usually shackled to a computer.

EC-130: Electronic warfare-outfitted C-130.
EEI: Essential Element of Information. The info-nuggets on which a mission is planned and executed.
EEO: Equal Employment Opportunity (Marcinko always treats 'em all alike—just like shit).
ELINT: ELectronic INTelligence.
EOD: Explosive Ordnance Disposal.

F^3: Full Fucking Faulkner—lots of sound and fury.
FIS: Flight Information Service.
flashbang: disorientation device used by hostage rescue teams.
FLIR: Forward Looking Infra Red.
FNG: Fucking New Guy. See **CANNON FODDER**.
Four-striper: Captain. All too often, a C^{2}CO.
frags: fragmentation grenades.

FUC: Fucking Ugly Corsican.
FUBAR: Fucked Up Beyond All Repair.
fuhatsu: (Japanese) misfire; dud.

Glock: Reliable 9mm pistols made by Glock in Austria. They're great for SEALs because they don't require as much care as Sig Sauers.
GNBN: Good News/Bad News.
Goatfuck: What the Navy likes to do to Marcinko (See **FUBAR**).
GSG-9: Grenzchutzgruppe-9. Top German CT unit.

HAHO: High-Altitude, High-Opening parachute jump.
HALO: High-Altitude, Low-Opening parachute jump.
HICs: Head-In-Cement syndrome. Condition common to high-ranking officers. Symptoms include pigheadedness and inability to change opinions when presented with new information.
HK: ultra-reliable pistol, assault rifle, or submachine gun made by Heckler & Koch, a German firm. SEALs use H&K MP5-Ks submachine guns in various configurations, as well as H&K 33 assault rifles, and P7M8 9mm, and USP 9mm, .40- or .45-caliber pistols.
Huey: original slang for Bell's AH-1 two-bladed helicopter, but now refers to various UH configuration Bell choppers.
HUMINT: HUMan INTelligence.
humongous: Marcinko's dick.
Hydra-Shok: extremely lethal hollow-point ammunition manufactured by Federal Cartridge Company.

IBS: Inflatable Boat, Small—the basic unit of SEAL transportation.
IED: Improvised Explosive Device.

Japs: bad guys.
Jarheads: Marines. The Corps. Formally, USMC, or, Uncle Sam's Misguided Children.

jibaku: (Japanese) suicide bombing.
JSOC: Joint Special Operations Command.

KATN: Kick Ass and Take Names. Marcinko avocation.
KH: KeyHole. Designation for NRO's spy-in-the-sky satellites, as in KH-12s.
KISS: Keep It Simple, Stupid.

LANTFLT: AtLANTic FLeeT.

M^3: Massively Motivated Motherfuckers.
M-16: Basic U.S. .223-caliber weapon, used by the armed forces.
MagSafe: lethal frangible ammunition that does not penetrate the human body. Favored by some SWAT units for CQC.
Mark-I Mod-0: basic unit.
MILCRAFT: Pentagonese for MILitary airCRAFT.
MOI: Ministry of the Interior.

NAVAIR: NAVy AIR Command.
NAVSEA: NAVy SEA Command.
NAVSPECWARGRU: NAVal SPECial WARfare GRoUp.
Navyspeak: redundant, bureaucratic naval nomenclature, either in written nonoral, or nonwritten oral modes, indecipherable by nonmilitary (conventional) or military (unconventional) individuals during normal interfacing configuration conformations.
NIS: Naval Investigative Service Command, also known as the Admirals' Gestapo (See: **SHIT-FOR-BRAINS**).
NMN: No Middle Name.
NRO: National Reconnaissance Office. Established 25 August 1960 to administer and coordinate satellite development and operations for U.S. intelligence community. Very spooky place.
NSA: National Security Agency, known within the SpecWar community as No Such Agency.

NSCT: Naval Security Coordination Team (Navyspeak name for Red Cell).
NSD: National Security Directive.
NYL: Nubile Young Lovely.

OBE: Overtaken By Events—usually because of the bureaucracy.
OOD: Officer Of the Deck (he who drives the big gray monster).
OP-06-04: CNO's SpecWar Briefing Officer.
OP-06: Deputy CNO for Operations, Plans and Policy.
OP-06B: Assistant Deputy CNO for Operations, Plans and Policy.
OP-06D: Cover organization for Red Cell/NSCT.
OPSEC: OPerational SECurity.

PDMP: Pretty Dangerous Motherfucking People.
POS: Piece Of Shit.
POTUS: President Of The United States.

RDL: Real Dirty Look.
RPG: Rocket Propelled Grenade.
R^{2}D^2: Ritualistic, Rehearsed, Disciplined Drills.

S^2: Sit the fuck down and Shut the fuck up.
SAS: Special Air Service. Britain's top CT unit.
SATCOM: SATellite COMmunications.
SCIF: Sensitive Compartmented Information Facility. A bug-proof room.
SEAL: SEa-Air-Land Navy SpecWarrior. A hop-and-popping shoot-and-looter hairy-assed frogman who gives a shit. The acronym stands for Sleep, Eat And Live it up.
Semtex: Czecho C-4 plastique explosive. Used for canceling Czechs.
SERE: Survival, Evasion, Resistance, and Escape school.
SES: Shit-Eating Smile.
SH-3: versatile Sikorsky chopper. Used in ASW missions and also as a spec ops platform.

Shit-for-Brains: any no-load, pus-nutted, pencil-dicked asshole from NIS.
SIGINT: SIGnals INTelligence.
SMG: SubMachine Gun.
SNAFU: Situation Normal—All Fucked Up.
SNAILS: Slow, Nerdy Assholes In Ludicrous Shoes.
SOCOM: Special Operations COMmand, located at MacDill AFB, Tampa, Florida.
SOF: Special Operations Force.
S&P: Spit-and-Polish.
SpecWarrior: One who gives a fuck.
SSN: nuclear sub, commonly known as sewer pipe.
STR: Smack The Rogue.
SUC: Marcinkospeak for Smart, Unpredictable, and Cunning.
SWAT: Special Weapons and Tactics police teams. All too often they do not train enough, and become SQUAT teams.

TAD: Temporary Additional Duty (SEALs refer to it as Traveling Around Drunk).
Tailhook: the convention of weenie-waggers, gropesters, and pressed-ham-on-glass devotees that put air-brakes on NAVAIR.
TARFU: Things Are Really Fucked Up.
TECHINT: TECHnical INTelligence.
THREATCON: THREAT CONdition.
Tigerstripes: The only stripes that SEALs will wear.
TIQ: Tango-In-Question.
totsugekijin: (Japanese) assault rifles.
TTS: Marcinko slang for Tap 'em, Tie 'em, and Stash 'em.

U_2: Ugly and Unfamilar.
UNODIR: UNless Otherwise DIRected.

VDL: Versatile, Dangerous, and Lethal.

Wanna-bes: the sort of folks you meet at Soldier of Fortune conventions.

Weenies: pussy-ass can't cunts and no-loads.
WTF: What The Fuck.

zhongdui: (Chinese) Naval reconnaissance commando unit of the People's Liberation Army.
Zulu: Greenwich Mean Time (GMT) designator used in formal military communications.
Zulu-5-Oscar: escape and evasion exercises in which Frogmen try to plant dummy limpet mines on Navy vessels, while the vessels' crews try to catch them in *bombus interruptus.*

Index

A^3, 11
ABSCAM, 185
ACOG (Advanced Combat
Optical Gunsight), 270
AK-47, 118
Ambush, 346–47
AMEMB (AMerican
EMBassy), 249
Andrews Air Force Base, 129
Antilaser goggles, 359
Appeasement, 16
Approach screwup, 105
APU (auxiliary power unit),
318
Army Field Manual 291–92
Arsenal ship, 283
The Art of War (Sun Tzu), 215
ASDF (Air Self-Defense
Force), 90
Asian mind, 291
Asian Wall Street Journal,
82, 103, 105, 176
ASR (Attack SEAL-in-
Residence), 18
Attrition politics, 83
Auditory exclusion, 272
Aum Shinrikyo cult, 80
AUTODIN (AUTOmatic
DIgital Network), 72
AV (area of vulnerability),
110–11, 271, 305, 344,
370

All entries preceded by an asterisk (*) are pseudonyms.

Backchanneling, 71
Baker, James, 103
Barrett, Everett Emerson, 30
BDUs (Battle Dress Uniforms), 49, 261
Beckwith, Col. Charlie, 66, 381
Ben Gal, Col. Avi, 20
Big Brother, 59–60, 64, 65–67, 72, 85–86, 122–23, 194, 232, 261, 283, 304–05, 324–32, 348, 352, 369
Bizon submachine gun, 269
Blauer, Tony, 160
Blueprint for the AirLand Battle, 291–92
Boehm, Roy Henry, 137, 162, 189, 193, 221, 266, 290–94, 304, 308, 324, 333, 374
Boehming, 189
Bolt cutters, 6
Booby traps, 346
Boomerang, 9, 12–13, 25–35, 46, 52, 64, 134, 136, 182–84, 225–26, 262–65, 270–83, 309–18, 324–32
Bootlegger's turn, 148
Brancato, Dave, 71–72, 78, 205
BRD (beyond a reasonable doubt), 19
Brendel, Bentley, 103–04, 173–78, 182–91, 195, 201–02, 209–21, 229–32, 248–51, 282, 380–81
Bridge (ship), 36–37
BUD/S, 9, 290, 378
Burundi, 147–48
Bush, George, 143

C-12 airplane, 318, 323
Carabinieri Nazionale, 259
Caving ladder, 35
C^{2}CO (Can't Cunt Commanding Officer), 93, 122
C^3 (Command, Control, and Communications) vans, 185
Cells, 95
Chi Haotian, 102
China, 83, 123
  activity in Pacific Rim, 15–20, 130–31, 194
  influence buying in U.S., 141–44
  intel ops, 98, 229–30
  interest in Senkaku Islands, 90–91, 303–04, 311, 322, 334–49
  political importance of, 15, 215
  stealth attack on Taiwan, 231–32, 288
  weapons dealings, 62
Chinese Embassy, 184
Christopher, Warren, 103
Chun Li, Gen., 224
CIA, 80, 99
CI (Counterintelligence), 180, 283
C^{4}IFTW, 58–59, 283
CINCPACFLT (Commander-IN-Chief PACific FLeeT), 78–79, 84, 203–04, 206

Cipher locks, 184
Clandestine missions, 66, 145
Claymore mines, 62, 347, 371
Clinton, Bill, 103, 142
CLIQ (combination lock in question), 55–56
CNN, 90
CODELs (CONgressional DELegations), 311
Code words, 57
Colby, William, 314
Cold War, 15, 20
Colonel Rolex, 281, 283
Color Clock Code, 273–74
Combat goggles, 6
Combat pack issue, 329
Compartmentation, 57–58
Condition orange, 152
Condition yellow, 151
Confidential material, 57
CONUS (CONtinental US), 85–86, 180
Core values, 76
Covert missions, 66
CQC (Close Quarters Combat) vest, 5, 25–26, 47–48, 55, 107, 113, 328, 358, 366
Crawford, Billy "Rommel," 233–38, 249
Crocker, Gen. Thomas E., 18–21, 66, 73–84, 99, 137–49, 190–91, 206, 220, 333, 367, 379
  attempt on life of, 232–53
  Rome NATO meeting, 254–59, 287
Cryptonyms, 57, 59
Cryptovault, 72
Cumshawed equipment, 329
C^2W^3, 58
CW/BW agents, 112
CYA (Cover Your Ass), 93

Deadly force, 180
Deception, 224
Def-Tec No. 25 flashbangs, 113, 117
Def-Tec TKO frangible slugs, 48
Delta hit, 110
Deng Xiaoping, 98
Dewey, Allan (Duck Foot), 8, 13, 27–52, 67, 182, 225–27, 262–64, 267, 274–82, 309–10, 322
DHS (Defense HUMINT Service), 97–98
DIA, 67–68, 98–99, 142, 195, 289
DiCarlo, Eddie (Nod), 9, 13, 27, 31, 33, 36–45, 52, 65, 182, 225, 260, 309–18
Diplomatic passport, 287
Diplomats, 214
DITSA (Defense Technology Security Agency), 73
Drinking water, 351
DS (Diplomatic Security), 256

EA (electronic attack), 304
E-2C aircraft, 345
E&E training, 236
ELINT (ELectronic INTelligence), 19
Enders, Cherry, 289

Er Bu, 102, 229–30
EWO (Electronic Warfare Officer), 11

Fast-roping gloves, 114
FBI, 184, 272, 359
First Amendment, 197
The First Principle of Victory (Sun Tzu), 225
Flaps and seals, 72
FLIR (Forward Looking Infra Red) night-vision device, 261, 353–54, 358–59, 368–72
Flora hotel, Rome, 259
Flotation bladder, 5
FN (Foreign National), 148
Foreign policy, 82
FORTE satellite surveillance, 18–19
Freelancing, 143
FS (Foreign Service), 254
F-two (file and forget), 76
FUBAR Zone, 34, 110–11
Fudo, 293
Fuel bladder, 27

Gerber Multi-Plier, 241, 322
GFs (goatfuck factors), 375
GLCMs (Ground-Launched Cruise Missiles), 61, 303, 343
Glock, 108
GNBN, 336
Go-Bar, 113–14, 116–18, 119–20
Grand Palace hotel, Rome, 257, 264–65, 268
Gray, Admiral, 89, 91, 94–95, 122, 188–89, 206
Grinkov, Viktor, 20, 139, 250, 256–58, 264, 268–85, 289
Grundle, Nasty Nicky, 9, 12–13, 26–27, 34–35, 36, 46, 52, 60, 63, 182

HAHO (High Altitude High Opening), 8, 14
HALO missions, 311, 336
HARP (High Altitude Release Point), 336
Harris, Half Pint, 9, 13, 27, 31, 35–36, 46–52, 182–83, 225, 260, 277, 309–15
Heckler & Koch MP5-PDW, 9, 49, 113, 116–17, 118
Heckler & Koch USP 9mm semiauto pistol, 6
HICs (head-in-cement syndrome), 139
Hideaway offices, 177
Hondamatic rice rocket, 183
Hong Kong, 15, 305
Huey UH-1H, 114
HUMINT (HUMan INTelligence), 19, 99, 130–31, 142, 204, 252
Hummer, 320
Hunan Number One restaurant, 155
Hunting, 354
Hussein, Saddam, 67
Hypoxia, 23

Ichiban beer, 289–90

ICRRC (Improved Combat Rubber Raiding Craft), 4, 9, 13–14, 24–29, 33–36, 111
IFF (Identification, Friend or Foe) transmitter, 68, 327
Ikigami, Hideo, 126
Indonesia, 194, 224, 287, 379
Industrial spies, 142
Iran-Contra affair, 143
IR lightsticks, 365, 368
Israel, 201–02, 300
Ivy Bells, 57

J-2, 99
Jakarta, Indonesia, 305
Japan, 79, 83, 130, 194, 224
  Kadena military installation, 306–27
  McDonald's hostage situation in Yokosuka, 87–121, 188–89
Japanese Red Army, 95
Jibaku, 89
JMSDF (Japanese Maritime Self-Defense Forces), 79
*Joseph, Alixe, 96–105, 112, 121–31, 173, 194–202, 206, 213, 224–30, 251, 289, 295, 380

Kadena, Japan military installation, 306–27
K-Bar assault knife, 5, 26, 44
Kennedy, John F., 193
Kid Armani, 171
Kielly, Arch, 310, 312–35
KISS (Keep It Simple, Stupid), 19, 162, 308
Korea, 194, 224, 287, 379
Kunika (Japanese National Police), 84, 301–02
Kydex sheath, 6

Lantos, Werner, 163
Laser-guided missiles, 283
Leadership, 333
Li Chimen, 101–05, 124, 130, 164–76, 182–86, 201–02, 209, 215–18, 227–32, 248–52, 282, 287, 302–05
  ambush of, 371–80
Li Chung, 213

Magellan GPS module, 7, 10–14, 21–23, 382
Marcinko, Richard
  assault on *Nantong Princess,* 30–69
  attempt on Gen. Crocker's life, 232–53
  flight from Kadena installation to Senkaku Islands, 320–33
  landing on Senkaku Islands, 334–49
  Li Chimen ambush, 368–80
  in Rome with Gen. Crocker, 254–87
  stolen USAF airplane at Kadena installation, 307–19
  in Tokyo, 299–305
  and Yokosuka McDonald's hostage situation, 87–121
  zhongdui ambush, 350–67

Mardigian, Ron, 73, 76
Mark 4 Mod-3 homing device, 70
McDonald's hostage situation, Yokosuka, Japan, 87–121, 188–89
MC-130E Combat Talon aircraft, 11
MC-3 parachute, 318
MC-5 parachute, 318
Mead, Piccolo (Pick), 9, 13, 27–46, 53, 182–83, 225, 262–64, 274–83, 309–18, 325–29
Mercaldi, Anthony Vincent, 64, 67, 73–76, 86, 136, 249, 251–52, 289
MERF (Marine Emergency Reaction Force), 89–90
Middle East, 300
Military, 332–33
Military Air Transport Service cargo flight, 129
MILPERS (MILitary PERSonnel), 143–44
MILSPEAK, 68
Mindfulness, 290
Mini frag grenades, 372
MIQ (Memo In Question), 202
Montgomery, Joanne, 146–49, 157–64, 225–27, 249–50, 286
Motorola, 73
Motor scooters, 257
M^3s, 112
Mussolini, Benito, 265
MVD (Ministry of the Interior), 62, 284
Naicho (Japan intelligence agency), 80
Nantong Princess, 30–69, 111, 122–24, 139–40, 142, 145, 195, 206, 224, 231, 247, 287–89, 303–05
National Security Council, 191
Naval Academy, 222
NAVSEA (NAVal SEA Systems Command), 37
NAVSOF (NAVy Special Operations Forces), 180–81
NAVSPECWARGRUTWO (NAVal SPECial WARfare GRoup TWO), 186
Navy, 57
Nixon, Richard, 15
NOC (nonofficial cover), 100
Nomex jumpsuit, 107, 115
Nonproliferation treaty, 16–18
North, Oliver, 143
No Such Agency, 19, 57, 67
NSC (NAVal Special Operations Component) forces, 204

O_2 bottle, 6–7
Officers, 93–94, 333
Okinaga, Toshiro, 84–122, 124, 130, 131, 189, 194, 226, 248, 251, 288, 299–318, 331
Okinawa, Japan, 307–08
Old Executive Office Building, 174, 193, 196
  hideaway offices, 177

Olshaker, Mark, 253, 255–59, 286–87
OMON (Special Purpose Militia Detachment), 256, 264, 281
OPCON (OPerational CONtrol), 149
Operation Desert Storm, 190
OPLAN (Operational PLAN), 20, 70, 149
OPSEC (OPerations SECurity), 145, 149
Op-sked (operational schedule), 29
Owen, Col. Mick, 273–74

PACFLT (PACific FLeet), 203
Pacific Rim, 19, 82, 98, 123, 194
Pads, knee and elbow, 108
PAO (Public Affairs Officer), 89
Paracel Islands, 231
Parachutes, 318
Parachuting, 335–40
Pave Low chopper, 87, 114
Pearl Harbor, 72
Pencil detonators, 5
Pentagon, 149, 180
Perot, Ross, 16
Philippines, 224, 287, 379
Pine Gap, Australia, 67
Plus-P load ammo, 6
Point-and-shoot digital electronic camera, 5, 53
POLAD (Political Advisor), 100
Pollard, Jonathan, 202
Powell, Gen. Colin, 147
PPD (Presidential Protective Detail), 177
P-7 pistol, 240
Prescott III, Pinckney "Pinky," 186–90, 206–07, 209–23
Presidential commission, 216
PV (point of vulnerability), 111

Quarters Six, 250

Radar-defeating unit, 64
Radios, 36, 255
Ram Air parachute, 330
Reagan, Ronald, 143
Red Brigades, 257
Red Cell, 88, 91, 266, 314
Red Seeds, 91, 95, 121, 123
Remington 870P Magnum, 48
Reynolds, Avenir, 198–99, 207
Right-to-know, 197
Rodent, 182–83, 225, 260, 309–15, 324
ROEs (Rules of Engagement), 314
Rogue Manor, 149, 224, 244, 301
Rome, Italy, 254–87
Ross, Kenny, 146
RSG (rear-security guy), 358
RSO (Regional Security Officer), 253
RS (relative superiority), 110, 293
RUMINT (RUMor INTelligence), 59

Russia, 231
Russians, 123

SAIC (Special Agent In Charge), 178
Salt-and-pepper team, 152
SAS 22 Regiment, 273
SATCOM, 65
Saturation training, 161
Schiavo, Mary, 147
Schwarzkopf, Gen. Norman, 99–100
SCIF (Sensitive Compartmented Information Facility), 138
SEAL Force Alpha, 203
SEALs, 86
- approach practice, 106
- body build of, 362
- combat pack issue, 329
- difference from other warriors, 277
- in Operation Desert Storm, 190
- readiness for WAR, 135
- seven phases of mission, 292–93

SEAL Team Six, 186, 266, 289
- shoot-and-loot, 110

SECDEF, 18, 83, 97–99, 139, 144, 225
Secrest, Arleigh, 124
Secret material, 57
Secrets, spilling of, 196–97
SECSTATE, 16–17
Secure phone, 66
Secure radio, 261
Security classifications, 56–57
Semtex, 5, 53, 62
Senkaku Islands, 90–91, 303, 311, 322, 334–49
S$_3$FA (short, shit-filled, slovenly, fat asshole), 163
Shellhammer, 89
Shepard, Gator, 8, 13, 27, 31, 35–46, 52, 63, 182, 227, 260, 309–15, 324
Shifty eye movements, 218
Ship-boarding, 36–37
Shooting schools, 159
SIGINT (SIGnals INTelligence), 19, 67
Silicon Valley, 142
Simon, Col. Arthur "Bull," 16, 215
Singapore, 194, 224, 287, 305, 379
Sino-Russian alliance, 123
SISMI (Service for Information and Military Security), 258–61
Skunkworks, 73
Skyhorse, 57–58
Snooping and pooping, 86
Somalia crisis, 92
Son Tay (N. Vietnam) prison raid, 16
South China Sea, 19, 22, 23, 205, 231, 295, 341
Soviet Union, 15, 99, 142
SpecOps, 11, 293, 344
- AV, 110–11, 271, 305, 344, 370
- RS, 110–11

SpecWar, 16, 60, 106, 148, 237, 277, 293

Fourth Commandment of, 135–36
Ten Commandments of, 292
Tenth Commandment of, 363
Spetsnaz Alpha Unit, 256, 275
S^2 (sit the fuck down and shut the fuck up), 291
Static opening, 13
Static surveillance, 185
Stealth aircraft, 283
Stiletto, 43
STOL (Short TakeOff and Landing), 323
Styr, 376–77
SUBOPS (SUBmarine OPerationS), 72
Sun Tzu, 43, 213, 215, 224–25, 229–31
Suppressed MP5, 260, 270–76, 358–61, 370–72
Suppressed weapons, 361
Surveillance van, 184
SWAT op, 110
The Sword (Fudo), 293

Tachypsychia, 272–73
Tactical driving, 160
TAD (Temporary Additional Duty), 78
T'ai Li'ang, 213
Taiwan, 232, 288
Tangos, 78, 90, 124, 230
Task Force Blue, 289
T & B (towed away & blowed), 174
TECHINT (TECHnical INTelligence), 19
Teheran rescue mission, 66
Thompson, Matt, 82–83, 98–99, 138, 178
Tiananmen Square, 17, 102
Tokyo, Japan, 299–305
Top secret material, 57
T pass, 176–77
Tracee Wink, 67
Training jumps, 331
Tremblay, Doc, 22, 359
*Trott, Hank, 99–100
TS (top secret) doc, 168
TS/SCI (Top Secret/Special Compartmental Intelligence), 96, 201, 217–19
TTB (top to bottom), 55
Tunnel vision, 272

UDT vest, 26
United States Air Force, 307
United States Secret Service Uniform Division, 174
UNODIR operations, 253, 264
UNPs (unknown nasty parties), 201
Untraceable equipment, 366
USGI (U.S. Government Issue) equipment, 366
USP Variant One, 380
USS *Scorpion,* 70–85

VBSS/H (Visit Board Search and Seizure), 37
Viet Cong, 221
Vietnam, 231
Vint Hill Station, Virginia, 68

Visualizing, 161
Visual slowdown, 272–73

War, 279, 283
War-gaming, 160–61, 166
Warrior Code, 85, 108, 167, 270, 319, 332, 378
Washington, D.C., 129, 171
Weapons, 16, 180–81
Weather Gable, 130, 201, 206, 222
Weaver, Ty, 177–79, 249
"What If" games, 161
WHA (White House Asshole), 93
WHCA (White House Communications Agency), 248
White House, 91–92, 138, 142, 192–93
  Lincoln Bedroom, 192
  Oval Office, 192
  press pass, 176
  West Wing, 175
White House Fellows, 146–47
*Williams, Brian, 313–14
Wirth, Tim, 147
*Wonder, Stevie, 54, 133–34, 136, 182

Xinhua (New China News Agency), 101–03, 176, 184, 248

Yokosuka, Japan naval installation, 78
Yoshioka, 106

Zhongdui naval recon forces, 8, 19, 51, 102, 247, 248, 350–82
Zhu Linfan, Maj. Gen., 102, 215, 229, 367

POCKET BOOKS
PROUDLY PRESENTS

OPTION DELTA

Richard Marcinko
and John Weisman

Available Now in Hardcover from
Pocket Books

The following is a preview of
Option Delta. . . .

Chapter 1

God, how I do love being cold and wet. And it is lucky that I do, because cold and wet (not to mention tired, hungry, and suffering from terminal lack o'pussy) is precisely how I have spent a large portion of my professional life. Take my present situation. (Oh, yes indeed. Please, *take* my present situation. All of it. Each and every molecule. Every single fucking bit.)

And exactly what *was* my current situation, you ask? Well, to be precise, I was one of four SEALs crammed inside a spherical steel tank built for two—we're talking roughly eight feet high, by five feet in diameter—in total blackness, squashed atop and against the three similarly chilly and claustrophobic occupants, and clinging to a ladder attached to the side of the cylinder so I wasn't stepping on the head of the man below me. Just to make things interesting, cold seawater from several vents was being pumped into the tank. Currently the water was at crotch level, and it was frigid enough to shrink my Rogue-sized balls to hazelnuts, even through a thick, black neoprene foam wet suit, which covered me head to toe.

I waited quietly, patiently, until the tank was completely filled. As the water came in, I could hear the air as it escaped through the collar of the air bubble hood manifold above me. Under what might be called normal circumstances, I could have monitored our progress on the chamber's interior pressure and air gauges courtesy of the two waterproof battle lanterns that are mounted six feet above the bottom hatch cover. But Mister Murphy (of Murphy's Law fame), or one of his Murphyesque minions, had already decided that light was an unacceptable component of the night's activity, and thus he had caused the lanterns to malfunction as soon as the bottom hatch had been sealed, the pressure equalized, and the water had begun to flow.

Even so, I might have followed the action by using my waterproof flashlight. But my waterproof flashlight was safely stowed in my equipment bag. And my equipment bag was being transported on the fucking deck of the fucking nuclear attack submarine on which I was currently a passenger, lashed to a cleat behind the sail, where I would retrieve it after I'd completed lockout.

Under normal circumstances, we wouldn't even have been in this particular fucking sewer pipe, which is how SEALs refer to subs. We'd have been aboard one of the retrofitted SpecOps craft, attack subs that have been specially outfitted for us shoot-and-looters. We'd have had the advantage of Mark-V SDVs, or swimmer delivery vehicles, which are carried on the decks of SpecWar subs in bulbous clamshell devices called DSS, or dry-dock shelters. But there are only three such boats available, given the current drawdown to our 296-ship, twenty-first-century navy. And so, we'd had to make do with what was on hand. Which was, to be precise, the USS *Nacogdoches* (SSN 767), a third-generation Los Angeles–class U-boat, equipped to kill other subs, launch Tomahawk missiles, lay mines, wage electronic warfare, and do many other, sundry top secret tasks. But the list did not include the capacity to accommodate and launch eight SEALs and all their equipment on a clandestine mission.

The result, as you can probably guess, meant that we'd had to jury-rig everything from our sleeping quarters (we'd hot-bunked in the forward torpedo room with the Tomahawk missiles, Mark 48 ADCAP—ADvanced CAPability—torpedoes, and Mark 67 SLMMs—Submarine Launched Mobile Mines), to having to store our weapons and other gear outside the sub, as the escape hatches were too narrow to allow us to exit with anything more than our Draeger LAR-V rebreathers. Even our method of egress was nonreg. SSNs have two escape trunks. This one (known formally as the stores hatch, because it was where the ship's stores are commonly on-loaded) was the most forward trunk. It was located just aft of the control room and abutted the triple-thick insulated, lead-shielded wall surrounding the nuclear reactor compartment.

SSNs modified for SpecWar have enlarged escape trunks so that SEAL platoons, which number sixteen, can lock out quickly. Unmodified SSN escape trunks are, as I have just pointed out, built for two men at a time. But given the parameters of my current mission, which included the necessity of a quick exit, I'd changed the rules. And so, we were locking out four at a time. Which currently gave the escape tank the crowded ambience of a frat-house telephone booth during a cram-the-pledges contest.

Thus, I stood immobile in the darkness, teeth chomped tight on my Draeger mouthpiece, trying not to stick my size ten triple-Rogue foot in Gator Shepard's size normal face, while trying my best to stay out of range of Boomerang's bony elbow (he has a nasty habit of flailing his arm like a chicken's wing when he's under stress), running and rerunning the night's schedule in my head. Oh, yes, it was much easier problem solving than thinking about my iced-down nuts and my other chill-packed nether parts. And so I stood there in the cold and the wet, anticipating everything that can, could, will, would, shall, should, may, might, or must go wrong, so I'd be able to outwit Command Master Chief Murphy who, experience has shown, likes to tag along on these kinds of ops.

Finally, I sensed the water flow had stopped.

When I was positive no air remained in the escape chamber, I flexed my shoulders, worked the cramp out of my neck, and then started to pull myself toward the steel ladder bolted to the escape trunk bulkhead. I knew that I had to climb three rungs, then reach above my head in the total blackness to the spot my mind's eye had muscle-memoried as being the first of the six dogs that secured the trunk's outer hatch cover.

Wham! My action was interrupted by a rude elbow (or other sundry Boomerang body part—it was dark after all, and who could really tell), which smashed into the right side of my temple. I went face first into the ladder rail and saw goddamn stars. Belay that. I saw the whole Milky fucking Way. Oh shit. Oh fuck. Oh, doom on Dickie. Which, as you probably know, means I was being fuckee-fuckeed in Vietnamese.

My mask came off—the back strap separating from the clasp and disappearing into the void between my legs. And then the sonofabitch hit me again—this time *smack* upside my wide Rogue snout, which knocked my mouthpiece clean out of my mouth. I gagged and snorted, which just about fucking drowned me, because as you will remember I was completely underwater, and gagging and snorting when underwater means inhaling what in SEAL technical language is known as the old double-sierra: a shitload of seawater.

It occurred to me that perhaps I should yell "CUT!" and start this process all over again. But that, of course, was impossible. This wasn't fucking Hollywood, where you get as many takes as you need to Get It Right. Or a goddamn training exercise, where you can take a time-out to regroup, rethink, and reapply yourself to the task at hand. This was for real. And there was a mother-blanking, bleepity-bleeping schedule to keep.

You what? You want to know what that schedule *was?* And you want me to explain it all *now?* When I'm in serious fucking pain?

Geezus, have you no sense of timing? Okay, okay—you paid good money for this book, so I'll be fucking accommodating. To be brief about it, the mission tonight was for me and my seven SEALs to lock out of the *Nacogdoches,* swim undetected roughly eighteen hundred yards to the northeast, and makc our way under half a dozen picket boats manned by armed and dangerous nasties. Then we'd locate *die Nadel im Heuhaufen*[1]—in this case it was a certain seventy-five-meter boat—board it, obliterate any opposition, and then capture a Saudi royal yclept Prince Khaled Bin Abdullah. We would do all of this *sans* any hullabaloo whatsoever.

The reason for our stealth was that Khaled baby was the forty-seven-year-old scion of the Abdullah family, third cousins of da king, and Saudi Arabia's sixteenth most wealthy clan. Khaled's annual income was somewhere in the $400 million range,

---

[1]That's Kraut for needle in the haystack.

which works out to something like thirty-three million U.S. smackers a month. Educated in Germany, England, and France two decades ago, he'd eschewed the lavish single-malt scotch, Cristal champagne, beluga caviar, and hooker-rich lifestyle most of his fellow princes took up. Instead, he'd somehow gotten involved with the campus radicals, e.g., assholes from the Baader-Meinhof gang, the Red Brigades, and others like them. So Khaled wasn't into conspicuous consumption like most of your Saudi blue bloods. Instead, he'd invested his profits from Microsoft, Dell Computer, Cisco, and Intel, his circa 1980 12.5 percent zero coupon bonds, and his ARAMCO oil royalties in transnational terrorism.

Khaled funded Hamas suicide squads, Algerian GIA (Armed Islamic Group) death squads, and Kurdish car bombers. You could say that his money endowed "chairs" in murder and assassination at two of the five "universities" the mullahs have set up outside the Iranian cities of Tehran and Qum to train transnational terrorists. He'd provided financial support and logistics to the Harakat-ul-Ansar's program to assassinate westerners in Kashmir and Pakistan. He'd even given money to American neo-Nazis, German radicals, and Puerto Rican ultranationalists. This scumbag was a real equal-opportunity tango.

And until now, between the reluctant but constant protection of the Saudi royal family (he was, after all, an illegitimate third cousin to the current Saudi ambassador to the United States, which made him a directly indirect relative of da king), and his residence in rural Afghanistan, where he was protected by a brigade of Come-Mister-Taliban-Tally-Me-Banana-clip-on-your-AK-47 gunmen, it hadn't been politically prudent, tactically practical, or diplomatically realistic to lay our hands on him without creating what the State Department tends to describe as "a deplorable, regrettable, and unfortunate violation of sovereign territory involving United States military personnel."[2]

But tonight, his illegitimate ass was going to be mine. Because my guys and I would nail him in international waters, where the State Department has no jurisdiction. Once he'd been properly TTS'd—which as you know means tagged, tied, and stashed—we'd turn him over to the proper authorities, i.e., a team of special agents of the Federal Bureau of Investigation, who were already

---

[2]Have you ever noticed that the fucking State Department has the habit of almost always taking the other guy's side whenever there's an international dispute? It has occurred to me to ask who the fuck these pin-striped fudge-cutting cookie-pushing bureaucrats work for. The answer, of course, is that they work for you and me—the citizens of the United States. But don't tell *them* that—most of our professional diplomats get upset if you require them to stand up for America.

waiting on a close-but-not-too-close VSV.[3] They'd ferry him to an aircraft carrier cruising off Malta, where he'd be put on a plane that would, through the marvel of in-flight refueling, not touch down until it reached the good old U.S. of A. Bottom line: he'd stand trial for financing the bombing of the Khobar Towers complex in Saudi Arabia a few years back and killing nineteen American military personnel.

Yes, friends, when it comes to terrorists, the United States has a long, long memory. And sometimes, despite the current State Department's best efforts to the contrary, we even act on it.

Ninety-six hours ago, Khaled, the TIQ[4], had been lured out of his safe haven in Afghanistan to these here international waters, which happen to be eighty miles due southwest of Akrotiri, Cyprus, by the promise of securing something he'd been trying to buy for the past decade: a ready-to-go, .025-megaton Soviet special demolition munition device, popularly described as a suitcase atom bomb (even though the goddamn thing does not come in a suitcase). The bomb was real—and the man selling it to him, a former Stasi[5] officer-

---

[3]Very Slender Vessel, which is a fancy way of talking about the kind of high-speed cigarette boats favored by drug smugglers and other stealthy types.

[4]As you can probably guess, it stands for Tango-In-Question.

[5]East German secret police.

turned-black marketeer, smuggler, and arms merchant named Heinz Hochheizer, was a bona fide no-goodnik. Neither Heinz nor Khaled realized they'd both been set up in a protracted, complex, and very intricate sting by the CIA, which thought that getting its hands on one of the old Soviet devices at the same time Khaled was being scooped up made an excellent idea.

It had taken more than nine months to get this far, but Khaled had finally nibbled at the bait, and the folks at Langley had allowed the hook to be set—hard. Still, Khaled was a smart sumbitch. He knew that Fawaz Yunis, one of the tangos involved in the hijacking of TWA 847 back in 1985, had been seduced into international waters by the lure of pussy. But as we all know now, the PIQ (look it up in the Glossary) had been a female FBI agent, an integral part of the FBI's aptly named Operation Goldenrod (sometimes the Bureau actually *does* have a sense of humor). And Khaled remembered all too well that Mir Aimal Kasi, the wealthy Pakistani who'd killed two CIA employees and then fled to his homeland, had been sold out by his fellow countrymen—his bodyguards, actually—and scooped up in the summer of 1997 by a joint task force of CIA officers, FBI Special Agents, and Delta Force shooters.

And so, Khaled was real careful about leaving his Afghan sanctuary, even with the wonderful prospect of securing an atom bomb staring him in the puss. It had taken three months of negotiation before he'd agreed to meet Heinz in a non-Islamic venue. Only the threat that others were interested in securing the weapon had finally brought him out of hiding. And Khaled had insisted on making all the arrangements for the exchange—arrangements that changed daily, sometimes even hourly, all posted in encrypted messages on the Internet.[6]

But he was being watched by a joint CIA/FBI team. And so, Khaled's progress was noted as he flew in his private jet from a small airstrip southwest of Meymaneh, to Tehran. He was shadowed as he'd driven through Damascus, to Beirut, where his chopper awaited him for the final leg of the journey. It was in Beirut that Mister Murphy showed up and our intrepid American gumshoes lost him. Khaled climbed into his limo and drove to the airfield where his chopper was waiting to take him on the final leg of this nasty odyssey, a 230-mile flight onto the deck of the transatlantic-capable, seventy-five-meter boat I'll call the *Kuz Emeq,* which had sailed from Cannes to the anonymous rendezvous point Khaled had chosen in the

---

[6]Though a great boon, the Internet is making the tracking of tangos much more difficult, as it is almost impossible to intercept encrypted E-mail and other postings. Note, however, that I said *almost impossible.* Our alphabet-soup agencies have developed certain proficiencies in recent years that keep 'em half a step ahead of the bad guys. Half a step may not be a lot—but it's enough.

middle of the Med. But when the big Mercedes limo pulled onto the tarmac, Khaled was nowhere to be seen. He'd pulled a fucking vanishing act that would have done David Copperfield proud.

The team panicked—and with good reason. This op had cost us a bundle—not to mention more than a dozen assets. The alarm bells went off, and our people combed the whole goddam Mediterranean from Libya to fucking Marseille. But Khaled had disappeared. And then, after thirty-six hours of nothing, they spotted another of his private choppers, a CH-3C with a range of more than six hundred miles that we'd originally sold to the Saudi Air Force. It was flying south, threading the needle between France and Italy. When it refueled at Cagliari, Sardinia, one of our people got a peek inside. And guess what? Khaled was there, sipping on his Evian water and reading the Koran. Two hours later, he was sitting in the main salon of the *Kuz Emeq* as it steamed eastward toward the rendezvous point, with us, and the USS *Nacogdoches,* in hot pursuit.

Khaled had arranged for the bomb vendor, Heinz the East German (he had Russian Mafiya ties, worked out of a mail drop in Frankfurt's red-light district, and, as I've just mentioned, was an unwitting accomplice in this little charade), to be brought in by another of his choppers, so even the Man with the Bomb would be ignorant of precisely where the meet was going to be, and therefore unable to bring any of his own hired guns along. For his part, Khaled made sure that his security people, six fast boats of well-paid Corsican Mafiosi, as well as a dozen fanatical Taliban shooters aboard the *Kuz Emeq,* were handy, and well armed. For a quick getaway, he had his chopper sitting on the *Kuz Emeq*'s chopper deck, its engine warmed up and its pilots ready to go *am geringsten Anlaß,* which is how the scumbag had learned to say "at the drop of a hat" at the Free University of Berlin back in the late 1970s.

But every once in a while the folks at Christians In Action (which is, you recall, how we SEALs refer to the Central Intelligence Agency), get things right. This was one of 'em. The Agency's sneak-and-peekers had managed to plant a beacon aboard the *Kuz Emeq* so subtly that even Khaled's head of security, a former KGB one-star technical guru, failed to spot it during his twice-daily ELINT/TECHINT/SIGINT[7] sweeps. And by modifying the sub's ESM—it stands for electronic support measures—equipment and then glomming onto the beacon's signal, the *Nacogdoches*'s skipper, a bright young Annapolis ring-knocker named Joseph Tuzzolino, aka Joey Tuzz, aka Captain Tuzzie, had stealthily slipped his boat to within just over a mile of Khaled's yacht.

---

[7]ELectronic INTelligence/TECHnical INTelligence/SIGnals INTelligence.

Now all that was left was for us to lock out of the sub, swim in, while keeping the beacon signal dead ahead of our position, slither onto the yacht, and perform the actual takedown. There were even a couple of bonuses for us if everything went right: that suitcase full of cash was one—I like being able to help pay down the national deficit—not to mention that compact, man-portable Soviet atomic munition device.

And, hey, this was gonna be a piece of cake, right? An easy swim followed by an effortless shoot & loot. Oh, *sure* it was—and if you believe that, I have this nice bridge in Brooklyn to sell you. Anyway, so much for background. Now let's get on with the fucking action sequence, shall we?